Final Venture

Also by Michael Ridpath

Free to Trade
Trading Reality
The Marketmaker

MICHAEL RIDPATH

Final Venture

MICHAEL JOSEPH
LONDON

MICHAEL JOSEPH
Published by the Penguin Group
Penguin Books Ltd, 27 Wrights Lane, London w8 5tz, England
Penguin Putnam Inc., 375 Hudson Street, New York, New York 10014, USA
Penguin Books Australia Ltd, Ringwood, Victoria, Australia
Penguin Books Canada Ltd, 10 Alcorn Avenue, Toronto, Ontario, Canada m4v 3b2
Penguin Books (NZ) Ltd, Private Bag 102902, NSMC, Auckland, New Zealand

Penguin Books Ltd, Registered Offices: Harmondsworth, Middlesex, England

First published 2000
1 3 5 7 9 10 8 6 4 2

Set in 12.5/15 pt Monotype Garamond
Typeset by Intype London Ltd
Printed in Great Britain by
Clays Ltd, St Ives plc

A CIP catalogue record for this book is available from the British Library

ISBN 0–718–14319–1

for Nicholas

Acknowledgements

Writing this novel involved talking to a great many people, most of whom were busy and yet were very generous with their time. I should like to thank in particular Toby Wyles, Anne Glover, Chris Murphy, Jonathan Cape, Paul Haycock, Hamish Hale and Lionel Wilson in London, and in Boston, Steve Willis, Chris Gabrieli, Christopher Spray, Sabin Willett and Rob and Pam Irwin.

1

I should have told her the night before, when I came home very late smelling of wine. Or that Friday morning, early, as I fought a thick head to crawl out of bed and into work for eight o'clock.

But I hadn't. If I had, she might, she just might, have stayed.

It didn't seem a big deal, then. Not to me, not to her. I was cooking supper when she came home from the lab. Shepherd's pie and baked beans. You can't get shepherd's pie in America unless you make it yourself. I needed the English comfort food to absorb the remains of the previous night's alcohol. Lisa would understand. She would eat hers good-humouredly, and we would have an alfalfa salad tomorrow.

'Simon?' she shouted as the door slammed.

'Yeah!'

I heard her steps make their way through the living room of our small apartment, and felt her arms slide round my waist. I turned and kissed her. It was supposed to be a quick peck on the lips, but it became something more. I broke away and turned back to the beans, which were beginning to bubble.

'Shepherd's pie?' she asked.

'Yep.'

'I never will get used to this sophisticated European food. Was it a rough night last night?'

'You could say that.' I stirred the beans.

'I need a glass of wine. Want one?'

'No thanks.' I watched her pour one. 'Oh, all right, I'll have some.'

She poured mine and brought it over to me. She was wearing a black V-necked sweater and leggings. There was nothing under the sweater, I knew; no shirt, no bra. I knew her body so well, small, pert, lithe, yet I couldn't get enough of it. In the six months we had been married, we had been all over each other all the time. Things just didn't get done around the apartment.

'I spoke to Dad today,' she said, a wicked smile on her face.

'Oh yes?' Dad was Lisa's father, Frank Cook, a partner at Revere, the venture-capital firm I worked for. I had him to thank for my job there, and then for introducing me to his daughter.

'Yes. He says he bumped into you last night. You seemed to be having an enjoyable evening. And there was I thinking you were slaving away at cash-flow statements or whatever it is you tell me you do at your office.'

I felt a rush of panic. Lisa saw it, but the amused smile remained on her face. 'He saw me?' I gulped. 'I mean, I didn't see him.'

'He was at the far side of the restaurant, apparently. You must have been too wrapped up in your date. He said it looked like you were having a good time.'

'It wasn't a date. It was Diane Zarrilli. We were both working late on one of her deals, and then she suggested we go out for a drink. We passed a restaurant, they had a table, and so we got something to eat as well.'

'That's not what you told me.'

'Isn't it?'

'Uh uh. You said you went out for a drink with some people from work.'

It was true, I had mumbled that to Lisa's back as I had crawled into bed after midnight.

'You got me,' I said.

'Dad seems to think I should be careful of this Diane woman.'

'She's nice. She's good fun. You haven't met her properly yet. You'd like her.'

'She's very attractive.'

2

'I suppose so,' I murmured. It was undeniable. Diane *was* very attractive.

'You lied to me, Simon Ayot,' Lisa said.

'It wasn't exactly a lie.'

'Yes it was.' She moved closer to me, pushing me back towards the cooker. I could hear the beans bubbling away behind me. I raised my arms. 'It was exactly a lie.' Her hand shot out and grabbed my balls. She squeezed gently.

'Ow!' I squawked. It seemed the right thing to say in the circumstances.

She walked backwards, pulling me out of the kitchen and towards the bedroom. She giggled, her brown eyes flashing up at me. We tumbled on to the bed.

Ten minutes later, the smell of burning beans drifted into the bedroom over the mess of clothes, sweat and bare skin.

2

'No.'

Gil Appleby, Revere's Managing Partner, and my boss, folded his arms across his chest, daring me to protest.

No? It couldn't be no. I couldn't let it be no.

While I had worked on many deals in my two years at the firm, this was only the second that had my name on it. My first, a PC home-leasing company, had been a lucky success in a record time. My second, Net Cop, was going to be a failure just as quickly.

I had promised Craig the money only a few days before. When we had initially invested in Net Cop six months previously, we had committed to provide more funds when the company needed them. Craig needed them now. Without our cash, his company would go bust.

I had given my word.

It shouldn't have been an issue. A regular item on the agenda of the Monday morning meeting of the partnership. This was where new investment opportunities were discussed, and any problems in Revere's investment portfolio dealt with. Net Cop wasn't supposed to be a problem. It was supposed to be an opportunity.

The meeting had started in the usual way, with Art Altschule talking about BioOne. Art liked to talk about BioOne whenever he could. It was Revere's most successful investment, and Art's deal, and he didn't want any of us to forget it.

I wasn't listening. My eyes were on a plane lowering itself gingerly through the sky towards an unseen runway at Boston's Logan Airport, two miles behind Art Altschule's closely cropped head. My mind was on what I was going to say about Net Cop.

Eventually, I became aware Art had stopped talking. I was on next.

Gil glanced down at the papers in front of him. 'OK. Net Cop. A three million dollar follow-on. Tell us about it, Simon.'

I cleared my throat. I tried to be concise, low-key, objective.

'As you no doubt remember, Net Cop plans to make the switches that direct the billions of information packets that fly around the Internet every day,' I began. 'They've completed the design of the switch, and they need a further three million dollars from us to go on to the next stage of their development, building something that they can show to potential customers.

'Frank and I made the initial investment six months ago. At that time we agreed to put in further funds provided Net Cop met various milestones. As you can see from my memo, they've met these milestones.

'Internet traffic is growing exponentially, and Net Cop has tremendous potential. In my opinion, Craig Docherty has done an excellent job, and we should continue to support him.'

In the six months I had worked with Craig, I had become more and more impressed with his abilities. I had also grown to like him. At thirty-two he was three years older than me, a wise old man in his business. He had vision, drive, energy, and an absolute determination to see Net Cop succeed.

The facts spoke for themselves. And the facts said 'Invest more money.' Or at least I thought they did.

There was a brief pause as I finished. My eyes flicked round the room. Everyone was watching me. The five partners: Gil, Frank, Art, Diane and Ravi Gupta, the firm's biotech expert. And the other two associates, Daniel and John, my friends and colleagues who I knew would support me, but who I also knew didn't have a vote.

No matter how many presentations I made, the board room didn't get any less intimidating. It was where all the important decisions in the life of Revere Partners were taken. Soft lighting reflected off cream walls with abstract sunsets. One set of windows overlooked Boston Harbor to the airport, the other the great canyon that was Franklin Street, with the colossus of the Bank of Boston building guarding one wall. Looking thoughtfully over Gil's shoulder, as if weighing the pros and cons of the discussion round the table, was a bust of Paul Revere himself. Silversmith, patriot, energetic horseman and finally wealthy entrepreneur, he mocked the computer geeks and disgruntled middle-managers who came before him. He didn't seem too impressed by my arguments either.

My eyes rested on Gil. He sat stiffly in his usual place at the middle of the table, leafing through the briefing papers I had prepared. I knew he would have studied them thoroughly over the weekend.

'The original plan called for a follow-on investment to be made after one year. We are only six months into the deal. Why so soon?'

His accent was clipped, almost English, what I had come to recognize as the hallmark of the Boston 'brahmins' who had run the city for three centuries.

He looked up and peered at me through his thick glasses. The lenses made his eyes look unnaturally small and hard. I had seen him use this effect many times before to unsettle hopeful entrepreneurs. It was working with me.

'As I mentioned, the market is hotting up,' I replied. 'There are more competitors springing up all over the place. Craig wants to make sure Net Cop is the first to ship product.' I cursed myself as I said this. I was beginning to sound defensive, always a bad position to find yourself in.

Gil's face, wrinkled and weather-beaten from countless days spent under sail in Massachusetts Bay or out in the North Atlantic, watched me, thinking.

There was silence round the table. No more questions. I began to relax. I was going to make it.

'Frank. You helped Simon with the deal, I believe. What do you think?'

I glanced over to the elegant figure of my father-in-law. Despite

6

his fifty-seven years his hair was still light brown, his body athletic, and his face handsome. He was wearing one of his dozens of suits, this one with a subtle check. But his eyes, which usually twinkled kindly, were agitated, worried.

'I don't know, Gil. I've got some problems with this one.'

What? This was not supposed to happen. Frank was supposed to be on my side.

The silence intensified. Everyone looked from Frank to me.

'Yes?' said Gil.

'Simon has laid out the information here well enough,' Frank said, gesturing to the paper in front of him, 'but I think he's drawn the wrong conclusions. There's much more competition out there now than there was six months ago. Maybe we should think about that.'

'But Craig *has* thought about it,' I said. 'That's why he's sped up the development process! His team is better than any of the small companies, and the big boys are just too slow.'

Frank shifted in his chair. His deep voice commanded attention. 'I'm not sure about Craig Docherty, either.'

Out of the corner of my eye I saw Gil flinch. Venture capitalists are proud of backing people, not businesses. Once you begin to doubt the person, then it is very hard not to doubt the business.

'You liked him six months ago, Frank,' Art said. 'What's changed?' Art was always quick to spot an opportunity to criticize Frank's judgement. He and Frank jostled in a most subtle way for the position of Gil's right-hand man.

'That's true. We all did.' And indeed Craig had made a presentation to the assembled partnership that had gone very well. His energy, dedication and total grip of his business had come through with great force. 'But from what I've seen of him since then, I think he's unreliable. He believes so much in the success of his company that he loses track of what's going on around him. The original plan was for twelve months to the development of a prototype, and that was tight. You can't do it in six without cutting corners. And you can't cut corners in this business without screwing up the product.'

7

'But he's been working eighteen-hour days, seven days a week!' I protested. 'The guy barely sleeps. And his staff are all working just as hard.'

'So he's driving them too hard,' said Frank. 'He'll make even more screw-ups.'

'Are you saying we should drop Net Cop?' asked Gil.

Frank paused. He leaned forward and rubbed his chin in the way I had seen him do a hundred times before turning down some hapless entrepreneur who had come into our offices looking for us to finance a dream. My eyes sought his, but he avoided them. 'We took a risk with the first two million. That's what we're supposed to do as venture capitalists. But the market's moving away from us, and the entrepreneur's losing perspective. The deal looks different. It would be a big mistake to drop another three million now.'

The bastard! I began to panic. Unless I did something immediately Net Cop would be dead. It was a good deal, I knew it. I just knew it. And more importantly I had given my word. Net Cop was Craig's life, and I had promised to support him. I wasn't prepared to go back on that.

'I disagree,' I said. I felt as much as heard a quick intake of breath from Daniel Hall, the associate sitting next to me. Associates didn't disagree with partners at Revere. 'I'm sorry Frank, but Craig seems to me to have done exactly the right thing. The market thinks that his switches are better than everyone else's. He has easily the most advanced security and encryption features, and that's exactly what the big telcos and ISPs want these days. He's got a winner here.'

Gil listened. When I had finished, he glanced across to Frank.

'He's got a higher spec than the competition,' said Frank. 'But we don't know whether he can deliver it – '

'That's why he needs the money for the prototype!' I interrupted. 'So that he can prove it works!'

Frank was silent. Then, for the first time that morning, he smiled. 'I admire Simon's enthusiasm. I've got to admit this looked like a good deal when we invested. But not any more. Sorry, Simon.'

The deal was dying, dying. 'But we can't back out now!' I protested. 'We told Craig we'd invest the next tranche when he met

8

his technical milestones. He's met them. It was in the investment agreement.'

'There's always a way out of an investment agreement, Simon,' said Frank. 'I can think of a couple of clauses in there that could give us an out.'

I paused. I was floundering badly. I felt a nudge under the table. 'Give up,' whispered Daniel, very quietly out of the corner of his mouth. But I couldn't.

'Frank,' I began. 'We made an agreement. We have to stick to the spirit as well as the letter of it. We both know that Craig thought we were committing the second three million dollars. I thought that too.'

Frank didn't answer. He glanced at Gil.

Gil took a deep breath. 'OK, do we go ahead with the extra three million? Frank, I take it you say no?'

Frank nodded.

'Art?'

'No.'

'Ravi?'

Ravi glanced down at my memo through his half-moon reading spectacles. With curly grey hair, a bow-tie, and a large fleshy brown face, he looked more like a professor than a venture capitalist. He thought for a moment, but he could tell the mood of his partners. He shook his head.

'Diane?'

Diane had been listening closely to the exchange. Now all eyes were turned to her. She sat there with perfect poise, her thick dark hair framing her high cheekbones, her small delicate lips puckered in thought.

'I think we should go with it,' she said at length. 'I take Frank's points, but I remember when we did this deal. We knew then we were in for five million. It's an exciting market, and maybe we have got a winner here.'

I gave her a quick smile. The support was too little too late, but I appreciated it.

Gil listened to her with respect and nodded. 'Thank you, Diane.'

The room was silent as Gil studied the papers in front of him. We let him think. Then he sat back, folded his arms and delivered his verdict.

'No.'

All eyes were on me. It felt like a physical slap in the face. I had lost a deal. Somewhere I had gone wrong, and I had a feeling that it had little to do with Net Cop and more with Revere. I should have taken the time to prepare the political ground more carefully, to square Gil. I shouldn't have allowed myself to be ambushed by Frank.

Gil took some pity on me. 'I'm sorry, Simon. I go with Frank on this one. When a deal turns sour, you should take your losses. We've learned that lesson over the years the hard way. I'd like you to get hold of the lawyers and work out how best to present this to Net Cop. But I don't want to lose our two million if we can avoid it.'

'Without the extra three, Net Cop's finished,' I muttered, pursing my lips.

'Well, salvage what you can,' said Gil.

My first bad deal! That was a blow to my ego, but I could live with it. In fact it was probably an essential part of my education as a venture capitalist. What I couldn't live with was going back on my word.

'I can't do it,' I said.

Gil looked at me sharply. 'I don't think you understand, Simon. You've made your points. We've listened. We've decided to pull out. Now it's your job to do just that.'

'We made a moral commitment to give Net Cop the funds. I made a moral commitment. I can't go back on that.'

Art, who had been quiet throughout this, suddenly burst in. 'Hey, quit playing the English gentleman with us. This is business. We back winners, and when they stop being winners, we drop them. It's tough, but that's how we make money for our investors – '

Gil held up his hand to stop Art. 'OK, Art, OK,' he said calmly. He turned to me. 'I appreciate your sense of integrity, and I think there is a place for it in the way we do business at Revere. And I agree we had a moral commitment to invest more money, provided we were happy with the way the business was being run. But we're not.'

Gil looked to me for a response. I didn't give him one.

'Investment decisions must be based on the commercial realities,' he went on. 'And the reality here is that the partnership doesn't want to invest. It's not your decision, it's ours. All we ask is that you carry it out.'

They were all staring at me. 'I can't,' I said, and picked up my pen and pad and left the room.

I sat at my desk in the empty office I shared with the other two associates, my brain tumbling over what had just happened.

I had been at Revere just over two years, joining straight from business school. From the beginning, I had been determined to succeed, to make the serious money that American venture capitalists can earn, to break out of the traditional constraints of my past: my father's title that had now become mine, public school, university, the army. In my middle twenties I had realized that my life of tradition and privilege, which since boyhood I had been told was the pinnacle of human civilization, was for me a cold prison cell.

There was something beguiling about being an officer in the Life Guards: the sense of belonging to an elite, a sense of superiority that had been carefully honed by centuries of regimental pomp, ceremony, myth and *esprit de corps*. But I didn't want to be beguiled. Soldiers were thankfully becoming increasingly irrelevant in the modern world. I didn't want to be irrelevant. I wanted to be in the middle of things. So I had escaped, leaving the army and winning a scholarship to Harvard Business School. America was a land of opportunity for anyone who believed they had ability and who wanted to make a success of themselves, untrammelled by their past lives in the old country.

I was definitely one of those people.

And I had been doing well. PC Homelease had made eight million dollars for Revere in six months out of a half-million initial investment, and had won me recognition in the firm as someone who was either smart or lucky. Gil thought highly of me, and until today, so had Frank. I badly wanted to make partner; that was where the big money in venture capital was made. At a lunch a few months before, Gil had hinted that this was a definite possibility. Was I now going to throw it all away?

But I had given my word. I couldn't go back on it.

Why couldn't I? Was this just another one of those precepts that had been programmed into me at school and in the army, that a gentleman's word was his bond?

No, that wasn't it. I knew plenty of gentleman liars. It was just that in life there were some people you could trust, and some you couldn't, and I thought it was important to be one of those you could.

The other two associates returned from the meeting.

'Have you got a death wish, or something?' asked Daniel, as he threw his legal pad on to his desk by the window. Short, thin, with dark hair and pale skin, he was the most aggressive, and probably the brightest of us. 'Once they say no, they mean no, you know that.'

I shrugged.

'Man, that was rough,' said John, putting a hand on my shoulder. 'They mauled you in there.'

'It certainly felt like it.'

He powered up his computer. 'I think you were right, though. If you say you're gonna do something, you've gotta do it.' He gave me a friendly smile.

'Bullshit!' Daniel said. 'Art's right. You've always got to do what makes financial sense. That's what the investors in our funds pay us for.'

I ignored him. There was no point in arguing with Daniel on the question of ethics. He was the personification of the concept of 'market forces' as a religious system. If something's price goes up it's good, if the price goes down it's bad. We had both been recruited from Harvard, and despite the compulsory ethics courses we had attended there, we had been given plenty of academic justification for the supremacy of the pricing mechanism as a moral tool. Daniel didn't need any of this, though. He was a natural believer.

John was very different. Tall and athletic, with mousy brown hair and big blue eyes, he looked younger than his thirty years. He had been at Revere the longest of the three of us. His father, John Chalfont Senior, was one of America's richest men. He had built up Chalfont Controls into a multi-billion dollar corporation, and for a couple of decades had made regular appearances in the business magazines, where his views on hard-working Americans, corrupt politicians and unfair foreign competition were stridently broadcast.

But John Junior had little interest in hard work or money, managing to do just enough to scrape into an Ivy League college and business school. His ambition seemed to be to lead an ordinary life, free of hassle, which, given who his father was, was not easy to achieve. Joining Revere had kept his father happy. Daniel said John would never make it at the firm; he didn't have enough interest in money. Daniel was probably right. But John did what he was asked to do competently enough, and it was hard not to like him. He did a lot of work for Frank, who seemed to be happy with him.

'What are you going to do now?' he asked.

I sighed. I had been thinking about that ever since I had walked out of the board room. 'I don't know. I'm thinking of resigning.'

'Don't do it, Simon,' said Daniel. 'Seriously. Shit like this happens. It's going to happen wherever you work. Just because Frank woke up in a pissy mood this morning shouldn't mean you have to give up your career. What's with him anyway? I've never seen him so mean.'

'Neither have I. What do you think, John?'

'I don't know,' he said thoughtfully. 'Something's bugging him.'

Frank would normally have backed me up on something like this. And if he had disagreed with my conclusions, he would have gently guided me to what he believed was the right answer before the meeting, not waited for the moment of maximum humiliation.

It had to be me and Diane. That was the only logical explanation. Frank loved his daughter, and was very protective of her. In this case overprotective.

My phone rang. It was Gil.

'Simon, can I have a word tomorrow morning? Say nine o'clock?' His voice was friendly.

'Gil, I'd like to talk to you now – '

Gil interrupted. 'There's no need for that. Let's talk tomorrow, when you've had time to think about this morning. OK? Nine o'clock tomorrow then.'

His voice brooked no argument, and anyway what he said made sense. 'OK, I'll be there.'

Daniel glanced across the room at me. 'Gil's going to give you a chance to dig yourself out of this hole. Take it.'

'We'll see.' I picked up the Net Cop papers on my desk and tried to focus on them.

'Do anything over the weekend, Daniel?' John asked.

'Yeah,' said Daniel. 'Went to Foxwoods. Played blackjack all Saturday night, and came out with a thousand bucks more than I went in with. What more could you ask? What about you?'

'Nothing so exciting. I caught the Monet exhibition at the MFA. Pretty good. You should go.'

'Sign me up!' said Daniel.

'Daniel, have you ever been to an art gallery?' I asked.

'Sure. My parents took me to some museum in Paris when I was a kid. I threw up over a sculpture of a man and a woman making out. My mother was convinced my innocent sensibilities were upset by such an obscene composition. I suspect it had more to do with the Pernod I sneaked at lunch. Anyway, it was a real mess. Museums don't agree with me.'

John snorted. 'I'm sure they don't.'

My phone rang again. This time it was an external call. 'Can you take that John?'

He punched a button and picked up the phone. He listened, and glanced up at me, mouthing the word 'Craig'. I shook my head.

'I'm sorry Craig, he's in a meeting . . . It may last all day . . . I'm not sure what exactly it's about . . . I'm sure he'll be back to you when he has some news . . . OK, goodbye.'

'Thanks,' I said, as he put down the receiver. 'Craig's going to be calling all day. Would you two mind picking up my phone today?'

'Us pick up your phone?' said Daniel. 'We can't do that! We need a babe to pick up your phone. I'll call a temp agency and get one for you. Now what do you need? Redhead? Blonde? Let's get a blonde.'

'You'll do fine, Daniel,' I said.

I glanced down at the Net Cop papers in front of me. I had told Gil I couldn't carry out his decision, but that decision had been taken, and I had to face up to the fact. I couldn't leave it to someone else at Revere, or even worse, some hard-nosed lawyers to tell Craig. I had to do it myself, face-to-face; I owed him at least that much.

3

Net Cop was located in a modern industrial park in the romantically named Hemlock Gorge, a small wooded valley just off Route 128 in Wellesley. The whole company was basically a room of engineers in cubicles on the first floor of a low, brown, all-purpose building. I received a wave from Gina, the company's only secretary, and looked for Craig. At this stage of the company's life, all the work was being done on computers. On one side of the room sat the hardware engineers, and the software engineers sat on the other. They were different breeds of people who spoke totally different computer languages: the hardware guys used Verilog, and the software guys C++. Craig needed to get these two groups working together. This was achieved by a small team of bilingual engineers who sat in the middle of the room with a handsome golden retriever called Java.

Many of the staff were surprisingly old, some of them even had grey hair. Craig liked to hire experienced people, the enthusiastic nerds of the eighties who now had wives, children and a little common sense.

It was a good team. A great team, Craig said. And from a standing start they had already achieved more in six months than much bigger firms' R&D departments had achieved in two years.

I spotted the man himself drawing at breakneck speed over a double whiteboard in the corner. Boxes and arrows spread across the large white surface in bewildering confusion, and Craig finished off his point with a resounding question mark, scribbled with such emphasis he almost broke the pen. Two engineers were listening to him: an Indian with a greying beard, and a large man with a bulging yellow T-shirt and hair that was receding at the front, and advancing rapidly down his back.

I crossed the room and coughed gently.

Craig turned round. 'Hey, Simon! Howya doin'?' Despite his MIT education, he sported one of the dozen or so local Boston accents, which he clung on to tenaciously. He was grinning broadly, as though he were genuinely pleased to see me. Perhaps he was.

'I'm fine, Craig. How are you?' I replied, nervously.

'So, when do we get the dough?'

'That's what I wanted to talk to you about. There's a problem.'

'A problem? What kind of problem?'

The two men Craig had been lecturing were watching us with interest. In fact, I could feel eyes from all around the room resting on us.

'Can we talk about it in your office?'

Craig paused, looking around him. 'OK, come on,' he growled, and led me over to his small glass corner office.

He closed the door behind me.

'What's the problem?'

I took a deep breath. 'Revere has decided to make no further investment in Net Cop,' I said. 'Sorry, Craig.'

'What do you mean, you're not going to give us the money?' Craig's face reddened, and his thick neck bulged even further, the veins clearly visible. His muscles tensed large under his T-shirt. He struck the small conference table in his office so forcefully I thought it would break.

'You gotta give us the fuckin' money! You gotta!'

'Craig, I'm sorry, I've discussed it with the partnership. We can't.'

'Why the hell not?'

He took a couple of steps forwards and stared up at me. He was only five feet six inches tall, but he worked out regularly. He looked more like a squaddie than a brilliant coder. He was strong and tough, and very, very angry.

17

I groped for words. 'We feel that the market has changed. It's become more competitive. Too many companies are out there and it's hard to tell who the winner will be.'

'Jesus, we've been through this a million times. You wanna know who's gonna be the winner? We are!'

Spittle darted from his lips as he pounded his chest with a meaty thumb. I was aware that outside the glassed-in office all the engineers had stopped their work. Some of them were drifting over to watch.

I wanted to tell him that I thought he was right, that Revere should have given him the money. But that would have been unprofessional and a betrayal of the partnership. Besides, it would have made a messy situation even messier. Gil was right: while I worked for the firm I had a duty to carry out their decisions. Whether I agreed with those decisions or not was between them and me.

'I'm sorry,' I said. 'But there it is.'

'You can't do this, Simon. You're committed in the investment agreement.'

'Not quite.'

'It says if we meet the milestones, Revere will put in another three million bucks. We've met the milestones. Where's the money?'

'We don't feel that the ASIC has been tested sufficiently.'

'That's crap! I'm satisfied, what more do you need?'

'We need it to be tested in real working conditions for a period of three months. To see whether it works in a real system.'

'That's impossible, and you know it! Anyway, I say it works fine, and that should be enough!'

Reluctantly I tossed across a copy of the investment agreement, with the words 'will be determined at the sole discretion of Revere Partners' highlighted in yellow.

Craig glanced at it and then scowled. Suddenly his finger jabbed the page. 'What about this then? "Such approval not to be unreasonably withheld." I'd say you assholes are being unreasonable.'

I sighed. 'Your lawyers can spend money with our lawyers discussing that if you like. It doesn't really matter. We'll win, and even if we don't, there are two more clauses we can use. Face it

Craig, if we don't want to put in more money, we don't have to.'

Craig threw the agreement on to the table and moved over to the window overlooking a car park, and behind that the small ravine that was Hemlock Gorge.

'You gave me your word that we would get the money, Simon,' he said quietly, his back towards me.

'I know,' I replied. 'I haven't been able to deliver. I should never have made you a promise it wasn't in my power to keep.'

'I've put everything into this business, Simon,' Craig said. 'And not just all my money. I gave up a good well-paid job with stock options at a successful company. I hardly see Mary and the kids, now. And I'm not the only one. What about those guys out there?' He waved his arm towards the small crowd gawping at us through the windows of the conference room. 'I promised them Net Cop would be a success. That if they worked their asses off for a couple of years, it'd be worth their while. And if I have to let them down, because you've let me down, I'll . . .'

He stopped himself. He stood silently for several moments, rocking on the balls of his feet. He was a tight bundle of muscle in jeans, trainers and a black T-shirt with a white dumbbell across his chest.

'Who was it, Simon?'

'What do you mean?'

'Which one was it? Who turned us down? Gil Appleby? Frank Cook? That woman, whatever her name is? The Indian guy?'

I was impressed with Craig's memory of the people who had heard him present earlier that year.

'It was a partnership decision. A consensus.'

Craig spun round. 'Don't give me that bullshit! You at least owe me the truth on this one. Now, who was it?'

He was right. Loyalty to the firm could only stretch so far. I owed as much, or more, to Craig.

'Frank Cook,' I said.

'The bastard! The fuckin' bastard!' Craig shook his head.

'Craig,' I said.

'Yeah, what?'

19

'You'll get the money.'

'Oh, please! We're screwed, and you screwed us.'

'It's a great opportunity for someone.'

'Oh yeah. Like, some other VC is just gonna leap in with a ton of money once you guys have pulled out. Come on!' Craig's face was filled with contempt.

'You can try. I'll give you the best reference I can.'

'Like they're gonna call you! They're gonna talk to Frank Cook, and you know what that cocksucker's gonna say.'

Craig was right. Frank would make clear his reasons why Revere had pulled out. Craig glared at me, his small blue eyes burning underneath the folds of his brow, his short hair bristling. 'You make me sick, you know that? Just get outta here.'

'Craig, I can help – '

'Just get out!' he screamed.

I nodded slowly and left, passing a series of angry, puzzled faces on my way out. I managed to keep my expression firm until I was safely outside the building. But as the door shut behind me, I slumped back against the wall, cursing Gil and Revere and myself. I vowed never to get myself into that situation again.

When I arrived back at the office, Daniel was scanning a list of stock prices on his computer. He had an ability to recall price histories for certain stocks going back years, just from looking at them every day.

Daniel and I had hardly known each other at business school. He did well in class, and he talked a lot about his investments. For the most part these seemed to be remarkably successful. He had an uncanny knack for spotting take-overs before they would happen, and for anticipating the rapidly changing fads of technology investors. He made no secret that his ambition was to make many millions very quickly, and he saw the stock market as the quickest way to that end. He had supreme confidence in his own investment abilities, but all the risks he took were carefully calculated.

Revere had liked the look of him, and he had liked the look of venture capital, although, as he once told me, this was as much because it would give him better information about the markets as because he thought he would make big money out of it directly.

'Craig wasn't too happy, huh?' He looked up from his paper. 'Did he try to kill you?'

'Nearly,' I said.

'Did you use that army self-defence shit on him?'

'No, Daniel. I just stood there and tried to be calm. I think I succeeded.'

'So, what are you going to do?' asked John.

I slumped into my chair. 'I don't know.'

'Tea?' John asked.

I nodded. 'Thanks.'

He was back a couple of minutes later with a cup of tea for me and some complicated latte-type coffee for himself.

'What about me?' squawked Daniel.

John struck his forehead. 'Darn it,' he said. 'I've forgotten again.' 'Huh!'

John looked over Daniel's shoulder at the stock quotes on his machine.

'Forty-three and a quarter, eh?'

We all knew what he was looking at. It was the same little number everyone at Revere looked at every day. The BioOne stock price.

'Edging up,' said Daniel.

John picked up a stack of papers from his desk, and dumped it on Daniel's. 'Enjoy.'

It was the 'cold deals' pile. These were the deals that arrived in the mail from the wide world of wacky inventors and crazy dreamers. There was a virtual pile, just as high, in our computer system, that had been received electronically.

Daniel groaned. 'OK. But I'm not going to read them. I find my rejection letter is so much more polite if I don't.'

'You have to read them. It's your turn this week. Gil insists.'

'All right.' Daniel grabbed the pile of letters and business plans, and began to go through it. 'They're all losers anyway.'

'You don't know that,' said John.

'Oh, come on. This is all crap.' Daniel tapped a business plan in front of him. 'Look, this is from a guy who wants to sell UFO scanners over the Internet.'

'I got that wind-power generation deal from the cold pile,' John said.

Daniel rolled his eyes. 'Precisely.' He had a point. Although John had been very excited about the wind-power deal, Gil had dismissed it out of hand.

'At least I've got an open mind,' John said.

'Wide open,' muttered Daniel.

I tried to concentrate on work, but it was impossible. I was being attacked from all sides. Firstly by Frank and the other partners, then by Craig. Craig I could forgive. Frank I couldn't.

Frank and I had immediately liked each other when he had interviewed me for a job at Revere. Once I had joined the firm, we had worked well together, and he had watched my developing relationship with his daughter with approval. It was only in the last six months, since the wedding, that his attitude to me had cooled.

He was besotted with Lisa, and had missed her badly when she had moved to California with her mother when she was fourteen. When she returned to Boston to work for a small biotechnology company they saw a lot of each other. At first I fitted into this arrangement very well, but somehow, once Lisa and I were married, things changed. Invitations to spend the weekend with him at his house by the shore had previously been haphazard and informal, but now they became more insistent. When I came too, I no longer felt welcome, and I was sure that Frank engineered times for him and Lisa to meet up when he knew I couldn't be there.

In a way, I understood his feelings. Belatedly, he had realized that once Lisa married me, he would cease to be the most important man in her life. This bothered him. And he bothered me. Lisa and I both worked hard, and I wanted to spend what little free time we had alone with her.

Frank's suspicions of Diane hadn't helped. To his fear of losing his daughter, and his jealousy of the time I spent with her, was now added concern that she might be mistreated by a philandering husband.

I might understand all this. But I didn't like it. Especially when it messed up my work. I needed to talk to him.

He was in his office. All the partners had their own, expensively kitted out with the mixture of high-technology and old furniture that Gil believed gave the impression of a leading venture-capital firm with money: sleek computers, old prints, discreet VCRs, leather chairs, conference phones, dark wood tables.

He was on the phone, and he waved me to a chair in front of his desk.

I waited. He continued talking, avoiding my eye. He moved his arms for emphasis as he spoke. The shrugs, the hand movements, the expressions were the only signs of his Jewish ancestry, and the only resemblance to Lisa I recognized in him. He looked the archetypal White Anglo-Saxon Protestant, while she took after her mother, with her dark hair and eyes and her sharp features. His father, a prosperous Boston doctor, had been born Koch and changed his name to Cook in a mostly successful effort to blend into the community around him.

At work, we had always treated each other as colleagues, or at any rate partner and associate.

Until now.

He eventually finished his phone call, and turned to me.

'I'd like to talk about this morning,' I began.

'There's nothing to say. We said it all at the meeting.'

'I don't think so. There's more to it than that.'

'You were wrong. You made a mistake. You'll learn.'

'I know you saw me having dinner with Diane.'

He leaned forward. 'Simon, understand this. Your marriage to my daughter has no bearing on how I treat you at work, and I resent the implication that it does.'

'What else am I supposed to think? We did that deal together. Nothing's changed, Craig's doing brilliantly, all the milestones we set have been met.'

'I disagree, Simon. As I said this morning, I think plenty has changed. And I'm beginning to have my doubts about Craig. All I was doing was preventing the firm from making a bad investment. It was a judgement call. I made the right one, you made the wrong one. Now, I don't want to have any more of this conversation.'

'Oh, come on,' I said. 'You might have disagreed with me, but there was no need to humiliate me – '

'I said, I don't want to have this conversation.' He looked down to the papers on his desk.

I knew there was more I should say, more that had to be said. But Frank didn't want to hear it.

'You may not want to talk about it now, but this is something we'll have to sort out some time,' I said as I left the room.

I swore under my breath as I made my way back to my desk. Diane passed me in the corridor.

'Cheer up,' she said.

'Why? I've just screwed everything up here.'

'No, you haven't. Here, come into my office.'

I followed her through a door a couple of paces further down the corridor. She closed it behind me. Her office was smaller than Frank's, and tidier. Cool, crisp and modern.

I slumped heavily into an armchair and put my face in my hands. She sat on the sofa opposite me, relaxed, an encouraging half-smile on her lips. Through my fingers I could glimpse her long legs, resting against the side of the sofa. Lisa was right. She was undeniably attractive.

'Everyone has a really bad day sometime in every firm,' she said. 'You have to live with it. It's like a rite of passage. You've had your good deal with PC Homelease. Now you've got your bad one. They'll all be watching how you handle it, you know. If you bounce back, they'll think the better of you.'

'We'll see,' I said. 'Thank you for your support in there, by the way.'

'I thought you made the right call. So I had to say so.' She smiled quickly. 'Now,' she got up and took a sheaf of papers from her desk. 'Take a look at this for me. It's a company called Tetracom. They have a new idea for microwave filters for cellular telephone networks. The technology looks very interesting to me. I've scheduled a trip to see them in Cincinnati next Thursday and Friday. Can you make it?'

I was just about to say 'yes, of course', when I hesitated. An overnight trip with Diane, however innocuous, would be bad timing.

'Um, I don't think I'll be able to,' I said. 'This Net Cop business is going to take some sorting out.'

'Oh, come on. It's only a day and a half. And I'd like you to work on it. I think we make a good team.'

When a partner specifically wanted you to work on something it was just stupid to refuse.

'Do you have a problem with travelling with me?' Diane looked at me sharply.

She was standing there, soberly dressed, next to her large desk, a partner of the firm I worked for. Telecoms was her area of expertise, and it was a field I was trying to specialize in myself. How could I have a problem travelling with her?

'No, of course not. I'll do my best.'

'Good. I'll have a word with Gil if Net Cop is a problem. This is an important deal you know.'

I smiled and left.

'I saw you slinking into Diane's office,' Daniel said as I returned to my desk. 'You two sure are spending some quality time together.'

'She's just trying to find out how well hung you are, Daniel,' I said. 'But don't worry, I won't tell her. I promise.'

'Tell her that's something she's welcome to figure out for herself,' said Daniel, smiling at the rows of numbers on his computer screen. 'Any time.'

4

I left the office at six, early for me, and walked home. My route took me up from the Financial District over the Common to Beacon Hill. It was a warm evening for early October, and there were plenty of people walking about in shirt sleeves or T-shirts. But there had already been a couple of cold nights, and the first of the leaves were beginning to turn.

I walked slowly, trying to relax, letting the low sunlight caress my face. There was no doubt that fall was the best time of year in Boston. And winter was the worst. In a couple of months I would be battling through the bitter cold to make my way home.

Beacon Hill was quiet, as usual. I stepped past a woman cajoling four dogs back from the Common to their various mistresses, and smiled politely at a man who gestured at the 'goddamned son of a bitch' who had taken two parking spaces with one car. Parking and dog shit were the two big issues on Beacon Hill. I was for one and against the other, but in this neighbourhood it was prudent to keep such opinions to yourself.

Half way up the hill to my right was where Gil lived, a sedate town house on Louisburg Square, supposedly the most expensive piece of residential real estate in New England. But our apartment was on the 'flat' of the hill, at the bottom, down a pretty little street of dappled sunlight, green leaves and black railings.

I had just broken out a bottle of Sam Adams from the refrigerator when Lisa came in.

'You're early,' I said.

'So are you,' she replied, and gave me a kiss. 'It's kinda nice, isn't it?' She hugged me. 'What's wrong? Bad day?'

'Horrible day.'

'Oh no. What happened?'

I got her a beer and we sat down together on the sofa. She tucked herself under my arm and listened as I told her about the meeting, about the way Frank had humiliated me and the stand I had taken at the end. Then I told her about Craig's reaction. I had been dying to talk to Lisa about it all day.

She exploded. 'I can't believe Dad did that! Let me call him right now.'

'No, don't do that.'

'Simon! He shouldn't jerk you around at work. That's way out of line.' She untangled herself from me and moved towards the telephone.

'No, stop Lisa!' I said. 'That'll only make it worse.'

She picked up the phone. I put my finger on the cradle.

She glanced at me, and seemed to calm down.

I pulled her to me and kissed her. 'It's sweet of you to be so concerned,' I said. And it was. For Lisa to come down on my side so unambiguously was exactly what I wanted. 'So far, I've managed to keep my relationship with him at work purely professional. I'd like to try to stick to that.'

'OK,' she said reluctantly. 'I bet he's upset about seeing you with Diane last week. But he's overreacting. No way should he have done that to you.'

'No, he shouldn't have.' I picked up my beer, and took a swig. 'Gil wants to see me tomorrow.'

'What are you going to say?'

'I don't know. Maybe I should resign. I promised Craig the money. I mean we promised it to him, Frank and I. And now Gil expects me to pull the plug on Net Cop. I'm not sure I can live with that.'

'Can't Craig get money from somewhere else?'

I shook my head. 'No other venture firm would touch him if Revere pulled out now.'

'What about his customers? In the biotech world small companies are always doing deals with the big pharma companies who market their drugs.'

I paused for a moment to consider the suggestion. 'We could give it a go. It'd be difficult. But it's worth a try.'

Lisa took a gulp of her beer.

'What do you think?' I asked her.

She was silent. I waited.

'Do you really want to quit?' she said eventually.

'No. But I think maybe I should.'

'But do you want to? Give up, I mean.'

'No, of course I don't want to give up,' I said. 'But sometimes you can be forced into a position where the only right thing to do is resign. I'm afraid that's what's happened to me.'

'I guess you can give up if you want to. And it sounds like you've got a real problem. You can either run away from it, or you can try to solve it. Your choice.'

I listened to what she was saying. 'You talk about "giving up". I was thinking that resigning was the honourable thing to do. The courageous thing to do.'

'Quitting is quitting,' said Lisa. 'Look, I'm not suggesting that you forget your promise to Craig. Sure, you've let him down. It wasn't your fault, but you've got him in a horrible mess. So you've got to get him out again.'

'Net Cop is history.'

'Not yet, it isn't,' Lisa replied. 'I've never seen such a determined guy as Craig. He's smart. So are you. You'll figure something out.'

Her confidence in me was touching. But misplaced.

'I'll think about it.'

The phone rang. I picked it up. I heard the clear English tones of my sister.

'Helen! What time is it? It's the middle of the night in London, isn't it?'

'I couldn't sleep. And I thought this would be a good time to get you at home.' She sounded tired. Tired and worried.

'What's up?' I said. It had to be bad news. Bad news always happened to Helen.

'I spoke to the lawyers today. They think we can appeal. I don't know what to do about it.'

'But we lost the case. What makes them think we'll win an appeal? More fees?'

'They've found two more expert witnesses who will say that the doctor was definitely negligent. They're good. Well respected. Lots of letters after their names.'

'They'll need to be paid, of course.'

'Of course. And so will the lawyers. Especially the barrister. That's the killer.'

It was. Helen had already spent all her meagre savings on the case. And I had spent all mine. And Lisa's. And I'd added all I could to my business school loan. Sixty-five thousand pounds had been swallowed up by the lawsuit. And after all that, Matthew still had cerebral palsy, and Helen had still been forced to give up her career in a television production company. She had taken on a job as a part time secretary so that she could spend most of her time looking after him.

'Have you spoken to Piers?'

Piers was Matthew's father, an unsuccessful TV scriptwriter who had disappeared from Helen's life just before the boy had been born.

'There's no point. He has no interest, and he has no money, and he's no bloody use at all.'

'What about Mother?'

'Come on! I haven't spoken to her for six months!'

Our mother, Lady Ayot, hadn't approved of her daughter having a baby out of wedlock. Besides which, she had no money either.

'What do you want to do?' I asked.

Helen sighed. 'If we win, we could get a large settlement. Enough for me to look after Matthew. And we'd get costs, so I could pay you back.'

'That doesn't matter,' I said.

'It does to me,' said Helen.

What mattered was how Helen was going to look after her son without a full-time job, a husband, or any money. That was what mattered. I was very fond of my younger sister. She had come through a cold upbringing very well. She deserved more than this.

'And if we lose?'

'I've lost everything anyway, so I don't care,' Helen said. 'But it's you I'm worried about. I was going to leave you out of it. Tell them that we couldn't afford to go to appeal. But . . . But, it's our only hope. And . . . well, I thought you wouldn't want me to make up your mind for you.'

'You're right,' I said. 'I'm glad you called.' I sighed. 'But I haven't got anything left, Helen. I've borrowed all I can.'

'I know,' said Helen simply.

Silence.

'How much?' I asked eventually.

'Fifty thousand pounds. Maybe less. But we should expect fifty thousand.'

We sat in silence, thousands of miles apart. We had to try. Somehow, we had to try.

'We don't have to decide right now, do we?' I said.

'No. We've got time.'

'Leave it with me,' I said. 'I'll think of something.'

'Thank you,' she said, a glimmer of hope in her voice.

I put down the phone.

'She wants to appeal?' said Lisa.

I nodded.

'And it's going to cost money?'

'Fifty thousand quid.'

Lisa winced. 'Where are we going to get that from?'

I shrugged. I had no idea where we were going to get the money. I slumped back in the sofa. I had done all I could for Helen, and it still hadn't been quite enough. A wave of despair swept over me.

'I can't believe how stupid your system is,' Lisa said. 'If this had happened here, we wouldn't be paying lawyers anything, and they'd have settled by now.'

She was right. The case had proved much harder to pursue than any of us had expected. There had been complications at Matthew's birth that had led to him being deprived of oxygen for a few minutes. The doctor had made some mistakes. When it became clear that Matthew had cerebral palsy, it seemed obvious that the doctor was responsible. Helen had decided to sue, with my support.

It had been an easy decision at the time. Abandoned by her lover, Helen was alone and angry. Mother was never going to be any help, and Matthew, now two, needed constant care. Helen had given up a promising career in television production and was faced with a life where every spare minute was taken up with either looking after Matthew, or scraping enough money together to pay for looking after him. She was finding it very hard to cope – if it hadn't been for Matthew's total dependence on her, I was sure she would have cracked by now. She hadn't deserved this.

The case had quickly become more complicated and the fees had risen. Although Lisa and I agonized over the money, it became harder and harder to pull out. In the end, I always came to the same decision: I wasn't going to abandon my sister.

'I'm sorry about all this,' I said to Lisa, taking her hand.

She squeezed it. 'Don't worry. I'd do the same for my brother, and I know he'd do it for me.'

We were lying naked in bed together, reading. Lisa was engrossed in *The Quincunx*, a thick, fiendishly complicated novel whose title I didn't even understand. I was skimming the Tetracom material Diane had given me, trying to keep my eyes open.

'We had some good results today,' Lisa said.

I put down my papers. 'Really?'

'Yes, the animal work on BP 56 is looking good. We'll be able to try it on humans soon.'

'That's great! So it really works?'

'We won't know until it has gone through the whole clinical trials process, but so far it's looking very good.'

'Well done, my love.' I leaned over and kissed her. It was Lisa who had first suggested that BP 56, some kind of small molecule called a neuropeptide that she had isolated, would have a beneficial effect on Parkinson's disease. And it now looked as if she was right. I felt a flood of pride at what she had achieved. 'Perhaps Boston Peptides will have a market cap of a billion dollars in a few years.' I smiled at her.

'All you venture capitalists ever think about is money! The best thing would be if we actually could treat Parkinson's. That really would be cool.'

'OK, you've got me,' I said, properly chastened. 'But I can still hope.'

She smiled. 'Poor Henry is so excited he can hardly control himself.' Henry Chan was her boss and the founder of Boston Peptides. 'But we're going to need cash from somewhere to fund the clinical trials. Venture First doesn't want to put up any more. I kind of sympathize with Craig.'

I winced. 'At least Venture First has an excuse. I think they've just about run out of money themselves.' They were a small venture-capital firm that had provided the initial funding to Boston Peptides. The rumours in the market were that their performance had been poor and they were having trouble raising more funds from their investors.

'So what kind of people do you get to take these drugs?' I asked.

'People with Parkinson's disease, of course.'

'No, I mean during the clinical trials. Who would want to be the first human ever to take a drug?'

'Oh, I see what you mean. Volunteers. Medical students, mostly. They get paid for it.'

'They must be mad.'

'It's perfectly safe.'

'How can you know until it's been tried on people?'

'We do very thorough tests on animals. If there's a major problem it will show up.'

'So why do the tests on people at all, then?'

'There are often some side-effects,' Lisa said. 'Headaches, nausea, diarrhoea.'

'You'd never catch me doing it,' I said.

'Someone's got to. And these volunteers really are doing something for science.'

'Mad,' I said. 'Brave, but mad.'

Lisa glanced at the papers I was reading.

'What are all these?'

'Oh, it's a deal called Tetracom that Diane is working on. It looks quite promising.'

'Diane, huh?'

'Yes.' I tried to come out with the next bit casually. 'We're going to Cincinnati next week to visit them. I'll be out Thursday night.'

She pulled back. 'OK,' she said, picking up her book again.

I watched as she studied the page in front of her intently.

'Do you have a problem with that?' I said at last.

'No.' She didn't look up from her book.

'I mean, I have to go. It's my job to work with Diane.'

Then she looked up, a spark of anger in her face. 'To tell you the truth, I do mind, Simon.'

'You shouldn't,' I said. 'There's nothing to worry about. You should know that.'

'You say there's nothing to worry about,' Lisa snapped. 'I think perhaps there is. A business trip to Cincinnati. The two of you alone in some hotel. If she has got her eye on you, that's when she'll make her move, Simon.'

'Lisa! She's a partner in my firm. A colleague. A boss.'

'She's done it before!'

'Who told you that?'

'Dad,' she said quietly.

'Huh,' I snorted. 'He put all this into your mind, didn't he?'

'No. I just don't trust that woman.'

'You don't even know her.'

'OK,' said Lisa. 'You go then.' She reached over and turned out the light.

We lay in bed, backs to each other. I was angry. I really had no

33

choice but to go. And Lisa really ought to be able to trust me to go on a business trip with a colleague, even a beautiful one.

I was still fuming, when I felt a finger brush gently up my spine.

'Simon?' she whispered.

'Yes?'

'I have an idea.'

'What is it?' I turned to face her.

She pulled herself close to me, her hands moving over my body. 'I'm going to wear you out so completely that Diane will have to dump you for someone her own age.'

She gave me a long kiss.

'Sounds like a good plan to me,' I said.

5

The scull cut through the river and the slight head wind towards the Boston University Bridge, where the Charles River narrowed. A mile behind me was the Union Boathouse from where I set off three mornings a week. I was into a good rhythm now. Legs, arms, shoulders, back, breathing all combined to produce the regular splash of wood in water on either side of me.

I had learned to row at school and had rowed again at Cambridge. In the army they had other ways of keeping you fit, but when I had arrived at Harvard it had not taken me long to find the river again.

On my left rose the Dome and Senate House of MIT, and beyond them the mysterious tall brown buildings of Kendall Square, housing the biochemical secrets of companies such as Genzyme, Biogen, and our very own BioOne. On my right was the long strip of green that was the Esplanade, then the noisy Storrow Drive, and overlooking that, the sedate apartment buildings of the Back Bay. The air was crisp, the water blue, and the sky clear. Out here, scudding through the middle of this broad river, I felt alone. I could think.

My conversation with Helen had depressed me. I knew she was near the end of her rope, and I wanted so badly to help her, but I just couldn't do it. If I could find the cash, and we did win the appeal, then her life would still be difficult but it would be bearable. I was the lucky one, with a wife I loved and a job I enjoyed. It wasn't fair. I wanted to share some of that luck with her.

Although the job wasn't going that brilliantly at the moment. My anger with Frank and the other partners was hardening.

I remembered the discussions Frank and I had had with Craig when we were putting the deal together. All three of us assumed that the extra three million dollars would be available. Sure, we had inserted the right to refuse to provide the funds in the legals, but my implicit assumption was that that was to protect us from Craig failing to get a team up and running.

From what I could see, he had done a great job. He was certainly volatile, but we'd known that when we'd invested. Frank was correct that in the last six months a number of companies large and small had begun work on the next generation of switches for the Internet. But none had the determination and sense of purpose of Craig. He lived and breathed Net Cop: it had become his whole life. He would get there first, I was sure. If only we would give him the funds to do it.

But the partners had made up their minds. There was nothing I could do to change it. I could disappear in a huff, my honour intact, my résumé a shambles, and try to find another job somewhere else. But I'd be throwing away a promising career at a place I liked, working with people I liked.

Or I could do as Lisa suggested. Try to sort the mess out myself.

As usual, Lisa was right. I would stay and help Craig. I wouldn't let Net Cop die.

I reached the Harvard boathouses and turned round.

Frank's opposition bothered me a lot. And so did Lisa's reaction to my going to Cincinnati with Diane. I supposed I could have said no when Diane had suggested dinner the previous Thursday night. But nothing had happened, no matter what Frank thought. And Frank had overreacted to what he had seen, or what he thought he had seen.

Lisa didn't have anything to be jealous about. Did she?

Diane was attractive. I liked her. We got on well together, we had had a great time at dinner the other night. But I loved Lisa. I loved her so much, so much more than I could ever imagine loving

36

someone like Diane. And I didn't want to do anything that would jeopardize that. I didn't want to end up like my father.

Sir Gordon Ayot (Bart) had never known his own father, my grandfather, who had died on the road to Arnhem. He had inherited a small estate in Devon, a baronetcy, and a desire to join the family regiment, the Life Guards, which he duly did. He did everything that a dashing cavalry officer was supposed to do. He gambled, entertained lavishly, womanized, found a beautiful wife, and learned to drive armoured cars round godforsaken parts of the world. Women loved him, and he loved women. This was clear to me from when I was quite a young boy. My parents did their best to keep the state of their marriage from Helen and me, sending us first of all to bed, and then to boarding school, but of course they didn't succeed. My father's expenditure easily exceeded his income, and the estate shrank until only a small cottage was left. My father felt let down, too. My mother was supposed to be rich, but her father had carelessly gone bust in the property crash of 1974. She tried hard to ignore her husband's recreations, and their expense, but when I was ten, they divorced.

I hated my father for hurting my mother. But I also admired him. Throughout my teenage years he used to take me off on a series of unplanned trips: scuba-diving in Belize, rock-climbing in Canada, and later when I was at university to nightclubs in London and Paris. Where the money came from for all this, I had no idea, and my mother could never find out. Then one morning at Cambridge I was called to my tutor's rooms. He told me that my father had died peacefully in the night, of a heart attack. He was only forty-five. I subsequently discovered that he had been drinking heavily the evening before, and there were two women half his age there to witness it.

Against my mother's wishes, I joined the Life Guards after Cambridge. I did it partly out of a sense of loyalty to my father and grandfather, but also because I thought soldiering would be fun. It was, and I was good at it, but in the end the layers of constricting tradition got to me, and I left.

I bitterly regretted my parents' divorce, and my father's part in it. At ten I had solemnly resolved never ever to do the same thing myself. And now, here I was, six months into my own marriage to a woman I loved, and my father-in-law was suggesting I was going the same way. It wasn't just that he was wrong: he had hurt my pride.

Lisa's parents were also divorced, of course. Frank had walked out from his wife when Lisa was fourteen. Lisa had never been given a satisfactory explanation, and like me, had never quite forgiven her father. But there the similarity ended. Although her mother quickly remarried and moved to San Francisco, taking Lisa and her brother with her, Frank had stayed single.

I wanted to make quite sure that neither one of us followed in our parents' footsteps.

I looked over my shoulder and saw the Union Boathouse speeding nearer. My arms and shoulders ached. It had been a good outing.

Gil's office was the largest in the firm. The walls were oak-panelled, the furniture antique. Pride of place was given to a portrait of a weak-chinned colonial nobody by Gilbert Stuart, after whom Gilbert Stuart Appleby had been named. The portrait had only arrived a year before. Gil no doubt liked visitors to assume that the picture had been hanging in the family home for generations. But Daniel had pretty good evidence that it represented the first premature expenditure of a chunk of the BioOne millions.

'Now, have you decided what to do about Net Cop?' Gil asked with quiet concern.

'I'm going to try to save it.'

Gil raised his eyebrows. 'How?'

I smiled. 'I'm not sure yet. But I'm not going to give up. I'll get the two million back somehow. And I'm going to try to make more.'

Gil watched me closely through those thick glasses. Then he smiled, the wrinkles rearranging themselves on his face. 'I admire your perseverance. Do what you can. But there won't be a cent more from Revere.'

I returned his smile. 'I understand that.'

Gil pulled out his pipe and began to stuff it with tobacco. The only place he smoked it was in his own office. These days in America you couldn't smoke a pipe in any semi-public place, even if you did own your own firm.

'You know the mistake you made, Simon?'

Plenty of responses leaped to mind, but I settled on 'No?'

'It wasn't suggesting the follow-on. That was just a matter of judgement. Nor was it your desire to keep your word. Despite what Art says, I find that admirable. It was making a promise that boxed yourself in. As a venture capitalist, you always have to leave a way out. Circumstances change, the unforeseen always happens.'

I wasn't absolutely sure of this. It seemed to me that if an entrepreneur had put his life savings, his house, his dream into a venture capitalist's hands, at the very least he should expect some sort of commitment back from the venture capitalist. But Gil had written the rule book.

So I nodded.

'Well, I'm glad you haven't decided to do anything rash. Good luck with Net Cop. Oh, one other thing.'

'Yes?'

'Is John Chalfont OK?'

'I think so. Why?'

'It's just he was pushing very strongly for that wind-power deal the other day. He should have been here long enough to realize we've turned down a dozen of those.'

'Just a temporary loss of perspective,' I said. 'Happens to all of us.'

Gil didn't look convinced. 'Hmm. Thank you, Simon.'

Encouraged that my career at Revere seemed intact, I left the room, ignoring the feeling that my doubts hadn't disappeared, but had only been suppressed.

Daniel was looking at the stock quotes on his computer. BioOne had edged up to forty-four dollars. I'd already checked. John was out.

Daniel glanced up. 'Do you still have a job?'

'I do.'

'Gil talked you out of it, huh?'

'Lisa did, if anyone,' I said.

'I'm glad one of you has some common sense.'

I grunted. 'Gil did ask me whether John was OK. I think that wind-power deal worried him.'

Daniel laughed. 'John's such an airhead.'

'Oh, come on, Daniel. He's not that bad.'

'Of course he is. Sure he's a nice guy. But what's the point of that? It's worth zero. He's a loser. He's going nowhere in this firm, it's obvious. You know he's only here because of his father.'

I shrugged. Perhaps Daniel was right. But I liked John and had no intention of writing him off as a loser.

Daniel noticed my reticence, and changed the subject. 'So what are you going to do with Net Cop?'

'Find it some money.'

Daniel raised his eyebrows. 'How?'

'God knows. Any ideas?'

It was always worth asking Daniel for ideas. Despite his cynicism, he could be very creative.

He paused for a moment. 'What about Jeff Lieberman? He invested in BioOne, didn't he? He might have a go at Net Cop.'

I thought about it. Jeff had been at business school with us. He was an able student, and he and I had had a lot of time for each other. He had headed off for Bloomfield Weiss, a big investment bank in New York, but he had watched my progress at Revere with interest. I had told him about BioOne, with Lisa's reservations, and he had made a significant investment in the Initial Public Offering.

'It's worth a try,' I said.

I looked up his number and dialled it.

'Jeff Lieberman.'

'Jeff, it's Simon Ayot.'

'Simon! How're you doing?'

'I'm fine.'

'And how's my little BioOne? The price isn't going down any further, is it?'

'Forty-four this morning. Way above where you bought it.'

'That's true. I can't complain.'

'Jeff, I was actually calling about another company we're involved in. If you thought BioOne was risky, you should see this one. But the pay-off will be huge if the company makes it.'

'Tell me more.'

So I told him all about Net Cop.

The deal caught his interest. It had those magic words 'The Internet' attached to it. I told him the risks, that Revere had backed out, and we would need more money to keep Net Cop afloat, but that just seemed to whet his appetite. For him, though, there was one important question.

'Do *you* like it Simon?'

I had hoped he wouldn't ask me. I would have to put my reputation on the line for this one. I swallowed. 'It's very risky, but yes, I do like it. Craig Docherty is a winner.'

'OK, well send me the information. I'll let you know.'

'I'll do that right away.'

'Oh, and thanks Simon. Let me know if you hear about any other promising deals.'

I put the phone down. Jeff might invest. But I still needed to find a lot more money. That would have to wait until Craig had calmed down.

'Was he interested?' asked Daniel.

'He might be.'

'I'm going to New York this weekend. I can see him if you like. Talk to him about it.'

'Thanks. Do that.'

I tried to call Craig, but he 'wasn't available', so I left a voice-mail telling him what I was doing. I could understand his anger, but he'd come round, especially if I actually did find some money for him.

Just then, John strolled in, whistling some hit song from the eighties and clutching a large latte.

'Still here, Simon?'

''Fraid so.'

'Hey, why don't you get John to invest?' Daniel said.

'In what?' John asked.

'Net Cop.'

'High potential returns, can't lose more than a hundred per cent of your money,' I added.

'Can't,' John said, sitting down at his desk.

'Why not?' asked Daniel.

'I don't have anything to invest with.'

'Oh, come on, John. You can spare the odd ten million.'

'When can you get it into your stupid head my father doesn't give me any money? If I want a dollar from him, I've got to wash his car.' John said this casually. We had been over the subject many times before, and Daniel never believed him. I did.

'Can't you suggest it to your old man? He can put his own money in.'

'Oh, please.' John glanced at the screen full of stock prices in front of Daniel. 'Doesn't matter how long you stare at it. It's not going up.'

'You never know,' Daniel muttered.

'You've got to own half of BioOne by now,' said John.

'Unfortunately.'

'Why? You must be sitting on a big profit now, surely.'

Daniel sighed. 'I bought a shit-load at fifty-eight.'

'Warren Buffet would be proud of you,' said John, smiling.

'It'll come back,' said Daniel irritably.

A shit-load to Daniel was a lot of stock. After the Initial Public Offering the stock price had shot up, increasing fourfold. For the last year it had marked time, hovering around sixty dollars, until the recent slump with the rest of the biotech sector.

'Still, our glorious partners are doing OK,' John said. 'I wonder how much their stake is worth?'

'About fifty-four million dollars between them,' answered Daniel immediately.

'Fifty-four million!'

'Absolutely. Revere invested five million in ninety-four. That five million is now worth about two hundred seventy-five million.

The partners get twenty per cent of the profits and there you are.'

Trust Daniel to have the numbers at his fingertips. I knew that BioOne completely dominated Revere's other holdings. There were some successes – mostly Frank's, some big losses – mostly Art's, and a mixed bag of other investments, but BioOne was the only one that mattered.

Fifty-four million to be shared between five partners! Of course Gil would get the most. Art would get a big chunk, because he had done the BioOne deal originally, even though everything else he touched was a dog, but Frank would get a lot too. The newer partners, Ravi and Diane, would have much smaller shares.

No associate had yet made it to partner at Revere. It was a situation I desperately wanted to change.

'So, what's it feel like to have a father-in-law worth millions of dollars, Simon?' Daniel asked.

'It's all paper profits,' I said. 'And anyway I get the impression I'm not the favourite son-in-law at the moment.'

Daniel smiled grimly. 'I kinda got that impression too.'

'What does Lisa think of BioOne?' John asked.

'Not much,' I answered.

'Why?'

'She had a friend who worked there who hated it. Apparently the Technical Director is a scumbag. You know, Thomas Enever, the Aussie. He runs a regime of total secrecy there. He's the only one who knows what's going on.'

'I think she's wrong,' said Daniel.

I shrugged. Boston Peptides was a much smaller firm than BioOne, and they operated in related fields rather than being direct rivals. But Lisa had strong views about the bigger firm.

'Enever's brilliant,' said Daniel. 'Touchy, but brilliant.'

'He must be,' I said. 'I don't know the first thing about bio-tech.'

'Neither does Art,' said Daniel, laughing. 'And it's the only investment he's made here that's worked.'

I smiled. Daniel occasionally helped Art out on BioOne,

especially when Art needed some number-crunching done, and so he was the only person apart from Art who had had contact with the company. Art had backed an old friend from his computing days, Jerry Peterson, to buy BioOne four years ago. Daniel was right, Art knew nothing about biotech, and it was debatable whether Jerry, now BioOne's chairman, did either.

It had turned out that BioOne had the most promising treatment for Alzheimer's disease, the chief cause of senility in old people. Alzheimer's was one of the most prevalent chronic diseases in the world, and although it had always existed, its diagnosis was growing all the time. Chronic diseases were good targets for a biotech company; patients just kept taking the pills year after year. That would turn into billions of dollars of sales once the drug was approved by the authorities. That was why BioOne was valued at one and a half billion dollars on NASDAQ, the high-tech stock exchange.

Art had got lucky and it was difficult to begrudge him that, especially since the whole firm was benefiting from it.

I was lying on the sofa in our small living room, an open book resting face down on my chest, my eyes closed, when I heard the door bang. I looked at the clock on the wall. Ten o'clock.

'Hi,' I said, sitting up.

'Hi.' Lisa kissed me quickly and plopped down next to me. 'It's dark in here,' she said.

It was. I had been reading by one weak lamp. I liked the room like that in the evening. The yellow light from the gas lamps on the street outside would flicker through the windows, casting shadows on the white walls and the old brick fireplace.

'Shall I turn some lights on?' I asked.

'No. It's nice. But you could get me a glass of wine.'

'Sure.' I opened a bottle of Californian red, and poured us a glass each. Lisa drank hers gratefully, and stretched out, kicking off her shoes.

'My brain hurts,' she groaned.

I kissed her temple. 'Better?'

44

She turned, pulled me down to her, and gave me a long slow kiss. 'A bit.'

'I wish you didn't have to work quite so hard,' I said.

'No choice. It's like a race against time. We have to get BP 56 to a point where we can attract more money before we run out of cash. We've got to get the animal data finished so we can go on to the human trials.'

'I thought you said the animal work was all done.'

'It is. And it's obvious what the results are. But we need to get everything written up for the FDA. It's a nightmare.'

'I bet.'

Lisa finished her wine, and poured herself another glass. 'You didn't resign, I take it?'

'No. You were right. I'm going to try to save Net Cop.'

'How?'

'I don't know. A guy from business school might put some money up. But we'll need a lot more than he's got.'

'You'll find it,' Lisa said. 'Any more ideas about Helen's appeal?'

'I'd like to go for it,' I said. 'She's trapped, and this really is her only hope of escaping. But we just don't have the money.'

'Do you trust her lawyers when they say they'd win this time?'

'I called the solicitor this morning. He is confident, much more confident than I've seen him before. Apparently this new expert witness is very convincing. If only all this had come up in a few years' time, when I was properly established at Revere. I'd be able to afford it then.'

'I'm sorry, Simon,' Lisa said, touching my hand. 'I wish there was something I could do.'

'You've let me blow all our savings. There's not much more than that you can do.'

Lisa seemed to hesitate.

'What is it?' I asked.

'I saw Dad today,' she said. 'For lunch.'

I felt a mild burst of irritation at this. It was another example of my wife and my father-in-law conspiring to see each other behind my back. 'You didn't tell me.'

'No. I wanted to ask him whether he could lend us some money. For Helen.'

I was shocked. My heart beat faster. 'What did he say?'

Lisa bit her lip. 'No.'

I winced. 'You shouldn't have asked him, Lisa. It was nice of you to try, but this is my family's problem. It has nothing to do with him. As he seems to realize,' I added bitterly.

'It wasn't that,' said Lisa. 'He doesn't approve of medical litigation. He thinks it's screwing up this country's medical system. I remember how Pop used to go on about it.' I had heard a lot about Pop, Lisa's grandfather, a doctor of forthright opinions. 'Dad just doesn't want to support it.'

'But Matthew's life was screwed up by some incompetent doctor!' I protested. 'Someone's going to have to pay for that for the rest of the boy's life, and I don't see why it should only be Helen.'

Lisa sighed. 'That's what I told him. But you know what Dad's like when he says no.'

I did. Frank was a kind, generous man. But years in venture capital had taught him to say no firmly and finally, without leaving any trace of doubt that no money would be forthcoming.

I would never have gone to Frank myself. I knew that I had no right to ask Frank for money, and he had no reason to give it. It was good of Lisa to try. But now Frank had said no, I couldn't help thinking of him as heartless.

'I said I'd go up and see him on Sunday at Marsh House,' Lisa said hesitantly. 'By myself.'

'Lisa!'

'Sorry, Simon I had to. He asked me before I'd had a chance to ask him about the money. I had to say yes then, and I couldn't very well back out afterwards.'

I shook my head. 'Look, I can't stop you seeing him every now and then,' I said. 'But we don't get enough time to see each other as it is. I mean, you'll be working on Saturday, won't you?'

Lisa nodded. 'Probably.'

'Well, then. It's as though he's trying to edge me out somehow.'

'Oh, Simon, don't be ridiculous.'

'I'm not being ridiculous.'

'We always used to see a lot of each other. I love him. He's my father. Why shouldn't I see him?' Lisa's voice was rising.

'I think it's unhealthy.'

'Unhealthy? Jesus! And after I went begging to him for money!'

'I didn't ask you to,' I muttered.

Lisa glared at me, put down her wine, and stood up. 'Good night, Simon,' she said, and marched from the room.

I sat there, in the half-light, feeling stupid. I let ten minutes pass before I went into the bedroom. Lisa was already in bed with the light off, and her body almost entirely submerged by the covers, her back to the middle of the bed.

I took off my clothes and crawled into bed behind her. 'Lisa.'

No response.

'Lisa? Lisa, I'm sorry. I've had a bad few days. We both have.' I kissed her softly under her left ear. She stiffened. 'It was really good of you to try to get the money for Helen. Of course you should go to see your father on Sunday.'

I kissed her again, in the same place.

Suddenly, her body relaxed, and she rolled over to take me in her arms.

It took three days before Craig would see me again. He still had enough cash to last a month or so, but he would need to buy and lease some expensive equipment if he was to come up with a prototype.

He seemed in a better mood. Following Lisa's idea, we drew up a list of customers, and began to work on a presentation for them. He also called some of the newer, smaller and more desperate-for-deals venture firms to try to elicit some interest.

It was seven o'clock on Friday evening, and I was preparing to leave.

'We'll get there,' I said.

Craig allowed himself a smile. 'Yeah, I guess we will.'

I looked at him closely. 'Have you got an idea you haven't been telling me?'

'Have a good one, Simon,' said Craig, grinning widely.

Wondering what on earth he could be up to, I left for home.

6

I had hardly seen Frank at all since our awkward discussion earlier in the week. We used to like and respect each other, but not any more. I was worried about the steady deterioration of our relationship, and I wanted to do something about it. So, with Lisa's encouragement, I decided to have another try. I left Lisa in her lab where she usually spent her Saturdays, liberated my Morgan from its expensive lodgings in the Brimmer Street Garage, and headed north, to Marsh House.

Woodbridge was a small town about twenty miles outside Boston. It had been a thriving port in the seventeenth century, but as the ships became bigger and the river became smaller, trade moved elsewhere and the town remained, a frozen relic of early colonial prosperity. Marsh House was four miles to the south of the town, nestled in the expanse of salt-marshes that filled many of the bays along this coastline.

It was quiet there, isolated, and very beautiful. The house had been bought by Frank's father, and Frank had spent much of his childhood pottering around in the creeks in sailing boats. He still came here almost every weekend to escape the bustle of Boston.

I turned off the road to Shanks Beach, and drove down a dirt track to the house, almost colliding with a small old lady in a huge station-wagon as she pulled out of her driveway without looking. She gave me an icy look. I waved and smiled, which only deepened her frown, and drove on down the bumpy track, wincing as a stone clanged against the bottom of the Morgan.

I parked beside an old dinghy, pulled up on to a patch of grass next to the small white wooden house, with its freshly painted green shutters. Frank's Mercedes was there. I rapped on the door.

Frank answered, dressed in a checked shirt and jeans. He wasn't pleased to see me.

'What are you doing here?'

'I wondered if you could spare me a few minutes?'

'You could have called first. You should always call first before you come and see me here.'

This took me aback. True, Lisa always called before she visited her father, but I hadn't wanted to give him the chance to refuse to see me.

'Sorry,' I said. 'Can I come in?'

Frank grunted, and led me in to the living room. The furnishing in the house was old, basic but comfortable. It was warm, wood was burning in the iron stove. Frank sat in 'his chair', a beaten-up old rocker, and I sat in a wicker sofa with faded cushions. Through the windows and the porch stretched the marsh, brown at this time of year, with streaks of gold, green, orange and grey. A wooden walkway made its unsteady way down to a creek a quarter of a mile into the marsh.

'What do you want?'

Frank looked tired, as though he hadn't slept the night before. His eyes were dark and strained, and he fidgeted as he sat rocking backwards and forwards rapidly. I began to regret coming. He didn't look in the mood for a reconciliation.

'I was bothered by the Monday morning meeting last week. I wanted to talk to you about it.'

'I thought we'd been through all that at the office.'

'I know, but because it touches on a personal matter, I wanted to see you outside Revere.'

He watched me impatiently.

I ploughed on. 'Well, I just wanted to say that you have nothing to fear about Lisa.' My throat tightened. 'I love her very much, and I would never do anything to hurt her.'

This was hard for me to say. Not because I didn't mean it, but because it was not the sort of thing that had ever been said in my family as I was growing up. But I felt it was important Frank should know it and believe it.

'Sure you do,' he said, dismissively. 'Is that it?'

'I think you're reading too much into my dinner with Diane.'

He held up his hands. 'Who you have dinner with is your own affair,' he said.

'Precisely.'

'As long as you don't hide it from my daughter.'

'I didn't hide it.'

Frank raised his eyebrows.

'I mean, I didn't tell her. But I would have. If it was important. Which it wasn't.'

Frank's eyebrows gathered together. 'If you think having a date with another woman without telling my daughter about it isn't important – '

'It wasn't a date! We were just having something to eat after work.'

'I've seen the way she looks at you.' Frank glared at me. 'That woman is bad news, Simon. A friend at Barnes McLintock told me she wrecked a marriage when she worked there. I don't want her doing that at our firm, and especially not when the marriage in question is my daughter's!'

I bit my tongue. There were things I wanted to say, but I didn't say them. I had come here to look for a reconciliation, not to pick a fight.

'OK, Frank, I understand. I give you my word I won't do anything to jeopardize our marriage. Especially not with Diane. And I don't want it to interfere with our professional relationship.'

'It won't,' said Frank. 'I told you that on Monday. And like I told you, that's not the problem. If I were you, I would concentrate on not making any dumb decisions like promising a company more money when you haven't got the backing of the partnership.'

I felt anger rise in me, but controlled it. I was getting nowhere.

'And if you've come here to ask for money, the answer's no. I'm sorry about your nephew, but as I told Lisa, I have a real problem with medical litigation. I told Lisa no, and I meant no.'

I stood up straight. 'I didn't ask you for money.'

'That's OK, then.'

'All right, Frank, I understand. Thank you for seeing me.'

I held out my hand.

Frank turned away as though he hadn't seen it, and moved towards his desk.

'OK. Goodbye Simon.'

'Goodbye Frank,' I said to his back, and let myself out.

I drove a couple of miles to Shanks Beach, leaped out of the car, slammed the door, and stomped along the sand. A stiff breeze blew off the sea, and the beach, which had been covered with sprawling bodies only six weeks before, was now virtually empty. The waves, whipped up by the wind, crashed against the shoreline, scattering the wading birds in front of them. I walked along the water's edge, head down, dodging the occasional wave that reached farther up the sand than the others. I kicked a chunk of driftwood as hard as I could, almost hitting a surprised sandpiper.

Frank, Diane, Helen, Craig and Net Cop tumbled over and over in my mind. Something was wrong with Frank; I had no idea what it was. But I could still keep things under control. If I concentrated on saving Net Cop, and limited my contact with Diane, then everything would blow over. Give it time.

Although I still didn't see any way I could help Helen.

I spent an hour on the beach, and then drove round Route 128 to Net Cop. I didn't arrive there until about half past five. I was told Craig wasn't in. Apparently he had been out all day. This was unusual for him, but everyone deserves a day off every now and then, I reasoned. So I headed home.

'Why don't you come with me to see Dad tomorrow?'

We were eating dinner, some kind of pasta dish Lisa had put together.

'No, you go,' I replied. 'I'll stay here. It'll give me a chance to get some work done.'

'Can't you come, Simon? Please. I don't like you two not getting along. You're both important to me. I'd like to straighten things out between you.'

I put down my fork and rubbed my eyes. I really didn't want to see Frank again that weekend. 'I tried it and it didn't work,' I said. 'I think it would be better to leave things alone. Besides, you know he just wants to see you.'

'That's typical of you, Simon,' Lisa protested. 'You never want to talk about your feelings. I'm positive it will help to talk it over with Dad.'

This was a common complaint of Lisa's, although actually I had talked more about how I felt with her than I had done with anyone else. But perhaps she had a point. Where I had failed to talk her father round, there was a chance she would succeed. It was worth a try.

'OK, we'll go,' I said.

Lisa rapped on the door of the cottage. No reply. She rapped harder. Still nothing. She turned the doorknob, and pushed. The door was locked.

'His car's still here,' she said, nodding towards her father's dark blue Mercedes, which was parked exactly where I had seen it the day before.

'He must have gone for a walk,' I said.

We looked around. In front of us stretched the marsh, a soft carpet of brown and gold grass. No sign of Frank. Behind was the wooded knoll down which we had approached the house. There was no sign of him there, either. In fact there was no sign of anyone. There were a couple of houses in the distance, at least two miles away, and although there were some closer dwellings behind us, they were out of sight in the trees.

'Come on! Let's go down to the dock,' said Lisa.

I followed her along the rickety wooden walkway down to the creek. The tide was out, so the dock itself had floated down below the level of the surrounding marsh. We sat on the end of the walkway, and looked around us.

It was a surprisingly warm day for October. Although there was no sound of human life, there was noise. The wind whispered through the marsh grass, and water lapped against the wooden platform below us. The warm smells of the marsh, salt and vegetation, rose up to meet us. An egret that had been standing tall and still as we approached, started and rose up into the air, beating its wings, as if struggling to keep a few feet above the long grass. You couldn't see the sea from here, the marsh was surrounded by thickly wooded islands, green with yellow fringes. Just beyond Hog Island, a mile and a half in front of us, was the ocean.

'I love this place,' said Lisa. 'You can imagine what it was like to be a kid here in the summer. Swimming, fishing, sailing. I really missed it when I went to California.'

'I can imagine,' I said.

Lisa had often talked about Marsh House. In fact it was here we had first met. I had only been at Revere a couple of weeks, and Frank was having a barbecue for a dozen or so people, me included. I was listening to Art talk about what he described as Massachusetts' draconian gun laws. I disagreed with him. Everyone else fell silent. At the time, I took this to be tacit approval of Art's views, but afterwards I realized that they just knew it was useless arguing with Art about gun control. Anyway, Art launched into a tirade about the constitutional right of Americans to bear arms, and the necessity of defending oneself when the criminal classes were armed to the teeth, when a slight, dark-haired woman leaped to my defence. Barbed comments flew back and forth for about five minutes, to the embarrassment of most of the onlookers, before Frank diplomatically suggested that the woman show me his old dinghies, kept in a dilapidated boathouse a few yards away.

She did as she was told, and we spent much of the rest of the evening together. I was drawn to Lisa straight away. I liked the way she said what she thought, I found I wanted to talk to her, and I found her physically attractive. She mentioned the only French film I had happened to have seen, and on the strength of my enthusiasm, suggested we see something else by the same director. I suddenly became very interested in French films.

She turned and kissed me.

I smiled. 'What was that for?'

'Oh, nothing.' She giggled.

'What is it?' I asked, nudging her.

'Did I ever tell you I lost my virginity here?'

'No! You can't have. Right out here in the open?' It was hard to think of a more public place.

'Not exactly here. Down there. On the dock. No one can see you. And you can hear someone coming along the boardwalk in plenty of time.'

I looked down the few feet to the wooden platform below. 'I don't believe you,' I said.

'Do you want me to prove it?' Lisa asked, smiling wickedly.

'What, now?'

She nodded.

'But your father will see us!'

'No, he won't. That's the whole point.'

'OK,' I said, a grin spreading across my lips.

And so we made love, the wind and sun caressing our bare skin, water lapping a few inches below us, and the wide expanse of the marsh all around us. It was wonderful.

We lay in each other's arms, recovering. Lisa pulled her shirt over her chest to keep warm; I let the goose-pimples grow on my skin. We said nothing. I felt at one with the marsh, and with Lisa.

I don't know how much time passed before Lisa said, 'Come on. Let's see if Dad's back.'

'He'll know what we've been doing,' I said.

'No, he won't,' said Lisa. Then she giggled. 'Anyway, what if he does? It'll stop him worrying about our marriage, won't it?'

She held my hand as we made our way awkwardly along the walkway, back to Marsh House.

Frank's car was still there. Lisa rapped on the door. No reply. 'Do you think he's all right?'

'Of course he is,' I said. 'It's just a long walk.'

'I don't know,' said Lisa. She looked around anxiously. 'It's strange he locked the door. He usually leaves it open when he's here. Let's see if we can see inside the house.'

So we walked round the building, looking in through the windows. The living room was empty, as was the kitchen. There was a small dining area between the two. The window was high, above my eye level.

'Here, get on my shoulders,' I said to Lisa, crouching down.

'OK.' She giggled, and climbed on to my back. I slowly straightened my legs, bringing her up to the level of the window.

The giggling stopped abruptly. She stiffened, and her fingers clawed at my hair. 'Simon,' she whispered. 'SIMON!!!'

I swung her down to the ground. Her eyes were wide, and she was gasping for breath. I leaped up and grabbed the window ledge with my fingers. I hauled myself up until my eyes were just at the level of the glass.

'Jesus!'

Someone was lying face down in the doorway between the kitchen and the dining area, two dark patches spreading across his back.

I dropped to the ground, sprinted round the house, and charged the front door.

The wood cracked. I threw myself at the door two more times with all my weight, and it burst open. I rushed over to Frank's body.

He was dead. Two bloodied bullet holes gaped through the back of the checked shirt he had been wearing the day before.

Lisa let out a shriek, the like of which I had never heard before. She pushed past me and threw herself on to him, grabbing his face, willing him to be alive, sobbing 'Dad, Dad, Dad,' over and over again.

7

'Just a few more questions, Mr Ayot. Or is it Sir Simon Ayot?'

Sergeant Mahoney sat on the sofa in our small living room. His card said he was from the State Police Crime Prevention and Control Unit assigned to the Essex County District Attorney's Office. He was a big man, running to fat, with thinning red hair and bright blue eyes. One corner of his mouth seemed permanently raised in a half-smile of mild amusement, or mild disbelief, I couldn't quite tell. He was probably pushing fifty, and he had the air of someone who had seen a lot, as he no doubt had. A female colleague had taken Lisa out for a cup of coffee, leaving the two of us alone in the apartment.

'Just call me mister,' I said. 'All that the "Sir" means is that my father died young.'

I had tried to suppress my title since I had moved to America. And Lisa never called herself 'Lady Ayot', except sometimes when drunk and naked in bed. One of my reasons for being in America, apart from Lisa of course, was that things like titles didn't matter. In England, I felt awkward using the 'Sir', and disrespectful to my father's family not using it. Here I could just forget all about it. It was only when people saw my passport, as Mahoney had, or when Gil managed to squeeze it into a conversation somehow, that anyone knew.

'OK, Mr Ayot. I'd just like to go back over some of the things you told me yesterday.' He had a thick Boston accent, but it was slightly different from Craig's. I still wasn't able to distinguish the local accents with confidence.

'Fine.'

'It looks like you were the last person to see Frank Cook alive.'

'Really?'

The blue eyes watched my every reaction. 'Yes. The coroner thinks he died sometime before ten p.m. on Saturday. Now you say you came to see him at about two thirty on Saturday afternoon?'

'I think that's right, yes.'

'That fits with the neighbour who says she saw you speeding down the dirt road toward his house.'

I smiled. 'I was doing about ten miles an hour. She just wasn't looking where she was going.'

'Fair enough. This isn't a traffic investigation.' The corner of Mahoney's mouth flicked upwards. 'Now when you arrived, was Mr Cook there?'

'Yes, he was there. He looked tired. On edge. He didn't seem too pleased to see me.'

'Why did you go to meet him?'

'I wanted to try to straighten out a few things between us.'

'What kind of things?'

I hesitated. 'Frank and I had had an argument at work. I wanted to try to sort it out.'

Mahoney looked at me closely. He knew I wasn't telling him everything. 'What was the argument about?'

'An investment.'

'I see.' He remained silent, holding my eyes, waiting for me to say more.

I had no desire to tell Mahoney about Frank's suspicions over me and Diane. But I had even less desire to be caught hiding them. This was a murder investigation: the questions would not go away. I decided it was best to be as straightforward as possible with the answers.

I sighed. 'I thought the real cause of the disagreement was that Frank suspected me of having an affair with one of my colleagues. I wanted to persuade him that there was no danger of that.'

'And were you?' The eyes peered into mine.

'No,' I said simply. This wasn't the time for righteous indignation. I would have to be very careful with Mahoney. Careful and precise.

'OK. Did Mr Cook believe you?'

'I don't know. I don't think so.'

'Did you have another argument?'

'Not exactly,' I said, truthfully.

'But you didn't leave best of friends?'

'No.'

Mahoney paused, but let his eyes rest on me. Then the questions came again.

'What time did you leave the house?'

'I don't know. Three o'clock, perhaps.'

'Where did you go then?'

'I went for a walk on the beach. Shanks Beach. And then I drove to the office of one of our companies, Net Cop.'

'Did you meet anyone on this walk? See anyone?'

'There were a few cars in the car park.' I thought hard. 'I think there were one or two people on the beach, but I can't remember them. I was too wrapped up in Frank and his attitude towards me.'

'OK,' said Mahoney. 'How long were you at the beach?'

'About an hour.'

'And then you drove to this company, what was it? Net Cop?'

I gave Mahoney the details of Net Cop and the people I had seen there. He promised to check with them. I was sure he would.

'Do you know how much Frank Cook's estate will be?' The change of tack surprised me.

'I've no idea.'

'Take a guess.'

I thought about it. Frank had had a successful business career, and had probably already made some good money at Revere. And then of course there were the BioOne millions that would come his way. Daniel was right. Frank must be a rich man. But I decided to undershoot for Mahoney's benefit. 'A million dollars.'

'Closer to four, we think. And Mr Appleby says that in another

59

year or two, Mr Cook would have had another ten coming to him from one of Revere's investments. That will still go to his heirs. Which brings me to another question. Who are Frank Cook's heirs?'

'I have no idea,' I said.

'Try.'

'Lisa I suppose. And her brother Eddie. Maybe her mother.'

Mahoney grunted. 'I'll leave it to his lawyer to confirm whether you're right. But let's just say you might expect to get some money coming to you as a result of Mr Cook's death.'

I sighed. 'I suppose so. But I've never thought about it until now.'

'Do you own a gun, Mr Ayot?' Another change of tack.

'No.'

'Do you know anyone who owns a Smith and Wesson model six forty, three fifty-seven Magnum?'

'No.'

'Do you know how to use a gun?'

I paused. 'Yes.'

'How's that?'

'I used to be in the British army,' I answered. 'They teach you how to use a weapon.'

'I see. So you know all about guns, right?' He thought for a bit. 'Have you ever killed anyone?'

'Yes,' I said quietly.

'Tell me about it.'

'I'd rather not,' I said.

'Was it while you were in the army?'

'Yes.'

'In Ireland, maybe?'

'Yes.'

The blue eyes hardened.

'I don't have to answer this sort of question,' I said sharply. 'Am I under suspicion, or what? Do I need a lawyer?'

Mahoney relaxed. 'Look, we've got a job to do here. We're just gathering information from whoever might be able to help us with this, that's all. Thank you for your help, Mr Ayot. I'll be back if I have any further questions.'

With that, he was gone, leaving me feeling distinctly uneasy. As I waited for Lisa to return, Mahoney's last question rankled.

I remembered the vehicle checkpoint in a quiet country lane in Armagh, the beaten-up Ford Escort slowing down, Lance Corporal of Horse Binns bending down at the car window, the look of surprise and shock on his face, the two shots in rapid succession, his head disintegrating, his body thrown backwards, the car engine revving, my own weapon raised to the window, the explosion of noise and shattering of glass as I emptied the magazine into the car, the vehicle careering out of control into the side of our Land Rover.

I had killed two members of the Provisional IRA. I wasn't proud of it, but it had been something to tell Binns's parents.

Frank's murder was entirely different. I might have shot two terrorists while on active duty, but that didn't mean I could murder my father-in-law in cold blood. Mahoney's insinuation that I could infuriated me.

I didn't have much time to worry about that, though. Lisa needed me, and I was reluctant to leave her alone. She seemed dazed, sometimes crying and sometimes just staring into space.

I did the best I could, but I felt helpless. I could see and feel and touch her pain. It stretched forward into the coming weeks, months and years. It scared me. I had no idea how Lisa would react, how badly she would be hurt, whether any of the damage would be permanent. I wanted to protect her, to wrap my arms around her and defend her from the horrible thing that had happened to her father. But no matter what I did, I couldn't protect her from the central fact. He was gone. Eventually her pain might lessen, become more bearable, but that day was a long way off. Things would probably get worse before they got better.

And I had my own feelings towards his death to deal with. Frank and I had got on so well at the beginning. Until recently, I had counted him as a friend and mentor: I had him to thank for my job at Revere, and then for my wife. He had liked me and respected me, I was sure. And then our relationship had deteriorated, culminating in the last time I had seen him when he had turned his back on me. Literally. I had heard that grief brings guilt with it. I was beginning to understand what that meant.

So far in our lives together, we hadn't faced anything more serious than a broken dishwasher. I wondered how Lisa would cope with what had happened. I was determined to do all I could to help her, however inadequate that might seem.

The door buzzer buzzed. It was another reporter. I told her, as I'd told all the others, that we had no comment, and Lisa was too upset to talk to anyone. Frank's murder had been in the morning papers, and on TV, and they were all looking for grieving-relative quotes or pictures. I knew it was inevitable, but it made me angry, as though Lisa and I were expected to meekly take our parts in a play that had been put on without our knowledge or consent. Still, it would probably have been worse in England.

There was a lot to be done. Frank was to be buried the next day. Lisa's mother and brother were flying over from California, and were staying at a bed and breakfast round the corner from our apartment.

We picked them up from the airport that evening in Lisa's Honda. They were easy to spot. Lisa's brother Eddie was tall and thin with dark hair cut so short it was little more than stubble. Their mother, Ann, was a bustling dark-haired woman who, with the help of careful attention to clothes, make-up and hair, was still striking. The three of them embraced, tears running down the cheeks of Lisa and her mother, Eddie's face a foot above them, his eyes blinking.

I stood awkwardly to one side.

When they eventually broke up, Lisa's mother gave me a hug. I extended a hand to Eddie, who shot me a cool glance before shaking it. We all made our way back to the car, Lisa tucking herself happily under Eddie's arm.

I cooked them supper in our apartment. Lasagne. A bottle of red wine quickly disappeared between the four of us before the meal, and I opened a second one as we all sat down.

Ann looked around her. 'I don't see how you two live in such a small apartment. You've got so many *things*. I don't know how you keep them all tidy.'

The answer was, of course, that we didn't.

'Oh, Mom. We couldn't afford a bigger place around here, you know that,' Lisa said. 'We fit everything in. But I'm really sorry there isn't room for you and Eddie.'

'Oh, don't worry about that,' Ann said. 'The B and B is delightful.'

'It's kind of nice to have a bed instead of crashing on your floor,' said Eddie, smiling at his younger sister.

Everyone helped themselves to the lasagne.

'What I don't understand,' said Ann, returning to the subject that was in all our minds, 'is why anyone would want to kill Frank. He never had any enemies that I knew of. He was such a *nice* man. Always.'

Then why did you divorce him? I thought, but didn't say. Ann's attitude towards Frank was poles away from my mother's attitude towards my father. My mother had been a reluctant attendant at her ex-husband's funeral, her face and manner betraying no emotion whatsoever. There must have been feelings in there, somewhere, but I couldn't guess what they were. There could be no doubting the genuine sadness Lisa's mother felt.

She turned to me. 'Didn't people like him at work?'

'Oh, yes,' I replied. 'We all liked him. And he was very well respected.' All of us but Art, I thought.

'Have the cops any ideas who did it?' Eddie asked.

'I don't think so,' I answered.

'Simon seems to be their best guess,' said Lisa. I glanced across at her sharply. 'The questions that Sergeant Mahoney guy has been asking. It's obvious what he's thinking.'

Eddie looked at both of us. Two years Lisa's senior he had dropped out of medical school several years previously and was in some kind of post graduate school at the University of California in San Francisco, studying social work. Lisa admired him for following a career path devoted to helping those in need, which paid little. I tried not to think middle-aged thoughts about perpetual students. He and I had never had much to do with each other. As little sister's boyfriend and then husband, he was both suspicious and polite to me. As a titled Englishman who worked for an East Coast financial firm, I was irredeemably uncool. Since his father had left the rest of his family, he had taken on the role of man in the family; his mother and his younger sister hung on his every word. I suspected he didn't like the way they showed every sign of hanging on mine, too.

And, of course, I had been introduced to Lisa by his father. This put me on the wrong side of the family divide that figured so prominently in Eddie's mind.

'But wasn't Simon with you?' he asked Lisa.

She shook her head. 'Uh uh. That's the problem. I was working in the lab. Simon was at Marsh House, seeing Dad. He was the last one to see him alive.'

'Really?' Eddie was looking at me closely.

'It's true,' I said. 'He and I had had an argument at work, and I went up to Marsh House to sort it out. I didn't get anywhere, so I left. Apparently he was killed sometime between then and ten o'clock that evening.'

'Really?' said Eddie again.

'Don't look like that, Eddie,' said Lisa, grasping my hand, finally aware of the difficulty she had raised. 'Of course Simon had nothing to do with it.'

'Of course not,' said Eddie, with an indulgent smile at his younger sister.

She smiled back, glad to clear up the misunderstanding. But from Eddie's glance towards me I wasn't at all sure she had done any such thing. 'The police will catch whoever did this,' she said.

'I hope they do,' said Eddie. 'I'd never thought I'd say this, but he deserves the chair. They've brought the death penalty back in Massachusetts, haven't they?'

Lisa didn't answer my question. I shook my head. 'I don't think so.'

'Really? I thought I'd read they had.'

Lisa concentrated on her lasagne. Ann looked adoringly at her son. I felt mildly irritated. Lisa knew very well that Massachusetts hadn't brought back the death penalty, but the last thing she was going to do was contradict big brother. All Eddie's pronouncements, of which there were many, were greeted with rapture by his mother and sister. He was an intelligent man, and often said interesting things, but sometimes he was just plain wrong.

I knew better than to contradict him. I had become involved in an argument with him the year before at Thanksgiving. It was over a small thing, whether Helmut Kohl was a Social Democrat. He thought he was, I knew he wasn't, Lisa and her mother were sure Eddie couldn't be wrong. I had stood my ground, and briefly spoiled what had been a very pleasant evening.

'Must have missed it,' I said, pouring Eddie some more wine.

There was a brief silence, then Ann spoke. 'I thought you got on so well with Frank,' said Ann. 'I'm sorry you parted on such bad terms.'

'So am I,' I said. 'I do feel bad about it. There's a lot I'd have liked to say to him before he died.'

'Me too,' said Lisa flatly.

We finished in silence, the shock and anger seated with us like extra guests at the table.

That night, as I lay in bed, trying to get to sleep, I felt the bed shudder gently. I reached over and touched Lisa's shoulder. It was shaking.

'Come here,' I said.

She rolled over into my arms. I felt her warm tears trickle down my chest.

'You know that shirt Dad was wearing? The plaid one?' she said. 'Yes?'

'I gave that to him for his birthday last year. He really liked it. And now it's covered with his blood.'

I squeezed her even tighter into my chest. She cried some more. Eventually, she broke away, sniffed and reached for some tissues beside the bed.

'It must be awful for Eddie,' she said.

'It's awful for everyone.'

'Yes. But he hasn't seen Dad for six years. He's barely spoken to him since he and Mom broke up.'

'Why do you think it got to him so badly? You had no problems with your father, did you?'

'I don't know. I really think it would have been better if they'd told us the real reason they split up. I mean they said they just didn't want to live together any more. Eddie thought Dad was running away from us. He never forgave him.'

'I wonder if we'll ever know why now.'

'I guess now I'd rather not. Now Dad's gone. I mean one of them was probably messing around with someone else. Mom, I guess. I don't know.'

'I suppose that's why Eddie's so angry,' I said.

'Because he feels guilty about not seeing Dad? Probably. But you know Eddie. He can get pretty angry anyway.'

Actually I didn't know Eddie that well. And I was quite happy to keep it that way.

'I'm angry too,' Lisa went on. 'It's just so *wrong* for someone to die like that.' Her voice had suddenly become hard and bitter. 'He wasn't ready to die. He had years left to him. What right has anyone to take another person's life? Mom has a point, there's no good reason why anyone should want to kill him. I don't know about the death penalty, but I sure as hell hope they get the bastard who did it. He's not fit to live, whoever he is.'

This outburst surprised me. Lisa had been so submissive up to now in the face of Frank's death. But she was right. Murder wasn't just evil. It was callous as well.

We lay in silence for a while. Then Lisa spoke; this time her voice was so quiet I could hardly hear it. 'When I was little and felt bad or scared, Dad used to sing to me. He had a terrible voice; he never liked to sing in front of anyone but me. I wish he could do it now.'

I couldn't sing to her. But I could hold her. I didn't let her go until, a long time later, I heard the regular breathing of sleep.

8

Frank was buried in a Jewish cemetery in Brookline, where the Cook family had lived when it was still a family. The ceremony was simple. After the *Kaddish*, mumbled with varying degrees of confidence by those present, the rabbi spoke of Frank in his younger days; I suspected he hadn't set eyes on him in many years. Gil made a low-key eulogy, short, honest and very moving. Only a small group of about twenty or so people were there: family and close friends. I was annoyed to see Mahoney standing at the back, his sharp eyes scanning the gathering. He caught my glance, and the side of his mouth twitched upwards. I looked away. It seemed wrong to me that he should be here at Frank's funeral. I would have thrown him out if I could.

The *shiva* or visitation, was held at Frank's sister's house a mile or so away. *Shiva* meant seven, and technically it should have lasted seven days, but Eddie had to get back to his studies, and Frank was at best a lapsed progressive, so the family had decided on the one evening. The mourners were joined by others who came to pass on their condolences to his family. It seemed as if hundreds of people were trying to cram into the modest house. I was amazed at how many people knew and liked Frank.

Frank's sister, Zoë, did her best as a hostess. She was a tall, black-haired woman, with a gentle smile and kindly eyes. She stood smiling and nodding, patting hands and being patted. I extricated her from an earnest man wearing dark glasses and a yarmulke who had been talking to her for several minutes, and brought her a piece of cake.

'Oh, Eddie, thank you so much,' she said. 'I know these people, but half the names don't come. And I don't want to offend them.'

'You're doing very well,' I said, not bothering to correct her.

She smiled. 'It's such a shame about poor Frank. Had you seen much of him lately?'

I wasn't sure whether by calling me Eddie she had just got my name wrong, or whether she thought I was Lisa's brother. So I decided to answer blandly. 'Quite a bit,' I said.

'Aunt Zoë!' Lisa rushed up and gave her aunt a huge hug. The older woman beamed. 'Has Simon been looking after you?'

Aunt Zoë looked momentarily confused and then glanced towards me apologetically. 'Yes. Yes, he has, dear. How are you?'

'Oh, fine, I suppose.'

'And how are your potions?'

'Bubbling away,' she answered. 'Can you believe all these people? I don't recognize most of them.'

'Neither do I. It's extraordinary to have so many of Frank's old friends here at one time,' Zoë said. 'I wish he could be here to see them all.' She looked around the room, somewhat bemused. 'I wonder how long we've got to go. What time is it, dear?'

Lisa glanced down at the watch on her aunt's wrist, before looking at her own. 'Nine thirty.'

Aunt Zoë seemed to sigh.

'It's very good of you to do this,' Lisa said. 'We couldn't possibly fit everyone into our apartment.'

'Oh, don't worry about it,' Aunt Zoë said. 'I'll miss him.'

Zoë was accosted by a childhood friend of Frank's who wanted to talk to her. Luckily, she remembered his name.

'She looks OK,' Lisa said.

'Yes,' I said. 'But she called me Eddie.'

'No, really?'

'And you saw how she had to ask you the time.'

'It's so sad,' Lisa said. 'I remember so clearly playing with her when we were kids. She used to come up to Marsh House and stay with us before she was married. She was so much fun. We used to play all kinds of games exploring the creeks and the marshes. And in a year or two she might not remember any of it.'

'Yes, she will,' I said. 'Don't they always say that old people forget what they had for breakfast, but remember clearly everything that happened decades ago?'

'She's not old, Simon. She's fifty-two. She's ill.'

Aunt Zoë was suffering from the early symptoms of Alzheimer's.

'Are you talking about Zoë?' Carl, her husband, had joined us. He was a heavy man with a grey beard, several years older than his wife, who wheezed after any sort of exertion. He was a professor at Northeastern University in some kind of social science.

'Yes,' said Lisa. 'How is she?'

Carl sighed, a heavier wheeze than usual. 'You know she lost her job at the Library?'

'Oh, no,' Lisa said.

'But she's not too bad yet. She forgets names of people, names of books – that was her problem at the Library, and she has some trouble telling the time. But she still remembers me, and she always knows where she is and what day it is. There's a lot further to go. Unless the drug Frank recommended really works.'

'Drug? I didn't know Dad recommended any drug?'

'Yes,' said Carl. 'It's a new drug for Alzheimer's they're testing.'

'Is it neuroxil-5?' Lisa asked. 'Made by a company called BioOne?'

'That's right.'

'Does it work?' I asked.

'It seems to. She's been taking it for seven months now, and it looks like things have stabilized. She doesn't seem to be getting any worse. She had to take something called a Mini-Mental State exam, and they'll check her again in a few months to see how she's doing.'

'That's good news,' I said.

'I've seen some of the other patients at the clinic,' Carl went on. 'It's scary. Some of them have forgotten everything. Who their spouse is, where they live, their children. They get really angry and frustrated. One woman said her husband had lost his smile. I pray that never happens to Zoë.'

69

He glanced across to where his wife was talking to Frank's old friend, laughing at a shared memory.

I, too, hoped that neuroxil-5 worked.

The next morning, Lisa, her mother, brother and I all set off downtown for Frank's lawyer's office to discuss his will. As we waited in the law firm's smart reception area, an uneasy silence settled on us. Up to this moment, none of us had talked about Frank's legacy. Other things had seemed more important. We all knew he was wealthy: it had seemed in bad taste to discuss how wealthy he had been, and how wealthy we were going to be. The thought had probably not even occurred to Lisa. Eddie in particular seemed nervous, his long fingers played with the teaspoon by his cup. Lisa looked calm and Ann had an air of studied indifference.

After five minutes, the lawyer bustled in. His name was Bergey. He was a balding portly man, with a mild face, but intelligent eyes. He introduced himself and led us through to his office.

'Thank you all for coming in to see me today,' he said, having seated everyone round a table. 'I'm speaking to you in my capacity as Mr Cook's executor. Now, ordinarily I would simply mail a letter to the beneficiaries of a will, but in this case, I thought it made sense to take advantage of you all being in the same place at once, and explain the will in person.'

Bergey seemed nervous. Nervous and serious. He had our attention.

'First, Mr Cook held an insurance policy of three hundred thousand dollars, which is to be divided equally between his former wife and two children.' He smiled quickly at us, and cleared his throat. I had the impression we were coming to the tricky bit.

'Second, the will. It's actually very straightforward.' He looked down at the papers in front of him. 'Mr Cook's estate goes in its entirety to Elizabeth Rebecca Cook, his daughter. The value of the estate is difficult to determine at the moment, since so much of it comprises the carried interest in funds managed by Revere Partners. But excluding that, it should be at least four million dollars. As always, it will take a while for the probate process to run its course.'

He looked round the table nervously. We were all watching Eddie.

You could see the anger boiling up inside him. He grasped the teaspoon he had been fiddling with so tightly his knuckles were white. He glanced quickly at all of us, and then addressed Bergey. 'He can't do that can he? He can't leave everything to just one of his children?'

'I'm sorry to say that he can,' the lawyer replied. 'Of course, you will receive the hundred thousand dollars from the life insurance policy.'

'Yes, but his estate will be worth millions. I have a right to half of that.'

'I can well understand your concern, Mr Cook. But I drew up your father's will myself. He made it after careful consideration. He was quite clear in his intention, which was to leave his entire estate to his daughter.'

'How could he do that to me?' protested Eddie. 'Did he tell you why he cut me out?'

'No, he didn't do that,' said Bergey.

We all looked away. We knew why Frank had ignored his son in death. It was because his son had ignored him in life.

'You're behind this aren't you?' I continued looking at my hands. 'Yes, you, Simon. You're behind it.'

I glanced up at him. I hadn't realized Eddie was talking to me. 'What?'

'Eddie,' his mother put her hand on his sleeve.

'No, Mom. You should have gotten something too. You stood by him for all those years before he walked out on you. You deserve something from that.'

'I'm perfectly comfortable moneywise,' Ann protested mildly. 'Frank knew that.'

'OK. But what about me? Simon, you stole my inheritance from under my nose.'

'How do you get that idea?'

'I've seen how you worked your way into Dad's favours. Getting

71

the job at Revere, getting Lisa, being the perfect son-in-law. You kissed his ass and it worked!'

Given the deterioration of my relationship with Frank before he died, the irony of this comment made me smile. Big mistake.

'Oh, you just go right ahead and laugh about it. Just go ahead and deposit that fat cheque. It's pretty funny.'

'I'm sorry, Eddie,' I said. 'But Frank didn't consult me about his will, I can assure you of that.'

'Yeah, but you and Lisa spent so much time with him,' now he turned on his sister. 'The only reason he cut me out is because I stood by Mom. He should never have left us. I didn't go running to him. That's why I didn't get any of his money.'

Lisa looked shocked. She had viewed this meeting as just an administrative item that had to be got through before her family went back to California.

'Eddie, I loved him,' she said. 'I don't want his stupid money.'

'Oh, yeah, you loved him. Never mind Mom. And he . . .' he jabbed a finger in my direction, 'he will love his money.'

I could watch Eddie attacking me with something close to amusement. But not Lisa. 'Eddie . . .' I growled.

'No, Simon,' Lisa put her hand on mine. 'I really don't care about the money.' She turned to the lawyer. 'Mr Bergey. Isn't there any way I can renounce half of it? Give it to Eddie?'

'Hm,' the lawyer frowned. 'You do have the right to renounce all or part of your inheritance, up to nine months after the date of death. Your renunciation would not necessarily direct the funds to your brother, since he is not a named default in the will. So the funds would be disposed under the laws of intestacy, which means . . .' he paused, thinking it through, 'that since you have no issue, Edward Cook would be the next in line after all.'

'Great,' said Lisa. 'Let's do it.'

Bergey cleared his throat. 'I strongly suggest that you think carefully before you decide to take that course. After all, we are talking about Mr Cook's estate here. He was very clear that he wanted everything to go to you.'

Lisa glanced at Eddie. 'I'm sure it's what I want. But I'll think it over if you like. Perhaps I can see you next week, and we can figure out a way of getting this done?'

'Very well,' said Bergey.

Eddie breathed in. He smiled at Lisa. 'Thank you,' he said.

Lisa smiled quickly back. But a few minutes later, as we all got up to leave the room, I caught Eddie glaring at me.

I was eager to get back to the office while Lisa took the other two to the airport. I was looking forward to a dose of normality.

It was with relief that I immersed myself in the problems of Net Cop and Tetracom. But I was soon disturbed by a summons from Gil.

He sat me down on his sofa and poured me a cup of coffee.

'Thank you for coming in today, Simon. I know you must have a lot on your plate at home, but we can definitely use you here. There's plenty to do, and Frank leaves a big hole.'

'It's no problem. It's good to have the distraction, to be honest.'

'I'm sure,' said Gil sympathetically. 'How's Lisa?'

'Not great,' I said.

'No. It must be bad for her. And you?'

'Not too good, either. I just wish Frank and I had parted on better terms.'

'Don't beat yourself with that, Simon. Frank thought very highly of you. He told me so on many occasions. And although he's gone, I won't forget his opinions. They were always worth listening to.'

I tried to smile.

Gil cleared his throat. 'This is a difficult question, but I think it's important to clear the air. The police have been asking all of us here all kinds of questions about Frank, and about you. They haven't said anything directly, but from their questions I'd guess they view you as a likely suspect.'

'I know.'

'So my question is, are they correct?'

'You mean, did I kill Frank?'

Gil nodded. His eyes, shrunken by the thick lenses of his glasses, bored into me. I met them, held them.

'No, Gil. No, I didn't.'

Gil paused a moment, and then sat back. 'Good. I believe you. I thought so, but I wanted to ask for myself. I want you to know that you have my total support, and that of the firm. If there's anything I can do for you please ask.'

'Thank you,' I said. 'Um, Gil?'

'Yes?'

'There is one thing. I wonder if you could give me the name of a good criminal lawyer? I doubt I'll need one, but you never know.'

Gil looked at me strangely for a moment, as if wondering whether he had made a mistake in trusting me so quickly. Then he gave me a quick smile. 'Certainly. Hold on a moment.' He went over to his desk and rifled through his Rolodex. 'Gardner Phillips. He's an old friend of mine, and a fine trial lawyer. Here's his number.'

He handed me an index card, and I jotted down the details.

'Thanks. As I say, I hope I won't need him.' I made as if to get up.

'One moment, Simon. There's something else I wanted to talk to you about.'

'Oh yes?'

'Net Cop. What are you planning to do about it?'

'As I told you, I don't intend giving up quite yet. The company can continue for a month or so as it is. Craig Docherty and I are trying to find some other sources of funds to develop the prototype switch.'

'Any luck?'

'None yet. But we've only just started.'

'I see. I'm worried about Craig Docherty. I think Frank might have been right about him.'

I looked at Gil sharply. 'What do you mean?'

'He came to see me last week. He threatened me, said he would go to the press with the story of how Revere allegedly hadn't met its commitment to him.'

I groaned. How could Craig have been so stupid? 'What did you tell him?' I asked.

'I told him to leave my office. I won't be blackmailed by my entrepreneurs.'

'He was probably just upset,' I said. 'He was pretty angry when I told him we were going to pull out.'

'Oh it was clear he was upset. But as Frank said, it clouded his judgement. It wasn't smart to threaten me.'

'I think he's calmer now. I can make sure he doesn't do anything like that again.'

'It was stupid, Simon. If he did something that stupid once, he's going to do something just as stupid again.'

I saw Gil's point. 'What do you want me to do about it?'

Gil paused. 'Do you really think you can salvage something from this investment?'

'I think so. I don't make any promises . . .' I looked up at Gil, who caught the point and smiled, 'but I will do my best.'

'OK. Do this. Carry on with Net Cop. Get every last dollar you can out of it. But tell Craig Docherty that if he breathes a word to the press that might harm Revere's reputation, he'll be fired from Net Cop, and he'll never get venture backing from anyone in this town again.'

'I'll tell him.'

'What was that all about?' asked Daniel, back in the associates' office.

'Gil wanted to know whether I killed Frank. It seems I'm everyone's favourite suspect.'

'You're certainly mine,' said Daniel.

'Thanks for the support.'

'Do the police have any other ideas who might have done it?'

'Not that I'm aware of. I'm sure they'll find someone.'

'Poor guy,' said Daniel. 'Revere will be screwed without him.'

'I know what you mean.' BioOne excepted, Frank was easily Revere's most able investor. Gil's record was patchy and Art's was downright appalling, once again BioOne excepted. Ravi and Diane had made some promising investments between them, but it was too early to tell how they would do. But Frank was more than a good investor. He was the voice of caution, the voice of common sense, the voice Gil listened to when he had a difficult decision to make.

'Where's John?' I asked.

'Sick.'

'Huh. It must be serious. He's such a healthy sod, you don't expect him to actually take a day off work.'

'He's taken Frank's death pretty badly. You know how much they worked together,' Daniel said. 'Oh, by the way, I saw Jeff Lieberman in New York last weekend.'

'Was he interested in Net Cop?'

'He might be. Give him a call.'

I sighed. 'Maybe I will. After I've straightened out my favourite lunatic CEO.'

Craig had recovered his optimism and energy as he came bounding over to me, dressed as always in jeans, sneakers and T-shirt. 'Hey, Simon, howya doin'?'

'Not so good, I'm afraid, Craig.'

'Yeah. I heard about Frank Cook. I'm sorry. Come through to my office.'

We went through to the glass-enclosed space in the corner. 'So, is there any chance Revere might change its mind about the money now?' asked Craig.

I recoiled. 'You mean after what happened to Frank?'

'Yeah.' He looked at me expectantly.

'No, Craig, no chance at all.'

'Too bad,' Craig said. Only then did he seem to read my expression. 'Guess that was in bad taste, huh?'

'You could say that, Craig,' I replied. 'It also wasn't such a great idea to try to threaten Gil Appleby. What were you thinking of?'

'Hey. I was angry. I was desperate. I was willing to try anything.'

'Well, you didn't impress Gil. In fact, he told me to tell you that if you squeak a word to the press, we'll fire you.'

'You can't do that,' said Craig.

'We can, and you know it,' I said. Sadly, it was all too common for venture capitalists to fire entrepreneurs from the companies they had founded. Craig had come awfully close. Despite the faith in me he professed, the only thing holding Gil back had probably been his expectation that Net Cop would go bust of its own accord anyway.

'Oh, and after that he'll make sure you never get backing from a venture capital firm again,' I added.

Craig sighed. 'OK, I get the message. I'm sorry.'

A thought struck me. 'When I left Net Cop the day before Frank was killed, you seemed awfully cheerful. That had nothing to do with his death, did it?'

'No, of course not,' said Craig.

I looked at him suspiciously, but his face was all injured innocence.

He stood up and moved over to a whiteboard in his office. There was a string of names, venture capitalists in one column, and industry players in the other. Many of the names were crossed out.

'We're gettin' no luck with the VCs,' Craig said, 'but some of the equipment suppliers are nibbling. Nortel has said "no", but Ericsson and Luxtel sound interested. I've fixed up a meeting with Luxtel in New Jersey tomorrow . . .'

Craig rattled on, optimism returned, once again totally absorbed with the success of his company.

Inspired by Craig's enthusiasm, I called Jeff Lieberman in New York. He was pleased to hear from me. He liked the Net Cop deal. Daniel had indeed put a good word in over the weekend. In fact, Jeff had talked to a couple of his colleagues, and they had agreed to put in a hundred and fifty thousand dollars between them for an appropriate share of the company yet to be haggled over. It was much more than I had expected. Craig was impressed. Net Cop would still need more funds to develop the prototype, but Jeff and his friends had bought us a couple more weeks to find them. Not much, but it was something.

I took the train from Wellesley back to South Station and put in a couple of hours' work. I left the office early. I was worried about Lisa.

I went straight home, walking rapidly across the Common. I usually found that was the time when the problems of the day came crowding back into my mind, begging to be solved.

Gil's conversation with me jostled its way to the front of my brain. Mahoney hadn't said I was a suspect, but it was clear I was heading that way. I might need Gil's lawyer friend.

I approached a bench just above the Frog Pond in the middle of the Common. It was a grey afternoon and a few spots of rain spattered my face. There weren't many people about. I stopped suddenly, sat down on the bench, and looked behind me, back towards the elegant Georgian spire of Park Street Church and the giant buildings of the Financial District towering above it. An old lady stumbled by, muttering to herself. Behind her was a young Hispanic man in jeans and a dark jacket. His eyes darted up at me as I sat down, and he seemed to hesitate for a moment, then he walked past me, eyes on the pathway beneath his feet.

I was being followed. He was a policeman, no doubt. I decided not to say anything as he passed, head down, but I kept my eyes on him, until he had left the Common and turned right up Beacon Street. Only then did I continue home.

Lisa looked pleased to see me. She was wearing an old blue oxford shirt of Frank's he had lent her when we were painting the apartment just after we moved in. I hugged her.

'Did your mother and Eddie leave all right?' I asked.

She nodded. 'The plane was right on time. Mom wouldn't go without making me promise we'd visit her for Thanksgiving.'

'That's OK. We were planning to do that anyway, weren't we?'

'I thought so.'

'That was a pretty unpleasant meeting this morning, wasn't it?'

'I can't believe Dad left Eddie out of his will. That was so stupid.'

'It was very generous of you to cut him back in.'

'I didn't want Dad's death to cause any more strain on our family. And after Dad left, Eddie did so much to look after Mom and me. It's only fair to let him have his share. Don't you think so?'

'I suppose so,' I said.

Lisa looked at me. 'Do you think I was wrong?'

'If it were me, I'd have kept the money. Your father knew what he was doing. And Eddie was always going to get the hundred thousand bucks from the life insurance policy.'

Lisa frowned. 'But it's not right.'

'Don't worry, Lisa. It was your decision. And what you did was very generous. Eddie is very lucky to be your brother.'

Lisa smiled. Then her face became serious. 'You don't like him, do you?'

'It's more a case of him not liking me. But after a while, I have to admit I begin to feel the same way about him.'

'He's a wonderful person, really. After the divorce, I was the one who cried. I couldn't bear the thought of not living with Dad any more, or the idea that Mom and Dad didn't love each other. Eddie seemed to take it all so well: he never cried, he comforted. Whenever I had a problem, he was there. I was always going through those crises of self-confidence teenage girls suffer from. And Eddie always told me I was good enough to do whatever I wanted to do. He encouraged me to study biochemistry, to go to Stanford, to become a research student. He made me believe in myself again. Thanks to him, I did a pretty good job of getting over the divorce. I guess he never did. That's why he's so touchy about Dad.'

'It must have been rough on him,' I said, to mollify Lisa. What I really thought was that Eddie was a spoiled brat, who had thrown a temper tantrum and been rewarded with a couple of million bucks or more. But it was Lisa's money, and I really did admire her determination to be generous to her family.

'At least now we can help Helen out on her lawsuit,' Lisa said.

'If you're sure we can use that money?' I asked.

'Of course, Simon. I want her to win as much as you do.'

I smiled at her. With everything else that was going wrong, I was pleased that there might finally be some prospect of good news for my sister. She deserved it.

'You should call and tell her,' Lisa said. 'But remember, we'll have to wait till probate comes through.'

'I'll ring her tomorrow,' I said. 'She'll be very happy. Thank you.' I kissed her. 'How do you feel?'

'Lousy.'

'You're coping well.'

'Thanks to you.' She held me again. 'I'm *so* glad I married you. I couldn't deal with this alone.'

'It's the best decision I ever made,' I said, kissing the top of her head.

We held each other in silence. I remembered when I had made that decision. We were spending a long weekend in the Berkshires, a beautiful range of hills in western Massachusetts. We were walking up a path that ran alongside a small stream. I was in front, Lisa behind. Suddenly, I don't know where from, I got this strong feeling that I wanted to spend the rest of my life with this woman. I knew it was right. I wanted to turn round and tell her straight away, but I thought I ought to think it over first. But with every step I took up that hill, the surer I became. A rush of exhilaration flowed through me, and I smiled broadly to myself.

The gradient levelled off, and we emerged from the trees, into a clearing by a small lake, much like a Cumbrian tarn. It shone blue in the sunshine. We made our way over to its banks and sat on a large stone.

There was almost total stillness, apart from the occasional breath of wind ruffling the grass and throwing ripples across the tarn.

'You're very quiet,' said Lisa.

I didn't answer her, but I couldn't prevent the grin I had been trying hard to control spreading across my face.

'What is it?' she asked.

I said nothing.

She hit me playfully on the shoulder. 'What?'

I turned to her. 'Will you marry me?'

Her face went almost into shock. She clearly hadn't anticipated the question. I thought I'd made a big mistake. She didn't answer me. She clammed up.

'Lisa?'

She still didn't answer. For a moment I thought I had blown it completely, gone too far, totally misjudged our relationship. I sat there, helpless, trying not to stare at Lisa's silence.

The sun edged across the sky. Clouds came and went. Neither of us moved. Finally, Lisa turned to me.

'All right,' she said, smiling. 'I'll marry you.'

I let out a whoop, and threw my arms around her. We held each other tight, laughing, too excited to say anything coherent.

Now, a year later, she stirred in my arms.

'I think I'll go to work tomorrow,' she said. 'I can't stand hanging around here any more. And they need me there.' She broke away. 'Oh, I got a couple of visitors today.'

'Oh, yes?'

'Yeah. John Chalfont came round. He was very sweet. He didn't say much. Just that he was sorry about Dad.'

'Did he look ill?'

'Sick, you mean? No. He looked pretty sad, though.'

'He took the day off sick today. He and your father worked together a lot. I think he feels pretty bad.'

'He's a nice guy.'

'He is. Who else came?'

'Oh, the police.'

'Again?'

'They searched the place.' I glanced round the living room. It looked just as it had this morning when I had left. 'Don't worry, I put everything back.'

'Did they have a warrant?'

'They certainly did.'

'What were they looking for?'

'I don't know. They seemed awfully interested in some of your clothes. They had tweezers and little plastic bags.'

'Did they find anything?'

'I don't think so. Why, should they have found anything?'

'I don't know.'

'You look worried.'

'I am. I feel like I'm being surrounded. Like they're blocking all the exit routes before they attack.'

'They can't do anything to you. You're innocent.'

I looked down at Lisa's trusting face. She trusted me and she trusted the US justice system.

'Gil gave me the name of a good lawyer. If this gets any heavier, I'll give him a call.'

'It'll be OK, Simon. They'll find the real killer.'

'I hope so.'

'And when they do,' she said, anger flaring in her voice, 'I hope they kill the bastard just like he killed Dad.'

9

I met Craig at the airport the next morning, very early, and we made our way by aeroplane and rental car to a high-tech business park amidst the woods and highways of suburban New Jersey. We were making a presentation to Luxtel, a massive telecommunications equipment company that was a possible reseller of Net Cop's switches, and therefore, in theory at least, a possible provider of finance. I was there to field the difficult questions about why Revere had pulled out.

And they were difficult. I said that changes in market conditions had made Revere wary of making an additional investment in the business, but that we still had confidence in the quality of the product. It didn't go down well, but there was no way round that, short of outright lying. Craig, of course, had suggested this, but wasn't surprised when I said no.

Luxtel really liked Net Cop's switch. Craig promised 99.99 per cent reliability and this impressed them. They especially liked the encryption features, which they felt would be vital once more commercial traffic flowed through the Internet. Commerce meant money, and electronic money needed as much electronic security as possible.

But they felt it was too early to make a firm commitment to buy, let alone to invest. They needed to see working silicon first. It was the age-old mystery of venture capital. Which comes first, the prototype or the money?

Craig drove our rental car back towards Newark Airport in silence, his jaw set, meaty hands gripping the steering wheel.

I tried to sound optimistic. 'There's one definite customer, if we can get the money.'

'We'll get the money,' Craig said, more as an article of faith than as a forecast.

He drove on. 'I have to make this work, you know,' he said.

'I know.'

'No, you don't. This is just another deal for you,' he muttered. 'If it blows up, there will be others that come along. But I've put everything into Net Cop. I'll have to make it succeed. The alternative . . . there is no alternative.'

'You could get a job easily,' I said.

'Huh. I'm unemployable. I worked my ass off for Gary Olek. I'm not doing that again.'

Gary Olek had made tens of millions through the sale of his software company a year before. Craig had been the technical genius behind the firm. Olek, with his MBA, his charm, his financial acumen, had been CEO and major stockholder. Craig had made some money from the sale, all of which he had ploughed into Net Cop. Olek had made a fortune.

'Olek took my ideas and made millions out of them. That Net Cop switch is mine, and I'm gonna make the money this time. I'm not gonna let no banks or venture capitalists stop me. Of course Luxtel's going to buy our switches. So's every other motherfucker in the market. You hear what I'm sayin'?'

'I hear you.'

He relaxed a touch. 'I'm sorry, Simon. I know you're trying to help. But at the end of the day it's all down to me. I'll get the money. I'll sell the fuckin' switches. I'll make Cisco and 3Com and all those other fuckers sit up and take notice of Net Cop. Don't worry about it.'

I did worry about it. All the way back to Boston.

I didn't get back to the office until mid-afternoon. Daniel was out, something was hotting up at BioOne. I wasn't sure where John was. I surveyed the pile of papers screaming at me from my in-box. Tetracom. Net Cop. A former McDonald's executive who wanted to set up yet another chain of coffee shops. A proposal for a Swedish-goods-by-mail-order company. All needing urgent attention.

I pulled out the Tetracom pile. The deal was shaping up well. Diane was in Cincinnati, without me, visiting the company. I'd told her I didn't want to travel overnight because I ought to stay with Lisa, and she had understood.

I had been working for about a quarter of an hour when John burst in.

'Man, these quilt guys are something else!'

I looked up. 'Board meeting?'

'Yeah. Plus some kind of brainstorming session. It was wild.'

'What happened?'

The National Quilt Company was an ailing manufacturer of high-quality quilts that had been bought by a marketing man named Andy McArdle with the backing of Revere. His idea had been to turn the company round by realizing the potential of duvets, or 'comforters' as the Americans called them, for merchandising. Art had done the deal with John, and put John on the board.

'You know I told you about those merchandising deals they'd signed last spring for the fall season?'

'Yes.'

'It turns out some goon somewhere ordered a few hundred thousand Mutant Turtle comforters that no one wants to buy. Warehouse full. Lots of inventory. Big problem.'

'Sounds like it.'

'So, I suggest maybe they ought to go back to making comforters with cute patterns on them. Flowers and such like.'

'Radical.'

'Not as radical as McArdle. He's done a ton of research on the number of single-person homes, and the lack of comforters targeted at the under-thirties, and his conclusion is . . .' John looked at me enquiringly.

'I give up.'

'Go naked.'

'Go naked?'

'Yup. Go naked. Dump the turtles. We spread naked women all over these quilts. They get bought by the millions of young men out there who are sick of the choice of flowers or turtles on their comforters. National Quilt makes out like bandits.'

'Jesus. What did you say?'

'Why not naked men? I mean, single women buy comforters too.'

'Er. True. What did McArdle say to that?'

'He said that was an interesting idea, and he'd look into it.'

'Oh, dear.'

'Yes. Oh, dear.'

'Did you let him do it?' I asked.

'Yeah. On a small scale. The company's screwed anyway, and I'm curious to see what happens.'

'Have you told Art?'

'No point. He's lost all interest in this deal. He just doesn't want to know. It's my baby now. Tea?'

'Thanks,' I said, and John left the room to get it. A couple of minutes later he came back with tea for me and something brown under white foam for himself.

'Don't you think you should do something more positive?' I asked as he returned.

'I thought about it, but I don't see the point. I figure if this company goes down the toilet, then it's McArdle's fault, not mine. And that's the way I'd like to keep it.'

I wasn't convinced, but I let it pass.

Sergeant Mahoney came to see me that afternoon, accompanied by another detective whom he called a trooper, but who didn't look at all like the troopers I was used to. I took them into a small meeting room.

'How are you getting on?' I asked Mahoney.

'Slow but sure. Slow but sure,' he said. 'It's the best way, I find.'

'Do you have any suspects yet? Apart from me?'

'We're not quite at that stage yet. But we're making progress.'

There was clearly no chance of Mahoney telling me who he thought had killed Frank, even if he knew. I was curious to see where I stood in his list of possibilities.

'We have been able to narrow down the time of Mr Cook's murder. The phone records show he called John Chalfont at three twenty-four that Saturday afternoon. They spoke for only a couple of minutes. Mr Chalfont recalls the conversation. So we know he was alive at that time.'

'I had definitely left by then,' I said.

'Now, Mr Chalfont says he called Mr Cook back later on that afternoon. They were talking about a deal they were both working on, and Mr Chalfont had some responses. Mr Cook didn't answer the phone, but his answering machine did. The call was timed at four thirty-eight.'

'I see.'

'So where were you between three twenty-four, and four thirty-eight?'

'Walking on the beach. I told you. Actually, by four thirty-eight I was probably on the way to Net Cop.'

'Yes, you did tell us that,' said Mahoney. 'Trouble is we haven't found anyone who saw you down there. We did find a couple of people who said they were walking on Shanks Beach on Saturday afternoon, but neither of them remembers seeing anyone who fits your description. Nor the description of your car, which is quite distinctive.'

'Oh,' I said. Damn! Someone should have noticed the Morgan. Dark green, long and low, it looked like a roadster from the nineteen forties, although in fact it was only ten years old.

'Can you think of anyone else who might have seen you? Did you stop for gas? Go into a store somewhere?'

'No,' I said. 'I'm pretty sure there was no one manning the booth at the entrance to the beach . . .'

'There wasn't,' said Mahoney.

'Are you sure no one saw my car? You'd have thought they would have remembered it.'

'You'd have thought so,' said Mahoney. His blue eyes twinkled, and he smiled the irritating half-smile. He thought he'd got me.

'I definitely was there, Sergeant,' I said.

'All we're trying to do is confirm your story, Mr Ayot. Now, according to Daniel Hall, you and he discussed your father-in-law's wealth as recently as last week. Is that true?'

'No,' I replied quickly.

'He says you both discussed the money Mr Cook would make from Revere Partners' BioOne investment.' Mahoney raised his eyebrows, waiting for a reply.

Then I remembered the conversation. 'Oh, yes. That's right. We did discuss that. Or rather he did. Daniel is obsessed with how much money everyone makes, especially the partners. I wasn't very interested.'

'Not interested, huh?'

'No.'

'You have heard about the will now?'

'Yes I have.'

'And you've heard your wife is a very wealthy woman.'

'I suppose she will be,' I said flatly.

'That money will be useful for you, won't it?'

'I don't follow.' I wondered what Mahoney was driving at.

'To fight your sister's lawsuit. She needs fifty thousand pounds, doesn't she? That's, what, eighty thousand bucks? And you've sunk thousands in the case already. Isn't that true?'

'Yes, it is,' I said carefully.

'And how much have you already spent on your sister's lawsuit?'

'About forty-five thousand pounds. She's spent twenty.'

'Which you borrowed?'

'Partly. Part of it was our savings.'

'And unless you can find the money to continue with this lawsuit, then you can kiss goodbye to that forty-five thousand pounds?'

'That's right,' I admitted.

'OK. I understand that your wife asked Mr Cook for some money to help pay for this lawsuit.'

'So she told me.'

'But Mr Cook said no?'

'Apparently. But, listen. I didn't ask her to go to him. It was her idea. She didn't tell me about it until after he'd said no.'

Mahoney watched me closely. 'So then you went to see him yourself?'

'No. I mean, yes. But not about that. I told you what I wanted to talk to him about. We'd had problems at work that I wanted to sort out.'

'So you didn't talk about money?'

'No. Or I suppose Frank did. But I told him I wasn't interested in his money.'

'Oh. So Mr Cook brought up the question of giving you money, and you told him you weren't interested?'

I slowed down, took a breath. 'Frank thought I'd come to see him to ask for money. I hadn't. I told him that. And now I'm telling you.'

'I see,' said Mahoney. He paused. 'It's lucky that your wife is going to inherit all this money, isn't it? Now you'll be able to pay those legal bills.'

'No,' I said. 'No, it isn't. I'd much rather Frank were still alive. And so would Lisa.'

'Of course, Mr Ayot. Of course. Thank you for your cooperation.' The interview was over, and I showed Sergeant Mahoney to the elevators. The irritating little smile never left his lips.

It was very hard to get back to work. I was worried. Although Mahoney hadn't come right out and accused me of murdering Frank, he was steadily building a case against me. No one seeing me at the beach, needing the money for Helen's lawsuit, my argument with Frank. None of these pieces of information was damning in itself, but each was pointing Mahoney where I was sure he wanted to go.

I knew he'd find more evidence from somewhere. I was getting very worried.

Lisa must have told Mahoney about Helen's legal case. She probably didn't see the harm in it, just answering a straightforward question honestly. But I wished she hadn't.

All this reminded me that I had intended to call Helen that

afternoon to tell her about Frank's will, and Lisa's willingness to use some of the money to fund her legal bills. But something stopped me. Until I knew the results of Mahoney's investigation, I didn't want to get her hopes up. I still wanted to think that the justice system would inexorably grind on until I was cleared, and the true culprit found. But my doubts were growing. With some justification, as it turned out.

I tried to make it home by seven that evening, in case Lisa was back, but she wasn't there. She didn't arrive until nine. She looked tired and depressed.

'Can I get you a drink?' I asked.

'A glass of wine would be great.' She flopped on the sofa.

I passed her one. 'You did a long day's work.'

'Well, what do you expect?' she snapped. 'I've been out half the week. There's a ton of work to be done.'

I was taken aback by the outburst. 'I'm sure there is,' I said neutrally.

'You're not the only one with a stressful job, you know!'

'I know,' I said. I sat down beside her and put my arm round her.

She sipped her wine. 'Sorry, Simon. It's just that Boston Peptides is in real trouble. We're out of cash. I didn't realize how bad it was. I've agreed to no pay cheque this month, but that's hardly going to help.'

I sighed. 'Have they no leads on any more funds?'

'Not according to Henry. If only we could get all the animal work finished on BP 56. It would make us a much better proposition for any investor.'

This was bad news. Lisa had put everything into BP 56. If Boston Peptides went bust before the drug had met its potential, it would be a huge disappointment for her.

I squeezed her, and she pressed herself close into me. Then she began to cry. And she didn't stop.

I arrived at work a little late the next morning. Daniel hadn't shown up yet. I greeted John, who was looking over the *Wall Street Journal* whilst attacking a blueberry muffin.

'Forty-four and a half,' he said, without looking up.

'It's creeping back,' I said.

'Creeping is the right word for it.'

I checked the Chelsea web-page for details of the match they had played the night before. The Internet was a godsend for English football supporters trapped in America. The boys had won again, two–nil.

John interrupted me. 'Hey, Simon! Did you hear about Boston Peptides?' The whiff of gossip quickened his voice.

'No. What's happened?'

'BioOne's going to take it over. Art and Daniel were working on it all of yesterday.'

I put my head in my hands. 'Oh, Christ.'

John was surprised by my reaction. 'It'll be good for Lisa, won't it? She has stock options, right? And BioOne will give Peptides the backing to expand its R&D.'

'I don't think Lisa likes BioOne very much, John.' Where venture capitalists saw a high stock price, Lisa saw a big bad biotech company. And now she would be working for it.

Daniel strode into the office, bags under his eyes, and briefcase pulling down one arm.

'I heard about Boston Peptides,' I said. 'John told me.'

'It's a good deal,' said Daniel, arranging the papers on his desk. 'For BioOne.'

'And for Boston Peptides. It has a promising drug for Parkinson's, and BioOne has the muscle to see it through.'

I sighed. I could see the commercial logic.

'They're making a presentation this afternoon,' said John. 'You coming?'

'You bet.'

'It's at their offices in Kendall Square at two.'

'*Their* offices?'

Daniel grinned. 'Yeah. Enever said he didn't have time to come over here.'

It was unheard of for companies to make presentations to the partnership anywhere else but our offices. They came on time fully prepared. We showed up late, or cancelled the meeting. But in the case of BioOne, the balance of power had long ago shifted from investor to investee.

'Are you going?' I asked Daniel.

'Of course. I've been running all the damned numbers.'

'So if there are any mistakes, I know who to ask.'

'You do and you're a dead person,' Daniel said.

Despite his considerable mathematical ability, he had a tendency to transpose numbers, turning a 586 into a 568, for example. John and I delighted in waiting for the moment of maximum embarrassment to point them out.

I would keep my eyes peeled.

'Oh, Simon,' Daniel said. 'Art asked me to tell you to go see him first thing this morning.'

'About BioOne?'

'I guess so.'

Art was in his habitual position, leaning back in his leather executive chair, one hand pressing the telephone to his ear, the other clasping a can of Diet Dr Pepper. Art spent even more time on the phone than the other partners at the firm. It was the kind of work he liked. It involved talking, not thinking. You could easily spend a twelve-hour working day on the phone and not actually do or decide anything.

He beckoned for me to sit down. I perched on the small chair on the other side of his desk. I knew he wouldn't hurry on my account, and he didn't. He cut an imposing figure. He was a big broad man in his fifties with grey hair cropped close to his head. He exercised regularly, and most of his size was muscle, rather than fat. He had served in the Marines, as he had reminded me on many occasions, and he still affected a tough-guy attitude. He liked to tell it like it was.

Pride of place on his desk was given to a photograph of a young man in the uniform of one of the Midwestern football colleges. He looked like a younger but beefier version of Art. It was Chuck,

Art's son. Art was almost as proud of him as he was of BioOne.

Ten minutes later, he finally put the receiver down. 'I guess you heard. We're buying Boston Peptides.' By 'we' Art meant BioOne. He identified himself so closely with that company that in his eyes he was indistinguishable from it.

'Congratulations,' I said neutrally.

'Now, BioOne is a public company, and we're not quite ready to make an announcement yet. Also, we've been negotiating with Boston Peptides' VC backers, Venture First, directly. The management knows nothing about the deal. Are you with me?'

'But you'll need management support,' I said. 'Without Henry Chan, Boston Peptides is worth nothing.' And it's not worth much without Lisa, I could have added.

'Oh, they'll get a sweet deal. We just want to keep them out of the loop for the moment. So, it's very important that you don't tell any of this to Lisa.'

'I understand the importance of keeping price-sensitive information private,' I said. 'But it's OK to tell my wife, surely?'

'No, it is most emphatically not,' said Art, leaning forward. 'Particularly not in this case. Not only would it be extremely unprofessional, it would be disloyal to the firm. I've spoken to Gil about this case specifically, and he shares my concerns.'

I swallowed. 'OK,' I said. 'I understand.'

Art leaned back in his big chair. 'We're going to try to keep you out of this deal as much as possible, Simon, but in such a small office it's impossible to keep you entirely in the dark. Besides, that's not the way we work here.' He smiled briefly. 'But anything you do hear, you keep to yourself, OK?'

'I understand,' I repeated. I noticed he hadn't mentioned the presentation that afternoon. Well, if he wasn't going to, neither would I.

'Good. And can you tell Daniel to come in and see me, please?'

So dismissed, I left Art's office.

10

BioOne's building was a small, gleaming, high-tech block just behind its big brothers, Genzyme and Biogen, and within shouting distance of the Massachusetts Institute of Technology. Kendall Square was a prestigious location for a biotech company. Art, Jerry Peterson, and Enever had thought it money well spent. Daniel, who had crunched the numbers, said the rent played havoc with BioOne's expenses. But no one cared. Once BioOne had a treatment for Alzheimer's on the market, the dollars would flow in from all over the world.

John and I had made our way there together, and we were a couple of minutes late. The security was conspicuous: uniformed guards in the entrance lobby, a card-reader on every door, and fearsome signs announcing restricted access to just about everything. We were issued with temporary ID badges and ushered through to a reception area where a small group of people was waiting. There was Gil, Art, Ravi, Daniel and a small prim woman of about forty with short dark hair and very large glasses. Lynette Mauer, the firm's largest investor.

Like many other venture capitalists, Revere Partners didn't invest its own money, but managed a series of funds, each one of which was supposed to last ten years. We had finished investing the first three, and we were planning to raise a fourth fund in the new year. The money for these funds was raised from institutional investors such as insurance companies, pension funds, or family foundations.

Revere charged an annual fee for the work and took a twenty per cent cut of any profits. Lynette Mauer was Chief Investment Officer for the Bieber Foundation, a substantial family trust that was the biggest investor in our funds. Gil had no doubt brought her along to see our star investment at first hand.

When Art saw me he frowned. He whispered something to Gil who was sitting next to him. Gil glanced at me, and the two of them had a brief exchange of words, Gil's hand resting on Art's arm. I stood in the middle of the reception area not knowing what to do. Gil noticed my confusion.

'Hello, Simon, John. Take a seat. We're just waiting for Jerry Peterson and Dr Enever. You've met Lynette Mauer. Lynette, John Chalfont, Simon Ayot, two of our excellent associates.'

Mauer smiled in a friendly way, and Gil's charm dispelled the moment of awkwardness. But it was clear Art hadn't wanted me there. Tough.

A smartly dressed woman approached us and led us all through a series of corridors, flashing her identity card at winking green lights on the way. We passed silent workers in ones or twos, walking swiftly and purposefully in well-ironed shirts or pristine white coats. Corridors branched off to left and right, presumably leading to laboratories where mysterious biochemical processes were set in action. It was a far cry from the glorified hut where Lisa did her stuff for Boston Peptides. Eventually we reached a door marked DR THOMAS E. ENEVER, TECHNICAL DIRECTOR. The woman knocked, opened the door, and showed us in.

Two men greeted us. One I recognized. He had silver hair and a young fresh face, and wore an open-necked shirt and slacks, every inch the successful Route 128 entrepreneur. Jerry Peterson, BioOne's chairman and Art's old buddy.

The other man was tall and thin. What was left of his hair was oiled back over a shining brown forehead. He had a long narrow face, etched with deep downward sloping lines. He was wearing a bow-tie festooned with tiny balloons. The implied jollity was at odds with his dour expression. Dr Enever, I presumed.

Gil made the introductions, explaining that Mauer was there to understand a bit more about Revere's most important investment. Jerry Peterson ushered her across the large office to a group of chairs and sofas, and sat everyone down. There were enough seats for all of us. The smartly dressed woman produced a tray of coffee cups and filled them all up.

I looked round Enever's office. It was large and tried to combine serious scientist with international business executive. There were shelves with thick books whose titles were made up of words of more than ten letters. Periodicals and magazines were neatly filed. A large whiteboard was adorned with gibberish in tiny script. But there was also a big executive desk, a corner-office view of Kendall Square with a glimpse of the river, and a suite of executive armchairs. There was even some executive art, although somehow I doubted Enever had chosen it.

Jerry Peterson cleared his throat. 'Before I hand over to Thomas here, I'd just like to say that I'm real excited by this opportunity, and I know when he's spoken to you you'll be real excited too. In neuroxil-5, this company has a blockbuster drug, a world-beater. But people often ask me what else we have in the pipeline. The acquisition of Boston Peptides and its anti-Parkinson's drug, BP 56, will give us an exciting new prospect to talk about for the future. Thomas.'

Enever smiled thinly, as he sat stiffly in one of his armchairs.

Art caught his attention. 'Thomas, before you start, I wonder if you could just explain to Lynette here what neuroxil-5 does, and how it is progressing.'

'Why certainly,' said Enever, smiling thinly at Gil and Mauer. 'Alzheimer's disease is a complicated illness that no one really understands at the moment.' His accent was a hybrid of American and his native Australian. 'It strikes with increasing frequency as people get older. Over a period of many years, Alzheimer's kills millions of brain cells. At first the effect is too small to be noticed. Then the patient begins to forget small things, then larger things until they forget their own name, or the faces of their family. Eventually the body forgets how to function, and the patient dies. It's a horrible disease, for the sufferer who becomes increasingly confused by the world around him, and for the sufferer's family, who see their loved one's personality disappear with their memory.'

I remembered Carl's story about a woman at the Alzheimer's clinic whose husband had lost his smile, and his fear that that would happen to Aunt Zoë.

'There are a number of processes that develop in the brain of an Alzheimer's patient,' Enever went on. 'The pathways of one of the brain's neurotransmitters become blocked. A twisted plaque builds up in certain parts of the brain releasing molecules known as free radicals that attack the brain cells. Then the brain cells themselves become flooded with calcium. The result of all this is that the brain cells die, although it's hard to tell what is cause and what is effect. Most treatments focus on one or other of these processes.'

Enever's face was animated, as he talked fluently and coherently.

'But these are the symptoms, not the cause. What we have managed to do is identify a gene that, at a certain stage in a patient's life, begins to emit messages to the body that set in train these various effects. These messages are carried by molecules of ribonucleic acid or RNA. We have developed a molecule that neutralizes the RNA emitted by this gene, thus preventing the Alzheimer's from developing further. This is neuroxil-5.'

'So the patient is cured?' Mauer asked.

'Not exactly. Once the brain cells are dead, we can't resurrect them. But we can prevent the death of more brain cells, and hence slow down or even stop the progression of the disease.'

'And how many Alzheimer patients are there?'

'It's difficult to say. The government estimates there are four million in the US alone. They figure the cost to society at about eighty billion dollars a year. And of course those numbers will grow as other medical advances allow people to live longer and the population as a whole ages.'

'That's a huge market.'

Enever twitched a smile. This time his eyes smiled too. 'Billions of dollars.'

Lynette Mauer paused, blinking through her glasses. Gil shifted

97

in his seat, unsure whether she was about to say something, or if he could safely interrupt. Eventually, she spoke. 'Couldn't you give this drug to people with the Alzheimer's gene to prevent them from developing the disease? You know, almost a vaccine?'

Another smile. 'You're very perceptive,' Enever said. 'I couldn't possibly comment.'

God. I could see what Lynette Mauer was driving at. BioOne really could be worth billions if they were able to sell neuroxil-5 to any fifty-year-old who was worried about developing Alzheimer's in old age. I was pretty sure I hadn't heard Art mention that prospect for the company. It was obviously something Enever had up his sleeve for the future.

'And how is the drug progressing?' Mauer asked.

'The clinical trials are going excellently at the moment, although as you know, they are double blinded, which means we won't have a real idea of the results until the trials are completed next year. I'm afraid I can't go into anything more specific. We take confidentiality very seriously here at BioOne. But provided the trials don't throw up any problems, and frankly I don't expect them to, neuroxil-5 will be on the market by the end of next year.'

'Thank you, Dr Enever,' Art said. 'Now, perhaps you can tell us something about Boston Peptides.'

Enever launched into a similar description of BP 56. He was enthusiastic about its prospects for treating Parkinson's disease, but somehow managed to imply that the drug itself had been developed by accident. Then Jerry talked about the deal itself, and Daniel handed round his figures.

They showed strong revenues for BP 56 starting in year seven. As Lisa had always told me, biotechnology is a long-term business.

'How are you going to integrate Boston Peptides into your business?' Ravi asked.

'That won't be a problem,' said Enever. 'We're really just buying the drug. Many drugs are discovered like this, more or less by accident, but they need professional guidance to get them to market.' I stiffened. I didn't like this.

'Although Boston Peptides does have a very exciting new treatment for Parkinson's disease, it doesn't have the capital or the infrastructure or, quite frankly, the management expertise to develop this treatment to its full potential.'

My colleagues tensed. Art threw me a worried glance. I didn't like this at all.

I knew I should keep my mouth shut, but I couldn't. 'Management expertise?' I asked as innocently as I could. Out of the corner of my eye, I could see Art's glance turn into a glare.

'Yes. There are very few scientists who are able to take a drug all the way through from the discovery stage to marketing. At BioOne we are fortunate that we have people who can do that.' Meaning Enever himself, I assumed. 'Boston Peptides has a different culture. Less rigorous, less disciplined.'

'So you will have to make changes at Boston Peptides?'

'Oh, undoubtedly. We'll have to let some scientists go. They've done their part, now it's time for others to take over.'

Done their part! Lisa had devoted many years of her life to BP 56, as had her colleagues, and Enever was planning to shuffle them off before they had had a chance to see the fruit of their work. I did not like this man.

Art stepped in with a question about synergies or paradigm shifts or something. I fumed.

Although it was Friday, Lisa didn't return home until after nine again. She looked shattered.

She turned on the television, and said she didn't want any supper. So I cooked myself an omelette and ate it at the kitchen table.

Just as I was finishing, she came in.

'Hi,' I said. 'Change your mind about supper?'

She ignored me and put a muffin in the toaster.

'Are you going into the lab tomorrow?' I asked her.

She sighed. 'Yes. And Sunday too. I've no choice. There's so much to get done.'

I was worried that she was working too hard. Perhaps the work was helping her deal with her father's death, taking her mind off him. But she didn't look good at all. Her face was pinched into an expression of fatigue and cold despair.

'How are you feeling?'

'I feel really bad, Simon,' she snapped. 'My father's dead, I'm tired, my head hurts, and I just wish I was someone else someplace else.'

I shut up, finished my omelette, and fled from the silence to the chatter of the television in the living room.

I heard a cry from the kitchen. 'Damn!' A pause. 'Damned piece of shit toaster!' and then a crash.

I rushed through to see Lisa scowling at our toaster, which was lying on its side against a wall, smoke pouring out of it.

'What's the matter?'

'That stupid toaster's a piece of crap.' Lisa was shaking with anger. 'It's burned the damned muffin!'

I pulled the plug out of the wall socket, and looked in the toaster. The muffin was indeed stuck. I grabbed a knife and forced it out, sending the blackened bread spinning across the kitchen counter. I turned to see Lisa trying to hold back tears, her face red.

'I'm sorry, Simon,' she said.

I put my arms around her, and she buried her head in my shoulder. She began to sob.

I held her tight.

'It's only a stupid toaster,' she said.

'Shhh. Don't worry about it.'

She broke away. 'I need a tissue.' She fetched one, and blew her nose. 'I'm OK now.'

'Are you sure?'

'Yeah. Stupid toaster,' she mumbled, with a half-smile.

We sat on the sofa in the sitting room, my arm around her. I was shaken. Lisa was perfectly capable of losing her temper, but never over something so minor. I wanted so desperately to comfort her, to smooth over everything that was tearing her up inside. I could tell she didn't want to talk about it, but at least she let me put my arm around her. We just sat there for a long time, the TV laughing emptily at us.

I would have liked to have stayed like that all evening, but I had to tell Lisa about the take-over, no matter what Art said. Once it was made public, she would know that I had kept the information from her. That would really make her angry, and with some justification. It wasn't a good time, but no time seemed like a good time these days.

So I summoned up my courage and took a deep breath. 'I heard some news today,' I said.

'Oh, yes?' Her eyes were fixed on the television in front of her.

'It's about Boston Peptides. But it's highly confidential. If I tell you, you mustn't mention it to anyone at work. They told me to keep it quiet. Even from you.'

Lisa turned to me. 'What is it?'

'BioOne is going to buy Boston Peptides.'

'No! Are you serious?'

I nodded.

'Jesus! Does Henry know?'

'I don't think so.'

'But you can't buy a biotech company without talking to the people first.'

'They've been negotiating directly with Venture First. I think the idea is to sweeten the management afterwards. Which means Henry, of course. And maybe you.'

'I can't believe it,' she said. 'We need the money, but *BioOne*!' She glanced at me sharply. 'I suppose Revere is behind this?' Anger was rising in her voice.

'I assume so.'

'How long have you known?'

'I found out this morning.'

'This morning?' her eyes narrowed with suspicion. 'You didn't tell them what I'd said about our cash problems, did you?'

'Of course not!'

'Because if you did, and if you're the reason I'm going to be working for BioOne . . .'

'Lisa, I didn't.' I could feel my own voice rising in anger. I fought to control it. 'Look. At least you'll have the resources to finish working on BP 56.'

'Yeah, but Thomas Enever will take all the credit, and I'll be lucky if I'm doing anything more than washing out test tubes. That man's awful, Simon. I've heard all about him.'

'He can't be that bad,' I said, although from what I'd seen of him I feared perhaps he might be.

Lisa pulled away from me. 'You don't understand, do you? Everything I have worked for for the last four years has been sold out from under me to a total asshole. By my husband's firm, for God's sake!'

'Lisa . . .'

'I'm going to bed.'

With that she left me on the sofa, with the television's inane chatter, while she busied herself in the bathroom and bedroom.

I hadn't had a chance to tell Lisa what Enever had said about management rationalization. Given her mood, I was glad. Anyway, as I had thought about it that afternoon, I had decided there was little chance BioOne would be foolish enough to get rid of someone with Lisa's talent who knew more than anyone else in the world about BP 56. I waited half an hour, and then got undressed and crawled into bed. I could tell Lisa was still awake.

'Good night,' I said.

No response.

Usually, on those rare occasions when we fought, Lisa could soon be brought round. But that night I didn't even try.

Eventually I must have fallen into a deep sleep, because I awoke at a quarter to nine. Lisa was gone. To the lab presumably.

I pulled on my rowing gear and jogged down to the boathouse. I was five minutes late, and Kieran was waiting for me. He was a tall, rangy Irishman from Trinity College, Dublin whom I had met at business school. He was a good oarsman and most Saturday mornings we rowed pairs together. He had found himself a job at one of the many management consultancies in Boston.

'How are you, Simon?'

'I've probably been worse, but I don't remember it,' I said, as we slid the boat along the rack.

'I read about your father-in-law. I'm sorry.'

'Thanks.'

Kieran could tell I didn't want to talk, and knew to let it drop. 'Let's get this thing in the water.'

We threw the boat into the river, and I stepped in first. I was rowing stroke, Kieran bow. We soon set up a good rhythm. My muscles stretched and pulled, my heart pumped blood, oxygen and endorphins round my system, cool air flowed over my exposed skin and cool water underneath me. I began to relax. After ten minutes of concentrating on the rowing, my mind began to turn to Lisa.

I was worried about her. I had known Frank's death would fall very hard on her, and I had done my best to give her all the support I could. But work was getting at her as well. The timing was terrible. She seemed to be almost physically ill – tired, with headaches, and that dreadful look of despair. She had completely overreacted to the toaster burning her muffin. And it had been unlike Lisa to fly off the handle when I had told her about the take-over. It made no sense to blame me. But with all the pressure she was under, her outburst was hardly surprising. Perhaps she just felt that she had to blame someone for everything that was happening to her, and I was the easiest and safest choice.

Until now, when things had gone wrong, we had been able to rely on each other for support. Of course, nothing had tested us quite like the events of the past week, but I had hoped we would be able to deal with Frank's death together. It now looked as if things might not work out that way.

Well, Lisa needed me more than ever now. I would try to do everything I could to help her, and just put up with any moodiness on her part.

'Hey, slow down, Simon!' Kieran called behind me. 'I had a heavy night last night.'

'Sorry,' I shouted back. I had sped up without realizing it, so I reduced my pace to a more sedate thirty strokes per minute or so. 'That better?'

'That's fine. We'll win the Olympics next weekend, if that's OK with you.'

We glided along steadily, sliding underneath the graceful bridges spanning the Charles.

'Simon?' he called.

'Yes?'

'A bunch of the boys are getting together on Tuesday at the Red Hat. Do you want to come along?'

'I don't know. There's a lot going on at home.'

'Oh, come on. It'll be good for you.'

He was probably right. 'OK,' I said. 'I'll be there.'

But as we turned and headed for home, one other worry nagged me all the way back to the boathouse. Would Lisa tell Henry Chan about the BioOne take-over? Although I'd told her it was confidential, she hadn't acknowledged me. But I could trust Lisa. Couldn't I?

She arrived home at about five, looking exhausted.

'Hi, Simon.' She smiled and kissed me.

'Hi. How are you?'

'Tired. Very tired.' She took off her coat, and threw herself on to the sofa. She closed her eyes for a moment.

'I brought you some flowers.' I went into the kitchen and brought out some irises I had picked up on the way back from the river. She liked irises.

'Thank you,' she said, giving me a quick kiss. She disappeared into the kitchen, and returned with the flowers arranged in a tall vase, which she placed on her desk. 'Simon?'

'Yes?'

'I'm sorry I was so horrible to you yesterday.'

'That's OK.'

'No, it's not. I don't want us to become one of those snappy couples. I don't know why I did it, but I'm sorry.'

'You're under a lot of pressure,' I said. 'I understand.'

'I guess that must be it.' She sighed. 'I just feel hollow inside, like I'm empty. And then suddenly something seems to boil up somewhere in here,' she put her hand on her chest, 'and I feel like I want to shout and scream, or else just cry and cry. I have to work really hard to keep it all in. I've never felt like this before.'

'Something like this has never happened to you before,' I said. 'And I hope it won't happen again.'

She smiled up at me. 'Will you forgive me?'

'Of course.'

She looked at her watch. 'If we go now, do you think we might get into Olive's?'

I smiled. 'We could try.'

'Come on, then.'

Olive's was an Italian restaurant in Charlestown. It didn't take reservations, but we made it before the six o'clock rush, and were seated at a corner of one of the large wooden tables. As always, it was crowded, with lots of noise, warmth and excellent food.

We ordered, and surveyed the commotion around us.

'Remember the first time we came here?' said Lisa.

'Of course I do.'

'Do you remember how much we talked? They kept on trying to throw us out, so they could give the table to someone else, and we wouldn't go.'

'I do. And we missed the first half of that Truffaut film.'

'Which was crap anyway.'

I laughed. 'I'm glad you admit that now!'

I suddenly realized Lisa was staring at me. 'I'm so glad I met you,' she said.

It was the right thing to say. I smiled at her. 'And I'm really glad I met you.'

'You're nuts,' she said.

'No I'm not. You've done so much for me since we've been together.'

'Like what?'

'Oh, I don't know. You've pulled me out of myself, encouraged me to show my feelings, made me happy.'

'You were a tight-assed Brit when I met you,' she conceded.

It was true. And to some extent I probably still was. But Lisa had helped me escape from my old life in England, from parents who hated each other and wanted me out of the way, and from the ever-present traditions of Marlborough, Cambridge and the Life Guards, with their inescapable rules of how you should behave, how you should think, how you should feel.

'And I'm really sorry I've been such a pain,' she said.

'Forget it. You've had a really bad week.'

'It's funny. It sort of comes in waves. Thinking about Dad. One moment I'm fine and the next I feel awful. Like right now I . . .' She paused, and a tear ran down her cheek. She tried to smile. 'I was going to say I feel fine now, but look at me.' She sniffed. 'I'm sorry, Simon. I'm just a mess.'

I reached over and touched her hand. Despite the crowd, no one seemed to notice Lisa's distress. There was something about the barrage of noise in the restaurant that seemed to create walls around us, giving us our own little space of privacy.

She blew her nose, and the tears stopped. 'I wonder who killed him,' she said.

'Some burglar, probably. The house is pretty isolated. Maybe he thought he could get away with it in broad daylight and Frank surprised him.'

'I guess the police haven't got anywhere yet, or we'd have heard.'

'Oh, I didn't get a chance to tell you. Sergeant Mahoney came to see me a couple of days ago at the office.'

'What did he say?'

'He just asked me some questions about where I went after I left your father. Apparently your father spoke to John on the phone when I was walking on the beach. Mahoney wanted to try to confirm I was where I said I was.'

'Could you?'

'He hasn't found anyone who saw me. But I didn't get the impression he had made much progress in any direction. I think I'm still his number-one suspect.'

'Oh, Simon.' She squeezed my hand.

'Did you tell him about Helen's legal case?'

'Yes, I did. Why? Did he ask you about it?'

'Yes. He implied that it was convenient Frank had died, that now we can afford to fight the appeal. It makes me sick just thinking about it.'

'I'm sorry, Simon. He asked about money and whether we'd had any financial disagreements with Dad. I thought I should tell him the truth.'

I smiled at her. 'That's OK. I suspect it is best to tell the truth. Otherwise he'll catch us out, and it'll be even worse.'

'Don't worry, Simon. They haven't got any evidence.'

'Not hard evidence, no,' I said. 'But I have to admit, I am a bit worried.' The waiter brought a bottle of Chianti, and I poured us both a glass. 'Mahoney definitely has his sights on me. I wonder if it's because I'm British. Or rather because I served in Northern Ireland.'

'What do you mean?'

'He asked whether I had ever killed anyone. I said I had, in Ireland.'

Lisa shrugged. 'It's possible. He's obviously Irish. And even after the peace agreement, there must still be some strong pro-IRA feelings in this town.'

I sighed.

Lisa stole me a quick glance. 'Eddie thinks you did it.'

'No!' I was about to mutter something about what I thought of Eddie, and stopped myself just in time. In Lisa's eyes, Eddie could do no wrong. She had probably been reluctant to admit his suspicions to me. 'Well, he's wrong, isn't he?'

'Yes,' said Lisa. 'I know he is.' She looked at me, embarrassed. 'But I have to say in my darkest moments these last couple of days, I've wondered. You were there, you did have an argument with Dad, you do know how to use a gun, I'm going to inherit a lot of money. And the last person to see a murder victim alive is often the murderer.'

'Who says?'

'Eddie.'

Once again, I resisted telling Lisa what I thought of Eddie's idiotic theories. She didn't want to believe Eddie, she wanted to believe me. She was asking me for a reason.

'Lisa, you saw me when I came back from seeing Frank. Did I look like I'd just killed him?'

'No. No, of course not.' She smiled. 'Don't worry, Simon. I know you had nothing to do with it. Eddie's wrong, and I'm sorry I doubted you.'

Bloody Eddie. No doubt he felt guilty that he had got on with his father so badly in the years before he died. No doubt this self-recrimination had encouraged that basic human instinct to blame someone for his father's death, someone real, someone he knew and mistrusted. Me. Since the police seemed to be considering the possibility, and since I fitted into his half-baked ideas of criminology, I was the perfect candidate.

Lisa's closeness to her brother wasn't really surprising. He had always looked after her, and helped her through difficult times. I was grateful to him for having supported the woman I loved, but what I couldn't tolerate was him trying to turn Lisa against me.

The food came, and the conversation moved on. We didn't talk about Frank or Boston Peptides or BioOne for the rest of the evening. For a couple of hours we were as we had been before Frank's death. Eventually, they threw us out, and we decided to walk up the hill behind the restaurant to the Bunker Hill monument.

It was a warm evening for October, and we sat down under the tall obelisk, neatly hemmed in by black railings and crisply mown grass. We looked out over the Charles to the lights of Boston.

'I like it here,' I said.

'That's strange, considering it's where so many of the evil redcoats met their final destiny.'

'At the hands of a bunch of violent tax-dodgers.'

'Not paying taxes is a fine American tradition,' Lisa said, 'and one that our wealthiest citizens are proud to follow.'

'Anyway, wasn't the battle fought a few hundred yards from here?'

'Smart-ass.'

I smiled. I lay on my back, and looked up at the obelisk, tapering upwards into the night. 'No, seriously, things happened here hundreds of years ago. Wherever you walk in Boston you feel that. You can imagine the townspeople grazing their cows on the Common, or the clippers sailing into Boston Harbor. So many places in America have no history. Whatever was there before the latest strip mall was put up is obliterated, forgotten. But not here. As I said, I like it.'

Lisa kissed me. 'So do I'.

11

Lynette Mauer sat next to Gil, watching him through her large glasses with an expression close to awe, lapping up everything he was saying. This was a Monday morning meeting with a difference. The firm's largest investor was present.

It was also the first Monday morning meeting since Frank had died – the previous week's had been cancelled. The chair opposite Gil, Frank's chair, was empty. I could almost see him now, relaxed, cracking a joke, one long leg crooked over the other. His tenseness over the week before he died was forgotten. The old Frank, the relaxed, amiable but remarkably shrewd venture capitalist, would be the person we would all remember.

The meeting wasn't exactly rigged, and to be fair to Gil he had never told us to behave differently when an investor was present. But troubled investments were skated over rather than dissected, any disagreement was polite and swiftly resolved, and we talked a lot about BioOne.

This was good news for me, because I didn't have to talk much about Net Cop. It was good news for Art because he was allowed to expound upon his favourite subject. As usual, an open can of Diet Dr Pepper rested on the table in front of him, the dark purple liquid bubbling mysteriously in a glass. I had tasted Diet Dr Pepper once. It brought back memories of a particularly un-pleasant chemical cherryade from my childhood. Art guzzled it all day.

'The Street can't get enough of BioOne stock,' he was saying. 'The price is up to forty-five. Now that's not quite the sixty dollars we were at a couple of months ago, but the whole sector's been trashed.'

'OK, and at forty-five dollars a share, what's the value of Revere's holdings?' asked Gil, for Mauer's benefit.

Art paused as though he hadn't really thought about the question before. 'I'd say just shy of three hundred million.'

'Good. And we hold, right?'

Art smiled. 'We hold. Harrison Brothers is confident that the stock will be back up to sixty by year end. And we haven't gone wrong holding BioOne stock yet.'

'Good. Now I think you'll all agree that we had a very interesting meeting with Jerry and Dr Enever last week. The Boston Peptides acquisition will be a useful addition to the BioOne drugs portfolio. Can I take it we support the deal?'

There were nods around the table. It was pointless me protesting. This was just a formality, and anyway I wasn't a partner. I didn't get a vote.

'Excellent,' said Gil. 'Do you have any questions for Art, Lynette?'

Lynette Mauer glanced quickly up at Gil, fluttered a little, and then spoke. 'I enjoyed the meeting as well. It does seem to be a very successful investment, Art. Well done. I see you have been looking after our money well.'

Art beamed.

'I do have one question. It's something I saw in the paper at the weekend about Alzheimer's. After the meeting, it kind of jumped out of the page at me.' She smiled sweetly at Gil, who returned her smile encouragingly. 'Where is it?' She shuffled through her papers, and pulled out a piece of torn-out newspaper bearing the *New York Times* typeface. 'Ah, here.' She scanned it quickly. Art fidgeted with impatience.

'Yes. It's something about galantamine,' she pronounced this word awkwardly, 'which is some kind of drug extracted from narcissi bulbs. It's supposed to be a more effective treatment for

Alzheimer's than what's on the market at the moment. Do you think this might be a threat to neuroxil-5?'

'Ah, no, not at all,' replied Art quickly.

'Why not?'

Art replied slowly, as if addressing a child. 'Neuroxil-5 prevents the build up of beta-amyloid in the brain of an Alzheimer's affected patient. It is this beta-amyloid that eventually kills the brain cells. No other treatment has succeeded in attacking this beta-amyloid in the way neuroxil-5 does.'

'I understand that,' said Mauer. 'But it says here that this drug galantamine inhibits cholinesterase, which is what kills brain cells. So which is it?'

'Which is what?' asked Art carefully.

'Which is it that kills the brain cells? The beta-amyloid stuff or the cholinesterase stuff?' Mauer looked at Art ever so sweetly, as though she was completely confident he would be able to answer.

Art was stumped. He didn't have a clue. He was just about to open his mouth, when Ravi jumped in.

'As you know Ms Mauer, Art is our BioOne expert,' he began. 'But I did happen to catch that article about galantamine too.' He had all our attention. Ravi's approach to these meetings was usually to keep quiet until he was spoken to. But now, as he addressed Mauer over his half-moon glasses, he spoke quietly and with authority. 'I think the truth is that Alzheimer's involves a complex tangle of different biochemical reactions in the brain. It is difficult to separate cause from effect. It seems likely that drugs like galantamine delay the onset of Alzheimer's. But, as Dr Enever explained last week, BioOne believes that neuroxil-5 neutralizes a gene that is behind all these processes, including the production of beta-amyloid and cholinesterase, and a lot of others as well. We won't know for sure until the Phase Three clinical trials are complete, when we can look at the effect of the drug on over a thousand patients rather than just the hundred or so tested so far.'

Mauer smiled at Ravi. 'OK, I understand, thank you very much. I'll watch this one with interest.'

I felt as much as saw Daniel suppress a snigger next to me. Art was trying to smile. But he was furious. His neck was reddening as though any minute his head would begin to boil. Ravi had been hired as a biotech partner after Revere had invested in BioOne. Art had made it clear that he should stay clear of BioOne, and Ravi had scrupulously done just that. Until now. The trouble was, Ravi knew a lot about biotech, and Art didn't. We all understood that and now Lynette Mauer did too.

We moved on to new deals, of which the most interesting was Tetracom. Diane was an excellent presenter. She fed her audience information in such a way that they jumped to positive conclusions before she did. I knew there were still plenty of questions to be asked, but listening to her, it seemed that we should sign up on the spot. She finished her description with a note of caution, saying that she and I would be in Cincinnati the following week to clear up some detailed points. Mauer was impressed. We all were.

We came to the end of the meeting. Gil clearly thought it had gone well. He finished up by turning to Mauer.

'Lynette, perhaps you could tell us something about the Bieber Foundation's plans. As you know, we're raising a new fund next year. We look forward to welcoming you into it.'

Lynette smiled all round. 'Yes, there is something I'd like to say to all of you.' Gil stiffened first. This wasn't in the script. The rest of us looked on, our interest quickened.

'I'd like to thank all of you for the work you've done for us over the last few years. As you know, the Bieber Foundation has invested in your funds since the beginning. And your returns have been good, thanks in large part to BioOne.' A nice smile for Art. 'And of course to Frank Cook, who was responsible for so many successful investments.' She paused, out of deference to his memory.

There was a but. We were all waiting for the but.

'But we have had a recent change of policy. In future the Foundation will consolidate its investment in venture capital into two or maybe three firms. We will be reviewing all our venture capital investments, including Revere.'

The sweet smile stayed on her lips. Gil looked confused.

'I'm sure we can count on your continued investment in our funds, Lynette,' he said smoothly.

'Perhaps. But I wouldn't rely on it, Gil.'

'But, Lynette, our returns . . .'

'I have analysed your returns, and if you take out BioOne and Frank Cook's investments you are left with a performance that isn't quite as good as some of your competitors. You seem to have missed the Internet bus almost entirely.'

'Art, here, looked into that market, and concluded it was all hype. We firmly believe those companies are overvalued.'

'They've made a lot of people a lot of money,' said Lynette.

The firm had made some investments in the area in the early days. Frank had done a couple of successful small deals, and then Art came up with two spectacular disasters, which had set the firm's returns back significantly. Art's conclusion was that the problem was with the market, not his investing skills, and he had urged a policy of avoiding the sector. Frank and I had only been able to squeeze Net Cop through the investment committee by arguing that it was building the nuts and bolts of the Internet rather than an ephemeral 'community' in cyberspace. In truth, many of the Internet stocks had been hyped to the stratosphere. But most of our competitors had made money putting them there, and Mauer knew this.

'Perhaps we should discuss this in my office,' said Gil hurriedly.

'Why, certainly, if you like,' said Mauer.

The meeting broke up. Daniel strolled over to the small woman. 'Ms Mauer?'

'Yes?'

'Daniel Hall. I noticed you are a major investor in Beaufort Technologies. I just wanted to suggest that you should perhaps take your profits. The stock is due for a big correction.'

Mauer's eyes flicked up at Daniel. 'Why? What's wrong with Beaufort?'

'Nothing's wrong with the company,' Daniel said. 'It's just that the market's love affair with 3-D animation is wearing thin. It's going out of fashion.'

Gil was glaring at Daniel, but he had Mauer's attention. 'Thank you,' she said, and followed Gil out of the room.

'Talk about a death wish,' I said to Daniel as we made our way back to our office. 'You just about kissed goodbye to your career back there.'

Daniel smiled. 'Beaufort's going down. Lynette Mauer will remember I told her. And when it does fall, she'll be glad I warned her, and so will Gil.'

'Maybe. If we still have a firm by then. But if Bieber pulls out, so might some of the other investors.'

'Oh, Revere will survive,' said Daniel. 'And she saw right through Art, didn't she? That was just great!'

Maybe. Or maybe Revere was falling apart about our ears.

'Ayot, come with me! Gil's office. Now!'

It was Monday afternoon. I looked up from my work. Art was standing at the door to our office, his face was red, his short grey hair bristling.

John and Daniel turned open-mouthed. I slowly followed Art.

Gil was standing stiffly behind his desk as I came in, his weather-beaten face grim.

'Sit down, Simon,' he said coldly.

I took one of Gil's armchairs. The two older men seated themselves opposite me. Art could barely contain himself, his big forearms wrapped across his broad chest in an effort to suppress his anger.

Gil leaned forward towards me. 'Art tells me that you are responsible for a serious breach of confidence. Very serious.'

Oh Lisa, Lisa!

'Apparently someone has told the Boston Peptides management about BioOne's bid for the company. This has raised major difficulties with the negotiations, which were at a delicate stage.'

'You bet it has!' Art couldn't contain himself any longer. 'We've had to cave in to management's demands right away. We'll have to make a public announcement tomorrow morning. This is going to cost us money!'

'Art believes you were responsible for this leak. Is he correct?'

The eyes peered at me through those lenses. I wouldn't lie to Gil.

I nodded. 'I'm sorry.'

'Sorry!' screamed Art. 'I tell you not to do something, and you go right ahead and do it anyway! Sorry isn't good enough. Anyway, couldn't you have gotten your wife to keep her big mouth shut?'

'I did ask her to – ' I said.

'And she took no notice. If you can't trust your own wife, you shouldn't have spoken to her! Stupid bitch.'

'Hey!' I rose from my chair, the anger boiling up inside me.

'That's enough!' Gil put his hand on my arm. 'That's enough, Art. I know you're angry but let's keep the personal comments out of it. Take it easy, Simon.'

I glared at Art and sat down.

Gil turned to me. 'What you did today was a serious breach of trust. The firm has gone out of its way to back you up these last few days. We expect loyalty in return. *I* expect loyalty in return.'

'I know. I'm sorry, Gil. It's just it was the kind of secret I didn't want to keep from my wife.'

'That's not good enough, Simon, and you know it,' Gil said. 'Art suggested that we should try to keep the whole deal away from you until it's announced publicly. I told him no. We're a small firm, and we have to be able to trust each other. Frankly, I thought we could trust you. And it's not a question of us making you lie to your wife. We were just expecting you to behave ethically and professionally. That's not unreasonable is it?'

I sighed. 'No, it's not.'

'OK. At many firms this would be enough to get you fired. But we don't work that way here. Let this be a warning to you. I don't expect to see any signs of a breach of trust in your colleagues again.'

'OK, Gil. And I am sorry.'

I left his office seething. I marched straight back to my desk and picked up the phone, ignoring the stares of John and Daniel. I punched in a number.

'Lisa Cook.'

'You told Henry about the take-over, didn't you?'

There was a moment's silence. Then Lisa's voice, curt and crisp. 'Maybe.'

'What do you mean, "Maybe"? You either did or you didn't!'

'It was important to Boston Peptides. Henry told me he would treat the information carefully.'

'Well, he didn't, did he?' A small voice inside told me to calm down, get a hold of myself. But it was too late. It had been a stressful week for me too. 'Lisa, I can't believe you'd do that to me! I only told you about the take-over because I felt I had to. Because you're my wife, and I felt I could trust you. But I couldn't could I? The deal's blown wide open, Art's furious, and I just got a massive bollocking from Gil. It's lucky I wasn't fired.'

'Simon, I . . .' Lisa was clearly taken aback by my anger. I had never been that angry with her before.

'Yes?'

'I'm sorry, Simon.' Lisa's voice was cold now. 'I did what I had to do.'

'No, you didn't. What you should have done is keep quiet and wait for the news to get to Henry direct from BioOne. It's almost as though you place your loyalty to Boston Peptides above your loyalty to me.'

'And why shouldn't I, just for once? This is my career we're talking about. I started on this stuff long before I met you. Simon, I just don't think you understand that my job is as important to me as your job is to you.'

'Lisa – '

'Goodbye, Simon.'

And there was a click as the line went dead.

There was complete silence in the room as I stared at the receiver lifeless in my hand. Daniel and John were looking at me aghast.

'Don't tell me she forgot to fold your socks again,' said Daniel at last.

I smiled, deflated, and tried to go back to work.

That afternoon, Diane dropped by my desk. She was the only partner who managed to make her visits to the associates' office seem like informal chats, rather than missions to dispense orders or demand information. I hadn't spoken to her since her Cincinnati trip.

'How was Tetracom?' I asked.

'Fascinating,' she said. 'The product seems to do all they claimed. And the management team seems first class. I've got a good feeling about this one.'

'Excellent.'

'I'm going out there again next Monday. I'd really like you to come with me. I need some help, and . . . well, I'd like a second opinion.'

It was always flattering as an associate to be asked for an opinion rather than just spreadsheet time, and it looked as if Tetracom might go all the way to investment. Only a minority of the companies we looked at actually made it that far, and it was obviously smart for an associate to attach himself to a deal that eventually got done.

But, with Lisa in her current frame of mind, was it sensible to go on a trip with Diane?

Diane noticed my hesitation. 'It would be great if you could make it, but I'd understand if you have to be with Lisa.'

Be with Lisa? I didn't really have to be with Lisa. She could look after herself for one night. That bit about me thinking my work was more important than hers rankled. It simply wasn't true. She had betrayed my trust in her for the benefit of her career: I could go on a simple business trip for the benefit of mine.

'No, I'm sure she'll be fine,' I said. 'I'll be glad to come.'

Lisa arrived home at half past nine, by which time my anger at what she had done had subsided a little, and my concern about how she was behaving had grown. She looked terrible, lines of fatigue and misery ravaging her face.

'Lisa, I'd like to talk to you about the take-over.'

She dumped her bag on a chair. 'There really isn't any point, Simon.'

'But Lisa . . .'

'There's no point. Have you had dinner?'

'Not yet.'

Lisa ordered some Chinese to be delivered, and picked up her book. I turned on the TV. When the food came we ate in silence. I made a couple of half-hearted attempts to start a conversation, but with little success. I was still angry, so I soon gave up.

I had developed a headache myself. I rummaged around in the bathroom cabinet for Lisa's Tylenol. I had to remove a paper bag to get at it. Inside were two bottles of pills, unlabelled. I opened them, and poured out a couple of the tablets. They were un-marked. I forgot the Tylenol, and took the bottles into the living room.

'Lisa. What are these?'

She looked up. 'BP 56,' she said. She looked me in the eye, defying me to say anything.

'BP 56! But that hasn't been tested on humans yet.'

'It has now.'

'Lisa! Can't you wait for those volunteers to take it? It might be dangerous.'

'Of course it isn't dangerous, Simon. It's been thoroughly tested on animals. And how could I allow volunteers to take a drug I wasn't prepared to take myself?'

'Oh, Lisa.'

'Simon, if there are any problems with the drug, I need to know now so we can do something about them. We can't afford to wait until we've gone through all the paperwork with the FDA.'

'But is it allowed?'

'Technically, no,' said Lisa. 'And if you told anyone at work, I could get into big trouble. But this kind of thing has been done plenty of times. Jonas Salk injected his whole family with polio to prove his vaccine worked. I'm not doing anything as dangerous as that.'

'I don't think it's a good idea, Lisa. Why didn't you tell me?'

She sighed. 'Because I knew you wouldn't like it. But I have to do it, Simon.'

I put the pills back in the bathroom. It seemed to me foolhardy for Lisa to take this untried drug, especially in the state she was in, but I knew there was no chance of me persuading her.

The phone rang. I picked it up.

'Hello?'

'Can I speak to Lisa?'

I recognized Eddie's voice. No 'hello', no 'how are you?'

'Hold on.' I looked up. 'It's Eddie.'

'I'll take it in the bedroom,' Lisa said.

She emerged twenty minutes later.

'How is he?' I asked.

'I'd say he's quite upset,' Lisa replied icily.

'Did you discuss any more of his theories?'

'If Eddie wants to talk about Dad, I'll listen to him,' Lisa said, picking up her book again.

It angered me that Eddie and Lisa were talking about me as a murder suspect behind my back. But I bit my tongue. There was one thing I had to tell Lisa, though. I waited for a good moment, but once again there wasn't one. So I told her just as we were getting into bed.

'I'm going to Cincinnati with Diane next Monday. I'll be out one night.'

Lisa looked at me sharply. 'Next Monday?'

'Yes. We've been through this before. I have to go.'

'OK,' she said, climbing into bed.

'Come on, Lisa. I can't refuse to go.'

'You do what you have to do,' she said, rolling over.

'I will,' I muttered.

12

As Art had promised, BioOne made a public announcement the following morning about its intentions for Boston Peptides. Back at my desk, I called up the news service on my computer and looked at the press release there. The text was pretty bland, apart from one killer sentence.

'Daniel!' I called across to him.

'Yeah?'

'Have you seen the BioOne announcement?'

'Yes.'

'What's this about "substantial cost savings at Boston Peptides"?'

'BioOne thinks it can cut out some duplicated costs. It can move Boston Peptides into its building in Kendall Square. And other things.'

'Like firing people?'

Daniel shrugged. 'That's what happens in take-overs. You heard Enever.'

'But there was no need to announce it to the whole world, was there?'

'Why not?' Daniel smiled. 'Hey! The stock's up four to forty-nine.'

'Well, that's wonderful, then.' I put my head in my hands. Lisa was going to love this.

Sure enough, the announcement had caused uproar at Boston

121

Peptides, with rumours flying. But at least Lisa was willing to talk that evening.

'People are really upset,' she said. 'They're talking about resigning.'

'Is Enever really that bad?' I asked.

'Oh, yes. You know what they call him at BioOne?'

'What?'

'Enema.'

'Sounds attractive.' It was a good name. I remembered his pained, irritated demeanour.

'It turns out he didn't even discover neuroxil-5.'

'He must have the patent, surely?'

'Yes, he does. Or at least BioOne does. Most of the work was done at the institute he worked at in Australia. He was just one of a team. He took the idea with him to America and patented it here.'

'How did he get away with that?'

'Apparently, the Australians didn't know, or if they did, they didn't care. One of the other members of the team came to the US and tried to kick up a fuss. I don't think he got anywhere. Once a patent has been granted, it's very hard to prove prior art. Enema employs pretty fearsome patent lawyers. They argued that neuroxil-5 was slightly different from the drug the Australians had developed.'

'Sounds like a great guy.'

'Yeah. Also, there are rumours that some of BioOne's early research results were manipulated.'

'Jesus. Why the hell did we back him?'

Lisa sighed. 'He sounds convincing. The stock market loves him. I'm worried he'll muscle his way into running things at Boston Peptides, and hog all the credit for anything we produce.'

From what I had seen, that prospect looked quite likely. I hadn't yet told Lisa about Enever's little presentation. Somehow, it never seemed like quite the right time. 'I hope he leaves you alone,' I said.

Lisa gave me a withering look. 'I think that's highly unlikely.' She switched on the TV. 'Weren't you going out with Kieran tonight?'

'No, that's OK. He won't miss me. I'll stay here with you.'

'Don't worry about me,' said Lisa neutrally. 'You go, Simon.'

'I can stay – '

'Go.'

So I went.

The Red Hat was a frequent haunt of ours when Kieran and I were at business school. It was a dark basement bar only a few minutes' walk from our apartment.

Kieran was already there, with half a dozen others from our business school days who had found jobs around Boston. Daniel wasn't present. He had tended to avoid the group occasions at business school, and certainly avoided them now. Pitchers of beer were bought and drunk. There was some tedious talk at first of 'B-school', 'I-banks', 'VCs' and pay cheques, but then the conversation regressed a couple of years to women, drink and sport. I forgot Frank's death, Sergeant Mahoney and Lisa's problems, and my brain went pleasantly fuzzy.

I left early and arrived home at about half past ten, ready to tumble into bed. I didn't make it.

Lisa was sitting on the sofa. She was wearing her running clothes. She was crying.

'Lisa!' I moved over to sit by her on the sofa.

'Get away from me!' she cried.

I stopped in mid stride. 'OK,' I said. 'What's wrong?'

She opened her mouth to say something, then her bottom lip shook, and she bit it. Tears rolled down her face. I moved towards her again.

'I said, get away from me!'

I held up my hands in a calming gesture. 'OK, OK,' I said, and backed off to sit in the armchair.

I waited.

Lisa sobbed, and sniffed, and took a deep breath. 'I found it, Simon.'

'Found what?'

'What do you think?'

'I don't know. Tell me.'

'The gun. The gun that shot Dad.'

'What! Where?'

Lisa glared at me. 'Where do you think? Right there!' She pointed at the large closet embedded in one wall of the living room. 'I was looking for an old photo album I had as a kid, with pictures of Dad. I found it OK. But underneath was a revolver. A Smith and Wesson model six forty, three fifty-seven Magnum. I looked it up on the Smith and Wesson web site.' She pointed to our computer in the corner of the room. The screen was filled with an image of a short, stubby revolver. 'The police said that was the type of gun that killed Dad. And two bullets were missing. It's the gun all right.'

'You found it here?' I said. 'In the closet?'

'That's right. And I want to know how it got there.'

I thought quickly. I had no idea how it could have got there. 'Someone must have planted it.'

'Yeah, right. Like who?'

'I don't know. Hold on. Didn't the police search the closet last week? They didn't find anything then.'

'No. But it was definitely there this evening.'

'Let me see it,' I said.

'I threw it away. I didn't want it in the apartment. The cops might come back at any moment.'

'Where? Where did you throw it?'

'I went for a run and threw it in the river.'

'Oh, Jesus. Did anyone see you?'

'I don't know. It was in a plastic bag.' She looked up at me. 'Don't worry. I'm not going to tell the police.'

I put my head in my hands. Disconnected thoughts tumbled around my brain.

'You shouldn't have done that, Lisa.'

'Done what?'

'Thrown the gun away.'

'Why? Did you want to hang it on the wall?'

'I could have given it to the police.'

'That would have been dumb, wouldn't it? Give the police the evidence they need to arrest you?'

'But don't you see? It might have helped clear my name. If I gave it to them voluntarily, they would hardly suspect me, would they?'

'It's easy for you to say that now.' She shook her head, and more tears came. 'It was horrible to see it. The thing that killed Dad. I couldn't stand having it here in the apartment. I had to get rid of it right away. And I thought I was doing you a favour!'

This was ridiculous. 'Lisa, it's not my gun. I didn't put it there. I didn't kill your father.'

'It was there, right in front of my eyes, Simon. I can't ignore it.'

I rushed over to her, and put my hands on her shoulders. She tried to wriggle free.

'Lisa. Lisa! Look at me.'

Reluctantly, she did.

'How can you believe I murdered him? You know me. How can you think I'd do something like that?'

Lisa held my eyes, and then looked away. 'I can't bear to think about it.'

'It wasn't mine, Lisa. You must believe that.'

'I don't know what to believe.' Her hands reached my chest and pushed me away. 'Let go of me!'

I released her shoulders and stood back. Frustration at my inability to convince her boiled up inside me. 'Lisa. It wasn't me. I didn't kill your father. I've never even seen the bloody gun. I didn't kill your father!' I shouted.

She sat still, letting the echo of my denial reverberate though the small room. Then she looked up at me. 'I'm going to bed,' she said, and pushed past me to the bedroom.

She said nothing to me the next morning, as we both got ready for work. I tried to initiate some kind of communication, but with no success. Her face was set in stony misery, the corners of her mouth turned down, her brow furrowed. In the bathroom, while she was brushing her teeth and looking in the mirror, she burst into tears. I went to comfort her, I wanted to comfort her so badly, but as I touched her, her whole body tensed up, rigid, and she held her breath in tight, until I removed my hand.

A couple of minutes later, she left the apartment to walk to the Charles Street 'T' for the short subway journey to Boston Peptides' lab in Cambridge, and I set off in the other direction.

It was a long, cruel day at work. I couldn't focus on anything properly. I couldn't even focus on what the gun was doing in our apartment. All I could think about was Lisa. What would she do? How would she react? Would she believe me? How could I make her believe me? How could I calm her down, bring back the old Lisa?

Daniel and John must have realized something was wrong, but they left me alone. I was grateful.

Lisa didn't get home till eight. I waited for her with apprehension, fiddling about with a salad we would have for supper.

When I heard the front door of the apartment slam, I walked out to meet her, and gave her a quick kiss on the lips which she reluctantly returned.

'Hi,' I said.

'Hi.'

'Good day?'

Stupid question. 'Simon. BioOne is going to take the place apart. No it wasn't a good day.'

'Sorry. I made a salad.'

'Great,' Lisa said with little enthusiasm, and picked up her mail.

I went back into the kitchen, poured a couple of glasses of wine, and handed Lisa one. She grunted her thanks, and read a piece of junk mail from a credit card company with great interest.

'Supper's ready,' I said a few minutes later.

'Oh, I won't be a minute. I just want to call Eddie.'

She disappeared into the bedroom and shut the door. She was half an hour. I reread the newspaper and tried not to get angry, but failed.

Eventually she came out. She'd been crying. Her eyes were red, but she'd wiped away the tears. Her face was pinched, the corners of her mouth in what was becoming their habitual turned-down

126

position. I moved over to her to hold her. She didn't push me away, but she remained tense.

As we sat down, I felt a turmoil of opposing emotions. One was a powerful desire to pull Lisa towards me, to comfort her, to try to heal the terrible hurt she was feeling. The other was anger that she wouldn't let me do that, that she wouldn't trust me, that she was suspicious of me.

We sat in silence munching the salad. A tear ran down her cheek. At first she tried to ignore it, and then she sniffed and wiped it away.

'Oh, Lisa,' I said, moving my hand across to her. As I touched her sleeve she shook it off, and picked up her fork to stab a chunk of avocado. 'Talk to me.'

'What about?'

'About Frank. About me. About you and me.'

She put down her fork, and sniffed. 'What about you and me?'

'I need to know whether you think I killed your father.'

She put down her fork, and took a deep breath. 'I don't know,' she said.

Despite my resolution to control it, the anger flashed inside me. 'What do you mean, you don't know? You have to know! You have to believe me.'

Her eyes flashed at me. 'Yes, I guess I do have to believe you, don't I? If I'm going to live here under the same roof with you, I've got to believe you.'

'Well? Do you?'

Lisa shrugged, and looked down at her salad. 'I guess so,' she said.

'That's not good enough!' As soon as I'd said this I regretted it.

Lisa threw down her fork. 'I'm sorry that's not good enough for you, but it's the best I can do. The truth is, Simon, I just don't know. I've been thinking about it all day, and I'm totally confused. The police think you killed Dad, Eddie thinks you killed Dad, and I'm left wondering whether I'm just the stupid little wife, living with a murderer, sleeping next to a murderer. But you're right, how can I believe you'd do something like that? How can I even think something like that?'

'You have to trust me, Lisa – '

'Simon, I'd love to trust you. But don't you see, I can't.' She paused, taking in deep breaths, trying, and failing, to hold back the tears. 'Today I decided I'd just try to live with you, and ignore all my doubts, but I'm not sure I can do it.'

'You can, Lisa. You can.'

She sat in silence for a moment, the tears flowing freely. Then she shook her head. 'No. It won't work. I'm confused, I'm tired, I've never felt so miserable. Everything is just . . . falling apart. I don't have the strength to stay here when I don't know whether . . . whether . . .' She couldn't finish the sentence.

'But you need me to look after you.'

'Do I?'

'Yes, you do.'

She flashed an angry glance across the table, and then attacked her salad. She was so tense she was shaking. The plate clattered with each blow at the salad from her fork. She seemed to be making a superhuman effort to contain the turmoil within her.

I was losing her. I knew I was losing her.

'Lisa . . .'

She ignored me. Then after a few more seconds, she threw down her fork, pushed her plate away, and rushed from the room, head down, avoiding my eye.

I followed her. She went straight for the bedroom, slamming the door behind her.

I opened it. She was pulling a case down from the closet on to the floor.

'Lisa! What are you doing?'

'What does it look like I'm doing?'

'You can't leave!'

'Why not? I can't stay.' She stuffed clothes, shoes, washing things into the bag.

'Lisa. I'm sorry about what I said earlier. Don't go. Please stay here. We can work through this.'

I walked over to the case, and tried to pick it up.

'Leave that alone!' she screamed, and pulled at it. For an absurd moment, I held on, pulling it back towards me.

'Let go, Simon!'

I couldn't physically stop her if she wanted to go. So I loosened my grip.

'Thank you.' She snatched the bag. 'Now, let me finish packing my bag, and I'll be out of your hair.'

'Where are you going?'

'To stay with Kelly.' Kelly was a friend of hers from work. She zipped the bag shut. 'I'll get the rest later.'

'Lisa . . .'

She strode towards the door, carrying the bulging bag.

'Goodbye, Simon.'

13

I hardly slept at all that night. I needed to get out of the apartment, so I went in to work at Revere as soon as was decently possible, and stared at Tetracom papers without really taking in their contents. I more or less ignored Daniel and John. I waited for a quarter past nine, by which time Lisa would be sure to have arrived at the lab. Daniel was out of the room and John was on the phone.

'I'm just nipping out,' I called over to John. 'I'll be back in quarter of an hour.'

John waved as he continued talking.

I put on my jacket, took the lift down to the ground floor, and strolled out on to Federal Street. It was quiet, although the sounds of the 'Big Dig', Boston's heroic attempt to bury the highway that bisected the city, seeped round the giant buildings. I flipped open my cell phone, dialled Boston Peptides' switchboard, and was soon put through.

'Lisa Cook's phone.'

It wasn't her voice.

'Can I speak to her, please?'

'I'll see if she's available. Who's speaking?'

'Simon.'

Normally the response would have been: 'Yeah, sure, here she is.' I wasn't at all surprised when the voice told me Lisa was unavailable.

I waited five minutes, hands in pockets, shifting from foot to foot with impatience. Then I tried again.

'Lisa Cook's telephone.'

A different voice. Good. I put on my attempt at an American accent. 'Oh, hi, can I speak with Lisa please? It's her brother, Eddie.'

'One moment.'

There was a pause, and then Lisa's voice came on the line. 'Eddie! You're up early.'

'It's not Eddie,' I said. 'It's me.'

'Listen, Simon, don't you ever try to pretend – '

'No, Lisa. Listen to me. We were both upset last night when you walked out. We need to talk it through again when we're both calmer.'

There was a moment's silence. I prayed that she wouldn't hang up. Then I heard her sigh. 'Let me transfer you to a different phone.' A click and more silence, until I heard her voice again. 'OK, I can talk now.'

'I think we should meet somewhere so we can talk properly.'

'There's no need, Simon. I've been thinking about it all night. I've made up my mind.'

'But you can't leave me, Lisa.'

'No, Simon. I can't stay with you. Not when I think you might have killed my father.'

'You said "might". You're not sure then, are you?'

There was a pause at the other end. 'Look, I'm confused, OK? I feel lousy. Really bad. I just want to be away from you for a while.'

'I understand that's how you feel. But I don't understand why. Just think about it from my point of view for a second. I have a right to know why you're doing this. Why don't we meet for a cup of coffee, and you can explain it?'

'I'm not sure I can explain it.'

'You can try. I deserve at least that.'

There was silence on the phone. 'OK. I guess you're right. Can you get here now?'

'Yes,' I said immediately. 'I'll be there right away.'

I took a cab.

Despite its name, Boston Peptides was housed in a scruffy looking one-storey building in Cambridge, in the wasteland between MIT and Harvard. On one side was a small engineering company making castings, and on the other was an open patch of land that was temporarily being used as a soccer pitch. Backhoes churned up the plot in front.

Lisa was waiting on the steps. The tired look of misery I had grown accustomed to in the last few days was set firmly on her face.

'Let's walk,' she said, and we made our way towards the soccer pitch. Two teams of kids were playing, one in green and one in red. They weren't bad for eight-year-olds. One day, I thought, the United States is going to field a decent team in the World Cup.

We sat on a wall and watched them for a few moments, both of us nervous of starting a conversation that could, and probably would, end in disaster. The backhoes ground and clanked behind us.

'Well?' said Lisa.

'Why did you leave last night?'

She said nothing for a few moments. 'I need to get away for a bit. Sort myself out.'

'I see.' I forced myself to speak slowly and calmly. 'But why do you have to leave me to do that? Surely you'd be better staying with me? Then I can help you with your problems.'

'Simon, I think you might be the problem.'

'No, Lisa. It's not me. Your father died. You're worried about work. You're tired. You need me to help you.'

Lisa glanced up at me, and then back to the soccer players.

I waited for her to say something. She didn't.

'You shouldn't listen to Eddie. He hates me. He hates himself.'

'Maybe Eddie can see things more clearly than I can.'

I lost the calm I had been trying so hard to maintain. 'Lisa. You know me. I'm your husband. I love you. You know I'm not capable of killing your father.'

Lisa turned to me, her eyes moist. 'Then what was the gun doing there?'

'I don't know,' I said in exasperation.

Lisa looked ahead.

'Be rational about it, Lisa. I know you've been under a lot of pressure recently, but you must get a sense of perspective.'

'Oh, I am being rational,' she said through gritted teeth. 'Very rational. You're right, it's difficult with all that's been going on. But let's look at the evidence here, Simon.' She was talking fast now.

'One, you were the last person to see Dad alive. You were with him at about the time he died. Two, you and he have been getting along badly recently. You had a fight. Three, he was shot. You know how to use a gun. And four,' she looked at me defiantly, 'I found that gun hidden in our apartment.'

'That doesn't mean anything. Why would I kill him anyway?'

'I don't know. You need fifty thousand pounds to fight your sister's lawsuit. We'll have that now.'

'Oh, come on.'

'All right. Maybe you *are* having an affair with Diane. Maybe Dad found out. Maybe you wanted to keep him quiet. Maybe you wanted to keep him quiet *and* get your hands on his money.'

'That's absurd. I'm not having an affair with anybody. Can't you trust me?'

'I don't know,' she muttered.

'Anyway, why would I be so stupid as to leave a gun lying around the apartment where the police could find it?'

'I've been thinking about that, too,' said Lisa. 'It wasn't there when the police searched the apartment last week. Perhaps you were just keeping it overnight until you found a better place to hide it.'

'Don't be ridiculous. Someone must have planted it.'

'Like who? The police? The gun was in a *Boots* plastic bag. Do you think Sergeant Mahoney goes all the way to England to pick up his deodorant?'

I managed to get myself in control again. 'None of that proves anything.'

'It's a hypothesis. And a plausible one,' said Lisa. 'And I will go with it, until you can disprove it.'

'This isn't some scientific experiment, Lisa. It's me you're talking about. Us!'

'I know,' she said. 'But you said I should be rational. I'm trying to be rational about it. With all that's been going on in my head, the blackness I feel about everything, the way I just want to scream and scream and scream, it's all I can do. Be rational. So, let's test the hypothesis. Can you prove you didn't kill Dad?'

'No. But my point is, I shouldn't have to to you. You who know me better than anyone.'

Lisa looked at me, her eyes filling with tears. 'But I'm not sure I do know you, Simon – know who you really are.'

'But we're married, for God's sake!'

'Yes. But I've only known you, what, two years? I don't know anything about who you are, really, where you come from. I've only been once with you to your own country, and that was a disaster. I do know you come from a screwed-up family, but that's no comfort. I know you're clever, I know you can hold a lot inside without talking about it, but perhaps I don't know what really is there inside you.'

'That's ridiculous!'

'No, it's not,' Lisa said quietly. 'Of course the Simon I fell in love with wouldn't have an affair with another woman, or kill anyone. But did that Simon ever really exist?' She wiped her eyes, and then her nose with her sleeve.

I wanted to put my arm round her, but there was no point. I wanted to argue with her, but there seemed little point in that, either. How could I argue that I was just who I seemed to be?

'Come back,' I said simply. 'Please.'

Lisa took a deep breath, and shook her head. 'No, Simon.' She stood up. 'I've got to get back to work.'

And she left me standing there beside the makeshift soccer pitch, watching her slight hunched figure disappear into the Boston Peptides building.

I walked the couple of miles back to the office, through Cambridge, over the Salt and Pepper Bridge, and through the Common. It was a grey cold morning and the wind whipped off the water and threaded its way through the city buildings.

I played over our conversation again and again and again. Although I hadn't been able to understand the pressure Lisa had been under recently, the grief, the misery, the exhaustion, I had seen it in her face, heard it in her words, felt it with her. But to her, I had become part of that black world that seemed to surround and threaten her.

The bells of the Park Street Church chimed twelve o'clock as I plunged through the busy shopping streets of Downtown Crossing towards the office.

I didn't notice the people jostling around me. My anger ebbed, leaving a huge empty feeling of loneliness, of failure. My limbs felt heavy, my face taut. I still couldn't quite believe that Lisa had just walked away from me. But she had. I couldn't bear the thought of her believing that I had killed her father. Her love was the most precious thing in the world to me. The idea of it turning to hatred for me, hurt. It hurt a lot.

Somehow I had screwed up. Even my father had managed to keep hold of my mother for more than six months!

She had wanted to 'test her hypothesis'. Well, I would test her hypothesis for her. I'd prove to her that I was innocent.

Perhaps I should go to Mahoney? It was, after all, his job to find Frank's true killer. No, that was a very bad idea. I was clearly his favourite suspect at the moment, and it would be difficult to persuade him to look elsewhere. And I definitely shouldn't tell him, or anyone else for that matter, about the gun. If Lisa hadn't lost her head and ditched it, then I could have considered taking it to the police in the hope that if my honesty didn't clear my name, forensic tests might. But Lisa's actions just served to implicate me more. No, I couldn't rely on Mahoney to find out who killed Frank.

I would have to do it myself.

'You said you'd only be a quarter of an hour,' John said, as I walked in the door.

'Sorry,' I gave him a quick smile.

'Your voice-mail has been working overtime.'

'Thanks.'

But I ignored the winking light on my phone, and asked myself the vital question.

If I hadn't killed Frank, who had?

Could it have been a burglar as I had suggested to Lisa? Perhaps Frank had surprised him, and been shot? It was a tempting idea. But as I thought it through, I realized it was unlikely. The police hadn't mentioned any signs of a break-in, nor had I seen any. Frank had been shot in the back some way inside the house. It seemed most likely that he had known whoever had shot him, or at least that he had voluntarily let his murderer into the house.

I realized that I didn't know much about Frank's life away from Lisa and Revere. Presumably he had other friends, but I knew nothing about them. Lisa said there hadn't been any girlfriends since he and her mother had got divorced. She liked to believe that that was because her mother was the only woman Frank had truly loved, although he seemed to me to speak about his former wife with nothing more than indifference. Much of his time was spent at Marsh House. What else he did with it, I just didn't know.

I thought about the gun. It must have been planted. But how? I had checked the apartment for signs of a break-in. I wasn't an expert, but there was nothing I could see. The chipped paintwork round the living-room window seemed to my eye to have natural causes. And no one had been in the apartment since the police had searched it apart from Lisa and me.

In theory the police could have planted it. But would the American police really plant evidence on a suspect? Why? I didn't think Mahoney much liked me, but that wasn't much of a reason. Perhaps he wanted to improve his clear-up record? Perhaps a foreign national was an easy target? Anyway, if he had planted the gun, wouldn't he have 'discovered' it in his search of the apartment?

I now realized the *Boots* bag didn't mean anything. It was undoubtedly mine, in fact I thought it might have held some old school and university photographs, but whoever had been in the closet could have spotted the bag and taken the opportunity to stuff the gun inside it.

Ann and Eddie were on their way to San Francisco when the police had searched the apartment and found nothing. Not that I thought Ann could have killed her ex-husband. She seemed to me to have recovered from their separation quite successfully, and was now happily remarried. At the funeral, she spoke of Frank with a certain fondness rather than with passion.

But Eddie. Eddie was much more likely. He had never forgiven his father for leaving the rest of the family, and had barely spoken to him for years. Despite his professed indifference to money, the prospect of Frank's legacy seemed very important to him, as he had shown so clearly that morning at the lawyer's offices. And he was very eager to blame me for the crime. Eddie was definitely worth considering.

The other two 'family suspects' were Lisa and me. Lisa I just couldn't believe. Which left me.

There were rivalries at Revere. Frank and Art didn't much like each other, vying for position as Gil's right-hand man. The only other conflict that I was aware of at work was once again with me. But Revere was generally a civilized, pleasant place to work. It wasn't the kind of place where people stabbed each other in the back. Or shot each other for that matter.

With a sigh, I drew the same conclusion as Mahoney. I was the most obvious suspect.

I needed to find out more.

The first place to look was Frank's office. I walked down the corridor towards it. The door was locked. Hm.

I sauntered further along the corridor.

'Connie, I'd like to get into Frank's office. I need to see if he has some papers on Net Cop. Do you know who has the key?'

Connie occupied a large desk just outside Gil's office. She was a well-groomed woman in her forties who had been Gil's assistant since before he had set up Revere. She seemed to like me, which was at times very useful.

137

'I think Gil has it, Simon. Go right in, there's no one with him at the moment.'

I went in. Gil was on the phone. I sat and waited. After five minutes or so he finished.

'What can I do for you, Simon?' Gil smiled at me, his thoughts obviously still on the telephone call.

'I need the key for Frank's office. There are some files on Net Cop in there I need.'

For a moment, Gil looked at me half-suspiciously. Then, as if remembering his decision to trust me, he reached into his desk for a key.

'Here you are. Please return it as soon as you're done with it.'

I took it and unlocked Frank's office. It looked much the same as it had the last time I was there. My eyes were immediately drawn to a photograph of a seventeen-year-old Lisa, looking slightly gawky, but already with the smile that I loved so much. There was a smaller photo of Eddie graduating. Nothing of Lisa's mother. The office was reasonably tidy, but there were papers in his in-box, and on top of the wooden filing cabinets. Yellow Post-Its reminded him of things he would never now do. The office looked as if it were expecting him back at any minute.

I had worked with him closely enough to know my way round his filing system. The first thing I did was to look for his Net Cop file and pull it out. The only papers in it were ones prepared by me. I ignored the bulging files on his other deals and concentrated on his more personal stuff.

He didn't have any secrets. No locked drawers. No coded files. A very full diary, but none of the appointments seemed out of the ordinary. There was an interesting file labelled 'Recruitment'. In it was a sheaf of résumés, mine included. Curious though I was, I just skimmed it. And then there was a file labelled 'Fund IV'.

I flipped through analyses of Revere's existing funds' performance, completely dominated by BioOne of course. This was no doubt supposed to impress investors into taking part in the new fund. Then I came across a single sheet of paper.

It was a letter from Gil to Lynette Mauer, dated September 9. The second paragraph grabbed my attention:

As you know, I am planning to reduce my involvement with the day-to-day management of Revere Partners and its investments. While I will continue to provide advice related to investments made by our first three funds, I will take no role in the new fund which Revere intends to raise next year. You know the strong team of partners that I have been fortunate enough to assemble over the last few years, and I am confident that the performance of our fourth fund will be as strong or stronger as those preceding it.

I look forward to seeing you at our Monday morning meeting on October 19, when we can perhaps discuss this further.

The letter was signed Gilbert S. Appleby III.

So Gil was going to retire! With the twenty or thirty million that was his share of the BioOne loot, no doubt. Very interesting. And now that Frank was out of the way, his successor was obvious. Art Altschule.

No wonder Lynette Mauer was worried. She didn't trust Art. She saw BioOne for what it was, a fluke.

Art Altschule running Revere! I shuddered.

I stuffed the letter back in the file and continued my search. I had just turned on Frank's computer and was beginning to figure out how I might be able to get into his files when his office door opened. I looked up guiltily, half-expecting it to be Frank himself. It wasn't. It was Gil.

'What are you doing, Simon?' he asked, his forehead wrinkled. 'You've been in here a long time.'

'I'm looking for a memo Frank wrote when we originally invested in Net Cop,' I said, guiltily. 'I was just checking to see if I could get it off his computer.'

The small brown eyes bored into me through those thick lenses. He said nothing. I sat still, trying to keep a keen-associate look on my face. Inside I squirmed. I'm sure he saw the inside.

'I don't think you should be rooting around in Frank's computer. You've been in here long enough. If you haven't found it yet, you're not going to find it.' He nodded at the Net Cop file lying on Frank's desk. 'Why don't you take what you've got and go?'

I switched off Frank's machine, grabbed the file, and left, feeling very small. I should be much more careful in future. Gil had promised me his trust. It might be very useful in the coming weeks. I would be foolish to throw it away.

14

I made my way slowly home that evening, delaying my return to the empty apartment. On an impulse I stopped at the absurdly up-market 7-Eleven on Charles Street with its cream-coloured porticos, and bought bacon, sausage, eggs, the works. Within minutes, the sounds and smells of a gigantic fry-up filled the apartment.

The bell rang. I swore and answered the door. It was Sergeant Mahoney, accompanied by his trooper/detective sidekick. I let them in.

Mahoney sniffed the air. 'Smells good.'

He waited as if he expected me to offer him some. No way. That bacon was all mine.

'Hang on a minute. Sit down, while I sort out the stove.'

I rushed into the kitchen, and turned the cooker off. Supper would wait. When I returned to the living room, Mahoney was looking at Lisa's desk. His colleague stood in the middle of the room, shuffling from foot to foot. He was nervous, probably more of Mahoney than of me.

'I thought you'd already searched the place,' I said. 'Worried you missed something?'

Mahoney looked up. 'Oh, we don't miss anything,' he said. 'Nice uniform. A captain, eh?'

Mahoney was holding a picture of me in my Life Guards uniform, complete with red tunic and breastplate. It was Lisa's really. She had appropriated it because she said I looked dashing. I wasn't sure how I looked to Mahoney.

'Thank you,' I said. 'What can I do for you?'

'We'd like to ask you some more questions about Frank Cook's murder,' he said, sitting on the sofa. His sidekick perched next to him, notebook ready.

'I don't have to answer them, do I?'

'No, you don't. And you can end the interview whenever you like,' said Mahoney.

I thought about refusing to talk, or about insisting that I call the lawyer Gil had told me about, Gardner Phillips. But I decided to let him continue. Partly I still hoped that I would genuinely help him establish my innocence, and partly I wanted to find out certain things from him.

'OK. Go ahead.'

'Where's your wife, Captain Ayot?'

I didn't want to answer the question, but there was little point in avoiding it. It was obvious Mahoney knew the answer already. 'She left me. She's gone to stay with a friend.'

'Is this a permanent separation?' he asked, raising an eyebrow.

'Oh, no,' I said.

'You're expecting her back soon, then?'

'Yes,' I said, trying to sound confident, but failing.

'Why did she leave?'

'She's upset by her father's death. She says she needs some time alone. Or at least without me.'

'That's tough on you, isn't it?' Mahoney's voice was softer, almost kind. I didn't trust it.

'Yes,' I replied simply.

'But it's not what your wife says. She says that she's working on a big project with Kelly Williams, and it makes sense to stay with her for a while.'

I sighed. 'She's just trying to keep up appearances, I suppose. It'll blow over. She'll be back here soon.' I tried to make my voice sound confident.

Mahoney smiled. 'OK. I didn't believe her explanation, anyway. But then, I don't believe yours either.'

My pulse quickened. I kept my voice calm. 'No?'

'No, I don't.' He left the words hanging there for a while. 'Do you know anything about a gun?' he asked.

Too late I realized my own eyes had flicked towards the closet. 'What kind of gun?' I replied.

'A Smith and Wesson three fifty-seven Magnum.'

'No.'

'It was the gun that fired the bullets that killed your father-in-law.'

'You told me,' I said.

'Does your wife know anything about this gun?'

'No, why should she?'

'Why should she?' Mahoney leaned forward. 'You see, you and your wife had an argument last night. You raised your voice. You said,' here he examined his notebook, ' "I've never even seen the bloody gun. I didn't kill your father." Did you say those words, Mr Ayot?'

I closed my eyes. A neighbour must have heard me. This was a question I didn't want to answer. 'I think I'd like to talk to a lawyer.'

Mahoney glanced at the other detective. 'OK. I can understand that. Have him give me a call in the morning. In the meantime we have a warrant to search your apartment and your car.'

'What, again?'

'That's right.'

Mahoney handed me the warrant, and then he and his colleague efficiently took the apartment apart. It didn't take them long. It was a small apartment and they knew what they were looking for. I then led them the couple of blocks to the Brimmer Street Garage where my Morgan was stowed. There weren't many places you could hide a gun in that, and it only took them a few minutes to check them all. I was glad, after all, that Lisa had ditched the weapon.

'We'll be hearing from you or your lawyer tomorrow,' Mahoney said as we stood on the street just outside my apartment. It was dark, but we were standing in the pool of yellow light thrown off by the gas lamp. The shadows of trees, lampposts and railings criss-crossed the street.

I nodded. 'Before you go, I have a question for you.'

'Yes?'

'Yes. Who else are you investigating?'

'Oh, we're keeping an open mind.'

'Have you spoken to Frank's colleagues at work? To Lisa's brother?'

'We've spoken to a lot of people. This is a murder investigation.'

'Well? Have you found anything out?'

'I'm sorry, but our conclusions are our own business, Mr Ayot.'

I touched his sleeve. 'Look. Sergeant Mahoney. I didn't kill Frank. I want to help you find out who did. If you give me some information, perhaps I can help.'

Mahoney turned his bulky frame towards me. 'I am very confident we will find Frank Cook's murderer. And we won't need any help from you to do it.'

With that, he and his colleague walked a short way down the street, climbed into a car and drove off.

As I unlocked the front door of my building, I turned and saw two more men waiting in a parked car a little way down the street. Policemen. I couldn't run, even if I'd wanted to.

As soon as I was in the apartment, I telephoned Gardner Phillips's office. Fortunately he was still there, even though it was after eight o'clock.

I told him who I was, and more especially, who had recommended me, and he suggested meeting me at eight o'clock in his office the next morning.

Then I looked up Kelly Williams's number in the book and dialled it. She answered the phone with a cheery 'hello'.

'Kelly, it's Simon. Can I speak to Lisa?'

'Oh, hi Simon,' she said breezily, as though this was just a normal social call. 'I'll just see if she's around.'

There was a clack as the receiver was put down on a hard surface, and a long wait. Finally Kelly was back on the line.

'She's just stepped out, Simon. I'm not sure when she'll be back.'

'No, she hasn't. She's there and she doesn't want to talk to me.'

'Yeah, well. You're right. But that's what you expected, isn't it?' Kelly's reply was friendly but firm.

'Kelly, just put her on the line for a moment. It's important.'

'Sorry, Simon. I'm not going to spend all night running back and forth between the two of you. You want to talk to her, she doesn't want to talk to you, I don't have any say in the matter.'

'OK, OK. But can you at least give her a message from me?'

'Sure. What is it?'

I thought for a moment. There was so much I wanted to say to her. I was angry at her for leaving me, for suspecting me of killing Frank, for not believing me. But I wasn't calling her to tell her how angry I was. I was calling to get her back.

I thought of telling her about Mahoney, but then I suddenly realized the phone might be tapped.

'Simon?'

'Sorry, Kelly. Can you just tell her thank you for standing by me.'

'OK. I'll tell her.'

'Oh, and Kelly?'

'Yes?'

'Look after her, won't you?'

'Don't worry, I will,' said Kelly, and rang off.

I hoped Lisa would understand my message. It was clear she hadn't told Mahoney about the gun when she had spoken to him. I wanted her to know that I appreciated that. That there was still a lot between us. That I wanted her back.

I was glad she was with Kelly. She would be looked after. And I liked the way Kelly seemed to be impartial in all this, or at least she didn't seem to hate me.

My supper was cold and congealing in the kitchen. Cold bacon is bearable. Cold eggs aren't. I threw the lot away, and drank a beer instead.

What would happen next? Mahoney seemed only a step away

from arresting me. This was all going to get very serious. I could feel myself about to be sucked into the US justice system, and it scared me. I felt alone, and very foreign. I thought about what I knew about the American legal system, all taken from TV, of course. A murder trial was a long, gruelling process, I knew. And all those involved – police, lawyers, judges, juries, and above all, the press – would see me as an arrogant foreigner who had come to their country to murder one of their own.

Whatever the final verdict, the next year would be hell.

Gardner Phillips's office was in a modern building close to the Court House. It was only a small detour for me on my way to work.

Phillips himself was a decade or so younger than Gil, with a neatly trimmed beard and an air of confidence that I found very comforting. He listened carefully to my story, taking notes. I told him everything, including how Lisa had discovered the gun in the closet, and how she had disposed of it. He asked some pointed questions of detail, but never came right out and asked me whether I had shot Frank and hidden the gun in the closet myself. Somehow this disconcerted me.

When I had finished, he took a moment to scan the scribbles in front of him, before telling me his conclusion.

'There's no doubt they're trying to build a case against you. But they have a ways to go yet. They need to find the weapon, or a witness, or something else to tie you in.'

'I can't believe no one saw me at the beach. Someone must at least have seen my car.'

'We can do our own checks if necessary. But Mr Cook could have been killed any time before ten p.m. Just because he didn't answer the phone doesn't mean he was dead. He could have gone for a walk, gone to the store, been in the tub, anything. Mahoney was just trying to scare you.'

'He succeeded,' I muttered.

'The important thing is from now on not to talk to them unless I'm present, and even then say nothing.'

'Even if I can straighten them out on something?'

'Say nothing. I'll straighten them out if they need straightening out. I'll talk to Sergeant Mahoney this morning and tell him you won't answer any more questions. Don't worry, he won't be surprised. And let's just hope they don't make any more progress.'

I left Phillips's office, and walked the rest of the way to Revere very worried indeed.

It was a difficult weekend. I spent most of it in the apartment. I tidied up first, stuffing Lisa's small piles of possessions that were dotted around the apartment into her closets. I took the wilting irises out of the tall vase on her desk, and threw them in the bin. But then, when the place finally looked as tidy as I would have liked it, I missed her mess. It was so much part of her, part of our life together. So, I took a couple of her things out again, a coat, a book she'd just finished, some back-copies of *Atlantic Monthly*. I refilled the vase with water, and stuffed the drooping irises back in. Then I stopped myself. This was ridiculous.

It wasn't just that I missed her so badly. I was also worried about her. I couldn't help believing that the pressure of the last couple of weeks had been too much for her. She needed help, and I desperately wanted to give it, instead of being shut out like this.

I tried to call her, of course. But Kelly was an efficient guardian, and I got nowhere. Eventually they stopped picking up the phone. I considered staking out Kelly's apartment in Cambridge in the hope of physically forcing Lisa to talk to me, but I restrained myself. It might just make things worse. There would come a moment when I might do that: perhaps later when she had had a chance to rethink leaving me. Or when I had found out something more about Frank's death.

I felt I was making small progress there. I had been totally unaware of Gil's retirement, and the succession issue at Revere was much more important than I had realized. But I still had a lot more to find out. Once again, I wished I knew what the police had discovered.

My sister phoned. She commiserated with me about Frank, and about Lisa. I didn't tell her about Sergeant Mahoney. She didn't even ask me about the money for the appeal; but I still felt bad about not being able to come up with it. The way things were going, I wasn't inclined to count on Frank's legacy.

Not a great weekend.

15

After a businesslike Monday morning meeting, in which Art told us that BioOne was already into Boston Peptides, 'taking names and kicking ass', Diane and I headed off to the airport.

Tetracom was actually located in a suburb a few miles to the south of Cincinnati, over the Ohio River in Northern Kentucky. The company had bought and refurbished some old red-brick industrial buildings. From the outside the premises looked nothing like the gleaming high-tech ventures I was used to on Boston's Route 128.

Diane introduced me to the management team, and we were ushered into a shabby office. Diane had been given the tour the week before. The purpose of this session was just to nail down answers to some questions.

Diane asked detailed, difficult questions. She focused on the competition in a much more thorough way than Frank and I had done with Net Cop. The management coped well. The CEO, Bob Hecht, seemed to know both his product and his market inside out. He lacked some of Craig's energy, he was more of a 'corporate man', but he gave an air of supreme competence.

We had dinner with Hecht and his colleagues back at the Cincinnatian Hotel where we were staying. It was a credo of venture capital that you should get to know the management team thoroughly before making an investment. We usually stopped short of interviewing spouses, but it was important to understand the personalities involved.

Hecht had assembled a good team. They all believed in their product, an improved microwave filter that was used in cellular networks, and seemed determined to make it work. As cellular telephony spread around the globe, so did demand for these filters, and Tetracom's appeared to be better and cheaper than what was out there at the moment. And their technology was patented.

Hecht and his team left just before eleven. I was about to go to bed when Diane suggested a drink. We headed for the bar, and I ordered a single malt, Diane a brandy.

'So what do you think of them?' Diane asked.

'The management or the product?'

'Both.'

I gave Diane my analysis, which was that I was impressed, but that I was worried existing companies in the sector might come out with their own new technologies that could match Tetracom's. And, given similar products, customers would always tend to go with the more established supplier. We talked about that for a while, and then Diane asked me the four point seven million dollar question. 'Do you think we should invest?'

No deal was ever perfect, but this was closer than most.

I nodded. 'Provided we can get comfortable with the competition, yes.'

'Good. So do I. We'll do some more research on the competition as soon as we get back. And we can begin putting together an Investment Memorandum.'

Venture capitalists spend so much time saying 'no', it's always satisfying when there is a chance to say 'yes'.

I smiled and raised my glass. 'To Tetracom.'

'To Tetracom.' Diane sipped her brandy. Even though she had been up since six that morning and hadn't had a chance to change, she looked cool and poised in a simple but well-cut black suit. I suspected I looked knackered.

'What do you think about Revere, Simon?' she asked.

I glanced at her, wondering how much to confide in her. I

decided to trust her. And I hoped I might find out something about Frank and Art and who was to succeed Gil as head of Revere.

'I'm worried.'

'By what Lynette Mauer said last week?'

'Yes. But I'm not just worried about us losing an investor in our funds. I'm more concerned she might be right.'

'What do you mean?'

'Well, now Frank's gone we've lost the partner with the most consistent track record.'

'What about Gil?'

'Hm.' Once again I glanced at Diane. She was sitting back, relaxed in the comfortable armchair, watching me closely over her brandy. I decided to be open with her. 'I suspect Gil won't be around Revere much longer either.'

She raised her eyebrows. 'How do you know about that?'

I shrugged.

'Do the other associates know?'

'I don't think so. But Lynette Mauer is obviously worried, and I don't blame her. Without both Frank and Gil, Art would run the show. I think I would be concerned about that if I were an investor.'

'What about the other partners?' asked Diane.

'I'm sure you and Ravi will be very successful,' I said. 'And I think we associates aren't too bad either. But Art is going to dominate things. I just don't trust his judgement.'

Diane frowned, thinking over what I had just said.

'Do you think I'm wrong?' I asked.

Diane took a deep breath. 'No, I don't,' she said. 'In fact it's exactly what I've been thinking about a lot recently.'

We were silent for a moment. By saying what she had just said, Diane had implicitly criticized one of her partners in front of an associate, something Gil would definitely have disapproved of. I felt in a strange way honoured by her confidence.

'Tell me, what were relations like between Frank and Art?' I asked her.

She thought for a moment before answering. 'They were always polite to each other. Or at least Frank was always polite to Art.

And I never heard him say anything bad about Art behind his back. That's just not the sort of thing he did.'

'And Art?'

'Art was always polite about Frank, as well. But I think that's because Frank obviously knew what he was talking about, and Art would have gotten nowhere with Gil trying to undermine Frank's judgement. What he did try to do was to ease Frank out of the loop. He would schedule important meetings of the partnership for when Frank couldn't make it, he'd spend a lot of time with the investors, he'd get involved in policy issues and so on.'

'What was Frank's response?'

'Frank let himself be outmanoeuvred. He knew that ultimately he could rely on Gil's support.'

'How long have you known that Gil was planning to retire?' I asked.

'Not long. About six weeks. I don't think Gil had told Art before he told Ravi and me. But I wouldn't have been surprised if Frank had known for a little longer.'

'I see.' I paused before asking my next question. 'And if Frank was still alive, do you think he would have taken over from Gil?'

'Oh, undoubtedly,' Diane said. 'I think some way would have been found for Art to save face. I don't know, some new title or position or something. But Frank would have taken the important investment decisions.'

'Do you think that was Art's opinion as well?'

'I don't know. He certainly hadn't given up hope. He's been lobbying Gil hard over the last month. It's almost embarrassing really. And I'm sick to death of hearing about BioOne.' Diane laughed. 'Didn't you think that was funny with Ravi on Monday? I swear I thought Art was going to kill him.'

She drained her glass. 'Do you want another?' she asked. I nodded and she beckoned to the waiter. 'Why are you asking me all this?'

'I wonder who killed Frank,' I answered simply.

Diane drew in her breath. 'Isn't that for the police to decide?' she said carefully.

'They seem to have decided it was me.'

'That's ridiculous.'

'I'd love to be able to point them in another direction.'

'Toward Art, you mean?'

'He seems a likely candidate.'

Diane leaned forward. 'I can understand your concern. But be careful. Gil's right, if we start pointing fingers at each other over Frank's death, we'll tear the firm apart. He spoke to us about the police's suspicion of you, and said you had his total support. I don't think he meant we should support you and accuse someone else.'

'I can understand that,' I said. 'But what about you, Diane? Do you think I killed Frank?'

'Of course not,' she replied unhesitatingly.

I smiled back. 'Thank you.'

We sipped our drinks in silence. It had been a long day. The second whisky, a generous helping, was beginning to relax me.

'How's Lisa?' Diane asked.

I had not yet told anyone at Revere about Lisa and me. But the simple question seemed to beg a simple answer.

'She's left me,' I said.

'No!' Diane looked genuinely concerned. She didn't ask the question I would have had to lie to answer – Why? Instead she asked, 'When?'

'A couple of days ago.'

'How do you feel about it?'

I sighed. 'Lousy.' I drained my glass.

'I'm sorry,' Diane said.

I didn't want to talk about Lisa any more. And just for the moment I didn't want to think about her. It was good to be away from Boston and Lisa and the mess of Frank's death. The waiter hovered near by, and I grabbed his attention. 'Two more please.'

We talked of other things, of England, of New Jersey where Diane had grown up. I hadn't realized she was a classic example of poor girl made good. Her father was an electrician, yet she had managed to get herself into NYU and then Columbia Business

School where she had graduated top of her class. She had done well. The poise, the sophisticated clothes and the accent must all have been learned. To my admittedly foreign eyes, she had learned well.

It was nearly one o'clock when we finally called it a night. As we rode up in the lift together, Diane stood close to me. She reached up and kissed me on the lips. I was too tired, too confused to respond, but I didn't pull away either. Then, as the lift stopped at her floor, she flashed me a quick smile. 'Good night,' she said, and was gone.

I had another terrible night's sleep brooding about Frank, Lisa and now Diane. Guilt piled on to my anger. Whisky, fatigue and semi-consciousness chased my brain into all kinds of strange corners. I woke up still tired, and with a headache.

Diane met me at breakfast. She looked great, and apart from drinking several glasses of orange juice, acted as though nothing had happened the previous night.

Perhaps it hadn't.

Back in the office, the stack of papers in my in-box had grown higher, and I had several minutes of voice-mails to return. My computer informed me I had forty-six e-mails.

Several of the phone calls and e-mails were from Craig, so deciding that I could get rid of a number of messages in one go, I dialled his number.

'How's it going Craig?'

'I don't know, Simon. Good news and bad.'

'What's the good news?'

'Your friend Jeff Lieberman came through with the hundred fifty thousand. And he talked about some kind of fund for the Managing Directors at Bloomfield Weiss that might want to invest.'

'That is good,' I said, with as much enthusiasm as I could muster. The trouble was Net Cop needed more than a few private investors to build the prototype. It needed serious dollars from serious players. And that still left the bad news. 'How did it go with Ericsson?'

'Not so good,' said Craig. 'They like the idea, but they want to see working silicon.'

'And there's no way we can make a prototype any cheaper?'

'Not one that works.'

I sighed.

'It doesn't look good, does it?' Craig sounded unusually despondent.

'Hang on in there, Craig,' I said, trying to sound as confident as possible. 'We never said it would be easy.'

'I guess not. Speak to you later.'

Damn! I was not prepared to let Net Cop die. I just wasn't.

John wasn't having a good day either. He was looking seriously worried.

'What's up?' I asked.

'National Quilt is screwed,' he said.

'What's the problem?'

'The bank's getting antsy. They don't like all this inventory build-up. They want the working capital line of credit cleaned up by the end of the month.'

'And you're not going to make that?'

'No way.'

'What about the "Go Naked" strategy?'

'The bankers are not great fans,' said John gloomily. 'In fact I think it makes them even more worried.'

'Oh.' That sounded like a problem. 'What's Art's advice?'

'I started talking to him about it, and then he suddenly had an urgent phone call. He said if things were looking tough I should raise it at next week's Monday morning meeting.'

'Sounds like he doesn't want to know.'

'That's exactly what it sounds like. How's Net Cop?'

'I'd say it's screwed.'

John sighed. 'I guess this is all part of becoming a grown-up venture capitalist.'

'I guess it is.'

John headed off to Lowell to visit the ill-fated quilt company, leaving me to spend the day at my desk. I gathered together some pretty good information on Tetracom's competitors that seemed to suggest their product really was special. And I started on the Investment Memorandum, which would be the document that would, I hoped, eventually persuade the partners to invest.

But it was difficult. I spent long periods of time staring into space, thinking of Lisa, and worrying about Sergeant Mahoney.

Daniel was involved in some heavy-duty number-crunching. Eventually he stopped and stretched.

'So how was Porkopolis?'

'Porkopolis?'

'It's what they used to call Cincinnati. Great town isn't it?'

'I didn't see a pig anywhere. But I did see a very impressive company.'

'So you think we might do Tetracom, huh?'

'I think so. Or else I'm wasting my time with all this.'

'And how was the lovely Diane?'

'Missing you badly, Daniel.' I kept my composure. Or I thought I did.

'Naturally.' He smiled. 'Hey, how about a drink after work?'

'Yeah, why not? But can you get away?' I nodded at the piles of figures surrounding his computer.

'Oh, a couple of random numbers inserted in the right place will sort those out,' Daniel said with a grin. 'Hey, don't worry, Simon. It can't possibly get worse.'

But of course it could.

We went to Pete's, a bar on Franklin Street, in the middle of the Financial District. By the time we got there, the crowd of big loud brokers had already downed a lot of alcohol. Daniel found us a table in the corner and a cold Sam Adams each.

Every now and then Daniel and I had a drink after work. Despite his tendency to be obnoxious, I found him good company. He was funny and intelligent, and a good source of gossip. Once, we'd even been to Las Vegas together, crawling from casino to casino following a set of obscure gambling rules that Daniel called his system. He was a great person with which to live the tackiness of Las Vegas for a night. I had lost two hundred bucks, but enjoyed myself immensely. Daniel claimed he had come out five hundred dollars ahead. My impression was he had lost thousands, but maybe I had missed something.

'So how come you were staring into space all afternoon? Net Cop getting to you?' Daniel asked.

I took a long draught of the cool beer. 'That tastes good,' I said. 'No, it's not that.' I glanced at Daniel. 'Lisa's left me.'

'Oh, no! I'm sorry. Why did she do that? Did she find a one-eyed leper who was better looking?'

'Thanks, Daniel.'

'If she's free, so am I. I'd like to make some new friends. I've always liked her, you know. Have you got her new number?'

I ignored his comment, but I didn't mind Daniel's kidding, however offensive it was, and it could get pretty offensive. It eased the gloom a bit.

'She thinks I killed Frank.'

Daniel winced. 'Oooh. That could take some forgiving. I do hope she's wrong.'

'Yes, she's all wrong.'

'Oh, well that's all right then.'

'But the police seem to agree with her.'

'What, that nice Sergeant Malone who asked all those questions?'

'Mahoney. That's right. He says I had the opportunity and the motive. I was at Marsh House the afternoon Frank was murdered, and I inherit half his fortune. Or rather Lisa does.'

Daniel frowned. 'That all sounds a bit circumstantial, doesn't it? Did they find the gun?'

'No,' I said, keeping my promise to myself not to tell anyone about Lisa's discovery.

'Pity.'

'Why do you say that?'

'If they found the gun in the middle of South Boston or some-where, it would suggest that you weren't the guy who used it.'

'That's true.' For a moment I wished that Lisa hadn't thrown it away. Then I could have hidden it conveniently in Art's garage.

But the moment passed. That would probably just have got me in deeper trouble.

There was one question I needed to ask Daniel. 'Did you tell Mahoney we were talking about how wealthy Frank was just before he died?'

Daniel winced. 'Yeah, I did. Sorry. But he did ask whether we'd had a conversation like that, and I had to tell him the truth. Did it get you in trouble?'

I sighed. 'Not really. I think Mahoney was pretty convinced anyway. It'll just give him some more ammunition.'

'Sorry, Simon. I didn't realize. He was asking all these bullshit questions, and I never imagined you as a suspect. At least not then.'

'Don't worry.' I sipped my beer. 'But what interests me is, if I didn't kill Frank, who did?'

'Good question,' said Daniel. 'All I know is it wasn't me. I was in New York.'

'No need to be so smug about it. What's the office gossip? I don't seem to hear any of it any more.'

'People usually steer clear of the subject. It's like it was in bad taste or something. And Gil did say he didn't want us suspecting each other.'

'And when they don't steer clear of the subject?'

Daniel gulped his beer. 'There's one name that comes up quite consistently.'

'Mine?'

Daniel nodded.

'But people can't really think I murdered Frank?'

'I don't think they do. Which leaves us kind of stuck.'

'What about Art?'

Daniel thought for a moment. 'Not a bad choice for second favourite. He hated Frank, although he was always polite to him. But where was he when Frank was killed?'

'I don't know,' I said. 'Mahoney won't tell me anything. And I could scarcely ask Art himself.'

'You could ask his wife. You know how much she likes you. You charmed the panties off her at last year's Christmas party.'

158

'Oh yes. I just ring her up and say, "Hello, Mrs Altschule. I just want to check whether your husband murdered my father-in-law. Do you know where he was on Saturday the whatever-it-was of October?"'

'Hm,' said Daniel. 'I see your problem.'

'You've worked with Art more than I have. Do you know much about his background?' Daniel was curious to the point of being nosy. I was sure he had picked up much more about the people at Revere than I had, even though we had both been in the firm the same length of time.

'He's known Gil a long time. I think they were at school together.'

'Harvard?'

'Yeah. After that they both went to Vietnam. Gil was in a regular army unit, and Art was in the Marines. I think Art saw some pretty hairy action, and Gil had a relatively quiet time of it.'

'I've heard about the Marines,' I said. Art loved to refer to the service.

'Yes. But he never talks specifically about what happened there. Even when I asked him.'

'I can understand that,' I said. There were one or two things in my own short military career I would rather not discuss.

'I guess so,' said Daniel. 'But it was still kind of strange. You know how Art likes to brag about stuff. I'd have expected a couple of stories about how he took out three gook villages single-handed.'

'I see what you mean.'

'Anyway, after Vietnam he got an MBA, and then worked for Digital Equipment in Maynard. Eventually he left there and started some company selling mini-computers. According to him, it did brilliantly well. Although I'm not so sure.'

'Really, why not? Whenever I've heard him talk about it, it sounded like it was the biggest thing since Compaq.'

'He sold the company for something like twelve million bucks to ICX Computers. But once ICX got in there they found they had bought a can of worms. The accounts were rotten. ICX hit Art and his partner for ten million under the warranties they had given to ICX when they had sold out. Art's partner killed himself. Dark days.'

'Jesus.'

'The story is that Art didn't know anything about it. And I can kind of believe that. There's quite a lot Art doesn't know. Then Art's old buddy Gil started up a VC firm, and asked Art to join him. Art arrived a few months before Frank, I think. Then he had several years mediocre investing until he lucked out on BioOne.'

'Sounds like he and Frank were destined to clash.'

'I'd say it was unavoidable,' said Daniel.

We drank our beer. I thought through other possibilities. 'Gil?' I suggested.

'I don't think so,' said Daniel. 'He's so straight. And they were friends.'

'Besides, why would he do it?'

'No reason I can think of.' Daniel sipped his beer thoughtfully. 'But what about Diane?'

'Diane?' I said. 'Why would she want to kill Frank?'

'I don't know. She seems charming on the surface. But she's cunning. Devious. A skilful political animal.'

'Where did you get that idea?'

'Charlie Dyzart from B-school went to Barnes McLintock. He told me a bit about her.'

'Like what?'

'She was a very good management consultant. She became one of the youngest partners at Barnes McLintock. Certainly the youngest female partner. But she left some collateral damage in her wake.'

'What happened?'

'It seems her boss advised Pan United Airlines to change their image to appear more international and less American. They lost a quarter of their passengers within six months. They tried to sue Barnes McLintock. Diane somehow persuaded Pan United that she had always thought it was a bad idea, and she came up with some smart ways to fix the problem. Barnes McLintock didn't get sued, they kept the client, her boss got fired, and she got promoted.

Charlie said the guy didn't stand a chance once Diane had him in her sights.'

'I see.' I remembered Frank had said something about how Diane had broken up a marriage at Barnes McLintock. It was something I had tried to forget. 'She didn't have an affair with him, did she?'

Daniel laughed. 'No, but there was something with an associate,' Charlie said. 'A young guy. Married. He walked out on his wife and left the firm. Then she dropped him a few months later. Everyone knew about it.'

'Hmm.'

Daniel looked at me curiously. 'You'd better watch yourself with Diane, Simon.'

'Oh, come on, Daniel. There's nothing between us. I like her. I respect her. She's a good venture capitalist.'

'She's after you.'

The trouble with Daniel was you could never tell whether he was joking or being serious. But either way I knew he was right.

'I still don't think Diane would kill anyone,' I said. 'That goes way beyond political scheming. No, I think Art is our best bet.'

Daniel allowed the subject to be changed. 'There is one interesting thing about Art,' he said.

'What's that?'

'I think he used to be an alcoholic.'

'I've never seen him drink,' I said.

'Precisely,' said Daniel. 'And he doesn't act like the temperance type. In fact he seems more like the hard-drinking type to me.'

'You mean he must have given up?'

'Absolutely. Maybe Vietnam had something to do with it.'

'It must have been horrible.' Nothing in my military experience came close, certainly not Northern Ireland. 'But Art being a former alcoholic doesn't prove anything.'

'Except I think he might be back on the booze.'

'Have you seen him drunk?'

'No, but he's called in sick unexpectedly three times in the last three weeks. I know because I had to cover for him. And on Tuesday morning I could swear he smelled of whisky.'

'That's not good. Do you think some recent event might have started him off again?'

'It's a theory,' said Daniel. 'But it's nowhere near as convincing as the theory that you did it.'

'Great,' I said, and drained my beer.

An hour or so later, we left Pete's, mellow but not drunk. The nights were beginning to get cold. Daniel had his raincoat, but I was wearing just my suit. I hunched my shoulders and pushed my hands deep into my pockets. It was late, and it was quiet in the heart of the Financial District.

Two big men in jeans approached us along the narrow sidewalk. We paused to let them pass by. But they didn't pass by. Their eyes locked on Daniel and me.

I heard rapid footsteps behind us. Too late I pulled my hands out of my pockets, too late to prevent a heavy blow to my stomach. The air burst out of my diaphragm, and I doubled up, gasping. Two more punches followed, and I slumped backwards against the wall.

They bundled Daniel into an alleyway. In front of me stood a big hard man, his fists clenched. Daniel was suffering, I heard the blows coming thick and fast. He cried out. My head slowly cleared. The man in front of me was watching me closely, his fists ready to strike again. I closed my eyes, and allowed myself to slump downwards, letting my weight fall on to my right leg. Then I spun round, and thrust my fist upwards with all my strength into the man's face. The blow caught him on the side of the head, and sent him stumbling. I hit him a couple more times, and he staggered backwards into the street.

Out of the corner of my eye I could see the other two leave Daniel, and move towards me. I turned to face them.

Then one of them muttered something in a foreign language that sounded like Russian, and they backed off.

'Jesus, Daniel, are you OK?' I crouched over him. He was conscious but groaning.

'No,' he muttered between his teeth.

'Here, I'll call an ambulance.'

Daniel sat up. 'No, don't do that. I think I am OK. It just hurts.'

'Where?'

'Everywhere. But I don't think anything's broken. My arm hurts like hell. Get me a taxi, Simon. I'll go home.'

His face was a mess. His nose was bleeding, and so was his lip, and he had a huge red mark on one cheek. I picked him up and half-carried him to a busier street. We waited a couple of minutes for a taxi, and after I had assured the driver there was no chance of us getting any blood on the upholstery, I gently placed Daniel in the back seat.

'Here, I'll go with you,' I said, climbing in with him.

'You're a great guy to be out in Boston at night with,' said Daniel, trying to stem the flow of blood from his nose with his hand.

'They didn't know who we were, did they?'

'Didn't they?' said Daniel. 'Did they steal anything? I've still got my wallet, I think.' He patted his pocket to make sure.

I checked mine. It was still there.

The thought that people I didn't know might want to beat me up bothered me. But Daniel was right. They hadn't taken anything.

'Did you hear them at the end?' I said. 'One of them was speaking a foreign language. Russian I think.'

'No,' Daniel said. 'I was out of it.' He groaned and rubbed his ribs. 'This hurts.'

'What would a bunch of Russians want with me?' I said.

'Face it,' said Daniel. 'Nobody likes you.'

16

The sun rose cold and clear the next day as I walked into work. The leaves of the trees on the Common were at the peak of their colour: oranges, yellows and browns. The previous autumn, Lisa and I had spent as much time as we could outside Boston, in the back roads of New England, amongst the extraordinary foliage. But not this year. This year, the leaves would fall unremarked. The cold greyness of a Boston winter was close.

My body still ached from the blows it had received. Why would some Russian thugs want to beat me up? Daylight and a clearer head didn't help answer the question.

If they'd beaten me up once, they could do it again. I'd have to be careful. No more walking down dark alleys half-drunk. But if someone wanted to get me, they'd find a way, however careful I was. A depressing thought.

I left the open spaces of the Common, and made my way through clogged streets downtown. I was walking past the Meridien Hotel with its line of red awnings over the ground floor windows, when I saw Diane coming the other way. She crossed the road at the junction, and disappeared into the entrance. I wasn't surprised; it was the favourite breakfast haunt for downtown venture capitalists. Then, as I reached the junction myself, I saw the diminutive figure of Lynette Mauer, clutching a *Wall Street Journal* and a briefcase. I turned, walked up the street for a few yards so she wouldn't see me, and watched. She too headed for the entrance of the Meridien.

Interesting. Of course it might just be a coincidence, Diane and Lynette Mauer could both be having breakfast with different people at the same time at the same place. Or, they could be having breakfast together.

I arrived at work before Daniel. When he made his entrance, I saw the bruises on his face had flourished. A black eye had materialized from somewhere, his cheek shone purple and red, and his bottom lip had a nasty black-red scab.

'Very attractive,' I said.

'Thank you.'

'Jesus! What happened to you?' exclaimed John.

'Some guys tried to beat up Simon. I got in the way,' said Daniel.

'You don't know they were after me,' I protested.

Daniel just scowled at me.

'Did they get you too?' John asked me.

I nodded. 'You just can't see the damage.'

'Superman here held them off, while I got the shit kicked out of me,' Daniel grumbled.

'Why did they want to beat you up?' John asked me.

'I wish I knew,' I muttered.

Work had to be dealt with. No matter what happened to me, it was always there, piling up. I went to see Diane with some analysis I had prepared on Tetracom's competition. I had done a good job. It clearly impressed her.

Just as I was about to leave her office, I paused. 'Oh, I think I saw Lynette Mauer this morning going into the Meridien. She didn't see me.'

'Oh, yes?' said Diane neutrally.

'You didn't see me either, I don't think.'

Diane smiled. 'OK, you caught me. Actually I did see you, but I didn't want to delay you on your way to work. I know you're an important guy and you have big deals to do.'

'Yeah, right. So what were you and Mauer talking about?'

'Oh, women's things. You wouldn't understand.' Diane's smile broadened.

I raised my eyebrows.

165

'Mind your own business, Simon,' she said. 'You'll find out soon, I hope.'

'Sounds intriguing.'

'Let's just say someone had to take the initiative around here. Now, see what you can find on Pacific Filtertek. I'm a bit worried about how fast their market share is growing.'

'Certainly, Madam,' I said in my best butler-speak, and withdrew.

Back at my desk, I checked Yahoo Finance on my computer for BioOne's stock price.

John saw what I was doing. 'Forty-eight and five-eighths. Down an eighth, going nowhere,' he said.

I looked up. The previous night I had asked Daniel about Frank's murder. Now seemed like a good time to ask John.

'John?'

'Yeah?'

'Who do you think killed Frank?'

He looked at me sharply, surprised by the question. 'I don't know. I haven't thought about it much, I guess.'

'You must have some opinion.'

He looked uncomfortable. 'Not really.'

'What about me?' I pushed him.

He took a deep breath. 'It did cross my mind when the police asked all those questions about you. But it didn't make sense to me when I thought about it. To tell you the truth, Simon, the whole subject is something I'd rather not think about.' He swallowed. 'I liked Frank. We did a lot of work together. I just can't believe . . .' He paused. 'He was a good guy, you know. A great guy. He wasn't just a good venture capitalist. He was a great person. Kind, generous, smart, honourable. But you know all that. I'm going to miss him.' He tailed off.

I was a little surprised by his emotional reaction to my questions. But I had been thinking about Frank's death too much in terms of what it meant to me and Lisa. There was genuine sadness at Revere that I was in danger of ignoring. I decided not to push him any further.

'The police said that Frank phoned you the day he died?'

'That's right.'

'What about?'

For a moment John looked confused. 'Oh . . . a deal we were working on.'

'What was that?'

'Um . . . Smart Toys, I think it was. Yes, that's right. He called me asking for some information. I had the papers at home. When I called him back a bit later, there was no reply. We all know why, now.'

Frank must have called John just after I had left. I tried to remember if I had seen any sign that Frank was working on a deal. I couldn't, but that didn't mean anything. 'Did he say anything about my visit?'

'No,' said John. 'It was strictly business. Get the information and call him back.'

'I see,' I said.

John and I looked at each other uncomfortably for a second or two, and then he turned back to his work.

I turned to mine. But something wasn't quite right with what John had said. I dug through the agendas for recent Monday morning meetings, and found the one for October 12. There was a section at the back labelled 'Dead Deals'. There all the deals that were being worked on that had been turned down in the previous week were listed, together with the date they were killed. Sure enough, there it was: Smart Toys, up-market toy retailer, FC, 10/8.

Frank had killed the deal on 8 October, the Thursday before he died. There had been no reason to work on it over a weekend.

I glanced up at John who was absorbed in a phone conversation. He had lied to me. And to the police. Why?

I decided not to confront him, at least not yet.

I had work to do. I attacked my e-mails. Amongst the dross was one from Jeff Lieberman. I opened it curiously. It said some of his firm's managing directors were interested in investing in Net Cop, and could Craig and I meet them that afternoon?

I was just mulling the message over when the phone rang.

It was Craig. 'Hey, Simon. Have you checked your e-mail?'

167

'I'm just looking at it now.'

'Good news or what?'

I hesitated. I hated to dampen Craig's spirits, but it was important we keep a sense of perspective. 'It's nice, Craig. But don't get your hopes up. Even if we do get in another couple of hundred thousand, we're still a long way off the three million we need.'

'Yeah, but these guys are investment bankers, right? I mean Bloomfield Weiss is one of the biggest investment banks in the world. They got to have dough.'

'I'm sure they have, Craig. But they're unlikely to want to put all of it into Net Cop. Jeff said we're just talking about these people as individuals here. It's not the firm's capital they're putting up.'

'We still go see them, right?'

'I'm not sure. I mean I don't know whether it's worth going all that way at this late stage. Maybe we should try some European telcos or something.'

'Simon, there's no one else to try. If these guys don't put up, then there's no Net Cop to save.'

'OK, Craig. In that case we go.' I looked at my watch. 'I'll see you at the airport for the one o'clock shuttle.'

Bloomfield Weiss's offices loomed over little more than an alley, just off Wall Street. Boston had some big buildings downtown, but New York's were huge. We were dropped off outside a fifty-storey black monstrosity, with the words 'Bloomfield Weiss' in small gold lettering just above the entrance.

A high-speed lift propelled us up to the forty-sixth floor, where we waited in a plush reception area for Jeff Lieberman. After some discussion, we had decided that Craig should wear his usual uniform of T-shirt and jeans. At least then he'd look like the brilliant computer geek he was, rather than a musclebound construction worker in his Sunday best. Although it was a 'dress-down' Friday, none of the investment bankers looked quite like Craig. But then he was wearing his favourite T-shirt, the black one with the dumb-bells on it.

Jeff met us, in a suit, and took us through a warren of corridors to a conference room. From the window I could look over the shoulder of a neighbouring block to glimpse the shimmering grey of New York Harbor.

More suits came in. Or more strictly they were shirts: half of them wore identical heavy white oxford shirts with bright ties, while the other half wore expensive polo shirts and slacks in honour of Friday. Craig was nervous. So was I. With the exception of Jeff, these were men in their forties and fifties, well-groomed, powerful men of money. Where Revere doled out the odd million here and there, Bloomfield Weiss sent billions spinning round the globe twenty-four hours a day. Not that I was intimidated or anything.

They dealt us a hand each of business cards, and then Jeff deferred to a tiny man named Sidney Stahl.

'So, Craig. Jeff's given me the red-herring bullshit. Tell me what you really do. You got ten minutes.'

His voice was thick and gruff, the New York equivalent of what Craig's might sound like in twenty years. I could see Craig found it reassuring.

'Sure,' he said, and he began talking. The Bloomfield Weiss hotshots were entranced.

Forty-five minutes later, there was a knock at the door, and a worried looking young man in a nice suit caught Stahl's eye.

'OK, OK,' he said. 'Sorry, Craig. I gotta stop you there.' He turned to look at the assembled group. 'I'm in. What about you guys?'

Heads nodded all round the table, with a mixture of deference and bravado. If Sidney thought it was a good risk, then so did the others.

Stahl stood up. 'You tell a good story Craig. I like you. You've got our money, but only if you and Jeff can agree on a deal. I don't think you'll find him a pushover.'

Craig and I shook Sidney Stahl's hand, and he left the room, followed by everyone but Jeff.

Jeff grinned at me over the table. 'I bet you didn't think it would be that easy, huh?'

I smiled broadly back. 'What was all that about? That's not the kind of investment committee you get in venture capital.'

'That's the point,' said Jeff. 'It's a kind of informal investment club of some of the big-hitters in the firm, with Sidney being the biggest hitter of them all. The idea is they invest in deals that are too small for Bloomfield Weiss to place with clients or do themselves. It's a kind of macho thing. Who's willing to put up their own money for a big risk.'

'So I noticed,' I said.

'But don't knock it,' said Jeff. 'These guys have had some spectacular home runs.'

'Um, there is one thing we didn't cover,' I said.

'Only one?' said Jeff.

'How much are we talking about?'

'How much do you need?'

My eyes flashed up at Jeff. 'Three million dollars.'

'Then I guess we're talking about three million dollars.'

Craig was ecstatic on the flight back. He gave himself and me a blow-by-blow commentary of what had happened, as though he still couldn't quite believe it. Jeff had hammered out a tough deal. The Bloomfield Weiss syndicate would end up with a large chunk of the company, Craig would keep a chunk, and Revere's holding would be diluted. Jeff would have a place on the board.

According to the investment agreement, the deal still needed Revere's approval, so the final word had to be left to them. But it looked very much as though Craig would get to build his prototype. And with working silicon, funding would come in from resellers like Luxtel and Ericsson. Net Cop was going to work.

'Thank you, Simon,' Craig said, finally.

'I never thought they'd come up with the whole amount.'

'But they did! They did!'

I stared out of the window at Long Island disappearing behind me. I was pleased about Net Cop. Very pleased. But it still left all my other problems out there.

Craig noticed my silence. 'Hey, Simon, what's up? You've been fighting for this as much as I have.'

I smiled at him. 'Yes. And I am truly very pleased.'

'So?'

So I told him about how I was everyone's favourite suspect for Frank's murder. I told him that Lisa had left me because of it, and that I needed to find out more.

'Perhaps I can help,' he said. 'My dad retired a few years ago, but I know a lot of people in the department. Hey, I come from a good Catholic family. I got more cousins than you got fingers and toes, and most of 'em are cops.'

'Perhaps you can,' I said. I took a moment to get my thoughts together. 'The man leading the investigation is assigned to the Essex County DA's office. Sergeant Mahoney is his name. He doesn't like me. It would be interesting to find out a bit more about him.'

'I'll ask around.'

'And can you get a look at any criminal records?'

Craig smiled. 'Of course not. That would be illegal. What do you want to know?'

'See if you can find out whether the following people have a criminal record. Do you have a pen?'

Craig raised his eyebrows. 'What do I need a pen for? I know pi to twenty-nine decimal places.'

'OK, sorry. The names are Arthur Altschule, Gilbert Appleby, Edward Cook – that's Lisa's brother, and,' I paused over the next name, but I remembered Daniel's words, 'Diane Zarrilli.'

'Nice to see you trust your partners.'

'Someone killed Frank, Craig. And it wasn't me.'

'OK, I'll see what I can do,' he said. 'Just as long as you have a drink with me when we get to Boston. And that will be champagne.'

'Ow!' A stab of pain ran down my shoulder as I swung the boat into the water. Although I didn't much feel like it, I had kept my Saturday morning appointment to go rowing with Kieran.

'Are you OK, Simon?' he asked.

'I got into a spot of bother a couple of nights ago. My shoulder still hurts.'

'A spot of bother? Do you mean a fight?'

'You could call it that. I was mugged on the street outside Pete's, downtown. With Daniel Hall.'

'Really? How much did they take?'

'It was odd. They didn't take anything.'

'Oh, I see. So they just didn't like your face?'

'I don't know what they didn't like.'

I puffed as we carried the boat to the river. My shoulder ached like hell.

'It was probably Daniel. Did he make some smart-arse comment?'

'I don't think so. He thinks it was me they were after. I've been in some trouble recently.'

'Must be some pretty bad trouble.'

'I suppose it is,' I said. 'But even so, I don't know why anyone would want to beat me up. One of them spoke Russian.'

'Really?'

'It sounded like it.'

We threw the boat in the water, and set off at a slow pace. I wanted to warm up gently.

'I read somewhere that the Russians are the new boys in town when it comes to organized crime,' said Kieran. 'Drugs, money-laundering, loan-sharking, cabs.'

'Are cabs a criminal activity?'

'When they're driven by Russians they are,' said Kieran. 'Do you remember that guy Sergei Delesov?'

'Yes.' He was a very able Russian in our class at business school. I hadn't known him well.

'There was a rumour he was mixed up with some of them.'

'Delesov? A Harvard graduate?'

'That was the rumour.'

'Where is he now?' I asked. 'Maybe he might know something.'

'I'm pretty sure he went back to Russia. I think he's already running some bank there.'

We rowed on at a slow, steady pace. The aching in my muscles eased a little as I warmed up, but I didn't want to push anything. We met another pair who asked us to do a 'piece' to the next bridge, something we were usually game for, but I declined. I apologized to Kieran for my tentative performance afterwards, but he told me not to worry, he could use a gentle start to his Saturday.

Weekends are tough when you love someone and they hate you. Especially if you're alone.

The full reality of Lisa leaving me was sinking in, bringing with it the awful thought that she might not come back. At first, it had all seemed absurd, almost unreal. Frank being murdered seemed absurd. I had never known anyone who was murdered. And then suddenly Lisa going, shattering our marriage out of nowhere. It was so unfair. My father had been able to womanize for over a decade and get away with it because my mother adored him. But despite my desperate efforts to avoid becoming my father, my own marriage wasn't going to last a year.

The loneliness of that thought crushed in on me.

It should have been a perfect marriage. We seemed to me completely compatible. No, we *were* completely compatible. No matter what Lisa said or did I would always believe that. Our respective mothers had doubted it from the start, but they were wrong.

The wedding had been a nightmare. Or rather, the wedding itself wasn't, but planning it was awful. When I told my mother that I was marrying an American woman, she was cautiously optimistic. I think she assumed I was following those many landed Englishmen who had found themselves a colonial dowry to keep the family estate intact. When she found out Lisa was Jewish, without a trust fund, and that she intended to keep her maiden name, the disapproval could have frozen the Atlantic. I took Lisa to England, partly to show my mother what a lovely person she was. My mother didn't notice, but insisted on talking about pork and Saturdays.

Lisa's mother tried to disapprove too, but did a much worse job of it. She had set her heart on a nice Jewish son-in-law, and my blond hair and blue eyes just didn't fit. But her pleasure at her

173

daughter's happiness, and the fact that she and I got on quite well, made her abandon her earlier hopes, or at least ignore them.

Over the first six months of our marriage, I thought we had proved them both wrong. I refused to admit now that they were right.

Craig burst in on my moping on Saturday evening.

'That was quick,' I said, getting him a beer.

'The Boston Police Department never sleeps,' said Craig. 'Or at least the computers still work at weekends.'

'So, what have you got?'

'Mahoney, first. My dad knew him. He worked in Boston for twenty years as a street patrolman and then detective. Then he got himself shot, and his wife demanded that he quit. He transferred to the State Police as a compromise.'

'I thought he looked streetwise,' I said.

'Oh, he was a good detective, my father says. He used to do things the old way. He'd get a hunch and he'd play it. Often he'd be right.'

Oh, great. I was obviously his hunch on this case.

'Do you know anything about any sympathies he might have with the IRA?'

Craig looked surprised. 'I don't know. I can check. I mean, he's Irish, like half the cops, especially the older ones. And most of the Irish in Boston do kind of think you should get out of their country. No offence meant.' I smiled thinly. 'Why? Do you think he's picking on you because you're a Brit?'

'Something like that,' I replied. Given Craig's own ancestry, I wanted to leave out my Northern Ireland tour of duty if I could.

'I can check if you like,' said Craig.

'If it's no trouble. Now, what about the others?'

'There are a coupla Edward Cooks with records in California, but none of them looks like your guy. Nothing on Gil. Nor on Diane Zarrilli.'

I was surprised to feel a small wave of relief when I heard about

Diane. I was also glad that Gil was clean. Eddie was a bit of a disappointment.

'And Art?'

'Now, this guy has an interesting file. He was involved with a company that sold UNIX boxes. His partner, a guy named Dennis Slater, liked to invent customers who he'd sell the same box to several times over. When they sold the company, Slater was found out, and he blew himself away, or at least that's the way it was left.'

'But the police investigated Art?'

'That's right.'

'Did they get anywhere?'

'They couldn't find enough evidence to arrest him, let alone convict him. He was supposed to have been at home with his wife. She supported his alibi, but no one else could. He said he was dead drunk at the time so he couldn't have done it. Once again there was no way of checking that.'

'How did Slater kill himself?'

'Literally blew his brains out,' said Craig. 'It's the kind of suicide that can be faked by someone who knows what he's doing, and can get close enough to the victim to place a gun to his temple. It's a messy job, but Art could have gotten rid of the clothes he was wearing. If he did it. And there's really no hard evidence that he did.'

'Can you get anything on the investigation into Frank Cook's murder?'

Craig winced and shook his head. 'Sorry, Simon. An ongoing murder investigation is a much bigger deal. Besides, it's Essex County isn't it?'

I nodded.

'It's going to be hard for my contacts to nose around there without being noticed.'

'That's a shame. I'd love to know if Mahoney has found out anything else about Art. Or whether there is a good reason to rule him out entirely.'

'You could always ask him.'

I looked sceptically at Craig. 'He's hardly likely to go on his knees and confess to me.'

'No, but he might tell you if there's proof that he didn't do it. If you ask him in the right way.'

'Maybe I will. Thanks, Craig, that's helpful.'

'No problem, buddy. Now, Monday's a shoe-in, right?'

I still had to get the partnership's approval for the deal I had hammered out with Jeff.

'I've learned my lesson,' I said. 'I'm never going to say any meeting is a shoe-in.'

Craig suddenly tensed. 'Look, Simon, if they jerk me around again, I'll – '

'Calm down,' I said. 'I'll call you on Monday if there's a problem.'

'Call me either way.'

'OK,' I assured him, and he left.

17

I decided there was little to be lost by talking to Art after all. And the best place to do that was at his home. So late on Sunday afternoon I drove out to Acton.

The Boston area is stuffed with the most prosaic place names from the South East of England. Acton, Chelmsford, Woburn, Billerica, Braintree, Norwood and of course Woodbridge, to name but a few. Driving around the area was a bit like being lost on the outer reaches of the Central Line. I hadn't found Chipping Ongar yet, but I was sure it was lurking there somewhere.

Acton was nothing like its West London namesake. Winding rivers, small bridges, stony fields of pumpkins lined up as if on parade, scattered brightly painted wooden houses, tiny blue lakes, and trees. Trees everywhere. The clear autumn light reflected brightly off the oranges and reds of the maples, and the yellows, browns and greens of lesser species. Despite the reason for my visit, my spirits rose as I drove up Spring Hollow Road to Art's large yellow-painted house, with the smart green Range Rover parked outside.

His wife, Shirley, answered the door. Although she must have been about fifty, she was trying to look twenty years younger. Counterfeit blonde hair, tight blue jeans, and careful make-up did their best, but didn't quite succeed. As Daniel had said, we had got on very well at the previous year's Christmas party, but it took her a second to recognize me. Then she gave me a broad smile.

'Simon, how nice to see you again!'

'I'm sorry to disturb you over the weekend, Shirley,' I said.

'No trouble at all. Do come in. I was just about to go down to the market, but Art's around.'

I stood in the hallway as she fetched her husband.

'What's the problem, Simon. A deal blowing up?' Art asked, almost with relish.

'No, it's not that. It's more, er, personal.'

'Oh yes?' Art looked me over suspiciously. He was dressed in neatly pressed khaki trousers and a denim shirt. He looked not exactly tired, but bleary eyed, as though he had a cold or something.

'Yes. Um, I wanted to ask your advice about something.'

After a moment's reflection, Art decided he was happy to play the role of wise uncle. He showed me through to the living room. A Big Ten football game was playing on the large-screen TV. He flicked a remote to turn the sound down, but not off, and picked up an open can of Diet Dr Pepper.

'Want one?'

'No thanks,' I said.

'Cup of tea?'

'Actually, yes please. That would be nice.'

I wasn't sure whether Art was mocking me, but I would prefer a cup of tea any day to the purple mixture of effervescent chemicals Art was drinking.

'Hold on a moment, I'll get Shirley to fix it.'

I sat down in an armchair, and let my eyes be pulled towards the huge screen. Michigan had just gone 23–22 ahead of Ohio State, and people were very excited. I idly wondered whether Chelsea had beaten Arsenal at the Bridge the day before.

'Good game,' said Art, returning from the kitchen. 'Chuck's playing Ohio State next week. What's the problem?'

'Well,' I began. 'It's about Frank's murder, actually.'

'Uh-huh.'

'The problem is, the police seem to think I'm responsible.'

I paused to watch Art. He didn't say anything at all at first, just looked at me carefully, as though he agreed with the police's assessment. But he decided to be polite and hear me out. 'But you were his son-in-law.'

'That's part of the problem. Lisa stands to inherit half Frank's estate. Including the BioOne profits.'

Art snorted as though he was displeased that Frank could have received any of the BioOne millions.

'And I went to see him at his house at the shore shortly before he died,' I continued. 'I was the last person to see him alive. Apart from his murderer of course.'

Art furrowed his brow. 'I can see how that might not look good. But Gil has made clear to all of us that he supports you, and so should we.'

Shirley Altschule appeared with a dainty Wedgwood cup of tea.

'Thank you, Mrs Altschule,' I said. 'I'm sorry, but can I just have a drop of milk?'

'Oh, why certainly,' she said, and retreated to the kitchen.

'But how can I help?' Art asked when she had gone.

I smiled quickly. 'I need to find out who did kill Frank. And to do that, I need to ask some questions.'

'Such as?'

'I wonder if you could tell me where you were on the Saturday he was killed?'

'What?' Art swigged his Dr Pepper. 'What kind of question is that? I didn't kill him.'

'I'm sure that's right, Art, but I just need to eliminate everyone in the firm.'

'I had to answer these questions from the police. Why the hell should I answer them from you?'

'I'm sorry, Art. The police won't tell me the results of their investigation apart from that they think I'm the most likely suspect. So I have to recreate their investigation for myself. I know it's a bore for you, but it would help me a lot.'

'Well, I was at home with Shirley all that day, wasn't I honey?'

His wife had just returned with a delicate jug of milk, which I poured into my cup.

'What day was that?' she asked.

'That Saturday when Frank Cook was killed.'

Shirley Altschule threw me a sharp look. 'That's right. You worked in the yard most of the afternoon, and then we rented a video in the evening. But we've told the police all this.'

'Yes, I know, hon, but Simon is making his own inquiries.'

'Was anyone else here that day?'

'No,' said Shirley. 'The kids are both at college.'

'And who collected the video?'

'I did,' said Shirley. 'It was a *Die Hard* movie. Art likes those, you know. But I don't know why you need to know all this stuff. Surely you don't think – '

'Of course I don't, Mrs Altschule. As Art said, I'm just trying to recreate what the police have done so far. Anyway, with what you've told me, I can cross Art off the list, even though he wasn't really on it to start with.'

She gave me a quick worried look. 'I'm just going down to the store, Art,' she said. 'I'll be back.'

'See you later, hon,' he said.

I waited until she had left, and then I continued my questioning. 'Have you any idea who else might have killed Frank?'

'No. I'm with Gil on this though. I can't believe it can have been anyone at Revere. It was probably some wandering psycho. The cops will get him in the end. I just hope they find him before he kills any more people.'

'I tell you though, it's horrible when you feel the police are after you,' I said. 'It shakes your faith in the justice system.'

'I bet.'

'I hear the same kind of thing happened to you once. After your partner committed suicide?'

'Who told you that?' asked Art, sharply.

'Oh, I forget who. It's just rumour. It's probably all wrong.'

Art looked at me. 'No, it's true.' He glanced at his watch, which must have said a quarter past five, and then towards the front door, through which his wife had recently disappeared. 'What do you say to a real drink?'

180

'It's a bit early, isn't it?' I said. Although a looser tongue might tell me more, I was reluctant to encourage a former alcoholic.

'Oh, don't be silly. Jack on the rocks OK with you?'

The truth was, if Art wanted a real drink, I couldn't stop him. I nodded.

Art reached behind a bookcase and pulled out a bottle. He found two glasses on a shelf, and some ice from a small refrigerator, which I could see was stuffed with Diet Dr Pepper. Within a moment a large drink was in my hand.

Art took a big gulp. 'Aah. That tastes good.' He slung the can of Dr Pepper accurately into the wastepaper bin at the far side of the room.

'Yeah, I've had my turn as a number-one suspect,' he said. 'It was a bad time. Everything seemed to be going wrong all around me. It turned out my partner had been ripping off our company for years. We were both being hit for a giant warranty payment. And then the stupid son-of-a-bitch went and killed himself. The cops blamed me.'

'They didn't have any evidence, though?'

'Not real evidence. But I had a motive, and my only alibi was Shirley, and they didn't believe her. They also held the fact that I had been in 'Nam against me. That really pissed me off. It was as though just because I had been out there fighting for my country, I was some kind of murderer.'

'I know what you mean,' I said. 'That's exactly what Mahoney holds against me.'

Art looked at me curiously. 'But you didn't fight in any war, did you? I thought you guys just pranced around on horses at the Queen's tea parties.'

'No, I never fought in any war,' I said. 'But I did learn to drive an armoured car. And I also spent a year in Northern Ireland. I think that's what Mahoney didn't like.'

'That figures,' said Art.

'But in the end they couldn't pin anything on you?'

'No. I got a good lawyer and they had to leave me alone.' Art snorted. 'That bastard Slater got me even after the grave.'

Art sipped his whisky thoughtfully.

'What was it like in Vietnam?' I asked.

Art looked at me suspiciously. 'It wasn't what I expected. It wasn't how a war should be fought. Not what we were trained for.' He took a large gulp of his whisky. 'I try to forget it. I don't always succeed, but I try.'

This reply was so unlike Art, so lacking in bravado and bluster, that it caught me by surprise. I thanked God I hadn't been asked to go anywhere like Vietnam.

He emptied his glass and refilled it. 'What about Northern Ireland?'

'That was pretty unpleasant,' I answered. 'You're there to keep one half of the population from murdering the other half, but you get the feeling they all hate you. There is so much hatred there. It's quiet ninety-nine per cent of the time, but then a bomb goes off, or someone fires a shot, and one of your men dies.'

'Do you think the peace process will work?'

I shrugged. 'I hope so.'

We were silent for a moment.

'It teaches you something, doesn't it?' Art said.

I didn't reply. I wasn't sure it did. Other than that every society has nasty jobs that it persuades its young men to undertake on its behalf. I felt a worse person for having shot those two men in the car, not a better one.

I swallowed the rest of my drink and Art refilled the glass. 'Hey, do you want to take a look at my gun collection? You were a soldier, you'd appreciate it.'

'I'd love to,' I said. Art's interest in guns was definitely something that interested me.

We left our glasses, and Art took me down to the basement. One wall was lined with sturdy-looking metal cabinets. Art took out a key, and unlocked one of them. There were half a dozen antique muskets, rifles, and carbines. Most of them were from the American Civil War, although he also had a long Brown Bess musket used by the British army in the Peninsular campaign.

The other three cabinets held more modern weapons, including some from the Second World War. There were assault rifles, semi-automatics, and a variety of handguns. No three fifty-seven Magnums though. I wondered if there ever had been one in his collection.

Looking at all this assembled hardware, I remembered with a pang when I had first met Lisa, when Art and she had argued about gun licensing laws.

After twenty minutes or so, we returned to the living room and our glasses. Art was mellow and relaxed.

'What did you think of Frank?' I asked.

Art took a deep breath. 'We had very different philosophies on how the firm should be run,' said Art. 'Frank was very analytical about everything. I'm more seat-of-the-pants. Sure, Frank was a bright guy. But my method works.'

'So did his,' I said, unable to leave Frank undefended.

'Oh, on a small scale, yes,' said Art. 'But for a real big winner like BioOne, you need something more. It's a kind of imagination, a willingness to take risks, courage, leadership. Call it what you will.'

I'd call it luck, I thought, but I bit my lip.

'Do you think he would have taken over when Gil eventually retires?' I asked. 'I mean if he was still alive.'

'Possibly,' said Art. 'Gil liked Frank a lot. But what Revere needs now more than ever is leadership, and that's something I can provide.' He poured himself another drink. 'I joined Gil right at the outset, I have the best investment track record at the firm. I think I'm the obvious choice. When Gil does retire,' he added, almost as an afterthought. As far as he was concerned I didn't know anything of Gil's plans.

'And if you don't get to be Managing Partner?' I asked.

Art looked at me strangely. 'Oh, I will,' he said, forcefully. 'Don't worry about that.'

Just then, there was the sound of a car pulling up in the driveway outside. A moment later, Shirley came in, carrying some grocery bags. 'Art, can you help me with these?' she called. Then she saw the whisky glass.

'Art!' she snapped.

'What?' His tone was angry. Belligerent. I looked at the Jack Daniel's bottle. It had been full. It was now half-empty. But Art's voice wasn't slurred, and apart from a slight flush in his cheeks, he looked completely sober.

'Art. We agreed.' Her voice was exasperated.

Art stood up, drawing himself up to his full height, which was about six feet four. 'Shirley, I'm just having a drink with my colleague here.'

She dropped the shopping, and grabbed the glass in his hand. She threw the whisky into a plant pot.

Art's face reddened. 'Don't do that,' he growled. His voice was low, sinister. His wife froze, as if she recognized this new tone. There was something close to fear in her face.

She seemed to take a second to summon up her courage. 'Art. No more drink, OK?' She threw a quick glance at me.

'Don't worry. He's just going,' said Art, glaring at his wife.

I tried to catch her eye. She was standing in front of him, trying to be resolute, but fear was creeping into her eyes, and the corner of her mouth trembled.

I couldn't leave her.

'Can I help you with the shopping, Mrs Altschule?' I said.

She glanced at Art. 'OK. That would be very kind.' She hesitated, then headed for the door. I followed her, with Art watching us.

Her car was parked in the driveway, the boot open.

'I'm sorry,' I said. 'He offered me a drink and I accepted.'

She sighed. 'It's not your fault. If he wants to drink he's going to drink.'

'I was worried in there,' I said. 'Are you going to be all right?'

She bit her lip and nodded her head, but the frightened glance she shot me made me not so sure.

'When did the drinking start?'

'About a month ago.'

'When Frank died.'

'No, a bit before then.'

'Do you know why?'

She looked at me hesitantly.

'I know Gil is planning to retire,' I said. 'He must have told Art about then. Did he tell him Frank was going to take over the firm?'

She took a deep breath. 'Art's very ambitious. He's always assumed Gil's job would be his eventually. When Gil sent a note to the partners saying he was going to retire, Art thought his time had come. Then a couple of weeks later, Gil told him Frank had the job. Art was going to be given some grand title, but Frank would have the power. I've never seen Art so angry. He went on about BioOne, and how it was such an important investment for the firm. He felt badly let down by Gil, I can tell you.'

There was something in Shirley Altschule's voice that suggested she agreed with her husband on that score.

'Anyway, he ranted on for an hour or so, and then left the house. He didn't say where he was going. He came back in a taxi at midnight, drunk.' She bit her lip. 'If only Gil had been *fair* to him.' She sniffed. 'It was the first drop he'd touched for nearly ten years, since that awful time when his partner killed himself. Once he started, he couldn't stop. And it's so *stupid*. It's not going to do anything for his chances.'

'But now Frank's dead, doesn't he think the job's his?'

'He says he does. But his confidence is shaken. He doesn't trust Gil any more. And the drink doesn't help.'

She glanced at me sharply, as though she regretted what she had just said. 'My husband didn't kill Frank Cook,' she said icily. 'I know that. He was here with me all the time. And he might be violent sometimes, but he's not a murderer.' She looked at me defiantly, daring me to contradict her.

'OK,' I said, mildly.

Then her eyes clouded with worry. 'Don't tell Gil, will you?'

'He's bound to find out.'

She sighed. 'Maybe. And I expect when he does he'll be understanding. But I'm still hopeful I can get him off it. I can't go through that again.'

We were standing by her car in the driveway. I saw some movement in the window. It was Art, watching us.

'What are you going to do now?' I said. I looked back towards the house. 'Are you sure you'll be all right?'

'Of course,' she said. For a moment there was fear in her eyes, but then she banished it, and steeled herself. She looked me straight in the eyes. 'We have to face this together. He needs me if he's going to get over this. Now, help me carry these in.'

I grabbed some bags and followed her back into the house. Art was standing in the hallway, his large frame almost blocking it. I squeezed past him, and put the bags down in the kitchen.

'Goodbye, Simon,' Art muttered.

I glanced at his wife. She nodded. 'Goodbye,' she said.

I wanted to stay there, to protect her, or force her to come away with me. But I admired her courage and her loyalty, and I had no right to prevent her from doing what she could to help her husband.

But I couldn't abandon her completely. I drove my car a few yards up the road and stopped. I jogged back to their house, crept up to the living room window, and peeked in.

Art and his wife were standing there, in the middle of the room, holding each other.

18

I was up early on Monday morning, and set out on the river just as dawn was breaking. I needed the exercise to clear my head. My shoulder felt much better than it had on Saturday.

I wished I had somehow stopped Art from drinking the previous night. His wife's courage had impressed me, and I hoped she wouldn't have to pay for her bravery. But if she failed to get him back off the booze, I was sure Art would be in no fit state to run Revere. I just hoped Gil would recognize that too.

I was pulling slowly and steadily back to the boathouse. The sun had risen and the morning air was crisp and clear. As I neared the boathouse, I passed some figures in wet suits on the Esplanade. I eased up and watched. They were divers.

With a heavy feeling in the pit of my stomach I knew what they were looking for. I prayed they wouldn't find it.

The Monday morning meeting started on a positive note. Diane wanted to bring the Tetracom management in to present to the partnership that Wednesday. She warmed Gil up nicely. On a non-biotech investment, Ravi would always follow Gil. Art stayed suspiciously silent, ignoring me completely.

Then we came to the two troublesome deals. Net Cop and National Quilt.

I started off with Net Cop. I outlined the deal I had struck with Jeff Lieberman. Revere's holding would be diluted, but we would still have something, and if Net Cop really did work as well as I hoped, we could still make a healthy profit on our original investment. Without Bloomfield Weiss, our holding would certainly be worth nothing.

Gil was pleased, and gave his blessing. The others added theirs.

Then came the National Quilt Company. John explained that owing to an unexpected build up of unsold inventory the company would be unable to pay off its working capital line of credit by the end of the month as the bank had requested. He said it was likely that the company would have to file for Chapter Eleven of the Bankruptcy Code the following week.

'What?' said Gil, frowning. 'I didn't know we had a problem here. I don't like this kind of surprise, John.'

John glanced at Art. Art was looking at the yellow pad in front of him. He had avoided my eye throughout the whole meeting.

'I think it kind of took the management by surprise,' John replied.

'But you're on the board aren't you? Couldn't you see this coming?'

John shrugged. 'I guess I missed it.'

Gil turned to Art. 'This was your deal originally, Art. What went wrong?'

'It's difficult to tell,' said Art. 'Three months ago the company seemed very stable. Unexciting, but stable. So I handed it to John. Since then the management seem to have gone off on some crazy strategy to put naked women on their bed covers. I guess that's what the trouble is.'

'What?' said Gil, turning to John. 'Is that true?'

'Uh. Yes,' said John. 'Or, at least, no. I mean . . .'

'Are they putting nude women on their bed covers or not?'

'Er, yeah, they are.'

Gil's patience was wearing very thin. 'And you let them do it?'

'Er, yes.'

'Why, for God's sake?'

John panicked. He could have said that the build up of inventory had been caused by purchasing decisions that were taken when Art was on the board. He could have said that the 'Go Naked' strategy hadn't started yet. He could have said that he had tried to talk to

Art about the company, but Art hadn't wanted to know. But he didn't.

'Sorry.'

Gil glowered at him. 'This is just the sort of company we cannot afford to lose. Especially now when we know that the Bieber Foundation is looking at what we do so closely.'

John cowered. These were strong words from Gil.

Gil turned to Art. 'I'd like you to see what you can salvage from this one.'

'Sure,' said Art. 'It sounds like it might be too late, but I'll see what I can do.'

'Well, I think that just about wraps it up,' said Gil, picking up his agenda.

'One thing, Gil.' It was Diane.

Gil paused. 'Yes?'

'I agree with you. Losing National Quilt is the last thing we need. And I think it's not entirely clear what went wrong. It's extremely important we take the time to learn from our mistakes.'

There was silence round the table. I watched, fascinated. There was trouble ahead.

Gil frowned. 'I think John explained the problem. Management was allowed to embark on an entirely inappropriate strategy.'

Art butted in. 'And I should take my share of the blame. I shouldn't have handed over this deal to such a junior member of the team.'

Gil nodded his approval. John sat still, his ears turning slowly red, whether from shame or anger or a combination of the two, I couldn't tell.

'I wonder whether there were any early warning signs we should have spotted,' Diane went on. 'Management, for example. Should we have backed them? And the original turnaround strategy for the company. Was it the right one?'

Silence again. Then Gil spoke. 'Yes, I think those are useful questions to ask. Art?'

Now it was Art's turn to redden. He took a moment to compose his reply. 'Those are absolutely the right questions,' he said in a forceful voice, full of confidence. 'But in this case I can safely say that until three months ago the company was doing great, the management seemed fine, and the strategy was working.'

'And then it all suddenly went off the rails?' Diane asked. 'Without any warning?'

You could almost hear the intake of breath around the room. Partners at Revere just didn't question each other like that. At least not in the Monday morning meeting.

Art leaned his large frame on to the table, and stared at Diane.

'Yes. That's about what happened. I've seen stranger things in venture capital.'

Gil was frowning now, the tension between his lieutenants was obvious, and he disapproved. 'All right, now we've had the discussion, I think the meeting's over.'

Diane smiled quickly at Gil, and gathered up her own papers. But the tension hung on in the room, like the air after one squall has passed but another is about to hit.

'Why didn't you stand up for yourself in there?' I said to John as soon as we were back in our office. Daniel had gone to see Gil about something. 'Art dropped you in it, and if Diane hadn't stepped in, he would have got away with it completely.'

John shrugged. 'There's no point in me picking a fight with Art. That would only make it worse. As soon as National Quilt started going wrong, Art made sure it had my name on it. There was nothing I could do.'

'You've got to stand up for yourself,' I said. 'I was mauled on Net Cop. I survived.'

John shook his head. 'National Quilt is going down the tube.' He slumped back in his chair. 'Diane was just making a political point. I couldn't do that even if I wanted to.' He shook his head. 'I swear, I've got to get out of this job.'

'Hey, come on, John,' I said. 'You can't give up just because one deal goes bad.'

'It's not just that,' said John. 'I've lost my taste for this place. I'm just not turned on by money like the rest of them.'

'What do you mean, not turned on by money? You've been to business school. You know it's the only thing that matters.'

John ignored my irony. 'That's what someone like Daniel might think. But not me.'

'Nobody's quite like Daniel,' I said.

John looked at me. 'You know he's a jerk. He's sometimes funny about it, but basically, underneath it all, he's an asshole. Sure he's amusing, sure he's smart, but he's always looking after number one. Plus, he thinks making someone else look stupid is funny. I don't know, I guess I don't work like that.'

This tirade was so uncharacteristic of John that I found it hard to answer.

John sighed. 'My father's exactly the same. He has his grand plan for me. Business school, venture capital experience, then I can make my own millions.'

'Is that a grand plan you're going to follow?'

John looked at me sharply, and then relaxed. 'The secret with my father is to do just enough to let him think I'm listening to him, and then stay well clear. I got into Dartmouth, business school, here. And for what? To be bawled out because I didn't take a bunch of Hugh Hefner wannabes seriously.'

'There are always jerks around whatever you do.'

'Maybe, but since Frank . . .' John paused, suddenly finding it difficult to control his emotion. 'Since Frank was killed, I just wonder what's the point. I guess there comes a time when I'm just going to have to tell my father who I really am, and lead my own life. Maybe that time is pretty soon.'

I smiled with sympathy. A death can mean different things to different people. It was natural, I supposed, that Frank's sudden departure from this world should make John wonder what it was all for.

I called Craig to give him the good news about Net Cop. But I found it hard to share his enthusiasm that morning. The divers worried me. If they found the gun I would be in big trouble. But there was nothing I could do about it, save collect my passport and head to the airport. It was a tempting idea, but I knew I had to beat this threat, not run away from it.

I struggled through till lunch. I was just finishing a bagel at my desk when I heard heavy footsteps down the corridor. I glanced up, and in marched Mahoney, accompanied by two other detectives, and Gil, looking stern.

'Afternoon,' I said, as I chewed my last mouthful of bagel.

Mahoney didn't return my greeting. 'I'd like you to come with me to the DA's office and answer a few questions.'

19

'Have you ever seen this before?'

Mahoney was holding a silver-grey revolver. I had never seen it before. But I said nothing.

We were in the DA's office in Salem. Mahoney had given me a formal warning this time, and I had exercised my right to have Gardner Phillips present. Mahoney had brought in reinforcements as well in the shape of an Assistant District Attorney named Pamela Leyser. She was a well-groomed blonde-haired woman in her late thirties, very crisp and businesslike. I shook her hand and smiled at her. She didn't smile back.

Gardner Phillips had absolutely insisted that I say nothing. He was watching Mahoney like a hawk, looking for a slip-up in his questioning. He seemed competent and in control, although during our hurried discussions before the interview, he seemed totally uninterested in my attempt to convince him that I was innocent. He just wanted to know what evidence the police had and how they had got it.

'It's a Smith and Wesson three fifty-seven Magnum. It was used to murder Frank Cook.'

No response.

'Do you know where we found it?'

Of course I did. I'd seen them looking. But no response.

'It was in this plastic bag.' Mahoney held up a bedraggled *Boots* bag. 'Do you recognize it? I believe it comes from a British store.'

No answer.

'We found the bag with the gun in it in the Basin by the Esplanade. On the route your wife takes when she goes running. How do you think it got there?'

Once again, no reply.

'She threw it there, didn't she?'

Nothing.

'We have a witness who saw her running out of your street carrying something heavy in a plastic bag. We have another who saw her running back toward your house from the direction of the river carrying nothing.'

That sounded pretty damning.

Mahoney carried on, piling up the evidence against me. It sounded convincing. There had been tension between Frank and me over the way he had treated me at work, over money and over his fear that I was cheating on his daughter. I needed money to appeal the judgement in my sister's legal case. Because of the success of BioOne, I had realized that Frank would be worth several million. I had gone to Marsh House, argued with him, and shot him. I had hidden the murder weapon, but Lisa had found it. She had gone jogging with the gun in a plastic bag, and thrown it in the river before the police had had a chance to search the apartment again. She had protected me, but because of what she had found, she decided she couldn't live with me any more. So she had left.

I wanted to tell him that he had got it all wrong. Or at least half of it. But I put my faith in Gardner Phillips and kept quiet. The Assistant District Attorney watched it all, unblinking. Although she said nothing, both Mahoney and Phillips seemed intensely aware of her presence.

Eventually the questioning ceased and I was led along a corridor. I still hadn't been arrested, and I was technically free to go, but Gardner Phillips wanted to have a few words with Pamela Leyser. I passed a small waiting area, and saw Lisa sitting there, a middle-aged man in a suit next to her.

'Lisa!'

194

She turned. For a moment she looked surprised to see me, but she didn't smile.

I moved towards her. 'Lisa – '

I felt some pressure on my elbow as Gardner Phillips pulled me away.

'But – '

'You don't think it's a coincidence you saw her here, do you?' he said. 'It's much the best thing if you say nothing to her, especially here. She's got a lawyer. I'll talk to him.'

I left her watching me, expressionless, as though I were someone she didn't know. It unsettled me.

I was put in a bare-walled interview room, with a table and a couple of chairs, while Phillips went off to talk to the Assistant DA.

It took a while. I was scared. Shut in this room, still free in theory to leave, I could feel my liberty slipping away from me. The process was starting. Arrest could not be far away. And with it jail, a hearing, a trial, a media feeding frenzy. Even if I was found not guilty, my life would probably be changed for ever. And what if they found me guilty?

I was glad Lisa had stood by me. But she was the one person I really needed to talk to about this, the person on whom I had learned to rely over the last couple of years. If I had felt she truly were on my side, all this would have been much more bearable. But she wasn't. Her reluctance to help the police stemmed from the last vestiges of loyalty to me, and scraps of doubt, rather than the total belief in me that I needed.

Eventually, Gardner Phillips returned.

'I've spoken with the Assistant DA,' he said. 'They don't have enough evidence to arrest you. It will be difficult to link the gun to you, provided you and Lisa say nothing. We can work on the witnesses who say they saw Lisa: one jogger looks like another in the dark. But they are close. Very close. I've agreed that you'll voluntarily give them your passport, and that I'll surrender you should they want to arrest you. That means I have to know where you are at all times.'

'Did you talk to Lisa's lawyer?'

'Yes. She's taken the Fifth Amendment, which means she has chosen to say nothing to avoid incriminating herself. Fortunately, she will also avoid incriminating you.'

'So what happens now?' I asked.

'The police will try to find more evidence against you. And believe me, they'll try hard. We just have to hope they don't find anything incriminating.'

'They won't.'

Phillips ignored my comment. I had the unpleasant feeling that he thought I had killed Frank. Or perhaps he just didn't care. His indifference was infuriating. What I wanted was for someone to believe that I was innocent. Only Gil had done that so far, and Diane.

Mahoney glowered as I followed Phillips to the entrance of the DA's office. 'You'll be back,' he said.

As I pushed out into the bright sunlight, I was surprised to see a small crowd of journalists waiting for me. Two bulky TV cameras were present.

'Simon, got a minute?'

'Mr Ayot!'

'Did you kill Frank Cook, Mr Ayot?'

'Sir Simon Ayot! Can you answer one question?'

'I don't know who told them about this,' muttered Phillips out of the corner of his mouth. 'Don't talk to any of them.' He pushed through the crowd, repeating the words 'My client has no comment,' until we reached his car. He bundled me in, and in a moment we were away.

He glanced at me as we slowed for a light. 'You did well.'

'So did you.'

He gave me a half-smile. 'Pammy Leyser hasn't given up, neither has Mahoney. I guess we'll be seeing a lot more of each other.'

'Do you think they'll arrest me?'

'If they find more evidence, most certainly. I didn't convince them that you were innocent. I just convinced them they don't have the evidence to arrest you.'

'And if they do arrest me, do you think I'd get bail?'

196

'We'd ask for it, of course. But in this case there would be no chance that you'd get it.'

'So I'd have to wait for trial in jail?'

'That's right.'

I suddenly felt cold. Jail scared me. 'I wish I could prove I didn't do it.'

Phillips smiled. 'You don't need to. All we need to do is make sure there's a reasonable doubt that you're guilty.'

I stared out of the window at the gas stations and shopping malls. That's all you need to do, I thought. But a reasonable doubt wasn't good enough for me. I was innocent, and I needed everyone to know it. In particular, I needed Lisa to know it.

I watched myself on television that evening, along with the rest of Boston. And I saw Pamela Leyser being interviewed. She said she was confident of an arrest in the next few days. An Assistant District Attorney wouldn't say that unless she was pretty sure, I thought.

Gardner Phillips had said that if they arrested me, I would have to wait for the trial in jail. Presumably that would be a local jail with other remand prisoners. I could just about handle that, I thought, provided I was let go at the end. But what if I wasn't? What if they found me guilty and sent me to one of those high security jails for convicted murderers? American jails scared the hell out of me. I had seen the films, read the magazine articles. The privations of my Sandhurst training would be nothing compared with what I would experience there. In a community comprising gangs of murderers, where violence, drugs, rape and suicide were everyday occurrences, I would stick out as an easy target.

And if I was sent away, I'd spend what was left of my youth, and presumably the better part of my middle age, in prison. Everything I'd aspired to, everything I'd lived for, would be gone. Lisa, my career, all those experiences that life had yet to show me. Gone.

I went to bed alone and miserable, and for the first time in my life, afraid.

Daniel acted surprised to see me the next morning. 'So you escaped.

Shouldn't you be heading off to Bolivia or somewhere? The cops in this country are pretty smart, you know. They'll probably find you here.'

'They let me go,' I said.

'Why?'

'Technical problems with the evidence. They don't have enough to arrest me.'

'So you're not cleared, then?'

'Far from it,' I sighed. 'I'm beginning to think I might end up in jail.'

'So what? You'll be fine. A big guy like you. You'll make a whole bunch of nice new friends.'

'Yeah,' I said. 'I'm worried, Daniel.'

For a moment, Daniel was serious too. 'I know,' he said. 'Good luck. I guess you need it.' Then he tossed across a copy of the *Globe*. 'Here, have you seen this?'

There I was, on page four. They had a picture of Frank. *Police are receiving assistance with their investigation into the murder of Frank Cook from a man identified as Sir Simon Ayot, 29, a British national who was Mr Cook's son-in-law and his colleague at the venture capital firm of Revere Partners.* The article was very light on detail and long on speculation.

It turned out Daniel wasn't the only one who had read the paper. After about half an hour my phone rang. It was Connie, telling me Gil wanted to see me.

He was sitting behind his large desk, the buildings of the Financial District standing tall behind him. He looked grim. Spread across his desk was a copy of the *Globe*.

'I heard you'd been released, but I didn't expect to see you back here so soon.'

'I've got a lot of work to do,' I said. 'It'll help take my mind off things.'

'This doesn't look good, Simon,' he said, nodding down to the paper in front of him. 'Not for you or for Revere. And I understand you were on the TV news last night.'

'That's true.'

'I called Gardner Phillips. I asked him whether he thought you were innocent.'

'What did he say?'

'He said he took pains not to consider the question.'

'He's a good lawyer.'

'I've asked you this before, but I have to ask you again. Are you?' He leaned forward over his desk, his eyes like small brown balls through his thick glasses.

'Innocent?'

'Yes.'

'Yes,' I said, meeting his eyes. 'I've never seen that gun before in my life. I didn't kill Frank.'

Gil sighed. He looked tired. 'OK. I have to trust my judgement. I'm going to stick by you and I'll make sure the rest of the firm does too. But do the best you can to keep our name out of the press.'

'Believe me, I will.'

'Good.' He waited for me to leave.

I did so with mixed emotions. On the one hand, his obvious doubts hurt. On the other, he had been good to me. Revere's public image was everything to him, and I had tarnished it. The evidence against me looked damning, but he had still stood up for me. He had put loyalty to his employees, his trust in me and his own instincts, before what was rationally in the best interests of the firm, namely to dump me. I was grateful. I didn't want to let him down.

After lunch, I finished the Investment Memorandum on Tetracom, and circulated it to the partners. Then I told John I would be out for the rest of the afternoon at a meeting, and took a cab back to the apartment. Lisa had a key to her father's house, which she kept in a small bowl above the fireplace. I took it, walked the few yards to the Brimmer Street Garage, and drove the Morgan out to Woodbridge to the scene of the crime.

Marsh House stood alone under a large sky of gathering rain clouds. A strong breeze blew in from the direction of the sea, flattening the marsh grass, and rocking the trees behind the house. Everything was more or less as it had been the last time I was there, the day Lisa and I had discovered Frank's body. Except for the Mercedes, which had disappeared, presumably taken by the police. They had finished their polishing and scraping, taken away their tape and left the house alone and empty. I wondered what Lisa would do with it. Would she keep it for its memories of life with her father, or sell it for its associations with his death?

I let myself in. I wore gloves. Whilst I assumed the police had finished their study of the place, I didn't want to add any unnecessary fingerprints for them to find later. I was nervous about coming here. The last thing I needed was for the police to find out I'd been here, and draw the wrong conclusions. But it was more dangerous to sit at home and do nothing.

The house was cold. It was dead quiet: even the grandfather clock that stood against the living-room wall was quiet, unwound. The imprisoned air had a musty smell to it, and a thin layer of grey film covered some of the surfaces. There were scrapings on the wooden floor where I had found Frank. Although the house looked natural, I had the feeling that everything had been picked up and carefully put down again.

Most of Frank's stuff was still there. Books, magazines, photographs of Lisa and Eddie, and even one of his wedding. There were two books on a table next to Frank's beaten-up rocker. A bird book by Roger Tory Peterson, and a book about the *X-Files*. Seascapes and prints of birds hung on the walls, as they always had done. I went over to his desk. This had been emptied. There were no papers left, no notebook or diary that might have given some clue of his thoughts before he died. Just a flower-patterned pencil box that Lisa had made for him when she was a girl, itself thinly covered in the grey-white sheen of dust. There was no sign of Revere.

I climbed the stairs. All the beds had been stripped. Once again, there was no paper in sight. Out of Frank's bedroom window, I could see the clouds thickening and darkening over the brooding marsh.

I tried to imagine what the house must have been like twenty years before, with the noise and bustle of a family on holiday. A small Lisa and a larger Eddie running up the stairs, playing on the porch, returning from an afternoon's swimming along the walkway across the marsh, hair wet, limbs tired, skin browned by the summer sun. But for the last fifteen years this had been Frank's sanctuary. The place where he liked to come alone as often as he could. It was a beautiful, peaceful spot. Why had he given up his family, I wondered. He loved his children. He seemed to at least like his wife. It was a mystery that had haunted Lisa, and one that I couldn't solve myself.

As I descended the narrow staircase, something caught my eye. It was one of the pens that lay in the patterned pencil box. I recognized it from somewhere, somewhere away from here. I picked it up. It was a maroon ball-point pen, with an acorn logo and the words OAKWOOD ANALYTICS embossed in gold lettering along its side.

I turned it round in my fingers, trying to remember where I knew it from. But it wouldn't come.

I took one last look around, and left the house, closing the door carefully behind me.

I climbed into my car, and drove up the dirt track that led a mile back to the road. The clouds were upon me now, and it started to rain. A number of houses were scattered along the track, nestling among the trees, with glimpses of the marsh. The majority were only occupied in summer. None of them had a direct view of Marsh House, but I wondered whether the occupants of any of them had seen anything the day he died.

The first house I came to was clearly locked up for the coming winter. The second was little more than a shack. It was guarded by the giant Ford that had almost collided with me that day. I pulled up outside, climbed out of my car, and ran to the door. I knocked. It was raining hard.

The door opened a crack. I recognized the old lady as the driver of the Ford station-wagon. It was clear she recognized me too.

'Good afternoon,' I said in my most polite English accent. 'My name is Simon Ayot. I wonder if I can ask you a few questions?'

'I know exactly who you are,' said the woman with a mixture of fear and resolve in her eyes. 'I saw you on TV last night. And I won't answer your questions.'

She began to shut the door. I was soaking in the rain. I put my hand on it, to stop her.

'I just want to – '

'You let me shut this door, or I'll call the police!' she protested shrilly.

I realized I was only going to get myself into more trouble, and so I backed away. She slammed the door, and I heard the click of a lock. I dashed back to the car, and continued up the track.

The next two houses were empty, but the third showed signs of occupation. A small car was parked outside, and some lights blinked out into the gloom.

Once again I braved the rain, and knocked.

This time the door was opened by a pleasant looking middle-aged woman, her grey-streaked hair pulled firmly back from her forehead. She reminded me of the doughty ladies you see in the rose gardens and on the public footpaths of England.

'Yes?' she said doubtfully.

'Hello. I'm Simon Ayot, Frank Cook's son-in-law. Did you know Frank Cook? He used to live in Marsh House at the bottom of the road.'

'Oh yes. Of course I knew him. Not well, mind you. That was an awful thing to happen to him. And you're his son-in-law? How terrible for you.'

I smiled. 'I wonder if I could ask you a couple of questions. May I come in?'

'Of course. Get yourself out of the wet.'

She led me through to an open living space with a good view of the marsh through the trees. You couldn't see Marsh House, but with a slight surge of panic I realized that you could just see the end of the walkway down to the creek, and the dock, where Lisa and I had made love what seemed like an age ago.

'Coffee? I have some brewed.'

I accepted gratefully, and soon cupped my hands round a

steaming mug. I sat down on an old sofa. The furniture was basic, but the room was clean and warm and very cosy.

'You're English aren't you?'

'Yes, I am. I'm Lisa's husband. Do you know her?'

'I thought I caught your accent. Yes, I do know Lisa. I've seen her around over the years. We bought this place about ten years ago. My husband works in Boston, but I like to spend time here, especially in the fall. I like to paint.'

My eyes scanned the walls, and I saw some reasonable depictions of scenes I recognized from the area.

'They're very good. I like them,' I said.

'Thank you,' she said. 'My name's Nancy Bowman, by the way. Now, how can I help you?'

'I wanted to ask you about the day of the murder. Whether you saw anyone strange hanging around.'

'The police asked me this,' she replied. 'Anyway, didn't I see they'd caught the murderer?'

Nancy Bowman seemed an honest, helpful woman. I liked her. I decided to take a risk and tell the truth. 'They thought they had. But it turned out they had the wrong man. I know, because it was me.'

'You?' Her eyes widened.

'Yes, I'm afraid so. That's why I want to talk to you. I want to prove that I didn't kill my father-in-law.'

The woman looked confused for a moment, as though she was considering whether to throw me out. She spent a few seconds looking me over with shrewd eyes. Then she decided to trust me.

'Oh, I understand. All right, let me see whether I can help you. My husband and I were both here that weekend. I do like to walk along the marsh, and I often walk by Marsh House. Ray likes to stay indoors more.'

'Did you see anyone?'

'As I told the police, there was one strange man I saw a couple of times that weekend. He seemed to be some kind of photographer, or perhaps a bird watcher. I saw him on the road out there, and down behind Marsh House. He seemed to be waiting for a bird or something. He had an expensive-looking camera.'

'What did he look like?'

'Young. In his thirties I should think. Short, but quite big, if you see what I mean. Not fat, just broad.'

'I see. And what was he wearing?'

'A T-shirt and jeans. I remember thinking he must have been cold standing still in just a T-shirt, but he looked like a tough fellow.'

'Have you seen him before or since?'

'No. Just that weekend.'

'And you told all of this to the police?'

She nodded. 'Oh yes. They seemed quite interested.'

'I'm sure they were. Did you see anyone else?'

'No. Not that I can remember.'

'You didn't see me, for instance?'

'No. But come to think of it, the police asked me whether I had seen a tall fair-haired young man. And they mentioned an old convertible. That must have been you, mustn't it?'

'I expect so,' I said. I stood up. 'Thank you very much, Mrs Bowman. That's very helpful. And thanks for the coffee.'

'Not at all. I do hope you manage to persuade the police they have the wrong man.'

'Thank you,' I said. I was touched. It was encouraging to have a stranger show such faith in me, even if it was just because I had an English accent and an honest face.

I left her, and rushed through the rain to my car.

I drove round Route 128 to Wellesley. Nancy Bowman's description was unmistakable. Craig.

Craig had been in Woodbridge the day Frank died. Craig knew Frank was opposed to further investment in Net Cop. I remembered that when I saw him just before Frank was killed, he had been smiling, as though he had found a solution to his problems. Was he already planning to murder Frank? Could he have been dumb enough to have murdered Frank in the hope that Revere would change its mind about Net Cop? With a shudder I realized that it was just conceivable that Craig when very angry might kill someone.

I knew how absolutely determined Craig was to make Net Cop succeed.

For a moment I considered contacting Mahoney. But I couldn't be certain that Craig had killed Frank. I liked him, and we had supported each other. I had to give him a chance to explain himself.

I turned off 128 in Wellesley, and drove down into Hemlock Gorge. I leaped out of the Morgan, and hurried into Net Cop's building. Gina, the secretary-cum-receptionist, smiled when she saw me and told me Craig was in New York. He would be in tomorrow. Impatiently, I drove back to Boston.

I was sitting at home at the computer, idly scanning the Chelsea web-pages, when I heard the key scrape in the door.

It was Lisa, and she looked angry.

I leaped to my feet, with a rush of joy at seeing her again, immediately tempered with worry by her expression. 'Lisa!'

'Can you help me with some cartons?' she muttered, scarcely looking at me.

'OK.' I followed her outside, where a man and a small truck waited. A dozen or so collapsible cardboard cartons lay in their collapsed state on the sidewalk. I took half of them and Lisa took the other half. The man promised to return in an hour.

'I take it you're not moving back in, then?' I said, tentatively.

'No I am not, Simon. I'm going back to California. Roger has offered me a job.' Roger was Roger Mettler, her old professor. He had been trying to entice her back to Stanford for years.

'California! But that's thousands of miles away!'

'A geographic genius,' she muttered.

I felt a rush of panic. At least when Lisa was with Kelly, I knew she was only a couple of miles away. But California! She'd be really gone. Once the time was right, it would take days, not minutes, to see her, to get her back.

'What about Boston Peptides?' I asked.

'Oh, don't pretend you don't know,' she spat.

'What do you mean? What's happened?'

'I've been fired, that's what's happened,' she said as she wrestled with the first of the cartons.

'No! I don't believe it! Why would Henry do that? It makes no sense.'

'Henry didn't do it, although I would have expected him to stand up for me. No, it was Enema.'

'But they need you, don't they? I mean you're responsible for BP 56. Boston Peptides isn't worth much without you.'

'Well that's not what Enema thinks. He thinks the company can do perfectly well without me. He says I don't fit into the BioOne way of doing things. And frankly, I think he's right. Damn this thing!'

She was folding the flaps of the box together in the wrong order.

'Here, let me,' I said.

'Leave me alone!' she snapped.

I left her alone. 'What happened?'

'I asked too many questions.'

'About neuroxil-5?'

'Yep.'

'What's wrong with it?'

She threw the half-constructed box to the floor. 'Simon, the drug stinks, BioOne stinks, and Revere stinks. If you're too stupid to see that, that's not my problem. Now let me pack my stuff and get out of here.'

'Lisa,' I said, taking her arm.

She pushed my hand away.

'Lisa, sit down. Let's talk for a moment. We should at least do that. Then I'll leave you alone and you can pack up.'

Lisa hesitated, and then sat in the chair. Her face bore the stony expression of misery it had worn since just after Frank died, the corners of her mouth pulled downwards, her eyes dull. A tear ran unchecked down one cheek. She sniffed.

I took hold of her hand and crouched beside her. This could be my last chance to keep her, but I tried to keep the desperation out of my voice, to sound controlled, sensible. 'Listen, Lisa. I know things have been tough for you. Very tough. But I love you. I want to help you. You must let me.'

Lisa didn't answer. She sat still and straight, the tears now streaming down her face. She wiped her nose with the back of her hand.

'We work well together, Lisa. We understand each other. Your life must have been hell over the last few weeks. You need me. Let me help you.'

'I need the old you,' Lisa said, her voice trembling. 'I need the old you so bad.'

'But you've got me.'

Lisa shook her head. 'I don't know who I've got, Simon. I don't know whether you killed Dad. I don't know whether you used me to sell out my company and get me fired. I don't know whether you've been unfaithful to me. I don't know whether you've lied to me. I don't know you. I don't know you at all. And it scares me.'

'Of course you know me, Lisa. I haven't changed. Ever since we met, you've known me all the way through. We are so good for each other. I love you, and you love me.'

Lisa shook her head. 'I don't know whether I love you or I hate you. I don't know anything these days. I just want to go back to California and leave all this behind.'

'Don't. Please stay.'

Lisa took a deep breath, fighting to regain control. 'If I stay here, I'll go crazy. I need to try to rebuild my own life, Simon. Now let me go. I'll come back and do all this tomorrow morning. Please make sure you're not here.'

She stood up, and headed for the door, leaving the mess of cardboard all over the floor.

Then she walked out.

20

The Red Hat was full. Someone was leaving as I arrived, and so I acquired a beer and a stool and started to drink.

Lisa was going. Really going. Not just across town but to California, two and a half thousand miles away.

She had said that I had changed, that she didn't know me any more. But she was wrong. I was sure that it wasn't me that had changed, but her. It worried me, but it also made me angry. She was holding me responsible for so much, when all I had done was try to help her. I hadn't killed her father. I hadn't cost her her job; in fact I had risked my own to warn her about the take-over. She had lost her own job by being difficult. And I certainly hadn't slept with Diane.

I drained my glass and tapped it for a refill. The barman was running a tab. He knew I was here for the long haul.

All this was so unlike her. The pressure was too much for her, and she wouldn't let me near her to help. It was so frustrating. I felt myself being torn, between anger and concern, a desire to let her go and sort out her own problems, and a stronger desire to keep her.

She had threatened to leave once before. Then everything had been so different. We had known each other for about six months, in a relationship that we both thought was fun but casual. Then, out of the blue, Roger Mettler had asked her to return to Stanford. At the time, Boston Peptides was going nowhere, and so she decided to fly out there and talk to him. She came back full of enthusiasm. We had dinner together. We were both bright on the surface, but underneath, I felt a deep gloom creeping up on me. I realized, almost to my surprise, that I didn't want her to go. But I couldn't tell her that. Her life was her own, we had made no commitment to each other, it wasn't up to me to disrupt her career.

So she accepted the job, handed in her notice at Boston Peptides, organized somewhere to stay in Stanford. She seemed full of enthusiasm for the new life ahead of her. I played along, but felt terrible. Then as we lay in bed together one Sunday morning, the time to her departure now measured in days not weeks, I finally spoke to her about how I felt. I told her I knew she must go, but I really didn't want her to. I will always remember the look on her face, as it turned from confusion to a broad smile. We spent most of that Sunday in bed.

She stayed.

And now, eighteen months later, she was gone.

I had to get her back.

I decided to leave the apartment empty for Lisa the next morning, and drove straight to Wellesley, calling Daniel at the office to let him know something had come up at Net Cop. Craig was pleased to see me.

'Hey, Simon! So they let you out?'

'I've got a good lawyer and their evidence didn't stack up,' I said. 'But I'm not off the hook yet.'

'That's too bad. Hey, did you know we signed the deal with the Bloomfield Weiss guys yesterday?'

I shook my head. Craig's attention span for anything outside Net Cop was about ten seconds. I wasn't surprised. That was, after all, why I had backed him.

'That's good, Craig. When are you getting the money?'

'Next Monday, according to Jeff Lieberman.'

'Great.'

'Yeah. We're starting on the prototype right away. I've been talking to Luxtel and – '

'Craig?' I interrupted.

'Yeah?'

'Do you mind if I ask you about something else for a moment?'

Craig looked a little annoyed to be stopped in full flow, but he nodded his head. 'OK.'

'Were you in the marshes at Woodbridge the Saturday Frank Cook was murdered?'

'Oh,' said Craig.

I raised my eyebrows.

'Yeah. You could say I was. Did someone see me?'

I nodded.

Craig looked thoughtful. 'Do the cops know?'

'Not yet.' They had no obvious way of linking Mrs Bowman's description to Craig. To them he was one of hundreds of people Frank came into contact with through his work.

'Good.'

I paused. This next question was a difficult one to ask, but I had to ask it. 'Craig. Did you kill Frank?'

He paused. Breathed in through his nose. 'No,' he said at last.

'Is that what you were thinking when you seemed so pleased with yourself just before he died?'

'No, it wasn't.'

'Well?'

'Well, what?'

'Well, what were you doing in Woodbridge?' I asked in exasperation.

'That's a little difficult to explain.'

'So try,' I said. 'Look, Craig. I'm the one who's facing the murder charge here. If you were there when Frank was killed, I want some answers.'

'I don't think you're gonna like them.'

'I need to know, Craig.'

'OK.' He shrugged, and moved over to a locked filing cabinet in the corner of his office. He took out a brown manila envelope and handed it to me. Inside was a sheaf of a dozen or so black-and-white photographs.

They were pictures of Frank with someone. A man. They weren't sexually explicit, but the nature of the relationship was obvious. In one they were holding hands. In another Frank's arm was round the other man's waist. A third showed an affectionate kiss on the cheek.

The other man was John.

I now knew what the word 'gobsmacked' meant. The pictures made no sense!

Or did they? As I thought about it, they did make some kind of sense. They explained why Frank had left Lisa's mother, for a start. They explained why we hadn't heard of any other relationship since then. A man as good-looking as Frank would have to work hard to avoid an entanglement with a woman. And it looked as though he had.

I now remembered where I had seen the Oakwood Analytics pen. On John's desk at Revere. I had used it to write his phone messages for him. And then there was the *X-Files* book that had been lying on a table in the living room: I knew John was a fan.

But could I believe Frank was gay? It had never occurred to me before. He didn't fit any of the gay stereotypes, except perhaps for a certain neatness in the way he dressed. And there was that holiday to Florida. I remembered he had been vague about exactly where he was going, but later we had realized it was the Florida Keys. A clue of sorts if you were looking for one. But I hadn't been looking for one, and neither had Lisa.

John was more obvious. Although we had worked together for a couple of years, I knew him much less well than I knew Daniel. He kept his private life very private. He had a mythical 'girlfriend' back in Chicago. In fact, I remembered Lisa speculating a year or so ago that he might be gay. I had disagreed, and then forgotten her comment.

Only two days before, John had told me that maybe it was time to tell his father who he really was. Now I understood what he meant.

A host of questions leaped to my mind. How long had this relationship gone on? Were they serious? It looked as if it was still going strong when Frank had been killed. And then of course the most important question of them all. Did this mean John had killed Frank?

'When did you take these?'

'The evening before Frank was killed. I followed him from Boston out to Woodbridge, and hung around with my camera. I got these pictures of them on the porch outside the house with a zoom lens.'

'And on the Saturday? Did you see him on the Saturday?'

'No. I came over about lunch time. John's car wasn't there. Frank spent most of the time outside working on a boat. He had just gone inside when you came along.'

'So you saw me?'

Craig nodded. 'I saw you arrive, and then I left. I figured his boyfriend was unlikely to show up and do anything photogenic while you were there.'

'So you didn't see who killed Frank?'

'No.'

I thought for a moment. 'Did you see anyone else come to his house?'

'No. I did drive down on Saturday night, but when I saw the boyfriend's car wasn't there, I turned round and came home.'

'When was that?'

'About nine, I should think.'

'Did you see signs that Frank was still alive?'

'No,' Craig answered. 'I mean, I assumed he was at home because his car was there, but I didn't actually see him. I just turned my car around and left.'

'Whew.' I put my head in my hands to think over what I had just learned. 'How did you know about Frank and John?'

Craig didn't answer.

'Craig! Tell me.'

'OK. I intercepted Frank's e-mail at home.'

'I didn't know you could do that.'

'I can,' replied Craig. 'It's not that difficult once you know how. Anyway, he was getting these messages from some guy called John that showed they were very good friends. They were supposed to be spending the weekend together in Woodbridge. So I thought I'd go up there myself with a camera and see if I could take any interesting photos.'

'To blackmail Frank with?'

'I didn't want money for myself!' protested Craig. 'I just wanted him to give the go-ahead for Revere to put in the investment they owed us.'

'That's blackmail, Craig.'

'Look. Frank had welched on a deal!' said Craig, his old anger returning. 'I had to do what I had to do.'

'No you didn't. Oh, Jesus.' I ran my hand through my hair. 'Did you tell the police any of this?'

'No,' Craig replied.

'Why not?'

'I thought I'd just get myself into trouble. I didn't actually get around to blackmailing Frank, but I was sure it wouldn't look good to the cops. And I didn't want to become a suspect myself.'

'But what about me? You knew I was in trouble. You could have helped me!'

'I thought about that, Simon. Honestly. But I thought what I had seen just made you a bigger suspect. I didn't believe you had killed Frank. But I didn't want to give the police any more evidence against you.'

'Oh, bollocks,' I said. 'If the police had known about John, that would have opened up a new line of inquiry away from me. You were just afraid of incriminating yourself.'

Craig looked uncomfortable.

'I'm going,' I said. 'Can I keep these?' I held up the photos.

'I'd prefer you didn't,' said Craig.

'I'll keep them. You've got the negatives. You can make some more prints if you need them.' I put the photos back in their envelope, and moved towards the door.

'But Simon. We need to talk about the prototype.'

'No we don't, Craig. I need to prove I'm innocent. You can worry about Net Cop if you like. Personally, I don't give a damn.'

It was nearly midday by the time I got back home. Lisa had already been and gone, taking her stuff with her. The apartment, normally so cluttered, felt even emptier and lonelier than it had before.

I pulled out the photos Craig had given me and looked at them again.

Had John killed Frank? If he had, why? It was possible that he and Frank had had a fight about something. But I had no evidence of that. And even if I had, John seemed an unlikely killer. But then, I just couldn't imagine John and Frank together in that sort of relationship anyway. Now I realized there was a whole side of Frank's life I knew nothing about, a side that might easily include a motive for murder.

What would Lisa make of this? We had no openly gay friends, but that wasn't by conscious choice. I knew she shared the liberal view that people's sexuality was their own affair. But when it was her own father? I had no idea how she would react.

I tossed the photographs on the table. I felt angry. Not because Frank was gay, but because he had deceived Lisa for all these years. All the time he was living this double life, and not telling her. That I hadn't known who he really was, I could live with; but that his daughter hadn't made me angry. His secret would be much harder to confront now that he was dead than it would have been when he was alive. Not only had he gone, but now Lisa's memory of him would be altered. She would see everything he had done in a new light.

I wasn't sure whether I would be able to keep what I had discovered entirely quiet. But I resolved to do my best to keep the photographs from Lisa for as long as I could.

21

Tetracom were making their presentation at three o'clock that afternoon. I had to be there. I arrived at the office at one o'clock, hoping for a quiet spell over lunch when I could talk to John. But he was out at National Quilt in Lowell.

Bob Hecht and the Tetracom management were slick. They had been to business school, they had made countless big-company presentations, and it showed. It was an interesting contrast with Craig's raw enthusiasm and absolute determination. I wasn't sure which approach I preferred – probably Craig's since it personalized the struggle. But Tetracom's method was tailor-made for a venture capitalist's investment committee. Even the bust of Paul Revere seemed to be listening in respectful silence.

Everyone was there apart from John: Gil, Art, Diane, Ravi, Daniel and me. Of course Daniel and I didn't get to vote. Art had arrived late back from lunch, a glassy look in his eyes.

When Bob Hecht finished, Diane thanked him and asked for questions. I checked Art, but he seemed absorbed in the bottom right hand corner of his yellow pad. Gil asked an obscure question about consolidation among Tetracom's customers leading to stronger purchasing power on their part and lower margins for suppliers. Hecht had a good business school answer; with a small smile I imagined what Craig's response would have been – 'Huh?' Ravi asked about threats from Far Eastern manufacturers. Daniel asked about the risk that the stock market might become fed up with communications stocks by the time Tetracom wanted to float. All good questions, all answered well. Diane looked pleased.

Daniel was just beginning to ask a follow-up question when he was interrupted by a low growl. We all looked towards Art, who was drawing ever thicker lines along the bottom of his pad, as though he were crossing something out.

Diane raised her eyebrows to encourage Daniel to continue speaking. Then Bob Hecht blew it. He smiled towards Art. 'Yes, sir?'

He probably thought he was being smart, bringing in all the decision-makers, getting their objections out into the open. He wasn't.

'Huh?' said Art, looking up as though he had just been woken. His eyes, which had been dull before, now glinted dangerously out of his red face.

'Do you have a question, sir?'

Art cleared his throat. 'Yes, I have a question.'

'And what's that?' Hecht's eagerness was wearing thin. Diane looked on in something like panic.

'Why does a chicken-shit company like yours have the gall to ask us for money?'

'Art!' snapped Gil.

'It's a fair question,' said Art. 'Answer it.'

'We believe that we have a unique . . .'

'Don't worry, Mr Hecht,' interrupted Gil. 'Art, I'd appreciate it if you asked a more specific question.'

Art looked at Gil. Looked at Hecht again. Smiled. 'OK,' he said. 'How many venture-capital investors have you been to see?'

'You're the first ones,' replied Hecht immediately. 'We wanted to go to the best first.' Diane smiled appreciatively.

'The first since when?' asked Art.

'What do you mean?'

'Isn't it true you went to a bunch of venture capitalists last year and they all turned you down?'

For less than a moment Hecht was struck by panic. It was no more than a brief flutter on his handsome, sincere features. But we all saw it. Diane's gaze switched sharply from Art to Hecht. Gil's crumpled face crumpled some more. Art smiled.

Hecht, composed again, answered the question. 'It's true that last year, before we had a business model that was up and running, we did have a couple of informal discussions with some VCs. Just to help with our planning, you understand.'

'How many?' Art demanded.

Hecht glanced at Diane for help. She didn't give it.

'About a half-dozen.'

'I said, how many?' Art repeated.

'Let me think,' said Hecht. 'Eight.'

'Eight, eh? And who were they?'

Hecht rattled off eight of the biggest names in venture capital, most of them West Coast firms. Diane's face reddened. She should have asked these questions. And so should I.

'I see,' Art said. We waited for the follow-up question. Art seemed to sway slightly in his chair. The silence was becoming uncomfortable. Eventually it came. 'And why didn't you go back to these firms when you had your model up and running, Mr Hecht? Was it because you knew they wouldn't give you money in a thousand years?'

'No!' protested Hecht. He surveyed the group of venture capitalists. He knew he was in danger of losing us. He sighed. 'There was another member of the team, then. He was a kind of non-executive chairman and he was willing to provide the seed money. I subsequently found out that he was the one the VCs didn't like.'

'Oh really? And what was his name?'

'Murray Redfearn.'

Art and Gil exchanged glances. So did Diane and I. It was clear that they had heard of him and we hadn't.

'Murray Redfearn was involved in a couple of spectacular disasters in the late eighties,' explained Gil. 'A lot of venture capitalists lost money on him. Our first fund even had a small piece of one of his deals.'

Hecht nodded. 'We only found all this out later. So we bought him out, developed the product further, and here we are.'

'You lied to us,' Art said.

'No, I didn't,' protested Hecht. 'I've just told you the truth.'

'But you lied to Ms Zarrilli.'

Hecht looked shaken. 'Diane?' He glanced towards her for help.

Diane paused. She had recovered her composure now. She had a fine line to tread. She didn't want to seem weak to Hecht or the investment committee, but she also didn't want to kill the deal. 'I didn't ask the question, Art,' she said, 'and I should have. But I must admit, Bob, it would have been nice if you had been more open with me on this.'

'Damn right,' said Art. 'Now why don't we tell these jerks to piss off and let us get back to work.'

Hecht reddened. One of his colleagues, the Chief Financial Officer, looked as though he was about to explode.

'Art!' snapped Gil. 'That's enough. Thank you, Mr Hecht,' he said, with a smile. 'That was a most interesting presentation. Diane will be in touch with you very shortly.'

There was an awkward silence as the Tetracom team picked up their presentation materials and filed out of the board room, followed by Diane. She led them to a conference room, where we had agreed they would wait for the committee's decision. Diane returned in a moment.

Gil was red-faced, glowering at Art. He set great store by the image of the firm, and behaviour like Art's was not what he wanted. He no doubt suspected Art was drunk. And he now knew his drinking could do serious damage to the firm.

'Could you leave us while we discuss this deal, Art?' His voice was icy.

'No way,' said Art. 'I have strong views about this deal.'

'I gathered that.'

'If I hadn't asked the questions, you'd never have found out the answers,' pointed out Art. 'And I'm a partner in this firm. I have a responsibility to investors. I have a right to be part of its investment decisions.'

Art was suddenly sounding coherent.

'All right,' said Gil. 'You can stay. What do you want to do, Diane?'

'First I should apologize,' she began. 'I should have asked the questions Art did. Thank you.' She smiled charmingly at him. He grunted. 'I still believe in the deal, though. So I'd like to ask for investment approval subject to checking out Bob Hecht's story.'

'He could be hiding anything,' said Art.

'I think he's probably telling the truth. But it'll be easy to check with the other venture capitalists. Which is what I'd like to do.'

'I can help you with that,' said Gil. 'I'd like to hear the answers myself.'

'Thank you,' said Diane. 'Simon and I have done a lot of work on this deal, and I think it is a truly great opportunity that any other firm would be quick to snap up if they had the chance. You've seen the management, you've seen Simon's Investment Memorandum, I'd like to get your approval.'

'You're not getting mine,' said Art. 'They're liars and scumbags, and I've never seen such an amateurish piece of work in my career.' He contemptuously flicked my memo with his fingers.

'That's enough, Art,' Gil snapped. 'OK, let's take a vote. Diane, I take it you're still in favour.'

Diane nodded.

'Ravi?'

Ravi had been listening to everything attentively. He did his best to avoid political posturing, but he wasn't afraid of making a difficult investment decision. And at a time like this, an unbiased investment decision was just what was needed. He took off his glasses, and began to polish them. 'I'd like to be absolutely sure that Hecht isn't hiding anything else,' he said. 'And I'd like to see the notes on the calls you make to the venture capitalists they spoke to last year. But provided those are OK, I think we should go ahead.'

'Art?' Gil turned to him warily.

'No fucking way.' Art stared at his Managing Partner belligerently.

That was probably his mistake. Gil was in a nervous frame of mind, and if Art had subtly played on that he might have succeeded

219

in killing Diane's deal. Frank would have known how to do it. But Gil would not tolerate open war amongst his people.

'We do the deal.'

I followed Diane to the conference room where the Tetracom people were waiting. Diane gave them the good news, and then gave Hecht a firm but polite roasting. She was trying to assert her authority at as early a stage as possible. Hecht seemed confident that Gil and Diane's checks wouldn't bring up any nasty surprises, and on that basis we started work on the term sheet.

We broke at nine for dinner. We went to Sonsie's, a chic restaurant on Newbury Street. Diane was charming. Although Hecht and his boys were pros, I could see Diane's technique working. She used a mixture of charm and firmness to get what she wanted. Rather like a good teacher in a difficult school, she managed to inculcate a desire to please her in the people she dealt with. She had Tetracom eating out of her hand.

We left at eleven with promises to meet up again at eight the next morning. I was walking into the street to hail a cab when Diane caught me.

'Simon, I know it's late, but I'd like to go through those financial covenants again – see whether we can live with management's figures. Could you spare a half-hour to go over the numbers now? I'm sure it'll help us tomorrow.'

She was right. It would. I was tired and I wanted to go to bed, but Diane was the boss, this was a deal, and venture capitalists didn't go to bed early if there was work to be done on a live deal. I wondered why not sometimes, but that was the convention.

'OK,' I nodded, 'I'll get a cab.'

'No need to go all the way to the office,' said Diane. 'My apartment is just around the corner.'

I gave her a sideways glance, which she ignored. I was too tired to argue anyway. 'All right,' I said. 'Lead the way.'

It was, literally, just around the corner. The electrician's daughter from New Jersey had done well. The furniture was either expensive and comfortable or expensive, antique and European. The art was expensive, modern and American or oriental. The whole thing was all very tastefully done, and very relaxing.

'Coffee?' she asked.

'Sure.'

She dumped her copy of the base case forecast on the mahogany dining table, and fiddled about in the kitchen area. I pulled out my laptop and crunched some numbers. She kicked off her shoes and sat down next to me. The legal documentation contained a set of financial minimum ratios. If Tetracom's management broke them, they would be forced to hand over most of the company to us. These ratios needed to be set at a level that was loose enough to be fair, but tight enough to ensure that we could step in before the whole company went bust. That was what we were in the middle of negotiating, and that was what Diane and I had to sort out before the next morning.

I knew Frank would never have bothered with financial covenants for such an early-stage company. His view would have been that the numbers were all fiction anyway. But Diane did things differently, and since it was Diane's deal, we had to do it Diane's way.

In less than half an hour we'd cracked it. I leaned back on the antique dining chair, and rubbed my eyes. 'I'm knackered,' I sighed.

'Such a quaint expression,' said Diane with a smile.

'OK, I'm shagged out then. Don't you ever get tired?' She looked as cool as she had during the disastrous Tetracom presentation several hours before.

'Sometimes. But the excitement of the deal keeps me going. Don't you find that?'

'I try. But no. Late-night deals send me to sleep. I think the Commonwealth of Massachusetts should pass a law that agreements negotiated after eight o'clock at night are invalid. It would save the economy millions on lawyers' fees.'

She smiled, and sipped her coffee. She suddenly seemed to be sitting uncomfortably close to me. Or too comfortably close.

'Simon?'

'Yes.'

'Remember in Cincinnati when we talked about the firm?'

'Yes.'

'Well, things are developing. And I think you should know how. Let's sit down. Can I get you a drink?'

'OK.' I was curious to hear what she had to say. 'Have you got a Scotch?'

'I'm sure I can find one.'

We moved through to the sitting area, and Diane produced a glass of Scotch stuffed with ice for me, and a similar glass of what was probably bourbon for her.

We sat opposite each other. Safe. She tucked her long legs discreetly under the armchair and leaned back, watching me over the rim of her drink.

'Art was blasted today,' she said.

'I noticed.'

'And it wasn't the first time. The guy has suddenly dredged up a drink problem from somewhere. He's sliding downhill fast.'

'Gil must have noticed.'

'He has. And he's worried.'

'Is he still planning to retire?'

'He'd like to. He's considering sending Art to a clinic, or perhaps postponing fund-raising for a year.'

'But that won't solve anything,' I said. 'Art would be a disastrous Managing Partner of Revere. He was pretty awful before this. But with an alcohol problem? Gil might as well shut down Revere now.'

Diane gave a small smile. 'That's an interesting point of view.'

'Oh come off it, Diane, it's obvious. You think that. I'll bet our investors think that.'

'As a matter of fact, they do,' she said, the smile still playing on her lips.

I remembered Diane's breakfast at the Meridien. 'I get it. You've spoken to Gil and Lynette Mauer about this haven't you? And other investors too, I'll bet?'

Diane didn't respond.

'Get rid of Art, and make you Managing Partner?'

Still no response.

'Do you think it will work?'

Diane allowed herself a grin. 'Yes, I think it will,' she said. 'Lynette is on board. Gil is wavering, but I'm working on him. But I'll need to build a team.'

'Yes, I see.'

'I'll need to recruit an experienced venture capitalist at partner level. And then there's Ravi, and you.'

'Me?'

'Yes. I need your help.'

'As a partner?'

'Yes. I'm sure you can handle it. I like the way you work. PC Homelease was a great deal. I think you'll succeed with Net Cop when the rest of us were going to write it off. I believe you'll be very good at this game.'

I sipped the Scotch, my mind racing. I badly wanted to be a partner of Revere. There was no point in going into venture capital unless you became partner. That was where the serious money was made, and where the serious decisions were taken. It was what I had wanted since I had joined the firm.

But I was wary of corporate politics. Diane was drawing me in, trying to get me to support her. Against Art. That was OK. Against Gil wouldn't be.

'You're hesitating,' said Diane.

'Oh, sorry. It sounds a great opportunity. I was just thinking it through. I don't want to become involved in some coup against Gil. I owe that man a lot.'

'He is a good man,' said Diane. 'And he likes you too. Art is putting a lot of pressure on him to fire you. But Gil wants to keep you on. So do I, of course.'

So Art wanted to get rid of me? Somehow I wasn't surprised. During our conversation the previous weekend he had seemed to trust me. But after avoiding me for a couple of days he was back to his old self. I hadn't appreciated that crack about my memo.

'Don't worry,' she continued. 'Gil and I are on the same side.'

'What about the police investigation?' I asked. 'Do you really want to have a suspected murderer as a partner?'

'I know you didn't kill Frank,' said Diane smiling. 'Eventually, so will everyone else. It will blow away.'

I was impressed by her confidence although I didn't share it. I was also grateful. I had no right to expect such trust from her. Ruefully, I thought I had every right to expect it from Lisa. 'Thank you. In that case, thanks for the offer. What do I have to do?'

'Not much for now. Make good investments, avoid bad ones, sort out Net Cop . . .'

'And keep myself out of jail.'

Diane winced. 'That would be nice if you can manage it. The main thing is, I need to know I can count on your support when I need it.'

'You've got it.'

She gave me a smile that warmed my tired body.

'So who did kill Frank?' she asked. 'Do you have any idea?'

'No. The police still think I did it, and they're doing their best to put a case together against me.'

'I know,' Diane said. 'They seemed to think there was something going on between us.' Her eyes twinkled in amusement.

I tried to keep cool. 'Yes. That's what Frank suspected. We had a row about it before he died.'

The amusement left her face, to be replaced by sympathy. 'You must have had an awful time. Frank dying. The police on your back. Your wife leaving you.'

I glanced up quickly towards her.

'It hasn't been great.'

'I know this is none of my business,' Diane said, 'but how could she leave you when you are in so much trouble?'

I stuttered an excuse. 'She was under a lot of pressure. She thought I'd killed her father. I can understand what she did.'

It was all true, but as I was saying it I felt a surge of anger. Diane was right. Lisa should have stayed with me!

'You look miserable. Let me get you another drink.'

I should have protested, but I didn't. My guard was dropping. Lisa had pissed off to California; why shouldn't I have another drink with a beautiful woman who was listening to me?

Diane disappeared, and returned with another glass. Somehow she had put some music on, Mozart or something. She sat down next to me on the sofa.

'Cheers,' she said.

I swallowed my whisky.

'Relax, Simon. You need to relax.'

Slowly she leaned over and pulled at my tie, taking it off. She let her hand rest against my leg. Her presence next to me was overpowering. Her scent, which a moment ago had seemed so subtle, flowed over me. I could hear the rustle of her silk blouse next to me. I turned to look at her. Small delicate face, flawless skin, full lips slightly apart. She leaned over and kissed me. It was a soft gentle kiss, safe, yet promising much more. I responded. I wanted much more.

She stood up, and smiled at me. 'Come on,' she said, slowly moving towards a closed door off the hallway.

I stood up, and began to follow her. Then the muzzy feeling of warm relaxation snapped. I suddenly saw what I was doing with complete clarity.

'No,' I said.

She stopped and raised an eyebrow, the smile still on her lips.

'Look, I'm sorry, Diane. This isn't right. I've got to go. Now.'

I turned, grabbed my tie and searched for my jacket and briefcase.

Diane leaned against the wall. 'Stay, Simon,' she said quietly. 'You know you want to. Stay.'

'I'm sorry. I just can't. It's not you. It's . . .' I blurted, unable to string together a coherent explanation of why I wanted to go. But I knew I had to leave.

I found all my stuff, and rushed for the door. ''Bye, Diane,' I said, and ran.

22

I was ten minutes late for the meeting. Everyone was as fresh as a daisy, except me. Diane treated me as though we hadn't been entwined on her sofa only a very few hours before.

I couldn't concentrate. I just wanted to get out of there and think. Once again I was following in my father's footsteps. I had meant my marriage vows when I had made them seven months before. Yet I had come very close to breaking them in less than a year.

The meeting ended at eleven to give the Tetracom people time to get to the airport for their flight back to Cincinnati. I didn't join Diane on the brief walk back to the office. Instead I headed for the Public Garden. I gave her no reason. I don't know what she thought.

It was a bright, brittle late-autumn day. A cool breeze brushed the trees, which tossed handfuls of yellow leaves to the ground in its wake. The sun was shining, but it scarcely warmed the air. Winter was not far off.

Had I really done anything wrong? Lisa had abandoned me to the police. She had rejected my support. She didn't deserve my loyalty. The marriage was over, she had implied that. Well, she could take the consequences if something did start between Diane and me.

I sat down on a bench by the lake, Boston's mini-Serpentine. Tufted ducks drifted through the fronds beneath the willow opposite me, cruising for breadcrumbs, while the upper floors of the Ritz-Carlton Hotel poked out above. I raised my face to the sun and closed my eyes.

I could feel my marriage slipping away. It wasn't surprising, it had happened to my parents, and to Lisa's, and to millions of people in Britain and America. I could quite easily let it slide: there was nothing to stop me sleeping with whomever I wished as often as I wished.

But what I really wanted was to get Lisa back. It would be difficult to do. I might receive no help from her, quite the opposite. I might have to swallow my pride, forgive her for walking out on me, forgive her for the things she had said and would say in the future. And I would have to make her believe that I hadn't murdered her father. All this would be difficult to do, maybe impossible.

Was she worth it?

I remembered her voice, her face, her laugh.

Yes, yes, yes!

I hadn't been back at my desk for more than five minutes when my phone rang. It was Diane. She wanted to see me.

I entered her office with trepidation. But she gave me a friendly smile, and immediately launched into a discussion about Tetracom. Gil had made two calls that morning to venture capitalists who backed up Hecht's story. They wouldn't touch Murray Redfearn with the proverbial ten-foot pole. One of them questioned Hecht's judgement for linking up with Redfearn in the first place. A fair point, but not enough to sink the deal. The remaining calls were to the West Coast, and they would have to wait a couple of hours, but Diane was now confident that Tetracom's cupboard was bare of skeletons. A deal was probably less than a week away.

Our conversation finished, I stood up to go. I was almost out of there, when Diane stopped me.

'Simon?'

'Yes.'

'About last night.'

'Um . . .'

She held up her hand. 'No, it's OK, I don't want to talk about it now. But why don't you buy me a drink sometime?'

'I'm not sure that's a good idea,' I said.

'Oh, come on,' Diane said, with a reasonable smile. 'You owe me at least that.'

She was right. I smiled quickly. 'Yes, of course.'

'Good. Friday?'

'Fine.'

'OK. Thanks for your help, Simon,' she said, and I was gone.

As I returned to my desk, I wondered what Diane was up to, what she wanted. Her reputation suggested she was used to conducting inter-office affairs. She certainly seemed to know how to handle them professionally. But what about me? Was she just in it for the sex? Was she looking for a toy-boy? Did she get a kick from snagging married men?

But despite her reputation, I had difficulty thinking of her as that cynical. We genuinely liked each other. There was an undeniable physical attraction between us. For my part, I didn't know whether it had always lurked there unacknowledged, or whether it had only developed after Lisa's departure. I wondered how Diane would take me pulling back. Perhaps it would harm my chances of making partner in the new regime? Well, if it did, that was just tough. It would serve me right. I had been wrong to go as far as I had with her, and I wouldn't do it again.

I wasn't looking forward to Friday.

I faced the work in front of me, and closed my eyes. How could I have let things go so far? Sure, we hadn't had sex, but we had come very close. How could I have jeopardized even further a marriage that I was fighting so hard to save? Even if Lisa never found out, I would always know. It would be something lurking between us, threatening to flare up at any time.

No. I would never, ever let anything like that happen again.

'What's up, Simon?'

It was Daniel, looking at me with extreme curiosity. 'Don't ask,' I replied. I glanced over to John's empty desk. There was a lot I needed to talk to him about. 'Where's John?'

'Out at National Quilt all day,' Daniel answered. 'He left a number.'

'That's OK,' I said. 'It will wait.'

I checked my e-mails. There was one from Connie saying I was invited to Gil's club for a drink at seven that evening. My first thought was panic. Gil had somehow found out about me and Diane. But it was extremely unlikely that Gil would choose that venue for a dressing down. I had never been invited to Gil's club before, and I didn't think the other two associates had either, although I knew Frank had been a number of times. I wondered what it was he wanted to talk to me about.

The Devonshire Club was almost empty. It was still early, only seven o'clock, and I was tucking into a beer and a huge array of crisps and nuts, dishes of which had been perched on the small table in front of me. The bar was small and cosy, red and leather. A comprehensive collection of obscure single malts guarded the entrance. The atmosphere was similar to a London club, a carefully contrived balance that made members feel at home, and guests feel slightly awkward. The club reeked of class, social exclusion, and, because this was America, not Britain, money.

Three men in suits and striped ties came and sat at the table next to me. Two sported beards the like of which you hardly see these days, full bushy affairs. If the men were born in the early nineteen fifties, their beards were at least sixty years older.

Gil arrived exactly ten minutes late. He shook my hand, sat down and caught the waiter's eye for a martini.

'Thanks for coming, Simon,' he said. 'How are you holding up?'

'OK, I suppose.'

'I'm sorry about Lisa being let go. How is she taking it?'

'Not well, I'm afraid. She's gone to California.'

Gil's weary brow furrowed in sympathy. 'Oh, I am sorry. But it really would have been inappropriate if Art had intervened to keep her on. I'm sure you understand.'

I didn't answer. Gil wouldn't want to hear my opinion that it was more likely Art had already intervened to get her fired. He thought personal enmity between Revere people just didn't exist. When faced with it, he always looked decisively the other way.

The martini came. 'Simon, I wanted to talk to you about the future of the partnership.'

'Oh, yes?'

'Yes. You may have heard, I'm planning to pull back from my involvement in Revere.'

'I had guessed that.'

Gil smiled. 'It's a small place. Word gets around. Now, obviously I want to leave the firm in as good shape as I can.'

'Of course.'

'But with my departure there arises the question of succession.'

This was getting interesting. 'I see.'

'My intentions would have been for Art to take over from me. Now Frank has passed away, Art is the most senior partner, and he was responsible for the firm's most successful investment.'

I nodded.

'But Art hasn't been well recently. I'm not sure whether he will be up to the job. Which leaves two choices.'

He paused to sip his martini. Two? I thought there was only one. Surely he couldn't mean Ravi? True, he was an able investor, but he seemed much more interested in being left to get on with his own deals than in taking responsibility for the whole firm.

'Diane, or . . .' Gil went on, 'find a senior venture capitalist from outside to take over from me.'

That was an eventuality Diane hadn't considered, I thought, or at least not one she had discussed with me.

'I can't ask you to take sides, Simon. In fact I'm asking you to do the opposite. I don't want Revere to blow apart once I leave, so I'd like you to give me your word that you will continue to work under whomever succeeds me. You're a good man, Simon. The firm needs you.'

He watched me for a reaction. It was difficult. I had as good as promised Diane I would pledge my support to her if asked. Now that I was being asked, what could I say?

'Can't you stay on a bit until all this becomes clearer?' I asked.

'In theory I could. But my kidneys are in a bad way. I'll be on dialysis soon, my doctors tell me.'

'Oh, no! How soon?'

'That they won't reveal.' He snorted. 'I think they're scared if they get it wrong I'll sue. It could be six months or it could be six years. Whatever it is, I want to enjoy my last few years of mobility. So does my wife. So I need to sort out Revere now.'

'I can see that.'

'So, will you promise to stay no matter who becomes Managing Partner? At least until he, or she, settles in?'

I owed Gil. I didn't really owe Diane. 'Yes, Gil, I will,' I said.

He gave a tired smile. 'Thank you.'

I went straight from the Devonshire to John's apartment. He lived in the South End, in an apartment in a three-storey row house next door to a gallery and a real estate agency. Many gays lived in this neighbourhood, but then so did many straight professionals.

He was surprised to see me, but let me in. He had changed out of his work clothes into jeans and a loose cotton shirt, which hung outside his trousers. I had only been inside his apartment once before. It was nicely if minimally decorated. A wooden floor, a glass table, some attractive modern lamps and bowls. Science fiction posters proclaimed books or films I had never heard of, let alone seen. A large picture of a bullfighter adorned one wall. There was a giant TV, and several shelves full of videos. I couldn't help checking the room for signs of John's sexual orientation, but I wasn't an expert at the code. It all depended how you looked at it, I supposed.

We sat down. He offered me a beer, which I accepted, and then opened one himself.

'What a shit day,' he said.

'Don't you like Lowell?'

'I swear I'm going to torch that place if I have to go there again. Why can't we let companies die quickly? We're planning to file Chapter Eleven to protect us from our creditors. My view is we should just give the bank the keys to the factory. Then they can give away a free Ninja Turtle comforter to every kid who opens up a new bank account.' He took a swig of his beer. 'So. What are you doing here?'

'I wanted to ask you about something that might be a little . . . awkward.'

John stiffened. 'What?'

'I've been to see a photographer.'

'Uh-huh,' said John, carefully.

'Yes. He gave me these.' I passed him the envelope. He opened it, and took out the prints. His face froze. Then he closed his eyes.

'So?' he said, blinking.

'So I'd like to ask you about him.'

'Why?' he asked.

'I'm trying to find out who killed him.'

'I don't know who it was.'

I raised my eyebrows.

John let his face fall into his hands. I watched in silence. Eventually, he looked up.

'I loved him,' he said.

I didn't respond.

'We had a fight the night before he died. The last time I saw him was when I stormed out that Saturday morning. I just wish I could have left him on better terms.'

'I'm sorry.'

'It's been awful,' said John. 'The worst part about it is I haven't been able to talk about it with anyone. Or at least anyone who knew Frank.' He was desperately trying to hold back the tears.

'What was the argument about?' I asked gently.

'Oh, I'd been seeing other men. Frank didn't like it. None of them meant anything. It was just casual. But he didn't understand.'

'But weren't you and Frank . . . ?'

'Yes. But I think I was Frank's only lover. I don't think he really admitted to himself that he was gay until he met me. He was very uptight about it. I tried to persuade him to be more open, but he wasn't interested. I think he felt guilty about who he was. It's

232

something we all have to go through, and the sooner it's done the better.'

'Wasn't that why his marriage broke up?' I asked.

'Eventually Frank admitted that that was the reason, but he didn't realize it at the time. He just thought he had no sexual interest in his wife any more. I think he thought he was different from other men. That he was asexual.'

I couldn't really understand. But what John was saying fitted with the way Frank had lived his life for the last fifteen years.

'I was good for him, Simon,' John said simply. 'I made him realize who he really was.'

'Do you have any idea who killed him?'

'No,' said John. 'I kind of thought it might have been you, though I couldn't believe you'd do something like that.'

'The police think I murdered him,' I said. 'But they're wrong. I just need to prove that. Now, I don't think you were involved either.' This wasn't strictly true. I had no idea of John's involvement, but I needed to show trust in him if he was going to trust me. 'But we can't escape the fact that someone did kill him. I know Frank meant a lot to you. You can help me find out who that someone was.'

John looked at me doubtfully.

'At least answer my questions,' I continued. 'It can't do any harm, and it may help.'

'OK,' John agreed reluctantly.

'Was there anything Frank was worried about before he died?'

'Yes, a whole bunch of stuff,' said John. 'He was under a lot of pressure. And not just work pressure, either. He wasn't taking it very well.'

'What sort of pressure?'

'It started off with you.'

'Me?'

'Yes. He was convinced you were having an affair with Diane. He asked me about it. I said I didn't know, but it was clear you two got on awfully well, and you were working a lot together.'

'He gave me a hard time over that,' I said. 'He seemed to be going a bit over the top.'

'I thought so too. But you know how much he dotes on Lisa. And I think he was scared of the parallels with his own situation.'

'What do you mean?'

'Him and me,' said John. 'You see, we were having a relationship through work, which Frank felt guilty about. And then he found out I was seeing other men. He found that hard to take. I kind of feel that he thought he had messed things up with his marriage and then with me, and he didn't want his daughter to get messed up in a similar way. He brooded over it, I'm sure. And then of course we had that big fight on Friday night when he just exploded.'

'What happened?'

'He told me that just because I was gay, he didn't see why it was OK for me to be unfaithful.' John paused. 'I told him I could change. But he wouldn't believe me. He wouldn't give me a chance. So I walked out.'

'When was that?'

'About one o'clock in the morning.' John flinched, successfully controlling himself. 'And I never saw him again.' He paused, struggling to maintain control. 'He called me the next day, but we didn't resolve anything. Then when I called him back, there was no reply.'

'I'm sorry,' I said. I realized that John desperately needed comfort, but I couldn't bring myself to give it. 'What about Revere?'

John took in a deep breath. 'There was something there that was bugging him, too. I don't know what it was. We tried not to talk about Revere and the people there too much. When we were working together we'd talk about the deal we were working on, and outside work we'd try to leave it all behind. But something was eating at him.'

'Do you think it had anything to do with Gil retiring?'

'Is he retiring?' John asked, his eyes widening.

'Yes, he is. Sorry. I assumed Frank would have told you.'

'No,' John replied. 'That's absolutely the sort of thing we didn't talk about.'

'What did he think of Art?'

234

'He thought he was a jerk. I don't think they liked each other much.'

'Did he talk about Art's drinking?'

'I didn't know Art drank,' said John. 'You seem to know a whole lot more about all this than I do.'

'Maybe,' I said. 'I'm amazed the police didn't find out about you and Frank.'

'They did.'

'What?'

'It took them a couple of weeks. They found my fingerprints at Marsh House. At first, I said I'd been there working on deals with Frank, and they believed that. But then the results of some of the other forensic tests came through, which suggested I was doing more in Marsh House than just working. I never went to Frank's apartment in Boston, he was too careful for that. But when the cops interviewed my neighbours, they soon realized we had been together here. Plus, they checked Frank's computer and found some e-mails that made the situation pretty clear.'

'So didn't that make you a suspect?'

John nodded. 'For a day or so. But a neighbour saw me that afternoon, and I went out with some friends in the evening. So, after a while they gave up on me, and started asking about you.'

I groaned. 'Did you tell them anything?'

'Only the truth,' John said. 'I did say Frank was worried about you and Diane, and that there had been some tension between you in recent months. They asked whether Frank was frightened of you, or if you had ever threatened him, and I said absolutely not.'

'I suppose I should thank you.'

John shrugged. 'I was only telling the truth.'

'But now they know he was gay, can't they investigate that angle?'

John's eyes flashed. 'What do you mean?'

'Oh, I don't know. Another gay lover, or something.'

'There was no chance of that,' John snapped. 'I was the only man Frank was with. I told the police I was sure of that.'

'But you said you weren't entirely faithful to him . . .'

'Yes,' said John angrily. 'And that's something I'm going to have to live with. But Frank was different. That's why we had the fight that night.'

I sighed. Far from my discovery about John pointing suspicion away from me, somehow it only seemed to reinforce what Mahoney already believed. 'The police have kept this quiet, haven't they?'

'So far they've been very discreet. There's Frank's family to consider. Lisa.'

'They're right.' The fewer people who knew about Frank and John the better for Lisa. I was very worried how she would take this. 'John, can you do me a favour?'

'What?'

'If you think of anything that might help me discover who killed Frank, let me know.'

'All right. I will.'

23

John and I were polite to each other at work the next day. We both had our secrets and suspicions, and it was easier just to pretend that the previous night's conversation hadn't happened. Mahoney came in, set up camp in Frank's office for the morning, and seemed to be interviewing everyone but me. John and Daniel each took their turn. I walked past a couple of times and saw two of Mahoney's assistants going through piles of Frank's files.

I wondered what else he had discovered that I didn't know about. It had come as a shock that there had been a whole line of investigation involving Frank and John that I hadn't been aware of. But, despite that, from what John had said I was still Mahoney's favourite suspect.

Mahoney was doing better than me. I was stuck. True, I had widened the field of possible suspects beyond just myself. Now there was Craig, Art, and perhaps John. Gil and Diane were possibilities, although unlikely ones. Eddie was also worth considering. But having widened the field, I now needed to narrow it down to just one name. Frank's killer. And I had no idea how to do that.

Several times I had considered trying to join forces with Mahoney, but I knew Gardner Phillips wouldn't allow it. If I kept quiet and said nothing to the police, he would keep me out of jail. If I talked to them, I was on my own.

As far as Mahoney was concerned, I was guilty. His job now was to prove it. And I could see his point of view, especially once he had found the gun. He knew Lisa had dumped it in the river. Which meant I must have killed Frank.

How had the gun got into the living-room closet in the first place? That was still a question I was nowhere near answering satisfactorily. No one had been in the apartment between when the police had searched it and when Lisa had found the weapon, apart from me, her and Mahoney. Maybe the bastard really had planted it.

Unless Lisa had hidden it there herself? No, I couldn't think that. Couldn't even begin to think that.

God, I missed her!

Daniel came back into the office. He had been with Mahoney for about half an hour. He smiled at me.

'What did he say?'

'He told me not to tell you.'

'Come on, Daniel.'

'OK. He asked lots of questions about you. And Frank. Nothing specific. He was just fishing. He went through deals you had done together. Net Cop, that kind of thing.'

That was interesting. If he was checking out Net Cop, I wondered how long it would take him to link Nancy Bowman's description to Craig.

Daniel sat at his desk, and clicked a couple of buttons on his mouse. Then he let out a whoop. 'All right!'

'What is it? Don't tell me BioOne is up an eighth.'

'No. But Beaufort Technologies is off another twenty per cent today. That means it's lost almost half its value. I was short.'

'Good for you. I trust Lynette Mauer will be duly thankful.'

Daniel smiled. 'It was the Bieber Foundation selling their stake that started the slide.'

'Daniel!'

'What?' he grinned. 'It was an accident waiting to happen. I just nudged it along a little.'

I shook my head in disbelief as I watched him chuckle at his computer screen.

'Is money all that matters to you?' I asked.

Daniel turned to me surprised. 'No, of course not,' he said.

I raised my eyebrows.

'Well, maybe. But these days in America, you've got to have money. If you have money, people take notice. And it's got to be big money. A mill won't cut it. You need tens of millions. Like John's father.'

John looked up from his work, decided to ignore Daniel and put his head down again.

'I've just got ambition, that's all,' Daniel went on. 'There's nothing wrong with that. Tell me I'm wrong. Tell me a famous American who isn't worth millions.'

My mind ran through famous Americans: film stars, TV personalities, politicians, sports players, writers, singers, religious leaders. He was right. Even Mickey Mouse was probably worth billions.

'See,' said Daniel, and turned back to gloat at his computer screen.

I couldn't stand working at my desk, knowing that down the corridor Mahoney was asking everyone questions about me, so I decided to get the train to Wellesley and see how Craig was doing.

The place was buzzing. After so much uncertainty, the engineers now felt confident that their designs would actually take on a physical shape. For something so expensive, the switch wouldn't look very impressive. It would be a box about eighteen inches wide by two feet long. Most of the cost would go into the ASIC or Application Specific Integrated Circuit. This was a wafer of silicon with millions of tiny electronic connections. It was what would make our switches different from anyone else's, and it was ownership of the design of these circuits that would create the real value in Net Cop as and when it was eventually sold or taken public on the stock market.

We needed to hire more engineers to oversee the assembly and testing. Craig already had people in mind, but they had to be persuaded to jump from their existing lucrative posts. I joined Craig in the sales job. It was fun.

I was interested to realize that I was beginning to think of

Net Cop as 'us' rather than 'them'. I really did feel part of it. I was now a bit more sympathetic of the way Art talked about BioOne.

We were in Craig's office late in the afternoon, when Gina popped her head in. 'There's a Sergeant Mahoney here to see you.'

'I'll be with him in a minute,' Craig said. Then he turned to me and raised his eyebrows. 'What shall I tell him?'

'He knows about Frank and John Chalfont. John told me.'

'Shit. Oh, I forgot to tell you. I heard some more about this guy. He was an active contributor to NORAID. Still is, for all my uncle knows.'

I frowned, but I wasn't surprised. NORAID had been raising funds for the IRA for years. A supporter was unlikely to have warm feelings towards a British soldier who had served in Northern Ireland.

'Good luck,' I said.

'Thanks. You'd better go get yourself a cup of coffee.'

I left Craig's office to find Mahoney resting his bulk on a chair outside. His bright blue eyes shot up when he saw me.

'I'm surprised to see you here, Mr Ayot,' he said in a half-friendly, half-ironic tone.

'Net Cop is one of my companies, you know.'

'Ah, yeah, that's right. You and Frank Cook had some kind of disagreement about that, didn't you?'

I didn't answer.

I ignored him and stalked off to find someone to play table-tennis with. The Net Cop company facilities included a bare room earmarked for future expansion, which housed a table-tennis table and a competition ladder prominently displayed on a whiteboard. Craig dreamed of a weights room, but the company would need to get a lot bigger before he could justify it.

Mahoney was in a long time. I lost three straight games of table-tennis. These coders were bloody good. And my concentration was poor. I wondered what Craig and Mahoney were talking about in there. Mahoney and his men had been doing a lot of leg work. Had they found anything else that would incriminate me? It wouldn't take much more to get me arrested. I hoped Craig wouldn't give them anything.

Eventually I heard the sounds of Mahoney leaving. Craig came looking for me, and led me back to his office, via the kitchen, where he grabbed a large cup of decaf cappuccino. I had a cup of tea.

'What happened?' I asked.

'Well, you were right. When he saw me he did ask if I was the person with the camera seen down by the marsh. I told him I was. I figured there was no point lying about something he could easily check on.'

I nodded my agreement. 'So what did he ask you?'

'What I was doing there with a camera.'

'And what did you say?'

'I told him the truth. I said I was following Frank because he'd turned down Net Cop and I hoped I might find something to use as leverage. I said it was a long shot, but I was so mad it was the only thing I could think of.'

'Did he buy that?'

'Not at first. He tried to tell me I'd murdered Frank. Not directly, but he implied it. He made me go through my story backwards and forwards. I told him the same thing every time. And I explained that it would be dumb to kill Frank. What I needed to do was to change his mind. If he died, then the "no" would still stand. Which is what happened, right?'

'Did you say you saw me?'

'Yes. He liked that bit.'

I smiled grimly. 'And John Chalfont?'

'Yep. I figured if he knew about him and Frank anyway, it was best to tell the truth.'

'Did he ask for the photos?'

'Yep. I gave them to him. And the negatives.'

'Was there one of me?'

'Of course. I got a picture of you arriving.'

'But not leaving?'

'As I said, I left right after you arrived.'

241

'Great.'

'Sorry, Simon.'

I waited for Diane with trepidation. The bar at Sonsie's was full of young professionals and wealthy students limbering up for a Friday night on the town. Rather them than me. I had considered cancelling, but there was no point. Diane had to be faced some time.

She arrived only a couple of minutes after me.

'Hi,' she said, as she leaned over and kissed me on the cheek. Her scent overwhelmed me, reminding me of her apartment, the music, the whisky, her.

'Hi.' My throat was tight.

I ordered her a beer to go with mine. She seemed relaxed and confident in a bright blue suit with a tight short skirt. I didn't feel relaxed and confident at all.

'How have you been?' she asked.

'Busy. Running around trying to find out who killed Frank.'

'Have you got anywhere?'

'It's a case of the more I find out the more questions there are unanswered.'

'What about the police?'

'Oh, they're getting somewhere. Closer and closer towards arresting me.'

Diane smiled sympathetically and touched my hand. It was just a gentle pressure, but it sent a shock through my whole body. 'You've had a tough time.'

I nodded stiffly.

'Has Lisa come back?'

'No,' I said, pulling my hand away. 'But I really wish she would. I miss her.'

Diane withdrew her own hand and watched me.

I took a deep breath. 'I'm sorry about the other night. I almost did something I didn't want to do. No, no, that's not right, I wanted to do it at the time.' I paused to get the words right. 'I mean, something I shouldn't have even started. I want Lisa back very badly. And I'm not going to make the same mistake again.'

I watched Diane for a reaction. For a long moment she remained still. Then she spoke in a low, reasonable voice. 'I guess that says it. But if she's stupid enough to let you go, then she has only herself to blame. I like you, Simon. I think we could be good together. Just remember that.'

'Sorry,' I said. I didn't know whether Diane was putting a brave face on her rejection, whether she didn't care one way or the other, whether she was trying to show her interest without scaring me off, or whether, in fact, she just meant what she said. That was the trouble with Diane. You never really knew.

'So, what are we going to do about Revere?' she asked.

'We?'

'Yes. You and me.'

'I don't think I have much of a future there, Diane.'

'That's baloney. They'll find Frank's murderer eventually, and you'll be in the clear. Gil will retire, Art will be out of it, which leaves me.'

Diane's confidence was good to hear, although I wasn't even sure I'd be out of jail when Gil retired, let alone back at Revere.

'Lynette Mauer has told me she'll continue to invest in Revere, as long as I'm in charge.'

'Well done,' I said.

'Has Gil spoken to you?' she asked.

'Yes. He took me for a drink at his club last night,' I said.

She smiled. 'I know. What did he say?'

'Don't you know that too?'

'I'm well informed, but not that well informed.'

'He wanted me to promise I would back whoever took over, whether it's you or someone else. He seemed to have discounted Art.'

Diane's eyebrows shot up. 'Someone else?'

'Yes. He's talking about perhaps getting in an experienced venture capitalist from outside to take over the firm.'

Diane frowned. 'Hmm.'

'You'd better move quickly.'

'Maybe I should.'

243

We finished our beers in silence as Diane's brain whirred. I was thinking about how much I could trust her. I really didn't know.

We left the bar, and Diane set off on foot back to her apartment, while I grabbed a passing cab. It was still only eight o'clock when I arrived home.

I knew that I should appreciate my liberty, since it was looking ever more likely that I would soon lose it. But I was finding the waiting very hard.

I surveyed the apartment, empty without Lisa and her things. I hadn't heard from her since she had left for California. I didn't even know where she was staying: Kelly wouldn't tell me, and neither would her mother, whom I had called twice. I'd even tried her brother's number, only to be told I had dialled incorrectly. He must have moved. I had called Information, but they didn't seem to know anything about him.

I couldn't face the rest of the evening alone in my own apartment, wrestling with Frank, the police, Lisa and Diane. So I went out to the Red Hat. Kieran was there with a couple of the boys. The beer, friendship and laughter helped.

I came home late, and a little drunk. The answering machine was winking. One message.

'Hi, Simon, it's John. It's about eight thirty. I think I've got something on BioOne you might find interesting. Can you come round to my place tomorrow evening, and we can talk about it? Say about eight? Give me a call. 'Bye.'

It was too late to call him back, so I tumbled into bed, and fell asleep.

24

I arrived at John's building in the South End at ten to eight, very curious about what he had to tell me about BioOne. I buzzed his apartment number at the entrance to the building, but there was no reply. I was a little early. He had said eight o'clock, and I had called his machine back earlier in the day to confirm I'd be there, so he shouldn't be long. I decided to wait for him on the street.

It was cold, and I cursed John under my breath. Pictures of Provence shone brightly out of the gallery next door. I tried to go in, but they were just locking up, and the woman inside shook her head at me. A couple of rain drops began to fall.

Then the door to John's building swung open, and a man came out. He was thin with close-cropped dyed blond hair. A diamond stud gleamed in his ear. I walked past him, attracting a suspicious glance, and climbed the stairs to John's apartment, to wait for him there. There were two doors leading off the hallway on the second floor. A crack of light seeped out of one of them into the dark hallway. It was John's, and it was ajar.

Wondering why he hadn't answered the buzzer, I pushed the door open.

'John?'

I walked in. 'John!'

He was lying face down on the floor in the middle of his living room, a blood-soaked hole high in his back.

'John!'

I rushed over to him. His face, always pale, was pressed against the floor, a pool of blood near his mouth. His eyes were open, staring dully at nothing.

Stupidly, I felt his neck for a pulse, desperately asking myself whether I should try mouth-to-mouth or CPR. There was no point. His neck was still warm, but he was very dead.

I couldn't take my eyes off the body. I felt weak. Time seemed to stand still as my brain struggled to take in what I was seeing. I dropped to my knees next to him, closed my eyes, and put my face in my hands. An image of that other body I had discovered only four weeks before leaped in front of me.

What a horrible way to die.

I heard a noise behind me, and spun round, fearful that perhaps the murderer had been in the apartment all along. A black woman in heels and a tight dress showing through her open coat stood in the doorway. She saw me, and screamed.

'He's dead,' I said. 'Call the police.'

She nodded and rushed from the apartment. I heard the door opposite slam shut.

I looked around the living room. There was no sign that anything was out of place. No gun, nothing tipped over or scattered on the floor. But John hadn't been dead for long. Perhaps the murderer was still in the apartment. I didn't want to hang around to find out; I knew he had a gun, and I didn't. Besides, I didn't want to disturb anything at the scene of the crime.

I left the apartment and rapped on the door opposite.

No reply.

I rapped harder.

'Yes?' The voice sounded scared.

She obviously wasn't going to open the door. 'It's me. The guy who found John. Have you called the police?'

'Yes! They'll be here in a moment!'

'Good,' I said, and hurried downstairs to wait for them outside the front of the building.

They were only a couple of minutes. A squad car with flashing lights pulled up, swiftly followed by another. I showed them up the stairs, and waited in the hallway while they checked the apartment, and crouched over John's body.

Over the next few minutes a stream of other people arrived. One of them, a detective named Sergeant Cole, asked me questions about how I'd found the body, and then asked me to wait in the tiny hallway of the building. A uniformed policeman stood next to me as I watched people tramp up and down the stairs.

After a while, Cole came down the stairs again. He was small, with a young face, but greying hair. He asked me to come to the station with him so he could take a full statement.

I agreed, and we drove off together in an unmarked car. Within a couple of minutes we reached a police station, and I was led to an interview room. Half an hour later, Cole joined me with another detective. They were both businesslike but friendly.

'Mr Ayot, do you mind answering a few questions?'

'Not at all,' I said.

Cole smiled. 'Good.' He reached for a card from his wallet and began to read from it in a hurried monotone. 'You have the absolute right to remain silent. Anything you say can and will be used against you in a court of law. You have the right to consult with an attorney, and to have an attorney present both before and during questioning. If you cannot afford to hire an attorney, one will be appointed by the court, free of charge, to represent you before any questioning, if you wish. You can decide at any time to exercise these rights and not answer any questions or make any statements. Do you understand these rights I have just explained to you?'

This took me aback. 'Hey, you don't suspect me, do you?' I was angry. I'd had enough hassle from the police.

'You were seen right next to the body,' said Cole. 'We don't know what happened until you tell us. We just have to warn you before you talk to us, that's all.'

'But I can explain what happened,' I protested. 'I found him there.'

Cole raised his hand in a placating gesture. 'That's great. But before you do, I need you to tell me you understand what I just said to you.'

247

'I do,' I replied.

'And are you willing to talk to me now?'

I took a deep breath. I knew Gardner Phillips would advise me to say nothing. But I was sick of being the cops' favourite suspect. It seemed to me best to tell them what had really happened so they could leave me alone, and go and look for whoever had killed John.

'OK,' I said. 'Go ahead.'

Cole asked me once again to go through how I had entered the building, why I was there, how I had found the door of John's apartment open, whether I had noticed anything else in the apartment other than John's body. He took down details of my description of the man who had let me into the building. With a shiver, I realized this could have been John's murderer.

'What did you do after you found the body?' he asked.

'I left the apartment and knocked on the neighbour's door opposite, to check she'd called you. Then I went downstairs to wait for you.'

'Why did you do that?'

I looked at him blankly. 'I didn't want to disturb the scene of the crime.' Cole raised his eyebrows. 'And I could see John hadn't been dead long. If there was someone else with a gun in the apartment, I didn't want to be there.'

'So how long were you waiting outside?'

'Not very long. A couple of minutes, maybe.'

'I see.' Cole looked at me long and hard. 'Can you tell me how you knew Mr Chalfont?'

'We worked together. At a venture capital firm. Revere Partners.'

'And you were going to meet him for what? A drink? Dinner?'

'No. He called me yesterday. He said he wanted to talk to me about something to do with work. He asked me to meet him at eight at his apartment. So that's what I did.'

Cole had caught something in what I had said. A slight hesitation, perhaps. 'Something to do with work? What exactly?'

I took a deep breath. This wasn't going the way I had hoped. But they would find out sooner or later, so I explained to Cole about Frank's murder, and John's phone call. Cole's interest was quickened. His colleague was scribbling furiously.

When I'd finished, Cole smiled. 'Thank you very much, Mr Ayot. We'll just type this up, and then you can sign it.'

They left me in the interview room. Badly lit, bare walls, bare table, uncomfortable chair, and a smell of urine and disinfectant and cigarette smoke. There were two plastic coffee cups on the floor by a wall, one empty, and one containing a cigarette butt bobbing about in a grey-green scum.

I waited.

I wondered who had killed John. It must have happened shortly before I had arrived. Perhaps it was the blond-haired man whom I had seen leaving John's building. I wondered who he was. I was no expert, but to me he looked gay. Perhaps he was the link between Frank's death and John's.

An hour went by. I began to get impatient. I imagined typing a statement verbatim would take some time, but I hadn't said that much. The guy must type at five words a minute! I asked a couple of cops in the corridor outside what was happening, and they promised to get back to me. Having seemingly satisfied Cole, I just wanted to sign the statement and get out of there.

Finally, the door opened. Cole came in with the detective clutching some neatly typed sheets of paper. Following him was a shambling form I recognized instantly.

'Great to see you again, Mr Ayot,' Mahoney said, his eyes twinkling.

'Yeah,' I mumbled, my voice rough.

Mahoney sat down opposite me. 'I know you've already spoken to Sergeant Cole about what happened this evening. But we'd like to ask you some more about your relationship with John Chalfont.'

I wondered whether to call Gardner Phillips. But I was tired, and I wanted to get out of there. I decided to answer Mahoney's questions. If things got difficult, then I'd call my lawyer.

'OK,' I said.

'Did you know that Frank Cook and John Chalfont had a homosexual relationship?'

'Yes.'

'How long have you known that?'

'Three days.'

'How did you find out about it?'

'Craig Docherty told me. He'd taken some photographs of the two of them.'

'What was your reaction?'

'Complete surprise. I never expected it.'

'I see.' Mahoney paused. 'Did you discuss this knowledge with John Chalfont?'

'Yes. On Thursday evening. At his apartment.'

'What did you talk about?'

'I told him I knew about Frank and him. I asked him whether he had killed Frank. He said he hadn't, and that you had proof that he couldn't have been at Marsh House when Frank was killed.' I looked inquiringly at Mahoney as I said this, but he gave no reaction. 'He talked about what he felt for Frank. I asked him whether he had any clue as to who might have murdered him.'

Mahoney gave a half-smile. I bet he thought that was funny. 'And did he have any ideas?'

'No. At least not then. But he did leave a message on my answering machine yesterday night that he had found out something interesting about BioOne. He wanted to see me at eight o'clock tonight to talk about it. That's why I went to see him.'

'I see. Can you let us have the tape from the machine?'

I shrugged. 'OK.'

'Thank you. Have you any idea what he might have found out?'

'No.'

'None at all?'

I shrugged. 'No.'

'As you know, John Chalfont was shot in the back. There was no sign that anyone broke into the apartment. We think it's likely the murderer was someone he knew. Just like it was with Frank Cook.' Mahoney paused. 'Mr Ayot, did you shoot John Chalfont?'

I looked Mahoney straight in the eye. 'No, I didn't.' I thought for a moment. 'Anyway, if I did kill him, what did I do with the gun?'

Cole answered. 'You could have disposed of it when you ran outside to wait for the police to arrive.'

'Have you found it?' I asked.

'We're looking,' said Cole.

'What about the man I saw leave the building?'

'He lives there. He was just going out for the evening. When he got home he told us all about you.'

Mahoney spoke again. 'Did John Chalfont suggest that he had found something that could implicate you in the murder of Frank Cook?'

'No!' I replied. I turned to Cole. I'd let this go far enough. 'I want to speak to my lawyer.'

Cole nodded.

A spark of irritation flared in Mahoney's eyes. 'We'll talk later,' he said, and left the room.

It took a while to track down Gardner Phillips. He was at his weekend house somewhere or other. I finally got through to him. As expected, he told me to keep quiet until he got there.

Which took two hours, spent alone in the poxy interview room. At least it wasn't a cell.

As I waited for Phillips, my optimism that they would let me go slipped away. I began to panic that I would never see freedom again. I had been afraid I would end up behind bars for Frank's murder; now it looked like it would be for John's. If they didn't get me for one, they'd get me for the other. My luck was constantly running against me. And now Mahoney was involved, he would do his best to keep me in here.

Phillips had said there was no chance of bail in a murder investigation. At least I was alone in this interview room. But jail, real jail with murderers, drugs, violence, rape, AIDS, seemed much much closer.

Phillips arrived at last, wearing a jacket and tie and looking as cool as if this were a regularly scheduled meeting on a Monday morning. I was hugely relieved to see him.

I quickly explained what had happened. 'Are they going to let me out?' I asked when I had finished.

'You bet they are.' He looked angry. 'They haven't arrested you yet. There's nothing to stop you from leaving right away. I'll go and talk to them.'

He was back twenty minutes later.

'OK, let's go.'

'They don't want to keep me here?'

'They can't. They don't have enough evidence. They're as suspicious as hell, but they haven't got enough to charge you.'

'It sounded to me as though they were getting close.'

'That's the way they like to make it sound,' said Phillips. 'But they couldn't find the gun anywhere in or around the building. The gallery owner confirmed that you had tried to get in as he was closing up last night at eight o'clock. And one of the residents thinks they heard something that sounded like it might have been a shot at about seven forty. It just made no sense that you would have shot John Chalfont, run downstairs, made the gun disappear, tried to get into the gallery, run back upstairs to look at him, and then waited for the cops.'

I smiled. 'Thanks.'

'We're not out of the woods yet. I'd say you're still very much on the suspect list.'

'Great,' I said. 'I've heard that somewhere before.'

Phillips's voice became stern. 'You know you shouldn't have spoken to them at all. They can't make you go anywhere or do anything unless they're willing to arrest you.'

'But I thought if I told them what had happened they'd forget about me and go after whoever did kill John.'

'It didn't work out like that, did it?'

I sighed. 'I suppose not. Sorry.'

He drove me back to my apartment, dropped me off, and took the tape from my answering machine away with him to give to the police. I went straight for the shower, trying to wash off the evening in the police station.

That Mahoney had tried to tie me into John's murder didn't

surprise me at all. And I knew Gardner Phillips was right: he wouldn't give up.

Would the police ask Lisa about Frank and John? I had no idea how she would handle that except that somehow, I felt sure, she would hold me responsible.

Inevitably, the press got hold of the story. John's father was a well-known figure, John's murder a big story. It hadn't taken them long to link this murder with Frank's, and my apartment was soon besieged by reporters wielding notebooks and mikes. I braved them, giving them terse comments that said nothing. The newspapers and the TV bulletins were rife with speculation, but the police were staying tight-lipped about any connection between the two murders. Fortunately, they also said nothing about me.

It was only when the press had gone that the full significance of John's murder really sank in. Until then I had been more worried about the police and Gardner Phillips and the questions I was being asked. Now I thought about John. It seemed so unfair. He was the archetypal nice guy, friendly to anyone and everyone. Only now that he was gone did I realize how much I'd liked him. His relationship with Frank didn't change the way I felt about him. If anything, the knowledge that he had meant so much to Frank confirmed that he must have been a good person. I would miss him.

I saw again those dull blue eyes, the pale face, the trickle of blood, the absolute stillness of death.

A cold feeling of revulsion and fear crept over me. People around me were being killed. Seemingly normal, harmless human beings.

Like Mahoney, I was sure that the two murders were connected. And also like Mahoney, I suspected I might be close to the connection. But I didn't know how. For the first time since Frank had died, I sensed that my own life was in danger.

If Frank and John both knew something and had died for it, then I was in danger of stumbling on the same thing. But I couldn't turn back. Not if I wanted Lisa back. And I now had somewhere new to look.

BioOne.

25

Monday morning was horrible. The meeting was short. Gil, looking exhausted, said a few words about John's death. Everyone was stunned, even Art. Gil spoke about the difficult time we could expect from the press over the coming days, and urged everyone to direct all comment through him. Despite having read all the newspaper speculation, no one at the meeting mentioned me, for which I was grateful.

There were some desultory remarks about BioOne's stock price, which had slid back down to forty-one dollars. Diane reported on her checks with the venture capitalists, which had confirmed Tetracom's story. Gil said the Bieber Foundation were in the middle of their review of venture capital investments, and so far there was no news from Lynette Mauer on how Revere was faring. Then it was all over.

No one yet knew the full story of John and Frank's relationship, and I didn't want to be around when they found out. I left the office as soon as I could, barely exchanging a couple of words with the shocked Daniel.

I had work to do.

I took the 'T' to Central in Cambridge, and walked the few blocks to Boston Peptides. Despite its august new owner, the building looked as scruffy as ever.

I smiled at the receptionist, who recognized me, and asked for Henry Chan. He was with me in a moment.

'Hello, Simon. How are you? What can I do for you?'

He had a huge moon face with very large square glasses, and eyes that always seemed surprised. He had been born in Korea, brought up in Brooklyn, and educated at the best universities the East Coast had to offer. His huge head seemed to be literally stuffed with brains, giving him the aura of almost extra-terrestrial intelligence. He had tempted Lisa out of Stanford to join him at Boston Peptides, and since then had acted as a kindly, but quietly demanding, mentor. He was dressed in a white coat as always, and underneath it a shirt and tie.

'Can you spare me a few minutes, Henry?'

'It's about Lisa, I take it,' he said. His accent had lost any traces it might once have had of Korea or New York, and was flawlessly East Coast academic.

I nodded.

'Come through.'

He led me rapidly down the corridor towards his office at the end, looking quickly from side to side, as if he was scared that someone would see us. We passed the door to Lisa's lab, and I hesitated in front of it.

'This way,' urged Henry, and I followed him.

Henry's office was a box of paper and computer equipment with a small desk and two chairs. I sat in one and he sat in the other.

Henry blinked at me. 'I hear Lisa's left you. I'm sorry.'

'So am I,' I said. 'I also hear she's left you. Or rather you dumped her.'

'It's true, we have gone our separate ways,' Henry said coolly.

'Why did you do that? Didn't she do the important work on BP 56?'

Henry sighed. 'Your wife is a very intelligent woman. She made a tremendous contribution here. We will miss her greatly.' He hesitated. 'I will miss her greatly.'

'Then why did you fire her?'

'I didn't fire her, Simon. BioOne is a very different company from Boston Peptides. She wasn't going to fit in. That became obvious.'

'But why didn't you stand up for her?'

'There was nothing I could do.'

'Henry! You were her boss. You could have gone too. But I suppose you didn't want to lose those stock options.'

Henry Chan's bewildered eyes suddenly focused on me. For a moment I thought he was going to throw me out before I had had a chance to ask my questions. Then he took off his glasses and slowly rubbed his eyes.

'You're right, I do have stock options. But I did seriously consider resigning. The thing is, Boston Peptides is everything to me. I've devoted my academic career to it. My house is mortgaged to the rafters for it. And with BioOne's support, I believe I can make something of it in a couple of years.'

'Boston Peptides meant a lot to Lisa too,' I protested.

'Oh yes. I know it did. But when BioOne took us over we both had a choice: we could either fight them and lose, or stick with them and make something out of our technology. Lisa decided to fight. I decided to stick it out. Believe me, I don't like the way they do things any more than Lisa does.'

'What is it Lisa didn't like?' I asked. 'She didn't tell me precisely. She just said something about how the company stinks. She wasn't specific.'

'I'm sorry, I can't be either, Simon. Remember I work for BioOne now.'

'You've heard about Lisa's father's murder?'

Henry nodded, a slow downward movement of his huge head.

'I'm sure you also know that I'm the principal suspect?'

Another nod.

'Well, now someone else at Revere has been killed. And I think the connection between the two murders might have something to do with BioOne. I'm trying to find out what that is.'

'You're trying to prove your innocence?'

'Yes. But not just to the police. To Lisa. I need to get her back.'

Henry looked at me thoughtfully. 'OK. But what I tell you doesn't go any further than this room, and you mustn't name me as your source, whoever you talk to.'

'All right. Tell me a bit about BioOne.'

'What do you want to know?'

'What's wrong with it? I've heard some of what Lisa has had to say about it, but I'd like your opinion.'

Henry paused. 'I think what we both find most difficult is the secrecy. You see in an ideal world scientists would share their discoveries with their peers as and when they make them. That way the scientific world as a whole can progress much faster than any one scientist working in isolation. But this isn't an ideal world, especially in biochemistry. Even in academic institutions scientists are jealous of their research. They're constantly afraid that someone else will steal their ideas, publish a paper first, attract research funding that should be theirs.'

'I can imagine,' I said. Lisa had frequently talked about the politics of academia.

'Now, once you start talking about companies with stockholders and stock prices and patents, then openness of information becomes even more difficult to achieve. To successfully file for a patent, a company must show that its process or drug is not "prior art". The best way of ensuring that is to tell no one anything about it until the patent is safely granted.'

'But all biotech companies must be secretive,' I said.

'That's true to some extent. Although at a place like Boston Peptides we don't make a big issue of it. We're not going to do anything stupid to jeopardize our patents, but we're all here to find a treatment for Parkinson's disease, and if we can help other scientists without harming the prospects for our own projects, we will.'

'So what's the problem?'

'BioOne is different. Their whole culture is permeated with secrecy. It's extraordinary. There are dozens of scientists working in different groups who are allowed no contact with one another. All their research results are passed to the centre, and they are only made available to others in the company on a need-to-know basis. And it's set up so most people don't need to know.'

'Why?'

'Divide and rule. Create an atmosphere of competition and insecurity that will produce results. But most of all, it concentrates all the power in the centre. With Thomas Enever.'

'Enema?'

Henry smiled. 'I have heard him called that. He's the only one who really knows what's going on in the firm.'

'What about Jerry Peterson, the chairman?'

'I dealt with him when we were selling out to BioOne. He has no idea what's really going on. Neither does your man, Art Altschule.'

I digested this information. 'But surely some things must be made public? The company is quoted after all. And doesn't the Food and Drug Administration need data from the clinical trials?'

'Oh yes. The FDA needs truckloads of information. But most of that comes from the Clinical Trials Unit, which is the most secretive department of the lot. They report directly to Enever and no one else.'

'What's this Enever like? I've only met him briefly. Lisa said he got caught fiddling some experiment results a few years ago.'

'That was never proved,' Henry replied. 'He published some research showing that neuroxil-3 might reduce the production of free radicals in the brains of patients with Alzheimer's.'

'Neuroxil-3 was an early form of neuroxil-5?'

'More or less,' Henry replied. 'Anyway, other scientists couldn't reproduce the results, and a year later Enever was forced to publish a retraction. It caused a bit of a stir, but Enever was never shown to have actually manipulated the data.'

'What do you think happened?'

'I think he succumbed to the oldest temptation for any scientist. Wanting a certain result so badly that he fails to notice contradictory data.'

'I can see Lisa wouldn't like all this. But how did she get herself fired?'

'You know Lisa. She asked difficult questions.'

'About neuroxil-5?'

'Yes.'

'What was wrong with it?'

Henry leaned back in his chair as far as he could, which wasn't very far in his cramped office.

'I don't think there is anything wrong with neuroxil-5,' he said carefully.

'But what about Lisa? What did she think?'

'She badgered Enever into letting her look at some of the research data for neuroxil-5. She wanted to see whether it could be used to treat Parkinson's. Then she had some questions about the data. You know what Lisa's like; she doesn't stop until she has the answers she wants.' Henry smiled to himself. 'You have to know how to handle her. I guess Enever didn't have the patience for it.'

'So he fired her?'

'Yes. She didn't know where to stop. I tried to tell her to give up on it, but she wouldn't listen.'

'And what specifically was she worried about?'

'I can't say,' said Henry, looking at me carefully.

'What do you mean, you can't say?'

'Look, Simon. Neuroxil-5 is at the heart of BioOne's research programme, you know that. I can't tell you anything about it that isn't publicly available. Especially if it is only unsubstantiated guesses.'

'So you think Lisa's concerns were nothing more than that?'

'Yes. Lisa had tremendous intuition for picking up on a possible line of research. But sometimes she forgot she was a scientist. If you test the hypothesis, and find the scientific data doesn't substantiate it, then it's nothing more than speculation.'

I had had this lecture before, from Lisa herself, many times. It was ironic that she was the subject of the criticism this time.

'And the data didn't support her hypothesis, whatever it was?' I asked.

'Not in my opinion, no,' said Henry.

I wasn't a scientist, I trusted Lisa's intuition.

'Simon, I'd love to have Lisa here working with me now,' Henry continued. 'But things are different than they were when Boston Peptides was independent. I don't think Lisa would ever have gotten used to that. She's gone to an excellent post with Mettler in Stanford. I'm convinced she'll be much happier there. In many ways I'd like to join her. But I have to see Boston Peptides through. And with BioOne's resources I can do that.'

I stood up to go. 'Lisa had a lot of respect for you, Henry,' I said. 'It was just another one of those little hunches of hers that turned out to be wrong. Goodbye.'

Henry's eyes blinked behind his large glasses in surprise and dismay as I left him. I was probably being a bit harsh on him, but I didn't care. Lisa had needed all the support she could get. Henry should have given it to her.

As I walked back past Lisa's old lab, I pushed open the door and looked in. I recognized the jumble of benches, mysterious shaped glass containers, paper and boxes of electronics, none of which I understood. Half a dozen scientists were working in there.

One of them, a tall red-haired woman, glanced up as I came in. Kelly. She rushed up to me.

'Simon, will you get out of here! If someone recognizes you we'll be in big trouble.'

'OK, OK,' I said as I was hustled out of the lab. 'Kelly, can I talk to you?'

'No way. Now get out!' She propelled me down the corridor.

'Do you know where Lisa's staying?'

'Yes.'

'Where?'

'I'm not telling you.'

We were in the reception area. 'Is she OK?'

'No,' Kelly answered. 'I'd say she's not OK.'

'Kelly, I've got to talk to you.'

'No you don't,' she said. 'Now please go.'

So I went.

*

I waited for her on Mass Ave, near the deli where I knew Lisa usually bought her lunch. It was a bit of a long shot. I had no idea whether Kelly frequented the same place, or even when she went for lunch. I staked out the corner of Mass Ave and Boston Peptides' street at twelve, and read the *Globe*. Then I read the *Wall Street Journal*. Then a three-day-old *Daily Mirror*. Chelsea had won the previous Saturday, and there was speculation that they might topple Aston Villa at the top of the Premier League. It was past two, and I was just debating whether to buy *Business Week* or a *National Inquirer* when I saw her.

I buried my head in the *Journal*, which was the biggest of my newspaper collection. I decided to let her buy her sandwich and to catch her on the way back, hoping she wouldn't have any other lunch-time errands to run.

She didn't. I fell into step next to her.

'Kelly!'

'Simon! I thought I told you to beat it.'

'You did. But I want to talk to you.'

'Simon, you are very bad news. Someone might see us.'

'OK,' I said, and grabbed hold of her arm. I steered her down a narrow alley to the left, and dragged her ten yards or so away from the busier street. 'They won't see us now.'

Kelly leaned back against a brick wall. She fumbled for a cigarette. 'I told you. I can't talk to you.'

'At least tell me how Lisa is,' I said. 'You said she wasn't good. I'm worried.'

'You should be.' Kelly's eyes were hard. 'Her dad's dead. She thinks her husband killed him. She's lost her job. The poor woman's a mess. And from what I hear, you made her that way.'

Anger and frustration flooded through me. I turned and kicked an empty garbage can. 'Kelly, I didn't kill her father. I didn't get her fired.'

Kelly took a drag of her cigarette, ignoring my denial.

I tried to regain my composure. 'Kelly, you're Lisa's friend, and you have to take her side in this. I appreciate that. I'm glad she was staying with you. But you have to understand my point of view.

She's got it all wrong. And I *have* to show her that, for her sake as much as mine.'

Kelly was listening, just, watching me suspiciously out of half-closed eyes.

'I think her father's death had something to do with BioOne,' I continued. 'Maybe something to do with whatever Lisa was asking questions about. I need to find out what that something was. Henry Chan didn't tell me anything. You have to help me.'

'No way,' said Kelly. She dropped her cigarette and stepped on the butt. 'I'm not going to talk to you about BioOne. You're not getting me into trouble too.'

She turned and walked out of the alleyway.

'Kelly. It's for Lisa's sake, too.'

'Bullshit. You're just trying to save your own ass. And I'm not going to help you.'

We were in the road leading to Boston Peptides, Kelly walking fast, me keeping pace with her.

'At least tell me where Lisa is staying.'

Kelly stopped. 'If she wants you to know where she's living, she'll tell you. Now beat it or I'll scream. And I can scream real loud.'

Kelly was serious. I gave up, and trudged back up the road to the 'T' at Central.

26

I returned to the office to find Daniel recovered and ready to gossip.

'Hey, Simon, what's up?' he said as I entered the room.

'Hi, Daniel.'

'God, can you believe what happened to John?'

'No. It was terrible, wasn't it?'

'Did you know he was a fag?'

I felt a rush of irritation. 'No, Daniel, I didn't. He's dead, OK? It doesn't matter.'

I glanced over at John's desk. Empty. It looked strangely tidy.

Daniel followed my glance. 'The cops have been all over it. They took a ton of documents away. They're going to be very bored, I promise you.'

I walked over to the desk, and had a quick look through it. There was nothing of any personal value left. All his working files had been taken too.

Daniel was watching me. 'The cops were asking all kinds of weird questions this morning. Like did I know he and Frank were doing each other. Frank! Can you believe it?'

I sighed. 'Daniel, the guy we worked with for two years has been killed. It doesn't matter what he did with his personal life.'

'No, of course not,' said Daniel. 'But Frank Cook! I mean, did you suspect anything? He was your father-in-law.'

'No I didn't suspect anything,' I answered, letting my irritation show.

'I heard you spent the evening in the police station? I guess they thought you'd killed John because you were the one who found him?'

'Something like that,' I said. 'But they had no evidence, so they let me go. Eventually.'

'It must have been rough.'

'I wouldn't recommend it.'

'There's been pandemonium here,' Daniel said. 'Gil is furious. I think he's just as angry about John and Frank having an affair as about John getting killed. Luckily the press hasn't got hold of that angle yet. Art went off for lunch and hasn't been seen since, and Ravi looks like a scared rabbit. Only Diane is keeping cool. And me of course.'

'Of course.'

'I mean, people are frightened. First Frank, then John. It could be any one of us next. Actually, it will probably be you.'

'Thanks a lot, Daniel. That possibility hadn't escaped me.'

'Be careful, Simon.' Daniel's tone was serious, for once.

'There's not a lot I can do,' I said. 'But can you do me a favour?'

'Sure,' he replied.

'Can you find out some stuff about BioOne for me?'

'BioOne? What's that got to do with anything?'

'I'm not sure. You know Lisa was fired from Boston Peptides?'

'Yeah. Art told me. He seemed kind of pleased about it, to be honest.'

'Bastard,' I muttered.

'Tell her I'm sorry when you see her.'

'That's unlikely,' I said. 'She's gone back to California.'

'Oh,' said Daniel. 'Not good.'

'Not good at all,' I agreed. 'Anyway, she was fired for asking Thomas Enever some awkward questions about BioOne's wonder drug.'

'So?'

I leaned forward. 'John phoned me before he died. He left a message on my machine. Said he had found out something about BioOne that might interest me. That's why I went to see him on Saturday night.'

'But you never got a chance to talk to him?'

'No.'

'I see. So what might interest you about BioOne?'

'I don't know anything, that's the problem. Is there anything funny going on there? Anything that might lead to Frank and John getting killed?'

Daniel shrugged. 'Such as?'

'Something wrong with neuroxil-5, perhaps? That was what Lisa was asking Enever about.'

'I don't think so,' answered Daniel. 'I just do the number-crunching remember, but I haven't heard anyone talk about problems with the drug. In fact they all seem to think it's working very well in the clinical trials. They're pretty confident.'

'By "they", who do you mean?'

Daniel paused. 'Everyone at the company that I come across. Art, obviously. Jerry Peterson, Enever, the CFO, even Harrison Brothers, the investment bankers.'

'You don't think they're hiding anything?'

'It doesn't look like it to me. But I'm no biotech expert. I can poke around discreetly if you like.'

I smiled thankfully. 'That would be great, Daniel,' I said.

'Is there anything else you think might be the problem?' he asked.

'I don't know. There are so many things it might be. Fraud. Insider trading, perhaps. Perhaps something to do with the Boston Peptides take-over.'

'I'll see what I can do,' said Daniel. 'It'll be tough, though. Art keeps all the information on BioOne strictly to himself.'

'I know,' I said. 'That's why I'm planning to ask him about it myself.'

Daniel winced. 'Now that will be fun. And if he comes up with anything interesting, be sure to tell me. The more I work with him, the more I think it could be a laundry detergent company for all he knows.'

Art's door was open. I knocked. He was back from lunch, on the phone. A faint smell of alcohol hung in the room. He waved me to a seat and continued talking. Usual Art conversation. It was actually about a new deal. Something to do with a company that did special effects for Hollywood. That sounded like it would have a sky-high bullshit quotient. A great deal for Art.

Finally the phone went down. 'That is a deal we have to do,' said Art.

'Good,' I replied, not willing to be drawn.

'What can I do for you, Simon?' He looked at his watch. 'I've got a few calls to make.' He and I had done a pretty good job of avoiding each other in the week or so since I had visited him at his house. But I needed to pin him down now.

'It won't take long. I just wanted to ask you about BioOne.'

Art frowned. 'What about it? If it's about your wife being let go, I had nothing to do with that decision. That was entirely Dr Enever's call. What he does with his people is his own affair.'

'Actually, it wasn't about Lisa's job. I wondered if you could tell me something. What's wrong with neuroxil-5?'

Art's frown deepened. 'There is nothing at all wrong with neuroxil-5. All the trial results so far have been excellent, and we are expecting great things when the Phase Three trial results are published in March.'

'There's nothing wrong with the drug at all?'

'Why do you think there should be?' asked Art crossly.

'Lisa seems to think there's a problem with it. That may have had something to do with why she was fired.'

'I checked up on the drug specifically last month, when Frank talked to me. I went through it all with Dr Enever. There is nothing wrong with neuroxil-5.'

'Wait a minute. Frank asked you about neuroxil-5?'

'Yes, he did,' Art said, looking as though he regretted mentioning it.

266

'What did he ask?'

'Same as you. Was there anything wrong with the drug?'

'Wasn't he more specific? Did he mention any particular potential problem?'

Art raised his hands. 'He may have. I can't remember. All I know is that I checked it out and there was nothing in it.'

'Have you told the police this?'

'No. Why?'

'Didn't you think it was suspicious?' I asked.

'What do you mean?'

'I mean Frank asked you a question casting doubt on Revere's most important investment, and shortly afterwards he was murdered.'

Art shook his head. 'No, Simon, I wasn't suspicious. I saw no reason to be. Frank was playing political games. Revere is what it is today because of BioOne. My investment. Frank wanted to discredit me, and so he went for my investment. Trouble was, he had no evidence.'

I bit back my frustration. 'You're sure you can't remember what Frank asked you about, specifically.'

'No, I cannot,' said Art angrily. 'And let me tell you something. BioOne is at a very delicate stage right now. The last thing it needs is for someone like you to go around asking difficult questions.' He licked his lips, and jabbed a finger at me. 'If you go suggesting to anyone, and I mean *anyone*, that there is something wrong with neuroxil-5, I'll have you out on your ass before you can say lah-di-fucking-dah.'

I stood up. 'No, Art. If there is something wrong with neuroxil-5, I'll find it. And you won't be able to stop me.'

Art stood up, glaring at me across his desk. 'Don't threaten me, boy. BioOne is *the* most important investment in the whole damn firm. You fuck with BioOne, you fuck with me. Your wife asked dumb questions and she lost her job. You ask dumb questions, and by the time I'm done with you, you'll wish you were still prancing around on ponies at the Queen's tea parties.'

I turned and left him standing at his desk red-faced and shaking.

*

267

I made my way back to my office deep in thought. Art had a point: asking questions about BioOne was dangerous. Both Frank and John had done it, and they were both dead. It was too much of a coincidence.

Gil passed me in the corridor. His weather-beaten face was even more worn than usual. I wondered whether his kidney problem was causing him pain. He nodded to me curtly, his mind preoccupied, presumably with John's death and the press.

On impulse, I stopped him. 'Gil?'

'Hm.' He focused on me, his eyes dull through his thick lenses.

'Do you have a moment?'

'What is it?'

I looked quickly around me. There was no one about.

'Are you confident in BioOne?'

Gil looked surprised. 'Why do you ask?'

'It was just something John was worried about before he died.'

'Yes, the police mentioned you'd told them that.'

'Are you sure everything really is as solid as it seems?'

'Yes, I guess I am,' Gil said. 'That's not to say there won't be hitches, there always are. But BioOne is a big winner, it's written all over it.'

'Don't you sometimes worry that there's nothing there?'

'What do you mean?'

'The company has never made a profit. It's only real asset is neuroxil-5. What if that turned out to be worthless?'

'But it's not worthless,' Gil said. 'It's medicine's best hope for treating a chronic disease that affects millions of sufferers.'

'But what if there were something wrong with neuroxil-5?'

'Such as?'

'Oh, I don't know. The drug didn't work or something. BioOne would be worth nothing, wouldn't it?'

Gil smiled tiredly. 'You're right to be cautious, especially with biotech. It's one of the cardinal sins of venture capital to count profits before they've been made. And there are dozens of biotech companies whose drugs have been shown to be no better than a pill made of sugar. But that's not the case with BioOne. I have a good feeling about this one.'

'I hope you're right.'

'So do I,' said Gil, 'or else we really will be in trouble.'

He headed off back to his office and his problems, and I to mine. But I wasn't convinced. If only I knew what Lisa had discovered about BioOne.

I pulled out my address book, and dialled her mother's number. 'Hello?'

'Ann? It's Simon.'

'Simon! I've told you before. Lisa doesn't want to talk to you. She doesn't want you to know where she is.' Lisa's mother didn't sound hostile, more frustrated, as much with Lisa as with me.

'OK, I understand that. Can you just give her a message for me?'

I heard Ann take a deep breath. 'OK. Maybe. What is it?' she asked suspiciously.

'Can you tell her I want to ask her some questions about BioOne. It's important.'

There was a pause. 'All right,' she said reluctantly. 'I'll tell her. But she's very upset. I don't think she will call you back.'

'If you could just try, I'd appreciate it.'

'OK. I'll give Lisa your message. Goodbye, Simon.'

I put down the phone. I was confident Ann would pass my message on. I wasn't at all confident Lisa would respond to it. I couldn't just sit back and wait for a reply from her that might never come. But what else could I do? How could I uncover the problem with neuroxil-5 myself?

I stared into space for a few minutes, and then an answer came to me.

Ask someone who was taking it.

I took the train out to Brookline. I found Aunt Zoë's house and rang the bell. She answered in a moment with a warm smile.

'How nice to see you,' she said. 'Come in, come in.' She called into the recesses of the house. 'Carl! We have a visitor!'

269

Carl bustled into the hallway. 'Simon!' he said. 'How's Lisa?'

'Fine,' I lied, admiring the neat way they had managed to deal with Aunt Zoë's failure to recognize me.

They ushered me into the living room. The last time I had seen it, it was crowded with Frank's mourners. It still bore some signs of that day. The mirror on the wall was covered with black cloth, and a photograph of Frank as a handsome young man had been pushed to the front of a crowd on top of the piano. In fact, looking at Zoë now, I could see a resemblance to her brother: she was tall, long limbed, with the same kindly hazel eyes. There was something warm and approachable about her. I saw why she was Lisa's favourite aunt.

Zoë made us all coffee, and I indulged in small talk with the two of them. I said Lisa was in California doing some research work, and left it at that. I had been lucky to catch Carl, apparently he was just leaving for the College. I was glad of his presence, although Zoë seemed to have no problems following the conversation at all. Apart from her initial well-disguised confusion over who I was, there was no sign that her brain was steadily decaying.

After a few minutes I steered the conversation round to the purpose of my visit.

'You remember my firm backed BioOne, the company that makes neuroxil-5?' I began.

'Oh, yes,' said Carl.

'I wondered if you had noticed any problems since Zoë started taking it?'

'I don't think so, do you dear?' said Carl, turning to Zoë.

'No,' she said. 'I have to go to the hospital pretty frequently so they can check up on me. But they haven't come across anything out of the ordinary, at least nothing they've told me about. Ever since Lisa called, I've been keeping a good look out for any problems, but I feel fine. And the good news is that I don't seem to be getting any worse up here.' She tapped her temple.

'That is good news,' I said, sipping my coffee. 'You said Lisa called you?'

'Yes,' said Carl. 'Last week. I assumed that was why you were here.'

'Er, no.' I said. 'As I mentioned, she's in California at the moment. She didn't tell me she'd spoken to you.' I smiled nervously. 'Breakdown in communication.'

Carl looked at me oddly for a moment. 'She said she wasn't sure, but she was worried that neuroxil-5 could have some dangerous side-effects. When I pressed her on it, she said she couldn't be specific. It sounded more like a hunch. Zoë and I talked it over with our doctor, and we decided that we'd carry on with the drug. I mean it's working in Zoë's case, and the doctor assured us that the FDA monitors these trials very thoroughly, so if there was a dangerous side-effect, they'd let him know.'

'Do *you* know something, Simon?' Zoë asked, a brief look of worry crossing her face.

I paused, pondering how to answer the question. 'Not really. It's just a suspicion from things I've seen at work. But I don't have any hard evidence, no.'

'Do you know what this side-effect might be?' Zoë asked.

I shook my head. 'No. Sorry. That was why I wondered whether you had noticed anything.'

Zoë turned to her husband. 'I don't know, Carl. Maybe I should stop taking the stuff.'

Carl took his wife's hands. 'When Frank introduced you to this drug, it gave us some hope that we might be able to beat this disease. I don't want to give up on that hope. Sure, it might not work. It might even be dangerous. But it's the best shot we've got.'

Zoë looked at her husband and turned to Simon. 'Carl's right. I don't want to lose any more of my marbles.' She smiled faintly at her own joke. 'But you will let us know if you discover anything more, won't you?'

I promised I would, and left.

27

I walked home that evening. It was clear, cold and windy. I buttoned up my jacket and hunched my shoulders. Everyone else I passed was wearing a coat. I had held out that morning, but it would be an overcoat from now until the spring. That seemed a long way away.

I wondered whether I would be walking through the Common next spring, or whether I would be sitting it out in jail somewhere, waiting for my trial. And would Lisa be waiting with me, or would she still be thousands of miles away in California, settling in to her new life?

She had said there was something rotten in BioOne. But what was it? And how could I find it?

Deep in thought, I turned off Charles Street into the warren of little tree-lined roads that make up the 'flat' of Beacon Hill. I turned the corner on to my short street. It was quiet. My apartment would be empty. I remembered the sensation of anticipation I used to feel coming home, the hope that Lisa might have arrived before me, the warmth of an evening together which would melt away the aggravations of ten hours at the office.

No longer.

I slowed to reach for my keys in my trouser pocket. I fumbled and dropped them. I bent down to pick them up.

At that moment, I heard a crack, crack, crack to my right, and the thud of brickwork shattering above my head. The fragments of brick spattered my face. I spun round and threw myself to the ground behind a parked four-wheel drive. More cracks of an automatic rifle, and the sound of bullets smashing into the metal of the car, and shattering the glass.

I crawled under the car, my body pressed down hard against the cold tarmac. My face stung hot. Silence. If the gunman ran from his hiding place to finish me off, I would have no chance. I strained my ears, trying to listen over the loud thumping of my heart. Then I heard the sound of rapid light footsteps on the other side of the road. Damn.

I pulled myself to my feet and, crouching low, dashed up the street behind the parked cars. An engine roared into life a few yards up the road. A burst of gunfire shattered windows above me. Close. Very close.

The car accelerated down the road. I heard shots, pistol shots. The sound of brakes, car doors slamming, people running. I stopped and peered out from behind a parked motorcycle, and saw a car in the middle of the road, doors wide open.

Sirens blared from all directions, and within a minute the road was a mess of flashing lights and burly blue uniforms. A young man in jeans and a casual black jacket ran up to me, fighting for breath.

'Are you OK?'

I recognized him as the Hispanic I had seen following me through the Common a couple of weeks before.

I stood up. 'Yes,' I said. 'I think so.'

My face felt warm and wet. I touched it with my fingertips. Blood.

'Are you hit?'

I shook my head. 'Just masonry. Thank you.' I managed a smile.

'No problem. Looks like the guy got away. He was a pro, you were lucky.'

I had been. Just like I had been that day in Armagh when a bullet had blown away Binns's face instead of mine. At least this time no one was hurt.

My hands were trembling so much it was difficult to pick up the

273

keys I had dropped. I stood upright and took a few deep breaths to try to slow my racing heart. I let myself into my apartment and poured myself a stiff whisky, offering one to my saviour, who of course refused it.

His name was Martinez. He asked me some basic questions about whether I saw anything or knew who might have been shooting at me, but it was more for form's sake than anything else. A parade of people came and went, Cole, Mahoney's Boston partner, a paramedic who cleared up my scratched face, and some others. Eventually Mahoney himself arrived.

'So, you were shot at?' he began brightly.

'I believe that's what happened,' I replied.

'Lucky we had some people watching you.'

'I didn't know I had my own personal bodyguard. How long has this been going on for?'

'Oh, three weeks or so. On and off. More off than on, really. It's expensive tailing people.'

'Well, I'm glad you had the spare cash this evening.'

Mahoney sat down. Martinez had whipped out a notebook. 'Any idea who it was?'

'Your friend here said it was a professional. I don't know any professional killers. For that matter I don't know anyone who owns an automatic rifle.' Except for Art Altschule, I thought suddenly as I spoke.

Mahoney noticed my hesitation. 'What is it?'

I told him about Art's interest in guns.

'We'll check that out,' he said. 'Is there anything else we should know about Mr Altschule?'

'No, not really. He doesn't like me.'

Mahoney raised his eyebrows. 'Why not?'

'I've been asking awkward questions.'

'About?'

'BioOne.'

'BioOne, eh?' Mahoney looked at me closely. 'The deal John Chalfont wanted to talk to you about.'

'That's right.'

'And what's the problem with BioOne?'

'I don't know. That's why I was asking Art. Don't you know?'

Mahoney's questioning was irritating me. I had just been shot at, my nerves were frayed, and although he was asking the right questions, I still felt he was trying to figure out how I could be responsible for shooting myself.

'We've been making inquiries,' Mahoney said stiffly. 'Assuming we're talking about a contract killer here,' he went on, 'who else do you think might have hired him?'

'I don't know. The person who killed Frank and John, maybe?'

'But that was someone who knew them. They were both shot in the back with handguns. This is a totally different MO.'

I shrugged. I was feeling tired. 'You're the detective. I'm just the poor bugger getting shot at.'

'Aren't you used to it by now?' Mahoney was watching me with that annoying half-smile.

He was referring to my time in Northern Ireland, I assumed. I felt a flare of anger, but I controlled it. I stared at him.

Mahoney stood up. 'We'll no doubt be talking again,' he said as he left the apartment. Martinez threw me a worried look and followed him.

It was hard to sleep that night. When I did drop off, it was into the graffiti-strewn streets of West Belfast. In reality, my tour of duty had been nerve-jangling anticipation for the shot that almost never came, then complacency, and finally the death of Lance Corporal of Horse Binns. In my dream, the streets were wider, with no cover, and I knew for certain that a sniper was lying in wait for me in a lone house fifty yards ahead. I had to walk on, my feet growing heavier and heavier, towards the house. I couldn't turn and run, but my steps became slower and slower until I wished I'd reach the house and get it over with.

Then I started awake. My mind turned somersaults along the blurred line between sleep and wakefulness. Time blurred as well, as minutes became hours and the night seemed to last for ever. Eventually I fell back to sleep and that never-ending road. This process repeated itself, until I gave up at five thirty, and crawled out of bed, my brain muzzy and tired. I checked the living-room window. There was a blue car parked right in front of the house, and one of the two men in it was alert enough to have noticed the movement in the curtains. I waved to him, and he nodded back. Mahoney had been good enough to leave me under surveillance, at least for the night.

I was in trouble. Someone wanted to kill me. Someone with the wherewithal and the contacts to hire a man with an automatic rifle. They would try again. I might well be dead within a week.

I hoped Mahoney would check out BioOne. Although he hated me, and would love to hold me responsible for my own murder, he wasn't stupid. But I couldn't rely on him to clear this up before a bullet hit me in the skull. With a shudder I remembered again the damage that could do.

I wasn't sure how long the police could or would protect me, or even if their protection was a guarantee of safety against a really determined killer.

I was in the office early, by seven o'clock. No one usually showed up before about a quarter to eight. Daniel and Diane were usually first in; most of the others came in between eight and half past. But I wanted to be finished before anyone saw me.

So I went straight to Art's office. A wooden filing cabinet had five drawers marked 'BioOne'. It was locked. Damn!

I searched around for a key. Couldn't find one.

All of Art's other filing cabinets were unlocked, but there was nothing interesting in any of them.

I tried his desk. The drawers were locked too. That was odd. People didn't lock their desks at Revere. I jiggled and pulled, but nothing. It was a feeble little lock and if I'd had any expertise I would have been able to pick it. But I hadn't.

I had an idea. I quickly strode back to my own desk, checking my watch on the way. Twenty to eight. No one was in yet. I opened my own desk drawer. In one corner, next to my spare set of house-keys, were my own desk keys, which I never used. I hurried back to Art's office and tried them on his drawer.

None of them worked.

I sat in Art's chair looking at his desk. His son glowered back at me. Next to the photo frame was a box of paper-clips.

I unravelled a large one, and poked it into the keyhole. For two minutes I bent and twisted the metal, gently pushing and pulling, but still nothing.

I checked my watch. Quarter to eight. I shouldn't be here, I should be at my own desk by now. I checked that the office was exactly as I found it, and slipped out.

Just in time. I passed Art in the corridor. 'Morning!' I said, with too much jollity.

Art just grunted.

I sat at my desk, trying to work out what to do. I couldn't force my way into Art's files, that would be too obvious. But I wanted to know what was in there.

The only person with a key was Art. And there was no reason for him to give it to me.

Unless.

I checked my watch. Five to eight. I thought I had heard Diane come in, but no one else.

I made my way back to Art's office and knocked.

'Yes?' He was drinking a cup of coffee and scanning the *Wall Street Journal*.

'Can I borrow your key to the supplies closet?' The supplies closet was a large cupboard behind the reception area where some of the more valuable office supplies were kept: computer equipment and so on.

'Can't you get a key from Connie?'

'Not in yet.'

'Is it locked?'

'Yes,' I lied.

'But it's never locked.'

I shrugged.

Art grunted, and pulled out his keys. He fiddled with one of them, trying to detach it. Damn. I needed the whole lot.

'I'll bring them right back,' I said.

'All right.' Art threw me the whole bunch.

I caught them, nipped out and checked the supplies closet. It was indeed unlocked. Then I took the elevator down to the street, and hurried round the corner to a small hardware store. There were three keys on Art's ring that looked like they might open filing cabinets or desk drawers. I had all three of them copied.

It seemed to take the man for ever, but eventually I was back up in Revere's offices. I knocked on Art's door, and handed him his keys back. He was on the phone.

He put his hand over the mouthpiece. 'Where have you been? You said you'd bring them right back.'

'Gil wanted to speak to me,' I lied again. 'Sorry.'

Art grunted and went back to his phone conversation.

I spent a lot of time in the corridor that morning. At about a quarter to ten I saw Art enter the elevator, jacket on. I waited five minutes, and then slipped into his office, closing the door behind me.

The first thing I did was check his diary, open on top of his desk. He had an appointment at eleven at Revere's offices. That meant he would be back within an hour. I would have to be quick. But I should have at least fifteen minutes. There was little that you could do outside the office that would take less than that.

I pulled out the keys I had had cut and tried them on the BioOne filing cabinet. The second one fitted. There were five large drawers. I started looking through them. There was so much information. The early papers on Revere's initial investment, a whole drawer full of documents related to the IPO, Annual Reports, monthly management accounts, forecasts, résumés, a thick file on the acquisition of Boston Peptides.

I leafed through these. It was taking too long, and I wasn't getting anywhere. If BioOne had secret misgivings about neuroxil-5, it wouldn't appear in these publicly available documents. Where would it be? Either in a copy of clinical trial results or in correspondence, and relatively recent correspondence at that.

I searched, but I couldn't find any clinical trial data. It wasn't surprising really. From what I knew of Enever he probably didn't let that information leave his office, let alone the building. But in the bottom drawer was the BioOne correspondence file.

I opened it. This was more interesting. Most of the correspondence was between Art and his old friend Jerry Peterson. As Daniel had suggested, it was mostly about numbers, in particular one number, the stock price. Art seemed to hold Jerry responsible for every swing in BioOne's stock price. His more recent letters had become quite upset about the downward lurch in the stock. Of course there was nothing Jerry Peterson could do about it, although Art urged him to make upbeat forecasts about the results of Phase Three trials for neuroxil-5. This, Jerry explained, BioOne could not do. The trials were supposed to be double blind, so that no one, not the doctors, nor the patients, nor BioOne, knew which patients were being given neuroxil-5 and which were being given a placebo. So it was impossible to make any comment until the code was broken at the end of the trial, and the data was analysed. That wouldn't be until March the following year. But Jerry did agree to giving analysts nods and winks that BioOne was optimistic about the results.

Nothing there to suggest that there were any concerns about neuroxil-5. I looked for any correspondence from Enever. There was very little, save for some cryptic notes to Jerry, which he had then copied to Art, and which were of little interest.

I put the file back, locked the cabinet and checked my watch. Ten o'clock. I should really leave now. But it wouldn't take a moment to check Art's desk.

I tried the remaining two keys. One of them worked. I slid open the bottom drawer, and my nostrils were hit by the sharp sweet smell of whisky. Three bottles of Jack Daniel's: one empty, one half empty, and one full. Maybe that was why the drawers were locked. A pitiful attempt to hide a sad secret. I hadn't felt any guilt poring through Art's filing system; after all, the information in it belonged to Revere. But when confronted with this, I did feel bad. It was like rummaging through someone else's dirty linen; it made me feel dirty too.

I slammed that drawer shut and opened the next one up. I would have to be quick now. It contained stationery and old diaries.

I picked up the most recent diary and then froze. I could hear footsteps in the corridor outside. Daniel? Diane? No, these were heavy purposeful footsteps. Oh, shit.

Art swung open the door to his office, and stopped dead when he saw me. My mind darted through a thousand excuses, and instantly rejected them all. I had been caught. This wasn't the time to lie.

Eventually he spoke. 'What the fuck are you doing?'

I sat up straight in his chair. 'Looking for information on BioOne,' I replied.

His heavy face reddened in front of me. The short grey hair seemed to bristle. 'Well what are you doing looking for it in my office?'

'I asked you about it. You wouldn't tell me.'

'So you thought you'd poke around among my personal belongings to see what you could find? How did you get into my desk?'

His eyes were on the bottom drawer. At least part of his anger came from the fear and now the knowledge that I would stumble on his whisky collection.

I looked down at the copied key still in the lock.

He felt for his keys in his pocket. 'You son-of-a-bitch.'

He lunged towards me hands outstretched. I leaped out of the chair, but he crashed down on top of me and pulled me to the floor. I hit my head on the side of the desk on the way down. I was dazed for a moment, which was long enough for him to pin me to the ground. He pulled back his fist and I just had time to move my face as he brought it crashing down on the side of my head.

Art was a big man, and strong. I bucked and wriggled, but I couldn't throw him off. He hit me again, this time on the mouth. I writhed, and as he moved his hand to pin down my shoulder, I lunged and bit it hard.

'Shit!' he screamed, and pulled his hand away. I bucked, he lost his balance, and I pushed myself out from under him. He climbed to his feet, and stood between me and the door, breathing heavily and clutching his injured hand.

'Calm down, Art,' I said, spitting some of my blood and his skin out of my mouth. 'Sorry I broke into your stuff, OK? Just let me leave and I'll forget everything I've seen.'

Art grunted, and reached for the top drawer of his desk, the only one I hadn't checked. He pulled out a small pistol, and pointed it at me.

Jesus! 'Art . . . don't use that thing. It's not worth it. If you shoot me, you'll be in jail for – '

'Shut the fuck up!'

'OK,' I said, holding my hands in front of me in a calming gesture. 'OK – '

'I said shut up!' he screamed.

I shut up. I didn't know what Art was going to do. Neither did he. With the gun waving towards me, he bent down, and pulled out the half-empty bottle of whisky. Wincing from the pain of his injured hand, he managed to undo the cap and took a long slug.

I backed towards the window, where a Lucite BioOne tombstone seemed my best chance for a weapon.

'Stand still!' Art barked. He took another swig of the whisky. 'What's wrong with you? Are you trying to destroy this firm? We should have gotten rid of you months ago. I should get rid of you now – '

'What the hell is going on here?'

It was Gil. He stood in the doorway taking in the scene before him. 'Art, put that gun down! And the whisky.'

Art turned slowly, looked at Gil, and put the gun down on the desk. He examined the bottle, as if deciding whether to take another pull, and then placed it next to the gun.

'Will someone please tell me what is going on?'

Art stabbed a finger towards me. 'This son-of-a-bitch was going through my desk. He broke into my locked drawers trying to steal confidential information. I caught him at it.'

Gil glanced at my bloody mouth and Art's injured hand. 'Is this true, Simon?'

I took a deep breath. 'Yes.'

'You, go back to your office and wait. Art, come with me to my office. And give that damn thing to me.' He nodded towards the pistol.

I left the room as Art handed the gun to Gil.

Daniel was in the corridor staring. 'What was that all about?'

'Art and I had a disagreement,' I said.

Daniel glanced at my chest. 'Art's right. The tie sucks.'

I ignored him and slumped in my chair, waiting for Gil's call.

Twenty minutes later, I was in his office. 'I'm very disappointed in you, Simon,' he said, staring at me from the other side of his large desk. 'We should be able to come to work at Revere without worrying about one of our colleagues going through our belongings. And you know Art's health is in a very delicate state at the moment. What were you doing?'

'I'm still trying to find out who killed Frank and John,' I replied. I had decided I shouldn't be specific about BioOne with Gil.

'Isn't that the police's job?'

'It is, but they're not doing it very effectively.'

'So you say. But it's not them I'm concerned about, it's you!' He jabbed an angry finger at me. 'I've had to send Art home: I can't have people waving guns around. I told you the other evening how important you are to this firm, how much we need you more than ever now, and what do you do? Snoop around, antagonize one of my partners, put the firm in jeopardy.' Gil was red now. I had never seen him so angry.

'Someone tried to kill me last night,' I said flatly.

'What?'

'Someone shot at me, just outside my apartment. They only just missed.'

Gil paused, at a loss for what to say. Then he spoke in a low, determined voice.

'You have your problems, Simon, and I have mine. You do what you have to do, and I'll do the best I can to ensure this firm survives.

But I don't think you can be of any further help to the rest of us. As of this moment, you are suspended from this firm until further notice. Please leave the building. Now.'

'But Gil – '

'I said now!' Gil stood up, and leaned forward, his hands on his desk, his whole body shaking.

'OK,' I said. 'I'm going.'

28

I walked home looking over my shoulder. There was someone following me, a blonde woman in jeans and a padded jacket. She was about thirty yards behind me, making no real effort to stay hidden. A policewoman, I presumed, although it annoyed me that I couldn't be sure. I turned and waved at her. She stopped, lit a cigarette, and watched me.

My emotions were a turmoil. My confrontation with Art had played havoc with my already frayed nerves. Having an angry alcoholic waving a pistol in my face had scared the hell out of me. Art was unstable and dangerous, certainly to himself, probably to me.

But I also felt angry with Gil. I understood his point of view. Going through your colleague's desk was not something that he expected of his people. Revere was in severe trouble, and I wasn't helping much. He had been decent to me, and I had let him down.

But Gil's support was important to me. He had trusted me when others hadn't, given me his backing when I needed it most. He was a decent man, and I respected him. And now he wanted nothing more to do with me.

I didn't know whether Gil would have me back. I enjoyed working at Revere, and I didn't want to leave, especially not this way. A month ago, Revere had meant everything to me. It was still important: a link with an untroubled past. The future didn't look good. No wife, no job, and unless I was very careful, a bullet in the head. I couldn't afford to sit around. I had to get whoever had killed Frank and John before they got me. Only then could I hope to get my life back into some kind of order.

When I arrived home the light on my answering machine was flashing. For a foolish second I thought it might be Lisa. It wasn't.

'Hi, Simon, it's Kelly.' Her voice, usually strong and confident, was subdued. 'I called you at work, but they said you'd left for the day. I'd like to talk to you if I can. Give me a call.'

I dialled Boston Peptides' number straight away, and was soon put through. Kelly wouldn't say what she wanted to talk about. We agreed to meet for lunch at a café near Harvard Square, safely out of reach of her work colleagues.

It was a vegetarian establishment, infested by students. Although I was early, Kelly was already waiting outside, nervously smoking a cigarette. We muttered greetings and then joined the end of the queue at the food counter in silence. I chose a salad, and Kelly some kind of quiche, and we sat down at the only free table.

Kelly pulled out a cigarette, and then put it away again before the waiter had a chance to assault her. 'I shouldn't have come,' she said.

'I'm glad you did.'

'Lisa wouldn't want me to talk to you. Neither would Henry.'

'You must have a good reason.'

'I think I have.'

I waited. Kelly picked at her quiche.

'Lisa's in a bad way, and she holds you responsible.'

'I know.'

'I've been thinking a lot about it,' Kelly said, 'and I'm not sure she's right. I kind of trust you. And I think you should know what Lisa was worried about. What got her fired. I don't care what you do with the information as long as you don't use it against Lisa. Or me. You never heard any of this from me, OK?'

'OK,' I nodded.

'As soon as BioOne took over Boston Peptides, Lisa wanted to get hold of some of the data on neuroxil-5. She wanted to see if she could use it in her work with Parkinson's.'

'So Henry Chan told me,' I said. 'But he didn't tell me much more.'

'At first Enema said no way. He runs everything with total secrecy, no one is allowed to know anything unless they absolutely have to. But Lisa can be pretty persuasive.'

I smiled.

'Somehow she got through to Enema. But he was very careful what data he would let her see. It was mostly just some of the early animal experiments, on aged rats.'

Kelly took a bite of her quiche. I waited while she chewed.

'The information was pretty useless, but it was all Lisa could get. As she studied it, she noticed something than Enema seemed to have missed.'

'What was that?'

'Several months after taking the neuroxil-5, quite a few of the rats died.'

I raised my eyebrows. Kelly saw it. 'Nothing wrong in that. Old rats die. It's kind of what you'd expect. Except that a higher number than usual died of strokes.'

'Strokes? Do rats get strokes?'

'Rats get many of the same kinds of diseases that we do. Especially in laboratories.'

'I see.'

'Do you know what a stroke is?' Kelly asked.

'Some kind of blood clot in the brain, isn't it?'

'Yes, it can be caused by that, or by the opposite, a haemorrhage in the brain. It can lead to paralysis, or death.'

'So this was serious?'

'Maybe.'

'What do you mean, maybe? If all these rats died of strokes, doesn't that make neuroxil-5 lethal?'

'It's not that easy. Most of the rats survived, or died of natural causes. It's just that a slightly higher proportion than usual died of strokes.'

'But Lisa thought this was significant?'

'She did. At first she spoke to Henry about it. He told her to talk to Enema. Which she did.'

I could see where this was going. 'And he said there was nothing wrong.'

'That's right. He said that Lisa's observations weren't statistically significant. When she asked for more data to check whether this was a real problem, Enema refused to give it to her. He said that it had been thoroughly analysed and there was nothing to be worried about.'

'But that didn't satisfy Lisa?'

Kelly smiled. 'You know her. She wouldn't be satisfied until she had seen the data itself. When Enema still refused to show it to her, she more or less called him a liar. She accused him of not checking the numbers carefully enough.'

'So he fired her?'

'Not surprisingly,' said Kelly.

It didn't surprise me at all. I knew that she had given Henry Chan a similarly difficult time over the years, but he had much more patience than Enever. I now understood why he felt that Lisa wouldn't fit into the new BioOne culture.

'Do you think Lisa was right to be concerned?' I asked Kelly.

'I didn't see the data myself; this is all stuff I heard from Lisa,' Kelly said. 'And I'd guess that statistically Enema was right. But I've worked with Lisa for two years. I trust her hunches. There may be something there, I don't know.'

'How can I find out?' I asked.

'You?' Kelly looked surprised. 'You can't.'

'Can you help me?'

Kelly looked down at her plate, now almost empty. 'I can't. Unlike Lisa, I don't have another job to go to if I get fired. Thomas Enever is a powerful enemy that I don't need right now.'

'Hmm. Have the clinical trials shown the same problem to be present in humans?'

'I assume not,' Kelly said. 'I mean all that data is shown to the Food and Drug Administration. The FDA would be pretty unhappy if everyone who took neuroxil-5 had a stroke the next day.'

'But what if it was just a few patients and it was several months later?'

Kelly thought about it. 'I don't know. The Phase One and Two clinical trials probably involved only about a hundred people, total. It is possible that something that affected a small minority of patients might slip through unnoticed. That's why they have these massive Phase Three trials, with a thousand patients or more.'

'And that's what's going on now, isn't it?'

'That's right. They end in March next year.'

'Do you have any idea about the results of these trials?'

'Are you kidding?' Kelly snorted. 'Only Enever knows. And at this stage, even he isn't supposed to.'

I remembered the note in Art's BioOne files about the trial being double blind.

'Is there any way of finding out?'

'No,' said Kelly. I paused to let her think. 'Not unless you actually go and talk to the clinicians who are conducting the trials themselves.'

'Can you get me a list of them?'

'No way,' Kelly said.

I was disappointed. I was sure Lisa had been on to something, but it was hard to see how I, single-handedly, could break through BioOne's wall of secrecy.

'There is one thing you could do,' Kelly said. 'I'm pretty sure that the Phase Two trial was written up in the *New England Journal of Medicine*. I remember the buzz in the industry when it was published.'

'So do I. That was when the BioOne stock price shot up, wasn't it?'

'Possibly. You're the money man. I just make the drugs.'

I acknowledged the dig.

'Sorry,' Kelly said. 'There will probably be a list of clinicians involved with the Phase Two trial there. Many of them will be signed up for the new trial. You could talk to some of them.'

'Thanks,' I said. 'I'll try it.'

We ate our food, Kelly hurrying so that she could get away without being seen.

'How's Boston Peptides getting on without Lisa?' I asked.

'We miss her. BP 56 is going well. We're getting the first responses from human volunteers. It looks like the drug is safe, although it seems to cause depression in some people.'

'Depression?'

'Yes. It can reduce the levels of serotonin in the brain. Kind of like the opposite of Prozac.'

Depression.

Lisa had been taking BP 56.

I remembered her fragility a week or so after Frank's death, the way she had lost her temper with me, her uncharacteristic irrationality, her black moods, and most of all, my total inability to help her. A chemically induced depression, combined with all those other pressures, must have been very hard to cope with. No wonder she had cracked and run away.

'What is it Simon?'

Lisa had said she wanted to keep the fact she was taking the drug quiet from everyone at work. I wasn't sure whether that included Kelly, but it was probably up to Lisa to tell her, not me. 'Oh, I was just thinking,' I said, vaguely. 'It's not serious enough to fail the drug, is it?'

'Oh, no,' said Kelly. 'There are ways around it. It may be as simple as prescribing Prozac in combination with BP 56.' She looked at her watch. 'I've got to go. Do you mind if you wait here for a couple of minutes before you leave? I really don't want anyone to see us together.'

'OK,' I said, deciding that there was no need for Kelly to know that she was being watched as she spoke. 'You go. And thank you.'

She smiled quickly and left.

I waited a few moments, and sauntered round the corner to a bar I used to frequent, just on the Cambridge side of the bridge from the Business School. My female tail stayed outside. I ordered a beer, and thought through what Kelly had told me.

So Lisa had been depressed. Not the kind of depression that comes from stress at work, and grief, and marital difficulties, but biochemically induced stress, which would make the world seem bleak even in the most normal of times. Given the pressure Lisa had been under, the world must have seemed a very dark place indeed.

In some ways, this news made me feel better. Without the drug, I should have a much better chance of persuading her to come back to me. But I still needed to prove that I hadn't killed Frank.

So the next question was, was there a problem with neuroxil-5? I had to admit that there was a chance that the answer was 'no'. That the numbers that Lisa had seen were not from a valid statistical sample, and just represented the kind of false coincidences that happened all the time. Well, if that was the case, then I was wasting a lot of time and effort.

But what if Lisa's hunch was right? What if neuroxil-5 caused occasional strokes in rats? What would that mean?

It could mean the drug was killing some of the people it was supposed to be curing. That would be a disaster. For the Alzheimer patients who were taking it, for BioOne, and for Revere.

I wasn't sure what Frank and John had to do with this potential catastrophe. Frank had little involvement with BioOne, Art had always seen to that. But there was Art's cryptic comment that Frank had been asking questions about BioOne just before he died. And of course there was the message John had left, saying he had discovered something about BioOne that I would find interesting. Could that have been that neuroxil-5 was dangerous?

At the moment it was a big if. What I needed to do was find proof one way or another. I polished off my beer and took the 'T' home.

The *New England Journal of Medicine* was on the Internet. I quickly found an abstract of the article Kelly had mentioned. I had to call the journal directly to have the full article faxed to me. The title was 'A Controlled Trial of Neuroxil-5 as a Treatment for Alzheimer's Disease'. There was a formidable list of authors, but the first name on the list was none other than Thomas E. Enever. It described the Phase Two clinical trial on eighty-four patients with Alzheimer's. The sample was too small to draw definitive conclusions, but the paper seemed to suggest that the results were encouraging. There were no statistically significant differences in the 'adverse-event categories' between the group that had taken neuroxil-5, and the group that had taken the placebo. At the end of an article was a list of six centres participating in the study, together with the clinicians responsible. Kelly had suggested that it was likely that most of these would also be involved in the larger Phase Three trial.

It took an hour of fiddling about on the Internet before I had the names and addresses of these six centres. Four of them were in New England, one was in Illinois, and one in Florida, no doubt a prime Alzheimer's location. It was five o'clock. I resolved to see the four New England centres the next morning.

I made myself a cup of tea, and picked up the pile of junk mail that had arrived that morning. There was one letter with an address in handwriting I knew very well.

Lisa's.

I sat on the sofa and opened the letter carefully, hardly daring to read it. It wouldn't be about BioOne: it must have been sent before Lisa's mother had passed on my message to her. It just might be something about how she was sorry, how she missed me, how she wanted to come back.

Or it might not.

It wasn't.

Dear Simon,

I have some news for you. I went to the drug store yesterday, and my family doctor today, and there is no doubt about it. I'm pregnant.

I felt you had a right to know as soon as I did. But you should also know that it doesn't change my decision to stay away from you in California. I want to put Boston, you and Dad's death as far away as possible from me. There are issues I can't face right now — whether you were involved in Dad's death, and whether I can ever trust you again.

Both our parents messed up in bringing us up. I don't want to do that with our baby. I hope that here in California I can start out again, create a new life for myself and for the baby inside me. I have felt so horrible recently, but at least now I have something to live for.

I know you've been calling Mom. Please don't try to contact me. I need to be away from you right now. I hope that I will get to the stage where I can see you again and talk to you again, but I'm not there yet.

Lisa.

I read the letter over again, just to make sure I had got it right. A turmoil of emotions bubbled inside me. There was a primal joy that I was going to be a father. That soon an individual human being would be born that I had a part in creating, that was part me.

If I ever saw it.

We hadn't planned it. We hadn't even really talked about children. We had both assumed they were something for the distant future. A potential conflict between us that we wanted to put off.

For each of us the union of different nationalities and religions hadn't been a problem. In fact it had been liberating, freeing us from the different traditions in which we had grown up. But for our future children? I felt a tugging desire to bring up our children with English accents, a public school education and an occasional acquaintance with the Church of England. This wasn't for my own benefit but rather out of a sense of duty to my family. My title, which I had neglected, should be passed on, and with it some of the traditions I had been brought up with. The trouble was, I suspected Lisa had similar, but opposite feelings. Judaism passes through the female line.

Anyway, that was all academic now. Lisa was pregnant. She was going to lay total claim to the baby and keep it in California with her. The irony hurt. I realized that I really was following in my family's traditions, fathering and then abandoning children around the world. Not for the first time, I wondered if I had any brothers or sisters my father hadn't told me about. How could I be so pompous as to get myself hung up on the stupid title? I was a fucked-up Englishman in danger of begetting more fucked-up Englishmen. The kid was lucky to escape me.

Oh, sod it. I didn't care whether my children were English, American, Jewish or Hindi. What I really wanted to do was have a child with Lisa. I knew I would be a good father, and she would be a good mother. I could imagine us all laughing together, the three of us, the baby an as yet unformed blur. We could build a strong happy family together, we really could.

If Lisa ever gave us the chance.

I wanted to spend as little time out on the street as possible, so I ordered a pizza and sat down to write Lisa a letter, care of her mother. I wrote several, tearing each one up, until I was interrupted by the door-buzzer. It was Martinez. I let him in.

'Want some?' I asked him, pointing to the pizza.

He shook his head. 'I stay away from junk food.'

'I'd have thought that was impossible in your job.'

'It's a challenge.'

I glanced at his physique. He did look lean and fit. 'Have a seat. I'm sorry I haven't invited you in before, but I thought you were happier on the street.'

'Yeah. That's what I wanted to talk to you about.'

'Oh, yes?'

'Sergeant Mahoney has called us off. He thinks he can't justify tailing you any more.'

I suddenly felt cold. I hadn't realized how comforting my semi-visible companions had become.

'But doesn't he know someone's trying to kill me?'

'Remember, technically we were putting you under surveillance, not protecting you.'

'Jesus,' I said.

'I shouldn't really be here,' Martinez smiled. 'It's not standard police procedure to inform a suspect that his tail is disappearing.'

'No, I can see that. Thank you. Doesn't Sergeant Mahoney care if I get shot?'

Martinez shrugged.

'He doesn't like me much, does he?'

Martinez shrugged again.

'What about you?'

'I'm just a dumb cop who does what he's told.' Martinez got to his feet. 'But I don't like seeing innocent people getting killed. So, if you get worried about something, give me a call.' He pulled a card out of his wallet and handed it to me. 'And be careful.'

'Thanks,' I said, taking the card. 'I will.'

It was very hard to get to sleep. Whoever had tried to kill me would try again. They were bound to. With my police escort, I had some hope of protection. Now I had none.

It might be that Mahoney had finally crossed me off his suspect list. But through the long night that thought gave me little comfort. Alone in my apartment, it was difficult to fight the fear. I had been very lucky that whoever had tried to shoot me the day before had missed. But they would try again, for sure. There was nowhere to hide. A bullet seemed unavoidable; the only thing I could do to delay it was to lock myself in, and the world out. Pull down the blinds, live on Chinese and pizza deliveries and wait and hope.

I felt small and alone in my bed, our bed. I so desperately wanted Lisa's warm body next to me, her embrace to give me comfort and courage. With her, I felt I could face the likelihood of death. Without her, that night, it was very difficult.

So I was going to be a father! I laughed to myself, a hollow bitter laugh. Who was I kidding? I wouldn't last a week, let alone nine months.

I pulled myself out of bed, and poured myself a Scotch. For a moment the whisky made me feel warm and almost safe. But then I poured it all down the kitchen sink.

Drinking myself into a stupor wouldn't save me. If I wanted to live, if I wanted my child to have a father, even one living thousands of miles away, I would have to do something. Soon.

29

Very early the next morning, I packed a bag and called a cab.

'Where to?' asked the Indian driver.

'Logan Airport.'

The traffic wasn't too bad, and I checked over my shoulder all the way. I didn't think I was being followed, but I couldn't tell. We soon approached the airport. I was so tempted to direct the driver to International Departures and take the first flight to London. I would be safe in England; I wouldn't be much of a threat to anyone three thousand miles away.

I had two choices: either to run away and forget Revere, BioOne and Lisa, or to go underground and try to take the battle to the enemy, whoever they were. What I couldn't do was wander around Boston until someone shot me.

Long ago I had decided I couldn't run away from Lisa.

Besides, the Assistant DA had my passport.

So, I had the taxi-driver drop me off at Departures, and spent half an hour dodging round the airport, trying to make sure I wasn't being followed, before ending up at the Hertz office. There I rented a bland white Ford. I drove round Route 128 until I came to a rest stop, and pulled up in the parking lot. I hadn't seen anyone following me, and it was a couple of minutes before another car pulled off the highway, so I guessed I was safe.

I sat in the car and went through the four Alzheimer centres on my list. I pulled out my cell phone and managed to make appointments to see three of them.

The first clinician on my list was Dr Herman A. Netherbrook of one of the smaller universities that littered Boston. His office was on the campus in a medical research unit named after a now deceased Massachusetts politician.

Netherbrook was about sixty, grey and uninterested, with the weary cynicism that afflicts stale school teachers and, presumably, academics. He welcomed me politely into his small office, and procured me a mug of instant coffee. I gave him one of my cards.

'Now, who is it you are with, Mr Ayot? I don't quite follow.'

'Revere Partners is one of the investors in BioOne, who of course are conducting the trial of their neuroxil-5 drug for Alzheimer's disease. A trial in which you are participating, I believe?'

'Indeed we are. We were involved with the Phase Two trial, so it seemed natural to continue with the Phase Three trial as well. But I'm not sure I can talk to you about any of the commercial features of this work. You had better discuss that with Dr Enever himself.'

'It's the safety of the drug I'm concerned about.'

'Yes, you mentioned that on the telephone. But we monitor the patients very carefully in all the trials we do.'

'Of course. And have you encountered any adverse events?' I knew from my research on Alzheimer's that adverse events had to be reported as soon as they occurred.

Netherbrook looked me over carefully, as if deciding whether to answer my question. Finally he walked over to a filing cabinet, and pulled out a folder.

'Let me see. We have thirteen patients enrolled in the study. We have had two adverse events in the year or so the trial has been running. One patient had a heart attack, and another is showing signs of developing diabetes. But in a sample of elderly patients, that is only to be expected. And all of them have survived so far.'

'Any examples of strokes?'

'Strokes?' He glanced at his file. 'No, none.'

'Nothing that you would consider suspicious or a cause for concern.'

'If I had a cause for concern, I would have notified BioOne immediately, wouldn't I?'

'Yes, of course, Dr Netherbrook. Thank you for your time.'

I left, feeling slightly foolish, and drove off to Springfield, in central Massachusetts. I hoped I was asking all the right questions. But if there had been no strokes amongst the patients enrolled, it was difficult to see how I could have missed anything.

There was a specialist Alzheimer's Research Clinic in Springfield. Dr Fuller turned out to be about thirty-two, blonde, with long eyelashes and very long legs. She seemed to me to be wasted on geriatrics, but perhaps if I were eighty I would disagree with that view. She had a soft southern accent, and purred quietly, rather than talked. I could scarcely make out what she was saying.

I did understand that one of her ten patients enrolled in the trial had suffered a mild stroke nine months after the trial had begun. Another had died from bronchial pneumonia, as old people sometimes do.

One stroke out of a total of twenty-three patients. That didn't prove anything.

Then on to Hartford and a Dr Pete Korninck. He was a genial man with a beard and iron-grey hair that curled over the tops of his ears. One of his sixteen patients had developed a liver complaint, and another had died of a heart attack.

'How about strokes?' I asked, knowing that if there had been any, he would probably have told me.

'None. At least not among the Alzheimer's patients.'

'OK.' I thought a moment. 'What do you mean by "the Alzheimer's patients"?'

'Well, we have some patients who suffer from multi-infarct dementia. That's a condition also known as "mini strokes". Small blood vessels in the brain can become blocked, causing areas of surrounding tissue to lose their blood supply. Over the years these can cause damage to the brain, which has similar effects to Alzheimer's. The two are often confused.'

'And these patients have "mini strokes" all the time?'

'Yes,' the bearded doctor replied. 'And sometimes they get big strokes.'

'Presumably you exclude these patients from your study?'

'Where we can, yes. But there's no doubt some of them creep in. You can only really identify Alzheimer's for sure after an autopsy.'

'Have you had to reclassify any of your Alzheimer's patients in this way?'

'Yes, three.'

'And you told BioOne this?'

'Of course.'

'Do you think there is anything significant about it?'

Korninck thought for a moment. 'It's impossible to say from my patients alone. There may be. But BioOne would be the only people to have enough information to be sure.'

I left Hartford, and drove east, stopping briefly for a cup of coffee and a burger. It had been a long day, with lots of driving, but I thought I might still have time to see the fourth clinic on the list, in Providence, Rhode Island.

Dr Catarro was unavailable, but his assistant Dr Palmer was. He agreed to meet me at seven fifteen at his office.

Dr Palmer was a dark thin man who could have been anywhere from twenty-five to forty. His young-looking face had lines that suggested a short life with a lot of worry, or a longer one with only an average amount. His voice, when he spoke, had the squeaky depth of a thirteen-year-old.

'Thank you for waiting for me, Dr Palmer.'

'Not at all,' he said. He looked tired.

'Hard day?'

'Since Dr Catarro passed away, every day has been a hard day.'

I sat up in my chair. 'Dr Catarro passed away? What do you mean?'

'Oh, I'm sorry, I thought you knew,' Palmer replied. 'My colleague, Dr Catarro, died in a car accident last month. It was a terrible tragedy. We haven't found a replacement yet.'

'I'm sorry,' I said. 'What happened?'

'He was driving home late one night, and he hit a tree on a road near his house. He was only a mile away from home. They think he must have fallen asleep at the wheel. He left his wife and two girls.'

'How awful,' I said, lamely.

Palmer's eyes dropped downwards, recognizing the words and their inadequacy. Then he looked up. 'Now, how can I help you?'

'Oh, yes. I believe Dr Catarro was taking part in a clinical trial conducted by BioOne?'

'Yes, he was.'

'I wonder if I could ask you some questions about it?'

'I'm sorry. I won't be able to help. We discontinued the trial after Tony died. It was his baby really and I had too much other stuff to do.'

'Do you still have the records from the trial?'

Palmer shook his head. 'Well at least not easily available. I sent the file back to BioOne. We will have the information on each patient's file, but it won't be easy to collate.'

I was disappointed. 'Do you happen to know if there were any adverse events?'

'Yes, there were,' said Palmer. 'Tony was involved in a disagreement with BioOne over the reporting of adverse events. Strokes.'

'Strokes?'

'Yes. A number of our patients had strokes. A couple of them were fatal. BioOne had suggested that the patients concerned had been misdiagnosed as Alzheimer's patients, and really suffered all along from mini strokes. The autopsy showed the two who died definitely did have Alzheimer's. They had the neurofibrillary tangles that you only get with Alzheimer's disease.'

'Do you know how this disagreement was resolved?' I asked.

'It wasn't,' said Palmer. 'It's something I really need to follow up, but I just haven't had the time. It was one of the reasons I decided to drop the trial.'

'Thank you Dr Palmer, that was very interesting,' I said. I was just about to leave, when I asked him one more question.

'Oh, by the way, do you know where the accident happened?'

'Yeah, on a little road near Dighton. It's about twenty miles away. Why do you ask?'

'Just curious.'

I was very curious. It was too much of a coincidence that Dr Catarro had died in the middle of asking questions about BioOne. Car accidents could be faked.

I checked Information for the number and address of a Dr Catarro in Dighton. There was one.

I drove straight there. I didn't feel good about barging in on a widow, but I had no choice.

I found the white-painted clapboard house and rang the bell. Mrs Catarro came to the door. She was small and blonde. Her face was carefully made up, but very fragile. I heard a television in the background.

'Yes?' she asked.

'Mrs Catarro, my name is Simon Ayot. I'd like to ask you a couple of questions about your husband.'

She looked at me doubtfully, but the smart suit, friendly smile, and English accent seemed to do the trick.

'Very well, come in.'

She led me into a living room. A girl of about fourteen was sprawled on the floor in front of a sitcom.

'Can you turn it off for a moment, honey?' Mrs Catarro asked.

The girl made a face. Mrs Catarro snapped. 'Brette, I said turn the TV off!' It was almost a shout. The girl grumpily did as she was told, and left the room, throwing me an angry glance.

The woman sat down on the sofa. 'I'm sorry about that. My patience is not what it used to be. Teenage girls, you know.'

I knew very little about teenage girls, but I smiled and nodded, and sat down.

'Were you a friend of Tony's?' she asked.

'No, I wasn't,' I replied. 'But I'm interested in a project he was working on before he died.'

'Well then you should talk to Vic Palmer at the clinic.'

'I have, Mrs Catarro. And he was quite helpful. But I wonder if I could ask you a couple of things, too?'

'You can try,' she said. 'But I don't have any medical training. I doubt if I can help.'

'Do you know if your husband was worried about the neuroxil-5 trial he was working on before he died?'

She thought for a moment. 'Yes, he was, as a matter of fact,' she said. 'He used to talk about that a lot. It made him quite upset.'

'Did he say what the problem was?'

'Yes, he did. As I recall, four of his patients had suffered strokes after taking the drug, and the company that made it, what was it, Bio something or other?'

'BioOne.'

'That's right, BioOne, didn't seem to care at all. It was doing all it could to hide the results, or confuse them, Tony said. He was worried that patients were dying unnecessarily all over the country. He had two who died in his clinic alone.'

'I see. And what was he going to do about it?'

'Talk to the company first. And then go to the Federal Authorities.'

'But it never came to that?'

Mrs Catarro looked at me suspiciously. Her thoughts were following mine. Her brow furrowed, her jaw tightened. 'You don't think . . .'

I decided not to alarm her. Not when I had no more than guesses to go on.

'It was a car accident, wasn't it Mrs Catarro? I'm sure the police investigated it thoroughly.'

'Yes,' she said. She looked as though she was about to cry.

'Thanks very much. If you do think of anything more to do with the trial, do give me a ring.'

I pulled out a card, scribbled in my cell phone number, and handed it to her.

She glanced at it. 'Oh, Revere Partners. You'll have known poor Frank Cook, then?'

'Yes,' I paused. 'Yes I did. You heard about his death?'

'I couldn't miss it.' She nodded towards the television set.

'Did you know him?'

'Yes. Well, Tony knew him better. He'd known him for years. In fact we saw him at some friends' house just before Tony's accident. Come to think of it, just before Frank was murdered.'

I froze. 'Did your husband talk to Frank about the clinical trial?' I asked.

She thought a bit. 'I think he did. In fact I think they had a long conversation about it. Frank was involved in it in some way. The same as you, I assume.'

I nodded. 'That's right, Mrs Catarro. Thank you very much.'

'Are you sure that Tony wasn't . . .'

She was adding two and two and I could see she couldn't avoid reaching four.

I sighed. 'I don't know, Mrs Catarro. But that's what I'm trying to find out.'

I left her on her doorstep, her fragile face looking as though it was on the verge of shattering.

30

I checked into a motel on the outskirts of Providence. Throughout the day I had been looking over my shoulder for a tail, but hadn't seen anyone. I had an anonymous supper in a cheap anonymous restaurant, and felt safe.

I was now pretty certain that I knew why Frank had been killed. Dr Catarro had told him of his concerns about BioOne. Frank had asked questions and someone had killed him. And then Dr Catarro, and then John. I had asked questions, and they had tried to kill me.

Who was responsible? The list of possibilities was long, but it was headed by two people: Art Altschule and Thomas Enever. But I had no proof. I still needed more information on the neuroxil-5 trial.

There was one more clinic I could visit. I wasn't sure where Aunt Zoë had been enrolled, although I assumed it was somewhere in Boston. She must have been enrolled in the Phase Three trial, so there was a good chance it would not be one of those listed in the article on the Phase Two trial in the *NEJM*.

Even though it was late, I dialled her number. Carl answered, sounding tense.

'Carl? It's Simon Ayot.'

'Oh, Simon, how are you?'

'I'm sorry I'm calling so late . . .'

'That's OK. I've just come back from the hospital.'

'The hospital?' I knew what was coming next. 'Is it Aunt Zoë?'

'Yes,' said Carl, his voice strained. 'She had a stroke last night.'

'Jesus! How is she? How bad was it?'

'It was bad,' said Carl flatly. 'She's still alive, but the doctors say the damage was massive. She's in a coma, and they don't think she'll come out of it. It's just a question of time.'

A wave of despair overwhelmed me. I couldn't say anything.

'Simon. Simon! Are you there?'

'Yes, I'm here,' I said quietly. 'I'm so sorry, Carl.'

There was silence on the other end of the line for a moment. 'That wasn't the side-effect you were thinking about, was it Simon?'

I wanted to lie to him, tell him I didn't know, let him think that he and I bore no responsibility for his wife's stroke, but I couldn't. He'd find out soon enough.

'Yes,' I said.

'Damn!' Carl exclaimed. Then he gave a sigh that shuddered down the phone. 'I guess I shouldn't have told Zoë to go on with the treatment, huh?'

'You didn't know, Carl. Neither did I. We do now, but it's too late.'

'Yeah. It is.' Carl sounded very tired.

'I'll leave you to get some sleep,' I said. 'But one last question. Which clinic was Zoë visiting?'

It was Dr Netherbrook's. The one I had seen first that morning, the one with no patients with strokes. When I had spoken to him, Dr Netherbrook wouldn't have heard what had happened to Zoë. But he would soon be filing an adverse event report. I wondered how Enever would ignore or suppress that one.

'Goodbye, Carl. Give my love to Zoë.'

'I will,' he said, and rang off.

I lay on my back on the bed in my motel room.

Another good person dying for the greater glory of BioOne.

I bought the *Wall Street Journal* the next morning and read it over one of those great American breakfasts that you can get in cheap diners. Out of habit I scanned the NASDAQ quotes. BioOne's stock was up nineteen dollars to sixty-three!

I searched the paper for the story. BioOne had announced a marketing agreement with Werner Wilson, a huge pharmaceutical company. Werner Wilson was going to sell neuroxil-5 in the United States, as well as 'a promising new treatment for Parkinson's disease, developed by BioOne'. That was Lisa's BP 56. The deal gave extremely favourable terms to BioOne, although it was contingent on a successful outcome of the Phase Three trial of neuroxil-5, expected in March. It would mean neuroxil-5 would be pushed out to doctors by one of the largest pharmaceutical sales forces in the country. The Wall Street analysts loved it, and so did the stock market, which was why the stock had shot up. If they only knew.

I finished my French toast, and went out to the parking lot and the little white Ford, which was doubling as an office. I called Daniel at Revere.

'What's up, Simon? Where are you?'

'On the road,' I replied. 'Listen, Daniel. I've been to some of the clinics that are participating in the Phase Three trial. And I think Lisa was right. There is a problem.'

'Jesus,' said Daniel. 'What kind of problem?'

'It looks possible that people taking the drug over a period of months suffer from strokes.'

'Ooh,' said Daniel. 'That's bad.'

'Very bad.'

'Did you see the BioOne stock price this morning?' he asked.

'Yes. Sixty-three.'

'It's not going to be up there very long if this gets out.'

'No, it isn't. But keep it quiet for now, Daniel. I don't have hard evidence. I really need the clinical trial data on the Phase Two trial, and the adverse events on Phase Three. There must be some way you can get that from BioOne. Revere is its biggest shareholder, for God's sake.'

'I don't know, Simon. You know what Thomas Enever is like.'

'It's important, Daniel. Steal it if you have to.'

There was silence at the other end of the phone.

'Daniel?'

'I'm sorry, Simon. This is getting heavy. You getting fired. People getting killed. I don't think it would be smart to steal BioOne documents.'

'Daniel! Come on, this is important.'

'Sorry, Simon. Got to run. Later.'

The bastard hung up.

Shit! I had expected too much of Daniel's friendship. As usual, he was thinking of himself first. Bastard!

We hadn't discussed Daniel's personal holdings of BioOne stock directly. At sixty-three dollars he was finally in profit. I was sure he would sell. If he did, I supposed he would technically be insider trading, but that was his problem, not mine. I was furious that I had given him the information to dig himself out of that hole, when he had been unwilling to lift a finger to help me.

Who else could I talk to at Revere? Art was out of the question. So was Gil. He had made clear his displeasure at my attempts to find out what was wrong with BioOne. I would go to him when I had proof, not before. Ravi? I didn't know him well enough to count on his support; he would be much more likely to follow Gil's line. And the last thing I wanted to do was go to Diane for help.

I started the car, and drove north to Cambridge. I stopped opposite BioOne's gleaming building. The information was in there, somewhere, but how could I get at it? I had seen the security. There was no way past that.

I had an idea. I called Craig, and persuaded him to meet me at Marsh House that afternoon.

I drove out to Woodbridge, bought some groceries at the Star Market, and drove on to Marsh House. It would be foolish to go back to my apartment in Boston if I wanted to stay alive. This seemed like a good place to lie low. But even here I didn't feel completely safe.

It was a crisp clear day. The autumnal light reflected off the yellows and oranges of the marsh grass, so that the marsh itself seemed to shimmer. The creek twinkled at the end of the jetty. No one was about. Just the white egrets and me.

I used Lisa's key to unlock the door. The house had not been touched since I was last there. It was cold. I found some wood, fed the stove, and lit it. I made myself a sandwich for lunch, and waited for Craig. The peace of the place settled around me.

Craig came armed with a powerful laptop computer. He set it up on the kitchen table, and in no time he was up and running, and looking for BioOne's web site.

'How long will this take?' I asked him.

'No idea. Hours. Days, maybe. We'll see.'

'Will you be able to get in there?'

'Oh, yes. At Net Cop we monitor all the new tricks as soon as they're discovered. That's the only way we can keep our own switching systems secure. Something will work here.'

I watched him as he nosed around the BioOne web site, taking note of e-mail addresses, and so on.

'Can I help?' I asked him.

'Yeah. Let's do this properly. Pizza. Extra anchovies. And good coffee.'

So I drove into Woodbridge and got a pizza. There was a kind of deli which ground exotic coffees, so I bought a quarter pound of arabica and returned to the house with it. The kitchen was soon full of the smell of brewing coffee and extra anchovies.

'How are you doing?' I asked him.

'I think I can see a possible way in,' he said. 'There's a new link between BioOne's network and Boston Peptides', isn't there?'

'Yes. BioOne took them over very recently.'

'Excellent. That means they probably haven't got a cast-iron connection. It would really help if I had the password of someone in the Boston Peptides network,' Craig said. 'You don't know Lisa's by any chance?'

'No. I could guess. But won't she have been kicked off the system by now?'

'Probably,' Craig agreed. 'Anyone else?'

'Hold on.'

I called Kelly. She didn't sound pleased to hear from me.

'You shouldn't call me at work,' she whispered urgently.

'Kelly, I need your password for the computer system.'

'You've got to be kidding!'

'I'm serious. I'm pretty sure now that Lisa was right about neuroxil-5. To be certain, I need to get into BioOne's computer. To do that I need your password.'

'But I don't have access to that data. That would be in the Clinical Trials Unit.'

'Don't worry about that. It'll give us somewhere to start.'

'No, Simon. I'll get fired.'

'Kelly. Patients will die.'

There was silence. 'OK. But it's kind of embarrassing.'

'Tell me.'

'All right. Leonardodicaprio. One word.'

'Ah. I see what you mean.' Craig passed a note in front of me. 'Oh, and try to use the system as little as possible over the next twenty-four hours.'

'How am I going to do that?'

'Please, Kelly.'

She sighed. 'OK.'

'All right!' said Craig. 'Now what I'm going to do is try to log in to BioOne's connection from here, pretending to be Boston Peptides' machine.'

'Can't the BioOne machine tell the difference?'

'Normally, yes. But using one of my programs I can guess the packet number from the Boston Peptides system. BioOne will identify my message as coming from Boston Peptides and send an acknowledgement back to them. So what I'll need to do is flood the Boston Peptides system with fake messages, so that it doesn't receive the BioOne acknowledgement and realize something's wrong.'

'How long will all that take?'

'With the program I have, about a minute,' Craig smiled. 'Watch.'

He typed furiously, and then with a flourish, pressed enter. Numbers were dialled, modems screeched, lines of meaningless letters and ungrammatical word combinations scrolled down his screen. After about a minute, it all came to a stop.

'We're in!' exclaimed Craig.

'I'm impressed.'

'There's a ways to go yet, but we're getting there. Let's start with this guy Enever's e-mail.'

It took a while, but eventually the screen was filled with Enever's e-mails. We opened a few at random. Enever was not one of the great e-mail diplomats. His missives were terse, rude and managed to phrase the most simple message as an order rather than a request.

'OK, which ones do you want?'

There were hundreds of them. 'I can't tell without reading each one,' I said, shaking my head.

'OK. We'll download the lot, then.'

Craig began the process of stealthily downloading Enever's e-mails from the BioOne server in Cambridge on to the Net Cop machine in Wellesley, all from the rickety kitchen table in Marsh House.

When he'd finished, he rubbed his hands. 'Now for the Clinical Trials Unit.'

I'd asked him to look for data on the Phase Two clinical trial for neuroxil-5, and any early results for the Phase Three trial. It proved to be difficult. After a couple of hours, he took a break.

'This is going to be much harder,' he said, pouring himself a cup of coffee. 'It's much better protected than Enever's e-mail.'

'I really need that clinical trial data,' I said.

'I'll get it.'

Four hours later, he still hadn't. It was nearly midnight. I was exhausted, but I felt morally bound to stay awake and be supportive.

'Shit!' shouted Craig. 'I don't believe this!'

'Still no luck?'

Craig rubbed his eyes. 'These bastards know what they're doin'.'

I yawned. 'Look, Craig. You've tried hard, I really appreciate it. But let's just give up.'

'No way,' said Craig. 'I'm not quittin' till I get you that data.'

'But you'll be up all night!'

'Probably,' said Craig. He smiled. 'I've done it before. Many times. But you get some sleep.'

'No, I'll stay up with you.'

'Simon. You yawning your head off a couple of feet from my ear does not constitute help. Trust me. Go to bed.'

He was right. I was exhausted and useless. At least if I got some sleep, I might not be quite so useless in the morning.

'Thanks, Craig. Good night. But wake me if you get anywhere.'

I went to sleep disappointed. I had pinned so much faith in Craig being able to get hold of hard data, data that would prove neuroxil-5 was dangerous, that would prove there was a major problem that someone had tried to cover up.

I had hoped to be woken in the middle of the night by a triumphant Craig, but it was the alarm clock that jolted me out of my sleep at six thirty. I pulled on some clothes, and went downstairs to the clatter of Craig's fingers on the keyboard.

'No luck?'

Craig turned to me. 'No,' he snapped. He didn't look tired, but he looked angry.

'Have you been at it all night?'

'I went for a walk about three. Didn't help.'

'Here, let me make you some breakfast,' I said. 'Toast, OK?'

'Yeah,' said Craig, getting up from his computer and stretching.

'Thanks for trying,' I said.

We cleared a space at the table, sat down, ate toast and drank coffee. Craig munched noisily, his eyes glazed, his mind still on the problem. I felt refreshed by my sleep and the coffee. The blackness outside was turning slowly to grey as dawn crept over the marsh.

'Don't worry about it, Craig,' I said. 'You never know, there might be some stuff in Enever's e-mails. Someone might have sent him some of the clinical trial.'

Craig stopped in mid slurp, spilling drops of coffee over his chin. 'That's it!' He exclaimed. He pushed the breakfast out of the way, and leaped back to his keyboard, fingers flying.

'What are you doing?'

'Composing a message from Enever, asking the Clinical Trials Unit for the data. They send it. We read it.'

The message was sent. It was still early. We had to wait for the people in the Clinical Trials Unit to get in to work, read their mail, and do something about it.

We stared at the screen, waiting.

At last, at 8.33 a.m., a response came. We looked at it.

Dr Enever

Here is the summary of the data you requested. Can I give you the rest in hard copy, or do you need it in spreadsheet form?

Jed

A large spreadsheet of figures was attached. It looked quite comprehensive.

'Well I think we need the rest in spreadsheet form, don't you?' said Craig with a smile as he composed a response.

We sent it and watched for a response from the Clinical Trials Unit.

It didn't come. Instead, *Message Sent* flashed on the screen.

'What message?' I looked at Craig.

He checked the 'Copy of Sent Messages' file. It was from Enever, the real Enever this time, to Jed in the Clinical Trials Unit.

Jed

What's all this data? I didn't ask for the data. Who told you to send it to me?

Enever

'Oh, oh,' said Craig. 'Time to go.'

He quickly downloaded Jed's first e-mail and its spreadsheet attachment, and left BioOne's system.

'Will they know we were there?' I asked.

'I hope not,' Craig said. 'But I don't want to risk going back in.'

'That's OK. I'm sure we've got a lot of good stuff already.'

Craig stretched and began packing up his computer and the scraps of paper he had been scribbling on.

'Are you going home now?' I asked.

'Oh, no. If I can't pull an all-night hacking run any more, I'm not fit to run the company.'

'Thanks again for all your help.'

'No problem.' He paused at the door. 'Stay alive,' he said, and was gone.

I started on the BioOne files right away, using my own laptop. Craig had given me a password so that I could access them in the Net Cop system any time I wanted from anywhere I wanted.

There was a mass of information. Many of Enever's e-mails had meaty attachments to them. And then there was the Clinical Trial Unit's data, columns of dense figures and statistics. If this was the summary, I wondered what the complete data was like. It was good stuff, but I couldn't understand most of it. I had to stop and think about what every document referred to. Someone else would have to look through this. Someone who would instantly be able to sort the interesting from the irrelevant, and who could analyse whatever they found there.

The time had come to see Lisa.

I had held off physically tracking her down until I had something concrete to give her, evidence that I hadn't changed, that I was still the man she had married, that I hadn't killed her father. I was now pretty close to having that evidence. And I needed her help if I was to make sure that more Alzheimer's sufferers like Aunt Zoë didn't die.

I was excited at the prospect, but also nervous. I was confident in my ability to persuade the old Lisa that I was innocent, especially with all that I had now discovered. But the Lisa who had turned her back on me, who had suffered so badly from her father's death and taken it out on me? I wasn't so sure.

From my conversation with Kelly, I guessed that part of her behaviour was due to the effects of the BP 56 she had been taking. Perhaps the greater part. If she had stopped the drug when she'd moved to California, perhaps she'd be more amenable to reason.

I could only hope.

I wrote a one-page note and stuck it in an envelope, packed my bags and left. I drove to the airport and left the Ford in a car park. There were seats on the next flight to San Francisco, and two hours later I was in the air.

31

Lisa's mother lived in a small wooden town house on Russian Hill with her second husband, an affable banker named Arnie. Technically, the house had a view of the Bay and Alcatraz, and it was true that from one of the upstairs windows you could just see some water and one corner of the fortress-island. Lisa and I had visited them three times, the last being at Thanksgiving almost a year before. Apart from my stupid argument with Eddie about Chancellor Kohl, it had been fun, full of an American family warmth that I was surprised to find attracted me. There were probably English families like that too, but mine wasn't one of them. Lisa and I had agreed to come again for Thanksgiving this year, only two weeks away. Whether I would be there or not depended on what happened in the next twenty-four hours.

I walked up to the freshly painted white door and rang the bell. There was no answer at first, and I wondered if she would be in. I knew she worked a couple of days a week at an expensive children's clothes store run by a friend of hers. I tried to stand as close as possible to the door, so she couldn't see me from any of the windows and pretend she wasn't there.

Finally she answered, patting her hair in place and smoothing down her dress. The automatic smile that came to her lips disappeared when she saw me.

'Simon! What on earth are you doing here?'

'I'm looking for Lisa.'

'Oh, Simon! You shouldn't have come all this way! You know I can't tell you where she is.'

'Well, I have. Can I come in?'

'Oh, yes, of course,' she led me into the kitchen. 'Do you want some coffee? I was just making some.'

'Yes, please.'

She busied herself with percolators and filters.

'How is Lisa?' I asked.

'Not good.'

'I'd like to help.'

'I don't think you can.'

'Why not?'

She turned to me. 'Her life has been turned upside down, Simon. Frank's death, losing her job, Frank's . . .' she paused, 'sexuality. Rightly or wrongly she holds you responsible.'

'So she knows about Frank and John?'

'Yes. A detective flew out here to interview her. And Eddie and me as well.'

'That must have been so hard for her.' I looked closely at her mother. 'But you knew all the time, didn't you?'

She nodded. 'It took a while to dawn on me. Mind you, I think it took a while to dawn on him. It was almost a relief when it did. You see, before, I thought there was something wrong with me. We stayed married for the sake of the kids for a while, but there was no point in it. So, in the end, we divorced.'

'And Lisa never suspected anything?'

'No. In retrospect, I wish she had. She's a strong kid, she would have gotten used to the idea eventually. But Frank was adamant we shouldn't tell the kids. And now . . .' Ann's chin shook. 'Now after Frank died in such a horrible way, it's just so difficult for her. And for Eddie, of course.'

She sniffed, and reached for a tissue from a box on the windowsill.

'So she holds me responsible? She can't really think I killed him, can she?'

'I don't know whether she thinks it through that rationally. She's afraid you might have. Everything else has gone wrong in her life,

315

so she thinks it will turn out for the worst with you too. She just wants to leave it all behind, Simon. Frank, Boston and you. Especially you.'

These were difficult words to hear. The coffee machine began to bubble and drip. Ann glanced at it, and then let it do its stuff.

'What about you?' I asked. 'You don't think I killed him do you?'

She composed herself, and then slowly shook her head.

'Then, can I tell you why I want to see her?'

'It's not a good idea, Simon,' she said.

'OK, but just let me tell you. The reason Lisa was fired from BioOne was that she suspected a drug they are developing is dangerous. I've been doing my own investigating, and I think she might be right. I've collected a mass of information about this drug that I don't understand. Only she will know what it means. I'd like her to look at it.'

'That's not all you'd like, is it?'

'No,' I admitted. 'But it could prove Lisa right. And more importantly, we could save lives. Did you hear about Aunt Zoë?'

'No,' said Ann. 'What happened?'

I wasn't really surprised that Carl hadn't contacted Ann. After Frank's divorce, there had been little linking Zoë and her ex-sister-in-law, apart from the funeral.

'She had a stroke. Carl thinks she won't make it.'

'Oh, no!'

'She was taking neuroxil-5. She suffered from the side-effects. There will be others. You know Lisa. You know how important this would be to her.'

Ann poured the coffee and then sat down. We sipped the hot liquid in silence. Then she seemed to make up her mind. 'What do you want to know?'

'Where she's living.'

She glanced quickly at me. 'With her brother.'

'I thought so! Do you have his new address?'

Eddie had always lived in Haight-Ashbury, since his days at the nearby UCSF Medical School. His new apartment was only a couple of blocks away from his old one, where Lisa and I had visited him the year before. I wanted to give Lisa time to return from her lab in Stanford, so I spent several hours wandering around the area, drinking coffee, eating a sandwich, browsing in shops, walking. The Haight had been the centre of the 1967 Summer of Love, and nostalgia for that time was everywhere, from Grateful Dead and Jefferson Airplane memorabilia shops to places to buy quaint drug accessories.

I was not looking forward to meeting Eddie. It was clear that he had decided I had murdered Frank, and the guilt and anger that he had felt at his father's death had been channelled into hatred of me. I was sure he had been a strong influence in Lisa's decision to leave me, and her staying with him could hardly have warmed her feelings towards me.

I pressed the buzzer at the entrance to his building, a pink Victorian row house. There was a camera. He could see me. There was no hope of bluffing my way in.

'What do you want?' his voice was harsh.

'To see you,' I said.

There was a pause. 'Come on up,' the buzzer said with a kind of vicious eagerness.

His apartment was on the second floor. He opened the door, wearing a red T-shirt and jeans. He flashed a broad ironic smile. 'Come in, come in, old chap.'

I followed him into the living area. It was a mess of magazines, mugs, glasses and some low furniture. I recognized Lisa's bag in a corner, and some of her clothes stuffed next to it. She was probably sleeping in here.

'Let me get you a beer.' He turned his back on me and headed towards the kitchen area and the refrigerator. I followed a couple of steps behind. Suddenly he spun round. I was too surprised to do anything, and he landed a blow on the side of my head.

It knocked me to one side. My first impulse was to fly back at him, but I resisted it, and stood up straight. He hit me again on the chin. It hurt, and left my brain muzzy, but I held my head upright and my eyes on his.

If he tried to hit me again, I would have to defend myself, but he didn't. He smiled, rubbing his fist. 'I've been wanting to do that for so long.'

'Good. Well, now we've got that over with, I take it Lisa isn't back from Stanford yet?'

'No. And she won't want to see you.' He took one bottle of beer out of the refrigerator, opened it, and drank. 'So fuck off.'

'I'd like to wait for her.'

'She doesn't want to see you. Fuck off.' He took a couple of steps towards me. He was about my size, but I was confident I could handle him. I had intended to avoid it if I could, but at that moment, beating the living daylights out of Eddie Cook didn't seem such a bad idea.

'Eddie! Simon! Stop it!'

I turned round. Lisa stood in the doorway. She looked very small. Her eyes were tired, her shoulders weary. I wanted to pull her to me and hold her tight, tight until she felt safe under my protection.

'Simon, get out,' she said, matter-of-factly.

'That's what I was just telling him to do,' said Eddie.

I knew there was no chance of talking her round now, and I hadn't planned to. I handed her an envelope with the note I had written at Marsh House that morning. 'Read this.'

I held the envelope out to her. She stared at it, and then reached out slowly to take it from my hand. Our skin didn't touch. Then, deliberately, she ripped it once, and threw it into the wastepaper bin.

I kept my cool. 'That letter contains instructions for how to get access to BioOne's files on the neuroxil-5 trials. You were right, Lisa, there is something wrong with the drug. Aunt Zoë had a stroke a couple of days ago as a result of taking it. I can't analyse the information. You can. It's all there.'

Her eyes widened. 'Aunt Zoë? No. Really?'

I nodded slowly.

'Is she going to be all right?'

'Carl doesn't think so.'

'Oh, no!' She glanced down at the bin, and then, with an effort, composed herself. 'I won't read your letters, Simon. I won't listen to what you have to say. I want you out of my life. Now go back to Boston.'

It was painful to hear these words from someone I loved so much, and someone who needed me so much. But I had expected them.

'All right, I'm leaving now. But read the letter. And meet me in the coffee shop round the corner at ten o'clock tomorrow morning.'

'I won't be there, Simon.'

''Bye,' I said, and without waiting for a reply that would not have come, I left the apartment.

32

I arrived at the coffee shop half an hour early, after an appalling night's sleep in a cheap hotel worrying about whether Lisa would come. The café walls were orange, adorned with posters of dolphins and whales gliding through shimmering seas. The food was vegetarian and organic, and the coffee came in the standard forty different combinations. The place was almost empty. There was a cool banker type with a fancy briefcase and a raincoat and hair slightly longer than the market average, two young women with metal-studded faces and short white-blonde hair, and an old man dressed in a beaten-up overcoat pretending to be a bum. The double latte he had ordered and the *Scientific American* he was reading gave him away as something else.

I asked for a simple cup of coffee and opened the *Wall Street Journal*. BioOne stock was down four to fifty-nine. Daniel had probably sold by now. In fact, knowing him, he had probably shorted the stock. I wondered if I could be implicated if he had dabbled in some insider trading. But that was the least of my worries.

I finished the coffee and ordered another. Ten to ten. Would she come? It wasn't even ten yet, and I was beginning to panic.

Ten o'clock came and went, then ten thirty, then eleven. I drank cups of coffee nervously, and my nerves jangled at the result. I tried to read and reread the same pages of the *Journal*. She wasn't coming. Lisa could sometimes be a bit late, but not that late. She obviously wasn't coming. But I couldn't leave. I was rooted to my chair; I couldn't even dash out of the café to a news-stand to get something else to read. Then I'd never know whether I'd missed her or not.

Another coffee, decaf this time. And an organic Danish. My stomach needed something for the coffee to bite into.

She wasn't coming, but I couldn't accept that. Everything I had done over the last month, the risks I had taken, the trouble I had caused, had all been with the intention of winning Lisa back. But what if she didn't want to be won back? Lisa was a strong-minded woman. What if I couldn't convince her? Even if I showed her that I hadn't killed her father, that she was right all along about BioOne, what if even then she didn't come back to me?

I couldn't accept that. I stayed put, as though remaining in that café was the only thing left I could do.

It started to rain. Big San Franciscan drops of water, that swiftly turned the street into a landscape of streams and lakes. Umbrellas rose outside, the windows fugged up, cars swished water at dancing pedestrians.

The café was beginning to fill with the lunch crowd. The waiters looked as if they were about to throw me out, so I ordered a grilled vegetable sandwich.

At two o'clock, I gave up. I barged out into the waterlogged street, raindrops cooling my overheated skin, and splattering my hair on my scalp. I didn't know where I was walking.

'Simon!' I almost didn't hear it, didn't believe it. 'Simon!'

I turned. It was Lisa running towards me, her bag swinging in the rain.

She stopped in front of me, panting. I tried a smile. She returned it quickly, nervously. Water dripped off her nose and chin.

'Thank God you waited. It's been hours. I thought you'd go back to Boston.'

I shrugged. I allowed myself to smile again.

Lisa glanced up at the rain. 'Let's go inside.' She looked back towards the café.

'I can't go back in there,' I said. I noticed a scruffy diner further down the street. 'How about that?'

She grimaced. 'OK. Actually, I'm starving.'

She ordered a hamburger; I was relieved to get away with nothing.

We sat in silence as we waited for the food. There was so much to say. So much could yet go wrong. For now I was just pleased to be with her.

'I read those files,' she said at last.

'And?'

'And I'm almost certain that neuroxil-5 causes strokes in some patients if used over a six month period or longer.'

At first I felt a wave of relief. Then I remembered the thousand or so patients who were taking the drug in the Phase Three trial. Including Aunt Zoë.

'Almost sure?'

'The statistics are difficult. I didn't have time to go through the data thoroughly, but my gut feeling is that when the analysis is done it'll show the drug is dangerous.'

'Why hasn't BioOne discovered that yet?'

'Good question,' she said. 'It's not that easy in an Alzheimer's trial. The patients are old, and a number of them will die anyway. It looks like the incidence of strokes doesn't increase until at least six months after the patients start to take the drug, possibly longer.'

'Aunt Zoë had been taking it for seven months.'

Lisa nodded. 'Poor Aunt Zoë. I'll really miss her. She was a great woman. I just wish they'd listened to me.'

'I don't think Carl will ever forgive himself.'

'Is there no hope?'

I shook my head. 'Not according to Carl.'

We were both quiet for a few moments, thinking of Zoë.

'Didn't Enever pick any of this up?' I said.

'Nowhere does he mention the problem directly. But from his actions, I'd say he began to notice that the stroke adverse events were getting out of line. He might have thought this was just a blip. But he persuaded some clinicians to reclassify their patients as suffering from mini strokes rather than Alzheimer's, then removed the strokes from the statistics.'

'So he knowingly fiddled the figures?'

'I wouldn't say that, exactly. He may have genuinely believed the patients were misdiagnosed, or he may have convinced himself. I can't tell.'

'Hm. Anything from Catarro?'

'Yes. There were some e-mails about the two stroke deaths. Enever suggested the patients might have suffered from mini strokes. There's nothing from Catarro about the autopsies.'

'They must have spoken on the phone,' I said. 'But the autopsy records should be easy to get.'

Lisa's hamburger arrived, and she munched on it nervously.

'You were right,' I said.

'Yes,' she replied. She gave me a small smile. 'Thank you for proving it.'

'You read in my note how Dr Catarro spoke to your father just before he died,' I said quietly.

Lisa nodded and bit her lip.

'I didn't kill him,' I said.

She looked down. 'I didn't want to meet you here, Simon. But you were right. This neuroxil-5 stuff is important. What I don't want to do is talk about us, OK?'

I sighed. 'How have you been feeling since you came out here?'

'Better,' said Lisa. 'I mean, I still feel awful about Dad. And I'm angry about Boston Peptides, and about you, and . . .' she paused. 'Sorry. We weren't going to talk about us. But the world doesn't seem quite as black as it did. Out here, I can see a new life. Some days, I almost feel human. It was the right thing to do.'

'Don't you miss me?' I asked, and then immediately regretted it.

She bit her lip, and ignored the question.

'Sorry. Can I ask you something else?'

'Maybe,' she mumbled, eyes lowered.

'Has Kelly spoken to you about the BP 56 trials?'

Lisa shook her head, but I had caught her interest.

'They're going well apart from one thing. Apparently, the drug causes depression in some of the volunteers who are taking it. It can reduce the levels of serotonin in the brain.' Now I had all her attention. 'When did you start taking it?'

'You remember. About a week after Dad died. We had all the animal data in, but we couldn't start giving the drug to volunteers until it had all been processed. We just didn't have the time to wait that long, so I started taking it myself to get an early indication of any side-effects.'

'And when did you stop? When you came out here?'

'Yes. When I was fired from Boston Peptides there didn't seem much point any more.'

I wanted to ask her again why she had been so stupid as to take an untested drug herself. But I didn't. I stayed quiet.

She put her head in her hands. 'That explains a lot. No wonder I felt so bad. Why didn't I realize that was what was happening?'

'There was a lot else going on,' I said.

'I guess you're right,' Lisa was shaking her head. 'How stupid! I mean, I was keeping a diary of how I felt, recording the tiniest change in my bowel movements. And there was I, feeling more miserable than I've ever felt in my life, and I didn't even notice it.'

'You weren't exactly in a position to think clearly.'

'I guess I wasn't.'

'And now you've stopped taking it. Maybe that's why you feel better now?'

She looked up thoughtfully. 'Maybe.'

'Now can I tell you why I didn't kill your father?' I said quietly.

'Simon, I said – '

'I have a right to tell you. Just once. All you need to do is listen, and then you can go back to Eddie and your job at Stanford.'

She took a deep breath. 'OK.'

'Three people have been murdered in the last couple of months: your father, John Chalfont and Dr Catarro. The one thing that links all three is BioOne.'

'You said Dr Catarro died in a car accident,' Lisa interrupted.

'Yes. But it could have been faked.'

'Could have been?'

I fought to maintain my patience. 'Yes. Dr Catarro discovered that too many of his patients were dying after taking neuroxil-5. He was going to make a big fuss about it. He mentioned this to your father at a dinner party. Your father made his own inquiries. He asked Art amongst others about the drug. Knowing Frank, he would have been quick to reveal his suspicions as soon as he knew them. So someone killed both of them.'

Lisa was listening quietly now.

'Then John discovered something suspicious about BioOne, which he wanted to tell me about. So he was murdered. And when I was getting closer to what has happened, they tried to shoot me.'

'Shoot you?' Lisa exclaimed.

'Yes. Outside our apartment.'

'Oh, my God!' She put her hand over her mouth. 'Why would anyone do that?'

'If neuroxil-5 fails to get FDA approval, BioOne will be worthless. That will be very bad for a lot of people. There's Enever and Jerry Peterson. And the company means everything to Art. He's been looking more and more unstable since all this started.'

I watched Lisa. She was listening closely. 'But what about the gun I found in our closet, Simon?'

'I don't know about that,' I said. 'Someone must have put it there.'

'But who? How?'

I shook my head. 'I don't know.'

Lisa was silent for a moment. 'Eddie's sure you did it.'

'I know. But what about John? And Dr Catarro? Why would I kill them? And why would I try to get myself shot?'

'I don't know.'

We were coming to the reason I had flown all this way. To the moment when I would know whether everything I had been doing over the last month had been worthwhile.

'I have one more question, and then you can go away and never see me again if you want,' I began. 'I can see how when you were so upset about your father and you were taking that drug you might have thought all kinds of things. But now, here, I want to know.' I took a deep breath. 'Do you think I murdered your father?'

Lisa looked down at the Formica table, and the debris of her burger. She fidgeted with a paper napkin.

'Lisa?'

'I don't . . .' she mumbled.

'Lisa. Look at me. Answer me. And then you can go.'

She looked up. A small nervous smile touched her lips. She shook her head. 'No,' she said. 'I don't think you killed him.'

I couldn't believe it! I was so happy, I wanted to leap into the air and shout. But I controlled myself. I knew I still had a long way to go.

I looked at her empty plate. 'A hamburger?' I asked. 'I thought you never ate that kind of stuff.'

'It's my craving,' Lisa said. 'You'd have thought it could have been something truly delicious like double chocolate chip ice cream. But it's burgers and fries.'

'How are you?' I asked. 'How's the baby?'

Her hand fell to her stomach. I thought I could perhaps see a slight thickening of her waist, but maybe I was imagining it.

'I'm lousy. I've been throwing up almost every morning. And in the evenings, too, sometimes.' Then she looked up and her eyes gleamed. 'I saw the baby, Simon. I had an ultrasound on Friday. It's real. It has a head and it moves and everything!'

I wished I'd been there, but I couldn't say it.

It had stopped raining outside. 'Come on, let's get out of here,' I said.

We left the diner and walked. I wasn't quite sure where we were, and I didn't care where we went.

'I wasn't going to come,' Lisa said. 'I took your letter out of the trash can, like you knew I would. Then I dialled into Net Cop's network. I was up all night working through those files. I realized there was definitely something wrong with neuroxil-5 after all. But I still couldn't face seeing you. I told Eddie I wouldn't go. And then ten o'clock passed, and I felt worse and worse. But in the end, after what had happened to Aunt Zoë and everything you'd done to get the information, I knew I had to see you,' she said. 'And you were still there!'

I reached for her hand and squeezed it. 'Only just.'

We walked through puddles, weaving our way past other pedestrians. Above us, blue sky was ripping through the black clouds. Isolated streams of sunshine illuminated the newly watered Victorian buildings of the Haight, giving the faded hippiedom of the shops and cafés a new glister.

'What have you been doing?' she asked.

I told her. I talked long and hard, about Revere, BioOne, Art, Gil, Craig, getting shot at, her. All the thoughts that had been rushing round my head over the previous week burst out in a torrent, as though a dam had been breached. Lisa was the only person in the world I had ever been able to tell everything to: it felt so good to talk to her again.

We entered Golden Gate Park. I assumed Lisa had steered us there, I had paid no attention to where we were going. We walked across to the Japanese Tea Garden, where Lisa had taken me on our first trip to San Francisco together. Because of the rain, it was virtually empty. We sat on a bench next to a miniature bridge over a tiny stream. The sun had emerged now, as the black clouds scurried over the Bay somewhere to the east. Water glistened on the moss-covered stones and lush green foliage, and gurgled through the stream beside us. I put my arm round her and pulled her close.

'I'm sorry, Simon,' she said. 'Am I forgiven?'

'Of course.'

'Can I come back?'

My heart leapt. I kissed her.

We took a taxi back to my hotel. We fell on each other, fulfilling each other's need, expressing with our bodies what we couldn't say in words. Joy, tenderness, fear, love, loneliness. Afterwards, as she lay softly in my arms, I didn't want to move, never wanted to leave this drab hotel room, this nondescript queen-size bed, and Lisa. Here was the woman I loved. Outside was all that had driven us apart.

Lisa sniffed. I looked down and saw a tear running down her face.

'What's wrong?'

'I was just thinking about Zoë,' she said.

'I know. It's very sad.' I squeezed her.

'I was really fond of her, you know.'

'I know.'

She lay quietly for a few moments, and then dabbed her eyes with the sheet. 'It was horrible without you, Simon.'

'It was awful for me too.'

'It wasn't that I'd left you. It was that I thought you'd changed. Become someone else. Or, even worse, that you never were the man I thought you were. The man I loved. You haven't changed, have you Simon?'

'No,' I said, stroking her hair.

'I'd lost Dad like that too. And he turned out to be a different man than I thought he was.'

'No, Lisa, that's not true.'

Her eyes flicked up at me in surprise.

'Your father always loved you,' I continued. 'That was always genuine. He had one secret he kept from you, but he kept it from himself also. And it had nothing to do with you. He never regretted being your father, you know that. Don't think of him as someone different. He would have hated it.'

A smile spread across her thin face. She kissed me on the cheek and nestled into my chest.

'I'm sorry, Simon. I must have been very difficult.'

'You were having a very hard time.'

Lisa sighed. 'You know what the worst thing about taking BP 56 is?'

'What?'

'I'm pregnant.'

'You don't think . . .'

'I don't know. In theory it should have no effect at all. But you can never tell with new drugs. I'm scared.'

So was I. After all this, I prayed that the baby would be all right.

'Was the ultrasound OK?'

'So far. I'm going to have all the tests I can. I'm sorry, Simon.'

I held her tight. She lay there in my arms for a long time.

There were two people to see before we headed out for the airport that evening. Lisa's mother was overjoyed. She kissed us both and wished us luck. She pleaded with us to keep our date for Thanksgiving and the only way we could extricate ourselves was by consenting.

Eddie was more difficult. I waited outside his building. Half an hour passed before Lisa came out.

'How did it go?' I asked, as we waited for a cab to appear.

She was silent for a bit. 'I'm lucky, Simon. I've got you, although sometimes I'm too stupid to realize it. Eddie doesn't have anyone.'

'You feel bad about leaving him?'

'Dad's death has torn him up.'

I looked her in the eye. 'Lisa. I don't want to force you to choose between your brother and me. When we've sorted this out, go back and stay with him for a while. I don't want to be his enemy.'

She glanced up at me and smiled. 'Thanks. Now, let's go.'

33

They were all there in the large conference room: Gil, Art, Diane, Ravi and Daniel from Revere, and Enever and Jerry Peterson from BioOne. Gardner Phillips had called everyone to his offices first thing on Monday morning at my request. He was also there, of course, together with one of his associates, an earnest-looking woman with pen and yellow legal pad poised.

He stood up, shook my hand, and indicated that we should take our seats at the head of the long table. He sat on my right. Although I still didn't know him very well, I trusted him. At that moment I needed a good lawyer, and I was thankful to Gil for getting me one.

'Thank you for coming, ladies and gentlemen. I think you all know my clients Simon Ayot and his wife, Lisa Cook. They have some information about BioOne that they would like to share with you. Simon.'

I smiled at the assembled group. Diane nodded and returned my smile, Ravi looked vague, Daniel fascinated, and the others all glowered. Gil stared at me through his thick lenses, his forehead pulled down in deep furrows over his eyebrows. Enever looked furious. Not exactly an eager audience.

'I have bad news,' I began. 'Lisa and I have uncovered evidence that BioOne's drug neuroxil-5 is dangerous to human life.'

There was a stir around the room. 'Prove it,' demanded Enever.

'We will,' I said, nodding to him. Then I told them the whole story. About Lisa's concerns about neuroxil-5, about John's message to me before he died, and about my own investigations at the clinics involved in the trial. I then said that Lisa had been able to get hold of more complete data that had confirmed her initial suspicions.

Enever was quick with the counter-attack. 'What data?' he shot at Lisa.

'I can't be specific,' she replied. Gardner Phillips had warned us to stay well clear of how we had got hold of the information. 'But I can assure you there can be no question as to the conclusions.'

Enever snorted. 'That's absurd. Your "conclusions" are all unsubstantiated. They have no validity at all. Let's all stop wasting time and get back to work.'

'Don't you have any concerns about the incidence of strokes in patients who have been taking neuroxil-5 for more than six months?' Lisa asked.

'No, of course not,' Enever replied.

'Do you deny that you attempted to get clinicians to reclassify patients who suffered strokes as non-Alzheimer's patients?'

'No. Where appropriate. It's easy to misdiagnose mini strokes as Alzheimer's.'

'What about Dr Catarro? He was concerned, wasn't he? And his two patients who died of strokes were shown to have Alzheimer's at their autopsies, weren't they?'

'Possibly. But these are elderly people. Two of them dying of a stroke is no more than a statistical blip. He was just being difficult.'

'It was convenient he had his accident, then, wasn't it?'

'Too right,' muttered Enever. Then, as eyebrows were raised round the table, he continued. 'Look, of course I'm sorry the guy died. But he was a fool, all right?'

Enever's insensitivity was playing into our hands with the people gathered round the table. But he hadn't admitted anything yet.

'Will you make your data available for an independent consultant to analyse?' I asked Enever.

'Absolutely not,' he said. 'This is commercially sensitive information of a highly confidential nature. Anyway, the FDA sees all the adverse event reports.'

'But in a population of elderly people like this one, the abnormally high incidence of strokes wouldn't necessarily leap out at them, would it?' Lisa said. 'Not until they analyse all the data at the end of the trial?'

Enever glared at her.

Gil spoke for the first time. 'Where did you get this data from, Lisa?'

'I can't say,' she said.

'Pure fabrication!' spluttered Enever.

Gil looked at both of us. 'You realize how serious these allegations are? If they are true, then neuroxil-5 will be withdrawn. BioOne's stock price would collapse immediately. The results would be catastrophic for all of us.'

'I know,' I said. 'I wish BioOne was a success. But it isn't. And the sooner we face up to that fact, the better.'

Jerry Peterson was watching me, not convinced I was telling the truth, but not convinced I was lying, either. 'Thomas, can't we analyse the data on Phase Three in-house?' he asked.

Enever shook his head. 'We'd have to unblind the data. The regulators hate that. Not only that, it would delay completion of the trial. Don't forget Werner Wilson is expecting results in March.'

Jerry Peterson remembered. He kept quiet.

'Every day this trial continues there's a chance that another one of the thousand or so patients will have a stroke,' I said. 'You can't hide from that.'

'Bullshit,' muttered Enever.

'You son-of-a-bitch, Ayot.' It was Art. He looked edgy. Sober, but edgy. 'You've always had it in for BioOne, just like Frank. You're jealous, that's all. But that's a damn stupid reason for destroying this firm's best investment.'

'Hold on, Art.' It was Gil. 'From what I've heard, there is a chance that people will die unless we act now to stop the trial until the data can be analysed independently. We can't gamble with other people's lives.'

'There's no evidence!' Enever interrupted. 'We're relying entirely on what these people say.' He jabbed a finger at Lisa. 'I fired her. She's just trying to get her own back.'

Gil threw me a sideways glance, but then continued. 'I've known Simon for a couple of years, Dr Enever. And Lisa is the daughter of a good friend of mine. While they might be making all this up, I'd say there's also a good chance they're telling the truth. Right now, we don't know. So what I suggest is that Dr Enever gives all the information he has to Ravi to look at. If Simon and Lisa's conclusions are found to be accurate, we will have to stop the trial. And I mean *all* the information, Dr Enever.'

'That's absurd,' Enever protested.

'Either that, or we stop the trial immediately.'

There was silence round the table, as the consequences of these words sunk in.

'Ravi?' Gil looked at him for his reaction.

'I won't know whether I will be able to draw any conclusions until I know what data is available. But safety is the most important issue in developing any new drug,' he said. 'From what Simon and Lisa say, there must be real doubts. We have to address those right away.'

'Diane? Do you agree?'

She nodded.

Gil took a deep breath. 'Art?'

'No way!' Art almost shouted. 'This will destroy the stock price. It will destroy BioOne. Hell, it will destroy Revere. You can't do it, Gil.'

Some of the weariness had left Gil's face. He sat up straighter, more determined. He knew what he was doing. It was as if, now that he was face-to-face with a difficult decision, he could summon the courage to go through with it, no matter what the consequences were.

'Jerry?'

Jerry Peterson's fresh face looked at Enever, who was scowling deeply, and Art, who looked as if he were about to leap from his chair and throw it at someone. Then he shrugged, and gave a small smile, as if to say 'easy come, easy go'.

'I want you to give all the information we have on neuroxil-5 to Ravi by tomorrow, Thomas,' he said.

'Thank you,' said Gil. 'I needn't remind you that what we have been discussing this morning is highly price-sensitive information. Anyone selling stock would be inviting investigation from the SEC.'

Enever sat there fuming. Art didn't look much happier. Everyone else let the consequences of the decision that had just been taken sink in. If I was right, it wasn't good for any of them.

'That still leaves one other important question,' I said.

They looked at me with expressions that ranged between dazed and furious.

'Someone killed Frank. And someone killed John. And someone probably killed Dr Catarro.' I paused, to let what I was saying have its effect. 'They were murdered because they discovered what I now know about BioOne. Now, the people who would lose most from neuroxil-5 being discredited are all in this room.'

Enever looked up. 'That's absurd,' he said. 'You don't think I killed them, do you? Why would I do that? There's nothing to hide. Neuroxil-5 is a perfectly safe drug.'

I glanced at Art. He glared back. 'Asshole,' he muttered.

Gil cleared his throat, once more taking charge. 'Gardner, I think it would be a good idea if you called in the police. Perhaps we should all wait here for them.'

'I'll do that,' Gardner Phillips said, and the meeting broke up.

Small groups formed. Jerry Peterson turned to Enever, and began asking questions. Both men looked angry, although Jerry was under much better control. Gil walked over to Ravi, and began an earnest discussion. He beckoned to Daniel to join them. Of all of us in the room, Ravi had the most experience of biotechnology. I suspected it would be he, and not Art, who would be picking up the pieces of BioOne.

Art remained seated at the table, drinking and refilling a glass of sparkling mineral water. This would not be good for his attempt to stay on the wagon.

Diane walked up to Lisa and me. I could feel Lisa stiffen.

'It's a bad day for Revere,' she said.

I nodded.

'But if there is a problem with the drug, we can't pretend it will go away,' she continued. 'Gil was right. We have to get Ravi to confirm it.'

'Revere will lose millions. Hundreds of millions,' I said.

'It was only ever paper profits.'

We stood together in silence for a moment, contemplating the gloomy future of the firm.

Then she glanced at Lisa and me. I could feel the tension in Lisa next to me, and I didn't dare to check her expression.

'Good luck, both of you,' Diane said with a quick smile, and turned to find Gil and Ravi.

'Bitch,' muttered Lisa.

I didn't contradict her. But I wasn't so sure.

34

It was wonderful to wake up the next morning in our own bed, together. It took us a while to get up, but eventually I stumbled into the shower and Lisa went hunting for breakfast. Twenty minutes later, I heard the door slam. I stepped out of the shower, and grabbed a towel. I was hungry.

'What did you get, Lisa? Did they have any of those black ones hot?'

Lisa always got whatever was freshest from the bagel bakery, which made breakfasts a bit of a lottery. But as long as it wasn't rye with caraway seeds I was basically happy.

No answer.

'Lisa?'

I walked out of the bathroom through to the kitchen. Lisa had put the bag of bagels on the table. She was staring at the newspaper. Wordlessly, she handed it to me.

'Biotech Boss Found Dead,' shouted the headline. Underneath was a picture of a grimacing Enever.

I scanned the article. Dr Thomas Enever had been found hanged in his apartment in Newton. The police were tight-lipped, but it was clear what had happened.

'Suicide,' I said.

Lisa nodded.

'Is there anything linking him to your father?'

'Nothing there,' she said. 'But I'm sure there will be.'

*

Gil called me later that day, and asked me to come in to Revere the next morning. All was forgiven, and there was work to be done.

Ravi's analysis confirmed Lisa's opinion. There was a significant chance neuroxil-5 might be dangerous. Indeed, there were signs that as the length of time a patient took the drug increased, so did the chances that he or she would suffer from a stroke. Taken over a period of years, the drug might kill most of the people who took it. Jerry Peterson was left with no choice. The trials were stopped immediately, the Phase Three data was unblinded for further analysis, and the FDA was informed, as were all the clinics participating in the trial. All this was outlined in a press announcement.

The market response was predictable. The stock dived from fifty-five dollars to one and three-eighths, slashing the value of the company from nearly two billion dollars to around fifty million. The value of Revere's stake was reduced from three hundred and forty million to eight and a half. Nobody had escaped unscathed, except possibly for Daniel. He acted as though he too had taken a bath, but without conviction. I was sure the bastard had sold at the top.

Of course BioOne's pessimistic announcement about the side-effects was only one reason for the fall in the stock price. There was plenty in the story of Thomas Enever's death to scare investors. The press dug deep, and quickly found buried secrets. The faked neuroxil-3 experiment. The hijacking of the Australian research institute's ideas. And the murders of Frank Cook and John Chalfont.

The police did their best to sound vague, but the press had found their murderer. Thomas Enever had killed to defend the drug he had devoted his life to developing – the drug that he had stolen from his Australian alma mater. The world of biotechnology was portrayed as an evil one, full of secrets and homicidal egos. Biotech stocks everywhere fell.

The press interviewed Lisa and me, but on Gardner Phillips's advice we said little. Neither did we tell Mahoney and his colleagues anything about the gun Lisa had found. Phillips felt we should only do this if the Assistant DA gave us immunity from prosecution, and this she was still reluctant to do.

I wasn't surprised. I wasn't entirely convinced the case was closed, either.

I called Helen and told her we would be able to fund her appeal. She was overjoyed. Apparently, her extremely expensive barrister was confident of victory, once we got round to paying him.

But all this was too late for Aunt Zoë. She died on Tuesday, a week after her stroke. For the second time in a month Lisa and I attended a *shiva* at that small house in Brookline.

We were in a sombre mood as we returned to our apartment after the funeral. I poured us both a glass of wine, and we sat down together in the dimly lit living room. We shared each other's silence, wrapped up in thoughts of our own, but grateful to be together in our introspection.

Finally, Lisa spoke. 'You know, Simon. We still don't know how the gun came to be in the closet. Enever can't have put it there.'

The thought had occurred to me, too. 'Because there was no break-in, you mean?'

'That. And also he didn't know either of us, then. I mean why pick on you? Or me? He wouldn't have known our address.'

'He could have found it, with a bit of research.'

'Possibly. But he would have had to know a lot about you and me, and our relationship to Dad, to pick on us as likely suspects and our closet as the place to hide his gun.'

'You're right,' I said, thoughtfully.

We sat in silence for a minute or so. Footsteps approached along the quiet street outside, tapping louder and louder, and then receding into the evening. Through the undrawn curtains a small tree on the other side of the road glimmered in the gaslight. I felt a tremor run through Lisa, and she pressed herself against me.

'Simon?'

'Yes?'

'I'm scared.'

It was Thursday evening. I rubbed my eyes, saved my file, and turned off my machine. I'd done enough work for one day. I was just putting on my coat, when I realized I didn't have my house-keys with me. Henry Chan had offered Lisa her old job back, and it was her first day. I knew there was little chance that she would be home when I got back. I was supposed to be meeting Kieran and the boys at the Red Hat later on that evening, and I wanted to go home to get changed. I was considering my options, the best of which seemed to be to go to the Red Hat early, when I remembered the spare set of keys I had stuffed in the corner of my desk drawer for just such an eventuality.

As I dropped them in my trouser pocket, it dawned on me. That was how the gun had been planted! Someone had let themselves into our apartment with my house-keys borrowed from my desk.

But who?

Not Thomas Enever. Someone at Revere.

It was a big night at the Red Hat. Kieran was there, of course, and half a dozen others, all ex-business school. I had asked Daniel along, but as I had expected, he had declined. He never had been a great group socializer.

I was asked lots of questions, and aided by plenty of beer rapidly drunk, talked freely. Frank and John's murder, Enever's suicide and BioOne's collapse for once made for a better story than job offers and stock options.

I remained the centre of attention for an hour or so, and then Greg Vilgren spoke up. He was an American who had been posted to London with a big investment bank, and was on a brief visit back to Boston.

'Hey. Did you guys hear about Sergei Delesov?'

Blank looks round the table.

'It was in the papers in London. He was murdered about a month ago.'

'Jesus. What happened?' Kieran asked.

'It was a contract killing,' Greg said. 'I didn't realize it, but apparently he was the youngest CEO of any bank in Russia.'

'Wow!' said Kieran. 'I always thought he was a bit of a shady character.'

Notes were compared on Sergei. Nobody knew him much. Then Kim spoke. She was a management consultant with one of the big Boston firms, and one of only two women at the table.

'Daniel Hall knew him, I think. He used to talk about his stock picks with him.'

'Really?' I said, leaning forward. I remembered that Kim had sat next to Daniel in class.

'Yeah. In fact, I think Daniel borrowed some money from Sergei, or from some people Sergei had introduced him to. To play the market.'

'Much money?'

'You know Daniel. It was more likely to be a hundred grand than ten.'

'Has he made his million, yet?' Greg asked me.

'He gets close, then he blows it all,' I said. 'But he's a bright guy.'

'Hey, did he ever hit on you, Kimmy?' someone demanded.

'Daniel! No way,' said Kim, and the conversation deteriorated to its usual late-evening level.

I watched Daniel in action. He was on the phone trying to say no to a hopeful entrepreneur.

The entrepreneur was persistent, and Daniel's patience wore out as it always did. 'I said no. No means no! N – O. No!' He slammed down the phone. 'These guys drive me crazy. What do they think we are, a fucking charity?'

'I can't think where they'd get that idea from,' I said. 'You don't exactly come across to me as the charitable type, Daniel.'

'Gee thanks.'

'Daniel?'

'Yeah.'

'Did you hear about Sergei?'

'Sergei?'

'Sergei Delesov. The bloke we were at Harvard with.'

'Oh, yeah. Sergei. What happened?'

'He was murdered. In Russia. Greg Vilgren told me last night.'

'Jesus! Not another one. It's a dangerous world out there. They're dropping like flies.' He didn't seem especially upset, but then you wouldn't expect that from Daniel.

'You knew him quite well, didn't you?'

'Nah. Crazy Rooskie. Eurotrash. Do you remember he wore those Gucci loafers all the time?'

'Didn't he lend you some money?'

Daniel looked up sharply. 'Who told you that?'

'Kim Smith.'

Daniel grunted. 'I was down a few grand on some Dell I'd bought on margin. He knew some people who could tide me over. The stock came back within a month.'

'Some people?'

'Yeah. A loan company.'

'Why didn't you just go to a bank?'

'Jeez, Simon. What is this? An IRS investigation?'

'It just seems strange to borrow a few thousand dollars from some friends of a Russian, rather than top up your loan from the bank.'

'I was up to my limit with the bank. And my parents decided I was a lousy credit risk long ago. It was no big deal. I paid them back.'

Daniel made a show of looking over the papers on his desk, and I left him to them.

'What are you up to this weekend, Simon?' he asked after a couple of minutes.

'Oh, Lisa and I are going to Marsh House to sort out Frank's stuff. There's quite a lot to do. What about you?'

'Don't know yet.' Just then his phone rang, and he snatched it up.

35

We drove up to Woodbridge first thing the next morning in my Morgan. I parked it beside the house, in the spot where Frank had always left his Mercedes, and we climbed out. The thin November sun burned through the last remnants of the morning fog to illuminate the browns and golds of the watery landscape. There was no wind, and the silence of the marsh lay like a heavy cloak all around us. The only movement was the occasional flapping of an egret hauling itself into the air. There weren't many left now; most of them had gone south for the winter.

It was cold inside. I wound the grandfather clock and lit the stove, and a steady warmth soon pushed its way out from the old contraption through the building. The house wasn't really built for winter habitation, but the beginning of November was unseasonably warm, and the place was quiet, and cosy, and peaceful.

I had tried to call Jeff Lieberman the previous day, whenever Daniel was out of the office, without success. He was in and out of meetings all day. I had the number of his Riverside Drive apartment, so I tried him again. This time I got through.

'Hi, Simon.' He sounded tired.

'I didn't wake you, did I?'

'Yeah, but don't worry, you just beat the alarm by a couple of minutes. I didn't get home from the office until four last night. And they want me in again at eleven. All so we can make a pitch on

Monday that I know we won't win. But you've got to go through the motions.'

'Jeff. Do you remember when Daniel came to New York in October?'

'Yes.'

'You definitely saw him, did you?'

'What do you mean? Yes, I did.'

'And that was the tenth of October, right?' The day Frank was killed.

'I don't know the exact date. I can check with my diary?'

'Please.'

I waited a few seconds.

'Yes. Here it is. October tenth. Brunch. We were supposed to have dinner together, but he changed it.'

'He changed it?'

'Yeah. He called a day or so before, and said he'd met some "babe" who lived in New York who he wanted to see that night.'

'Daniel? A babe?'

'It sounded a little odd to me. I did try to pry, but he wasn't saying much. But, hey, everyone gets lucky sometime. He spent most of brunch pushing Net Cop.'

That much, at least, Daniel had told me. 'Did you see him that afternoon?'

'No. After brunch he headed off. I don't know where. Why all these questions?'

'Oh, nothing.'

'OK. I'll see you at the Net Cop board meeting next week.'

'See you then. Oh, and Jeff?'

'Yes?'

'Don't mention any of this to Daniel.'

There was a pause as Jeff tried to work out what I was fishing for. In the end he decided to trust me. 'OK,' he said and hung up.

'Well?' asked Lisa as I put down the phone. She was perched on Frank's desk beside me trying to follow my end of the conversation.

'Daniel switched dinner to brunch.'

We looked at each other.

Lisa exhaled. 'So, what do we do now?'

'Well, we don't have absolute proof. But the cops can check him out. They should find something to nail him, if they know what direction to look in.'

'Do we call Mahoney?'

I sighed. 'I'd rather not.'

'What about the Assistant DA? What was her name?'

'Pamela Leyser. Maybe. But I think we should talk to Gardner Phillips first.'

I dialled his home. His wife answered, and said he was out on the golf course. She gave me the number of his cell phone. I tried it. It was switched off. I called Mrs Phillips back, gave her Marsh House's telephone number, and asked her to make sure her husband called me as soon as he got in. It was urgent. She expected him back by eleven fifteen, although she said he might be home before then. I looked at the grandfather clock. Quarter to ten. An hour and a half.

The waiting was difficult.

'Shouldn't we call Mahoney?' Lisa said.

'I don't think so. I know Phillips. He'd definitely want me to speak to him first.'

'But we've proof it was Daniel!'

'I know. And I'm sure Phillips will want us to pass that on to the police. But I've screwed this up before, I don't want to do it again. Let's just wait till he calls back, shall we?'

'All right. But I'm not hanging around here,' said Lisa. 'I'll go crazy. I'm going for a walk. Coming?'

'No, I'll stay here, just in case he does call back early.'

Lisa grabbed her coat and walked out the door. Through the sitting-room window, I could see her tramp along the edge of the marsh to the right of the house.

I went upstairs to make sure the storm windows were securely fastened, my ears listening out for the ring of Frank's ancient telephone.

Instead, I heard the front door bang.

'Lisa! Did you forget something?' I ran down the stairs. 'He still hasn't called . . .'

I stopped short. There, standing in the middle of the living room, his hands thrust deep into his city raincoat, was Daniel.

'Hello, Simon,' he said casually.

My initial reaction was to bolt back up the stairs, but I fought to compose myself. 'Hello, Daniel,' I said in feigned welcome, as coolly as I could manage. 'What brings you here?'

He wasn't obviously carrying a gun. But he wasn't taking his hands out of his pockets either. I wasn't sure what effect a gun would have if fired from within a coat pocket like that. But from a foot or two's range, I didn't want to risk it.

'Oh, I'm meeting some people for lunch at Woodman's in Essex, and I thought I'd drop by on the way,' he answered. An extremely unlikely story, I thought. 'Where's Lisa?'

'She had to go into the lab,' I replied. 'She'll be there all day.' If the worst came to the worst, I didn't want Daniel hanging around waiting for her to come back from her walk. 'Can I make you some coffee?'

'Sure.'

I moved past him to get to the kitchen. He backed off, keeping his distance. For some reason he didn't want to show his hand yet. Why could that be?

As I fiddled about with coffee and filters, I thought it over. Another murder now would blow the case wide open again, something Daniel would want to avoid. He was here to check up on how much I knew. If I played it right, he might leave again.

'It's still quite warm for November,' I said.

'Yeah,' said Daniel. 'And October was quite pleasant too.'

In different circumstances, I would have laughed at Daniel's weather small-talk. It wasn't his style at all.

We moved back into the living room, Daniel still keeping his hands in his pockets, and his body a few feet away from mine. We sat in chairs opposite each other. I had decided not to jump him, but hope that he would talk and then go.

'So this is where Frank was killed, huh?' Daniel looked around.

345

The words acted like a shock, a reminder of what Daniel could do, as well as bringing back memories of finding Frank's body.

'Yes. Just there.'

I pointed to the section of scraped and scrubbed floorboard in the dining area. One of the things Lisa and I had intended to do that weekend was to cover the spot with a rug.

'And they still don't know for sure who did it, huh?'

'Not publicly. But I'm pretty certain they think it was Enever.'

'And you? What do you think?'

'I think it was Enever too.'

'Are you positive?'

I pretended to consider this for a moment. 'Yes. He killed himself, didn't he? He had everything to lose from news about the side-effects getting out. I'm sure it was him.'

'And Lisa? What does she think?'

'Oh, she thinks it was him, too.'

Daniel watched me closely. Then, seeming to come to a decision, he pulled a stubby revolver out of his pocket.

'I don't believe you,' he said.

I stared at the gun. This was not looking good at all. I had blown it. If I had jumped him when we were both standing up only a few feet away from each other, he with his gun hidden in the folds of his coat, I might have stood a chance. But now we were sitting down, ten feet apart, and he was pointing the weapon at my chest.

I swallowed. 'Why don't you believe me?'

'Because you and Lisa are too smart for that. I'd have been happier with a story about how you knew Enever wasn't responsible but you'd stopped worrying about it once you'd cleared yourself. That's what I was kind of hoping for. After the questions you were asking me yesterday, I thought I ought to make sure you hadn't jumped to any silly conclusions. Turns out I was right to be worried.'

'I know you killed him, Daniel,' I said.

'Have you talked to the police?'

I needed to play for time. I wasn't sure which answer would give me most.

'Well, have you?'

346

I shrugged.

'I need to know who you have spoken to.'

'And I won't tell you.'

He jerked the gun at me. 'I'll pull the trigger.'

I glared at him. I wasn't going to let him get the better of me. 'I know you will. I still won't tell you.'

I braced myself for the shot. But it didn't come. Daniel looked confused. He was thinking.

'Where's Lisa?' he asked at last.

'I told you. At the lab.'

'But you said you were both coming up here for the weekend?'

'She's coming this evening. She's got more work than she planned.'

'I heard you call out to her when I came in.'

'I thought you must be her. I assumed she'd left the lab early.'

Daniel scanned the room. 'Is that your bag, then?'

He nodded towards Lisa's black bag, lying on the floor.

'No,' I said simply.

'You're not being very truthful, are you, Simon?'

I shrugged.

'We'll wait here for her. She'll tell me who you've told. Especially when she sees me pointing a gun at you. How long will she be?'

Once again, I shrugged.

He glanced at the old grandfather clock. It was five past ten. 'We'll wait till eleven. Then we'll see. This should be a good spot to watch out for her.'

And it was. From the living room there was a perfect view of the marsh. She would be bound to come into view on her way back to the house.

We waited.

I knew why Daniel wanted to know who we had spoken to about him. If we hadn't told anyone, as indeed we hadn't yet, then once he had got us out of the way he would stand a reasonable chance of continuing to lead a normal life. Provided, of course, he managed to escape blame for our murders. If anyone else did know, then his best bet was to kill us straight away and take the first plane to South America.

Either way we ended up dead. I just didn't want my last act to be giving in to Daniel. But he was right. Lisa would tell him the truth, once she saw him pointing a gun at me.

I thought through again what Daniel had done over the previous few weeks. I had pieced most of it together, but I wanted to fill in the gaps. 'Did Enever have anything to do with Frank's death?' I asked.

Daniel laughed. 'No. Of course not. I thought about asking him for help, but there was really no need. He was doing everything he could to ignore any evidence that neuroxil-5 was dangerous. I think he just couldn't accept the idea that there might be a problem.'

'But Frank knew there was something wrong?'

'Yeah. He met some doctor in Rhode Island who was going to make trouble.'

'Why did you have to kill them? Was it because you'd borrowed money from the loan sharks Sergei Delesov introduced you to?'

'It was worse than that. I'd told them BioOne was a sure thing. The day afterward, huge volume went through in the stock. Millions of dollars. If the bad news had broken about neuroxil-5 when they were still invested, I'd have been dead meat.'

'But they got out?'

'Yep. Thanks to your warning, I got them out in time, as well as myself.'

'And everyone was happy.'

'I wouldn't say they were exactly happy with me. It was hairy there for a while. I don't think we'll be doing business together again, shall we say. But I'm still alive.'

'Yes.' I looked at him squarely. 'You are. But quite a few other people aren't.'

He just grunted.

I thought through what must have happened. 'You changed dinner to brunch with Jeff in New York, and came back to Boston that afternoon to murder Frank?'

Daniel smiled thinly. 'Very clever. I even had time to get the last flight back from Logan to New York. The hotel could vouch that I spent the weekend there.'

'And afterwards you used my spare apartment keys to let yourself in to plant the gun in my closet?'

'Seemed like a good idea,' Daniel smiled smugly. 'It nearly worked.'

'Who killed Dr Catarro?'

'The Russians. And they were the ones who were supposed to deal with you.'

'What about John? Why did you kill him?'

'I had to. He'd remembered something Frank told him about neuroxil-5. He called me to ask about it. He said he'd called you, and you were coming round to his apartment to talk to him about it. I knew I had to shut him up, and quick.'

'So you shot him in the back?'

'Hey, this isn't the Wild West. I did what I had to do to survive. There's nothing wrong in that.'

'Nothing wrong in that!' I exclaimed in amazement.

'Simon. I'm alive, and I'll do what's necessary to stay that way.'

It was difficult to think of Daniel as a murderer. Thin, pale, nerdish, he looked more at home with a keyboard than a gun. But I knew Daniel. He was greedy, and he was overconfident in his own abilities. That was how he had found himself in a position where it was either Frank or him. And Daniel had quite a self-centred morality. He'd go for himself any day. If he thought he wasn't going to get caught, and if the alternative was some Russian killing him, I could imagine him resorting to murder.

And once he'd done it once, he had to do it again.

We sat in silence, waiting for Lisa. She had said she wanted to be home before Gardner Phillips called back at eleven fifteen. I remembered all the times Lisa had been late in the past. Please, God, please let her be late just one more time.

The percolator was bubbling away in the kitchen.

'Shall I get your coffee?'

'Leave it! Stay where you are.'

349

I stayed where I was. The clock between us ticked louder and louder against the wall. Daniel was trying to stay cool, but he was finding it difficult. He was fidgeting, and a film of sweat was building up on his upper lip.

I was finding it difficult too. My earlier bravado, when I had dared Daniel to shoot me, was hard to maintain. I didn't want to die now, especially after all I had been through in the last couple of months to avoid first prison, and then a bullet. Just when I had sorted my life out, it was going to end. Because of Daniel. The bastard! John had been right about him all along.

Half past ten.

The phone rang. A loud, pre-digital, old-fashioned clanging sound. Gardner Phillips. I moved towards it.

'Stay where you are!' Daniel snapped. 'Leave it!'

So I left it. Both of us stared at the telephone as it cried shrilly for attention. Phillips was persistent, that was for sure. Thirty rings. I counted them subconsciously. But finally it went quiet. Daniel relaxed.

My mind raced. I hadn't told Phillips where I was, just the phone number. With the help of the police, he should be able to figure out the address from that. He could have the cops here in twenty minutes.

But why should he? I had said it was urgent, not a matter of life or death. He'd wait half an hour and call again.

In half an hour I'd be dead.

Quarter to eleven. As the time grew nearer when Daniel would shoot me, so also did the chance that Lisa might not return until after his deadline. She might survive. Oh God, please let her survive.

Five to eleven.

Then I saw her. She must have come back along the path through the woods. She was approaching the house from the side, the side I was facing, but in a few seconds she would pass right in front of the big living room window, and Daniel couldn't fail to see her. Unless I distracted him.

I kept my eyes on Daniel, but through my peripheral vision I could see her getting closer and closer. She was smiling, trying to catch my attention: she couldn't see there was another person in the room yet.

When she was a couple of yards from the window, I made my move.

'I need that coffee,' I said.

Then deliberately, but not quickly enough to scare him, I stood up, and moved across the room towards the kitchen.

'I said stay where you are!' Daniel's eyes followed me.

I remembered that Daniel had shot both Frank and John in the back. Perhaps he was squeamish about shooting a friend face-to-face.

I walked on, slowly, my hands up in a calming gesture. 'OK. You can keep me covered. But I need that coffee.'

'Stay there, or I'll shoot!'

I could feel sweat breaking out all over me. He meant it. The bastard meant it.

Through the window, which Daniel was now turned away from, I could sense as much as see Lisa. I knew that the slightest flicker of my eyes towards her would cause Daniel to turn, and then we'd both be dead. I sensed she stopped. She saw Daniel, and then she ducked out of sight.

'OK, OK,' I said, and slowly moved back towards the chair.

'Simon. I'm going to kill you, you know that,' said Daniel. 'I don't want to do it quite yet, but I will if you give me no choice.'

I sat in the chair again to wait. I wondered what Lisa would do. Get the hell out of here, and call the cops, I hoped. I glanced at the old grandfather clock. Only two minutes to go. Too late for her to save me. But time for her to save herself and our child.

My own death, now just over a minute away, suddenly seemed very real. Of course I was frightened. But somehow, the knowledge that Lisa and the baby would survive gave me some strength. Strength enough to die.

Daniel, realizing that his self-imposed deadline was fast approaching, seemed to be steeling himself. He was tense, sweating. He didn't like doing this.

The clock struck eleven.

351

Daniel stood up. He licked his lips. The gun was held out in front of him, shaking.

'I guess she didn't come back,' he said.

'It doesn't look like it.'

I watched him calmly.

'Stand up!'

I stood up.

'Turn around.'

I didn't move. If I was going to die, it would be standing up, facing my assassin. I wasn't going to beg for mercy. Lisa had escaped. And our baby. And now I was going to die with simple honour. In these final moments of my life, that mattered to me.

'I said, turn around!'

Daniel almost screamed. I held his eyes. He wasn't enjoying this one bit, and I was glad.

Just then a car engine burst into life. I recognized the low growl of the Morgan's V8 engine. Lisa was going to get away! He couldn't stop her now.

'What's that? Lisa?'

I nodded and smiled.

Daniel licked his lips. 'Did she come back? Did she see me?' His voice rose in something close to panic. Outside, the car was put into gear.

'You bastard!' he said and raised his gun.

Outside the car engine revved and then slowed. Through the wooden walls of the house we could hear it growl and then explode, rushing towards us.

'What the fuck!' Daniel turned towards the wall of the living room. There was an almighty crash, and the house rocked. The wall erupted, and the dark green nose of the Morgan burst into the room. Wood flew everywhere, a chunk dealing Daniel a glancing blow.

I leaped.

He regained his balance and fired. I felt a sharp burn on my stomach, and was on him. He was thin and wiry, and fighting for his life. I was strong, and bigger than him, and fighting for mine. I grabbed the hand holding the revolver. Two more shots rang out, each smashing harmlessly into a wall. I beat his hand against the floor until he let go of the gun. I grabbed it, and belted him over the head with the butt. He slumped on to the floor.

I rushed over to the Morgan, which was half-in and half-out of the house. Steam was hissing out of the engine. The whole front of the car was concertinaed upwards. The windscreen was cracked but still intact. And behind the wheel was Lisa, motionless.

I was seized with panic. She was leaning back in the seat, a cut on her head bleeding heavily. She was still, her eyes shut. On her lap was an inflated life jacket, which she must have grabbed from the boathouse to cushion the impact.

'Lisa! Are you all right?'

Nothing.

I touched her gently on the shoulder, afraid of making an unseen injury worse. She didn't respond. I wanted to grab her, shake her back to consciousness, but I knew I shouldn't. So I stroked her face. 'Lisa! Lisa! Speak to me!'

She moved slightly and groaned. Her eyelids flickered. Relief flooded through me.

'Oh, Lisa, are you hurt? Please tell me you're not hurt!'

She shook her head. 'I don't think so,' she whispered.

I helped her out of the car and pulled her close to me.

'What about the baby?'

'I . . . I don't know.' She buried her face in my shoulder.

'Thank you,' I said, holding her tight. She had risked her life and our child's life for mine. I couldn't ask for more than that.

She pulled back, and tried to smile. 'I didn't want our baby to grow up without a father.'

Epilogue

I was ten minutes late for the Monday morning meeting. I had had very little sleep over the weekend, and I was exhausted. I was looking forward to a day at the office to recuperate.

Everyone was there: Diane, Ravi, Jim the new partner, and the two associates Kathleen and Bruce. No Gil. No Art. No Frank. No John. And no Daniel, who was into the second month of his life sentence.

Ravi was talking about Boston Peptides. Henry Chan and the rest of the management team, including Lisa, had bought the company out from the debris of BioOne, with Revere's backing. 'The prospects for BP 56 look excellent. We're planning to start Phase Two trials in September.'

'Any sign of side-effects?' asked Diane from her position in Gil's old chair at the middle of the table.

'It causes mild depression in some patients, but that's no problem if it's taken in conjunction with an anti-depressant. Apart from that, it looks fine.'

'Are you sure?'

Ravi winced. 'So far. But don't quote me on that.'

'Don't worry, I won't. Simon?' Diane said, turning to me. 'How's Net Cop doing?'

'Craig has customers slavering over his prototype. Now all he needs to do is gear up for production.'

'And the finance for that will come entirely from the Initial Public Offering?'

'That's the idea.'

'Any price talk yet?'

'Forty-five dollars.'

Diane did some quick mental calculations. 'That puts a value on the company of two hundred forty million, doesn't it?'

I nodded.

'That's incredible!' Jim said.

'It's a big market and Net Cop has the best product.'

'So what's our share?' Diane asked.

'We'll have ten per cent of that.'

'Not bad, Simon.'

And it wasn't bad. We would turn an initial two million investment into twenty-four million. Jeff Lieberman and the Bloomfield Weiss investors would do even better. When we had backed down, they had had the courage to step in and they deserved their returns. Craig had done best of all, of course. But he definitely deserved that.

'Lynette Mauer will be pleased,' Diane said. 'I think she might bite at a new fund next year. With Net Cop, Boston Peptides, Tetracom, and some of the others, we're beginning to convince them that we know what we're doing without Gil.'

Gil was sailing five days a week, and had yet to go anywhere near a dialysis machine. But we were all determined that the firm he had started would thrive without him.

I was exhausted as I made my way back home across the Common. I needed a full night's sleep badly. But I walked fast, eager to see Lisa and the baby. It was eight o'clock and still light when I arrived at the apartment. I opened the door and called out. There was no reply.

I dumped my briefcase, and went through to the bedroom. Lisa was lying asleep, a breast exposed, the baby breathing gently next to her. I took off my clothes and crawled in beside them.

355

I kissed Lisa on the forehead. She didn't stir. Then I kissed the baby.

'Goodnight, Frank,' I said, and fell instantly asleep.